Jessica Adams is the author of the bestselling *Single White E-Mail*, *I'm A Believer* and *Tom, Dick and Debbie Harry* and has worked as an editor on four more bestsellers for the charity War Child: *Girls' Night In*, *Girls' Night Out*, *Big Night Out* and *Kids' Night In*. She is the astrologer for *Vogue* in Australia and her TV work includes *The Secret Life of Us*.

Jessica Adams' website address is:
www.jessicaadams.com

Acclaim for
Cool for Cats

'If the soundtrack to your youth includes The Clash and Blondie, or your penchant for punk arrived later, then this book will have you surfing a wave of nostalgia. With her rock-chick heroine Linda Tyler, Adams proves that musical obsession isn't just a male affliction. Languishing in a sleepy backwater, Linda longs for excitement, never imagining she'll land her dream job as a music journalist sharing Knickerbocker Glories with Altered Image's Clare Grogan. Despite the lighthearted tone of her novels, Adams' outlook is never rose-tinted, and Linda's dreams come at a cost as her rock'n'roll odyssey wreaks havoc with relationships old and new. An eloquent look at the bitter-sweet nature of success'
Glamour

D1102552

'Funny and warm, thought-provoking, honest and down to earth'
Sunday Tasmanian

'A sparky, entertaining book – I found it funny, surreal and poignant, all at the same time'   Sophie Kinsella

'Absolutely magical . . . The characters were beautifully drawn . . . I'm desperate for a sequel'   Lisa Jewell

'A grin-a-minute, snuggle-down treat of a book. A book that will have you humming and ha-ha-ing'   Freya North

'Jessica Adams has excelled herself with a cast of warm, witty characters who'll have you thinking that moving to a small town in Tasmania is almost a good idea!'   Chris Manby

'*Tom, Dick and Debbie Harry* is a book you take everywhere: in the bath, on the bus, and to bed . . . Jessica Adams' witty, understated style feels exactly like a bunch of mates chatting to you. Clear-eyed, compassionate and very funny'   Victoria Routledge

'Jessica Adams has written an engrossing and utterly original tale which is both funny and frequently very touching'   Isabel Wolff

Single White E-Mail

'She gives Nick Hornby and Helen Fielding a damn good run for their money . . . thoroughly enjoyable'   *Daily Telegraph*

'Sexy, funny, smart. For any woman who has ever been single'
Cosmopolitan

'A blissfully refreshing treat. I found it very, very funny and quirky enough to be really original. It was *Muriel's Wedding, Sex, lies and videotape* and *Ally McBeal* all rolled into one, and I defy any woman of my age not to relate to Victoria'   Fiona Walker

'Fresh, frenetic and fun'   *Elle*

'A very funny novel for the 90s woman – read it and recognize yourself'   *New Weekly*

'A modern classic'   *19*

'Smart 'n' sexy'   *B magazine*

'Recommended . . . the e-mail of the species is deadlier than the male'   *Marie Claire*

'Meet Australia's answer to Helen Fielding's star character Bridget Jones'   *Sydney Morning Herald*

Also by Jessica Adams

SINGLE WHITE E-MAIL
TOM, DICK AND DEBBIE HARRY
I'M A BELIEVER

and published by Black Swan

THE NEW ASTROLOGY FOR WOMEN

and published by Corgi Books

COOL FOR CATS

Jessica Adams

BLACK SWAN

COOL FOR CATS
A BLACK SWAN BOOK: 0 552 77084 1

First publication in Great Britain

PRINTING HISTORY
Black Swan edition published 2003

1 3 5 7 9 10 8 6 4 2

Set in 11/12pt Melior by
Falcon Oast Graphic Art Ltd.

Black Swan Books are published by Transworld Publishers,
61–63 Uxbridge Road, London W5 5SA,
a division of The Random House Group Ltd,
in Australia by Random House Australia (Pty) Ltd,
20 Alfred Street, Milsons Point, Sydney, NSW 2061, Australia,
in New Zealand by Random House New Zealand Ltd,
18 Poland Road, Glenfield, Auckland 10, New Zealand
and in South Africa by Random House (Pty) Ltd,
Endulini, 5a Jubilee Road, Parktown 2193, South Africa.

Printed and bound in Great Britain by
Cox & Wyman Ltd, Reading, Berkshire.

Papers used by Transworld Publishers are natural, recyclable
products made from wood grown in sustainable forests. The
manufacturing processes conform to the environmental
regulations of the country of origin.

ACKNOWLEDGEMENTS

Mental As Anything and Altered Images made some of my favourite singles of all time so it means a lot to me to have Reg Mombassa and Clare Grogan in the book – thanks chaps. I am also grateful to Karen Moline for letting me raid her memories of the legendary New York party that later inspired an REM song, and for allowing me to fictionalize her encounters with Lester Bangs and Michael Stipe. Fantastic insider advice on music papers and magazines in 1979 came from Andy Cowles, David Hepworth and Neil Spencer, and for that I owe you all several beers. Cocktails with umbrellas to the other Gang of Four as well – Diana Beaumont, Stephanie Cabot, Fiona Inglis and Cate Paterson – and to Wendy Bristow, Freya North, Martina O'Doherty and Jane Pirkis, who have been so generous. This book is fiction (don't all authors say that?) but it was born partly from my experience as a music journalist. For that I would like to acknowledge Noel Crabbe, who hired me all those years ago and gave me the chance to interview Elvis Costello and Kurt Cobain.

Jessica Adams
Brighton 2003

CHAPTER ONE

It's the best job in England and I'm not going to get it.

MUSIC JOURNALIST WANTED
NO EXPERIENCE NECESSARY

New weekly music magazine needs writer
(over 30s need not apply), passionate about
Punk/New Wave for immediate start.
Enthusiasm/knowledge for Clash, Costello,
Jam, Buzzcocks, Pistols, Blondie, etc. more
important than experience. Females particularly encouraged to apply. Salary £4,000 a
year negotiable. Please write with your name,
age, address, phone number and tell us which
ten songs changed your life, and why. Closing
date 15 January. Write to, The Publisher,
NWW, 8A Wardour Street, London W1 6XZ.

OK. Let's just go over that again. It's £4,000 a year,
which is a lot bloody more than I'm earning now.
You have to be under thirty. They'd like a woman. You
have to like The Clash. You have to know about Elvis
Costello. It's in Wardour Street. You don't need any
experience. They just need to know the ten songs that
changed your life, and you need to post it by next
Monday. And it's for something called *NWW*, which
sounds almost like the *NME* – which is good enough

for me. *Oh my GOD*, have you ever seen something so right for you that you know, with a sick feeling in your stomach, that it's never going to happen?

I know the Withingdean Library round the corner has a typewriter. You write your name on a piece of paper on a clipboard, with a pencil on a string, and you can book it for half an hour at a time – maybe more, if the librarian isn't watching.

'Well that's not very Punk, using the Withingdean Library typewriter,' David says later, when we're in bed. He wants sex, I don't, and it's a familiar scenario, so we're just talking rubbish instead, him with his pyjama top off, me with my pyjama top definitely on.

I've been reading copies of *Cosmopolitan* at the library which tell you to, quote, massage your man if you don't feel like making love, unquote. But the point is, when he doesn't feel like it, he never massages *me*, so why should I bother? And anyway, I haven't got anything to massage him with. My free samples of pink hand cream from the local Avon lady have run out.

I try to think of all the reasons why I can't apply for the job. That way I can avoid the misery of trying for it and failing.

'They're not going to want me, David. People from bloody Oxford will apply for this.'

He nods.

'They won't want someone like me.'

'Well don't do it then.'

'But I'll kill myself if I don't apply for this job, David. It's bloody made for me.'

'Just make up your mind, will you?'

'Would you move to London with me if I did get it?'

'No,' he says flatly. 'There's nowhere to park, the pigeons have got diseases, and none of the phone boxes work.'

'Those aren't excuses.'

'What I want to know is, why are females particularly

10

encouraged to apply?' David asks, finishing his cigarette. 'I mean, why females? Is it the only way the editor can find a girlfriend?'

'Don't be funny,' I say, rolling the other way and closing my eyes.

Later, though, when David is snoring, and the TV has shut down for the night and the flat is quiet, I go down to the kitchen, find a biro, make myself a black coffee and start the list. He knew I would. That's why he fell asleep – just so I could get on with it.

Linda Tyler
Flat 4
108 Hutton Close
Withingdean
BN3 2NXS
Phone 05678 3556 383

Monday, 8 January 1979

To the Publisher
NWW Magazine
8A Wardour Street
London W1 6XZ

Dear Sir/Madam,
For what it's worth, here are the ten songs that changed my life.
No, you sound like a twat, cross that out and start again.

Dear Sir/Madam,
Here are the ten songs that changed my life.

1. 'BALLROOM BLITZ' – THE SWEET
The song, of course, began with Brian asking Steve, Andy and Mick if they were ready. To which the reply seemed to be variously 'Aha', 'Yeah!' or 'OK!' depending on their mood.

11

Steve was Steve Priest, who had been known to turn up for photo sessions in full Native American warpaint and a feathered headdress. Andy was Andy Scott, who had butterfly hairclips in his fringe, silver platform boots and two red circles under his eyes like Coco the Clown. Mick was Mick Tucker, who had an open suede waistcoat that showed his nipples. And the singer was Brian Connolly, who had a much nicer blond pageboy than any girl I knew, and a voice that was so offensively camp that my father used to stomp over to the radio with his arms folded, breathing hard through his nose, every time Sweet came on the radio.

'You're a bit old to be listening to this sort of stuff, aren't you, Linda?'

Well I was, I suppose. Which was why I was too embarrassed to go into Disc City in Withingdean and buy the bloody thing. I just had to have it though. As summer turned into autumn in 1973 there were only a few things that seemed essential – brown suede platform boots, a flat tweed cap that made me look like my tuberculosis-ridden grandfather in the Depression – and this. The biggest, dumbest, chunkiest-sounding, most fantastically addictive record of this or any other year.

It's hard to say what Brian Connolly actually sounds like on 'Ballroom Blitz' if I listen to it now. An hysterical housewife who's just found a severed head in the bath? A dalek who's suddenly been plugged into the wrong end of Battersea Power Station? A mental patient who's simultaneously assumed the personalities of Kenneth Williams, Liberace, Frankie Howerd and Danny La Rue, then taken quite a lot of amyl nitrate?

In 'Ballroom Blitz', Brian Connolly sounds excited, panicked, close to tears, on the edge of nausea, as camp as a row of tents and as mad as a brush, all at the same time. I mean, how many times can a grown man say 'Yeah!' in quick succession without beginning to hyperventilate?

I could hardly go into a record shop in my early twenties and buy that in public, could I? So I did the intelligent thing. I shoplifted it.

There is only one big department store near us; it's in Brighton and it's called Hillage's. On the ground floor you can buy perfume for your mother's birthday. Tweed, Caleche, Cachet (it's different on every woman who wears it, you know). If you go downstairs, they have saucepans and fondue sets; and if you go upstairs, they sell ladies' coats in Princess Anne and Princess Margaret colours. At the side of the store there is a funny L-shaped bit, which they've never known what to do with, but in 1973 somebody decided to glue glitter all over the walls and put rainbow stickers on the windows and call it Rave At Hillage's.

In Rave At Hillage's you could buy suede chokers with apples on them, and big floppy denim hats, and you could even sit around on huge corduroy cushions talking about all the crucial things, like how to mend your split ends, and how to get Radio Luxembourg. ('Tune into 208 metres on the medium wave, towards the right-hand end of the wave band.')

Rave was the only place to go in Brighton if you wanted to buy a crocheted poncho in purple nylon wool, or a hilarious Jackson 5 afro wig, or a Mood Ring. You could smoke in there, you could eat in there (people used to wander in with bacon sandwiches from the Snack Bar across the road) and it was even rumoured that you could snog in there. I suppose in days of old the youth of Brighton used to amuse themselves by throwing rotten cabbages at Queen Victoria or trying to get Rudyard Kipling's autograph – but when me and my friends were growing up, the only thing to do on a wet Saturday was hand around Rave.

There was a special counter in Rave At Hillage's with lots of strange things mixed up together – Swingers tights, and bright green Timex watches and Philips tape recorders (which everyone used to have a go on, amazing their friends by saying things like 'Piss off' and then playing it back). On the counter they had Lee Cooper Easy Waist jeans with fly fronts and flared legs, along with a straw basket full of Eyelure false eyelashes. And on the back wall there was the Rave Record Rack, which had every single in the Top 20, from Mud, to T-Rex, to . . . Sweet.

Because the female shop assistants in Rave At Hillage's spent most of their time pushing each other off the corduroy cushions and laughing at each other, it seemed entirely possible to shove a copy of 'Ballroom Blitz' up the front of your bomber jacket and walk out without anybody seeing you.

And was I planning my raid from experience? Well of course I was. I had done Hillage's before, in times of need. I'd begun with one navy blue display clog from the shoe department (start small) and then worked my way up to some red plastic cherries (39p if I'd paid for them) to put on my hat. It helped that some bloke I knew told me that big shops like Hillage's deliberately upped their prices to pay for the insurance that protected them against people like me – all of which made it seem harmless somehow. So from one clog and a bunch of plastic cherries, I graduated to shoving a wipe-off Snoopy memo board up the front of my jumper, then finally a string of pearls for my mother.

David arrested me, of course. That's how we met. I was shoplift-ing a copy of 'Ballroom Blitz', and he was sitting on a stool by the front door, doing his job as a part-time security guard.

'Excuse me, miss.'

'What?'

Keep on walking, Linda, just keep on walking. But he was already blocking the doors, waving away an old lady with an umbrella who was trying to get in from the other side.

'Please unzip your jacket for me, miss.'

'What? Why?'

Thump, thump, thump. It's weird how your heart can start bang-ing before your brain has actually clocked what's going on.

'Just unzip the jacket and give it back.'

'I haven't got anything.'

'Then would you mind coming into this room with me for a minute?'

Over in the corner the shop assistants were still shrieking with laughter and pushing each other off the corduroy floor cushions.

David was a tasty fella. That's the way my friend Hazel used to categorize men. Curly brown hair was tasty fella, sideburns were tasty fella, and Fair Isle V-neck sleeveless jumpers like Rod Stewart and Paul McCartney wore were *really* tasty fella.

David had all of those elements in place when I met him for a drink after work – after the arrest. His chest hair was pure Steve McQueen, too, even if he did spill our beer down the front of his shirt when he was carrying it back from the bar.

We started going out together a few days later, and here we are today, living with each other in Brighton. If 'Ballroom Blitz' comes on the radio though, I have to turn it off. My dad was right about that bit at the front. It just makes you want to breathe very, very hard through your nose.

2. 'REVOLUTION NUMBER 9' – THE BEATLES
Other people lose their virginity to 'Strawberry Fields Forever' or 'Norwegian Wood'. On Christmas Day I lost mine to 'Revolution Number 9'. It was all Gregory Bannerman's fault. He was an ageing hippy who'd bought all this foul-smelling medicinal cream called Tiger Balm on his summer holiday in India. And when he found out I had a cold, he insisted on rubbing great handfuls of it into my breasts, reading from the label to reassure me.

' "This product contains menthol, cajuput oil, camphor, cassia oil, clove oil, dementholized mint oil, paraffin and petrolatum. Fast and effective relief for headaches, stuffy nose, insect bites, itchiness, muscular aches and pains, sprains and flatulence." '

'Flatulence as well?'

'You haven't travelled in Asia, Linda. I have. This stuff is really essential.'

I gave Gregory a look.

'Not that I'm saying you've got flatulence of course, because you haven't, but even if you did, I wouldn't be worried about it. You know.'

'Thanks.'

From there it was a simple matter for Gregory Bannerman to take my knickers off as well, and then skip the needle on the record forward seven tracks from 'Sexy Sadie' to 'Revolution Number 9'. Shortly after this, some nag champa incense got lit, a cat came in and was shooed away ('Go, my gentle animal friend,' Gregory murmured. 'Go.') – and then suddenly Gregory was on top of me. I gave in, I suppose, because I couldn't be bothered protesting, and anyway, at the age of seventeen my time had come. The gentle animal friend, incidentally, got into bed with us while it was all happening.

Gregory Bannerman had only just bought the *White Album*, I remember, because he kept going on about it. He was extremely proud of the fact that his edition was No. 0110182 out of a limited edition of what? Two million?

You got a free Beatles poster folded up inside the sleeve of the record with every copy you bought, and Gregory had his stuck up on the wall, above the mattress on the floor. The poster was a collage – I can still remember the way Gregory pronounced it, with a poncy French accent – and on it there was a picture of John Lennon sitting up cross-legged in bed, stark naked, with Yoko Ono lying back on the pillows. Perhaps because of this, Gregory also made a point of sitting cross-legged and stark naked on the bed as he rolled on his rubber, with his underpants hanging off the top of the fringed lampshade exactly where he'd thrown them.

'What's the best gig you ever saw, Linda?' he asked, because it was taking too long to get the rubber on and he was worried I was noticing.

'I've never been to one.'

'Christ, I wish I knew you a few years ago.'

'Do you?'

'We could have seen some great bands together. 23rd Turnoff. The Amazingly Friendly Apple. The Attack. The Bunch. Nessa O'Neill's Irish Stew. Fairytale. The Jelly Babies. Felius Andromeda. Grapefruit. Muly. Orange Bicycle. Rupert's People. Virgin Sleep. We could even have seen The Tickle.'

'Goodness.'

'I saw Pink Floyd at the Royal Festival Hall once. That's my favourite gig of all time. "More Furious Madness From The Massed Gadgets Of Auximines". It was just so amazing, Linda.'

'Wow.'

At seventeen I was trying to be a free spirit – which according to most of the hippies I met in Camden meant taking all your clothes off *right now* – but there was a lot of childhood conditioning to get over as well. I mean, I'm English, aren't I. I can't just remove all my outer garments and start grooving to 'More Furious Madness From The Massed Gadgets Of Auximines'.

Don't tell me that Gregory Bannerman, or any of the other hairy nudie hippies I met at his parties, didn't have the same inhibitions as I did. At school they wouldn't let us have showers after cross-country, just in case someone accidentally caught sight of your armpit.

I didn't see my first buttock until I was sixteen, and even then it left me in total shock. It was a fat male Woodstock bottom, I remember, wobbling past the camera on a BBC documentary like a white blancmange being wheeled past on a dessert trolley.

Anyway, after Gregory had deflowered me (and you try doing it to 'Revolution Number 9', which is basically a Mellotron played backwards, the last chord of Sibelius's 'Seventh Symphony' and George Martin chatting in the control room), I realized something else. He spent so much time wandering around naked that sex was probably just a mild extension of his daily life.

For me to think that him taking my virginity was a big deal was rubbish. In fact, it was a total misreading of just how important it was to him – i.e. *not very*. Gregory ate without clothes. He cooked without clothes. When you live like that, sex must seem like five boring steps up from stewing lentils. It must seem like combing your hair, or getting up to turn the telly off.

When I tried to put my clothes on afterwards, running for the security of my tights, skirt and boots, Gregory wouldn't let me.

'Feel your body, Linda. Go with it. Relax. You're not in Withingdean now. Let your skin breathe.'

All very well for Gregory Bannerman, except he'd got the stinking Tiger Balm everywhere – in my eyes, on my tongue and in places where the Chinese never meant it to go.

'I want a wash. This stuff is burning me.'

'Well cool, but don't get dressed again just to take it all off, you know?'

He gave a low laugh. That was another thing about Gregory Bannerman. Quite apart from breaking into a pretentious French accent every five minutes, he couldn't laugh. No matter how funny something was, or how funny he thought he was being, there was always this strained, disappointing sound at the end of it. Like a sheep mourning its dead young.

'I'm not going out there in the hall without my bra on! What if Jimmy sees me?'

Jimmy was Gregory's flatmate or, more accurately, his squatmate. They had both been squatting in the same grotty house in Camden for two years.

'Jimmy's got his lady with him. He won't trouble you. Listen!'

Gregory cupped his hand over his ear and closed his eyes. Pootle, pootle, pootle. Jimmy was trying to play Jethro Tull on his recorder again.

'I think I'll go now, Gregory, if you don't mind.'

'Linda—'

'Yes?'

'You're beautiful. Are you bleeding?'

'No I'm not bleeding.'

Shut up, Gregory Bannerman, and let me get to the sink and wash this stinking Tiger Balm off, while you go back to the start of 'Revolution Number 9' and get your underpants off the lampshade. And stop talking like something out of *The Myths And Legends Of King Arthur*.

I don't know what's happened to Gregory, and I don't care. I know he can't still be wandering around naked in Camden, though. Not in this weather. They're not calling it the Winter of Discontent for nothing.

As I think about Gregory now, I realize how easy it is to draw a straight line from him to David. Not so much because it was a natural progression, more because David was everything Gregory wasn't. Fully clothed. Didn't give a stuff about Pink Floyd or even The Amazingly Friendly Apple for that matter. Fully employed. Sensible. Called his parents once a week.

Hazel thinks I'm with David because he's like my dad.

'I read it somewhere. All women marry their fathers.'

'Rubbish. You know I don't get on with Dad.'

'But you don't get on with David, either, so there's your proof.'

'Yeah Hazel, very funny.'

I wish Hazel wouldn't try to analyze me, but she did a unit of psychology once, when she was in teacher training, so my relationship with David is constantly under the microscope. To me, it's not that complicated. He's good-looking. He's also honest, dependable, faithful, intelligent and – oh, just tick all the right boxes in the *Cosmo* quizzes.

Sure, we fight a lot, and Dad and I fight a lot too. But this still has less to do with my love life than Hazel thinks. For my money, losing my virginity to Gregory Bannerman and his pot of stinking Tiger Balm was traumatic enough to make any woman head for someone like David.

'Revolution Number 9'. I still can't listen to it. It's eight minutes of rubbish in my opinion, and I'd say that even if I hadn't made a big mistake and lost my virginity to the wrong man.

18

It's so odd. I had a prolonged crush on Gregory bloody Bannerman. I was obsessed with him for three long months before Christmas Day arrived and we finally did the deed. But, as The Buzzcocks pointed out last year, 'Ever Fallen In Love (With Someone You Shouldn't've)'? Well, that was him. Come to think of it, Gregory Bannerman would have hated The Buzzcocks. Now there's a band you can't play on the recorder.

3. 'ITCHYCOO PARK' – SMALL FACES

My mother died of cancer in September 1967, which was the worst month, in the worst year, to die of anything. The sun was shining brilliantly, people were wearing orange terry-towelling shorts in the hospital gardens, there were daisies everywhere, and the Small Faces were singing 'Itchycoo Park' on the radio. All the songs that summer were chirpy, cheerful, and stupidly happy – 'All You Need Is Love', 'See Emily Play', 'Carrie Anne' – so the sicker Mum got, the more completely wrong the rest of the world seemed to be.

My dad, who was always shell-shocked after the hospital visits, used to whistle mindlessly to himself on the long drive back home. He wouldn't have known Steve Marriott if he'd run into him at a zebra crossing, but like everyone else at the end of that summer, he had 'Itchycoo Park' in his head. He thought the words were silly, which of course they were – all about ducks grooving about, and blowing your mind and feeding them with a bun – so he used to whistle it instead.

Mum never heard the lyrics to 'Itchycoo Park' correctly – when they had the hospital radio on, she thought they were saying nun, not bun, and that made her laugh, as anything about nuns always did. I didn't want to correct her mistake, because that would have stopped her laughing. Towards the end it was very, very hard to get my mother to laugh at anything. 'Itchycoo Park' didn't change my life though. The reason it's on my list is because it became the sound-track for something which did.

Mum died on 14 September. Hazel held my hand all the way through the funeral, because Dad was crying and Auntie Maureen was holding his hand instead. Hazel wore a yellow PVC mac with a

19

fur-trimmed bonnet and I had a red PVC mac with my hair tied in bunches. It rained, of course, on the day of her funeral.

4. 'MY GENERATION' – THE WHO

In 1965 my generation was actually playing snap and watching *Stingray*. You could be younger then than you can be now. I still liked The Who, though. And I liked the way I could sing along with Roger Daltrey and do the naughty f-f-f- bit. Kenneth Tynan could say fuck on the television that winter, but I couldn't even say bum at home – I found out the hard way, saying it to Hazel on the phone one day and then being grounded.

Other things I couldn't do in 1965 – shave my legs, watch *Peyton Place*, cut my fringe, take out a book called *The Kandy-Kolored Tangerine-Flake Streamline Baby* from Withingdean Library, use Hazel's mother's bubble bath, accept a strange man's invitation to play badminton, pop bubble gum, ask for a pair of kinky boots for Christmas . . . no wonder I ended up running away.

'Can I go to London on Saturday? Please, Mum. I'll find a phone box and call you when I get to Victoria Station. I've seen an orange coffee pot I want to get you.'

'What? No, Linda. You're too young to go there by yourself. And don't make up stories about orange coffee pots. Besides, anything could happen to you.'

By which she meant something like Myra Hindley might happen to me. But eventually it all got too much. I felt – rightly as it turned out – that something amazing was happening just a few miles away from Withingdean and I was being stopped from seeing it. So one Saturday morning, with the words to 'My Generation' running around my head, I got the bus to Brighton station and followed two girls in big furry white coats onto the platform – they had to be going to London, dressed like that. And after carefully removing a copy of the *Beano* from the seat, I then jiggled my way past sheep, train stations and trees to freedom, sitting on my hands with the excitement of it all.

God he's old, I thought to myself in defiant Who-style fashion as the ticket inspector gave me a look. He was probably in his early forties, but that seemed old enough. I was on the lookout for Mods and Rockers on the train too, hopefully beating each other's brains out, which would have given me something to talk about at school. But my only fellow travellers on the 9.20 to Victoria were the girls in the white fur coats – who attracted a leering 'What's up pussycat?' from the ticket inspector – and some old ladies with a tartan Thermos full of tea playing whist.

London was amazing. They were making doughnuts and cooking them on the spot, inside a little booth next to a newsagent. There were two women in green plastic miniskirts trying to spray you with free green perfume on the way to the tube. And they were playing Herman's Hermits over the radio in the station, so you could hear it wherever you went, even in the toilets. I felt like I'd landed on the moon.

After that, I got as far as Buckingham Palace then burst into tears and sat in the park, chewing my fingernails. I couldn't do it. Couldn't go to Carnaby Street by myself. Couldn't wander into a coffee bar to flutter my eyelashes at a beat poet. Couldn't face the terror of walking around Piccadilly Circus – what if the police stopped me? Good grief, I couldn't even find a public toilet in Green Park by myself without bursting into tears again, because all the loo paper was in a soggy mess on the floor, along with someone's old sanitary pad. I was useless.

In the end I wobbled back to Victoria Station, where I rang my parents from a telephone box. Dad answered and was so furious with me he had to hand the phone over to Mum.

'You don't understand, Mum, it's because you wouldn't let me go.'

'We've been worried sick.'

'I left you a note. On the table.'

Later, much later, when I had eaten baked beans on toast for dinner, and had a bath, and was sitting in flannelette pyjamas on the sofa, wrapped up in a blanket watching an old episode of *The Man From U.N.C.L.E.*, I felt safe enough to hum 'My Generation' again. At least in my head. F-f-f-fade away, the lot of you. But hey, these baked beans taste great. Thanks, Mum!

5. 'TWO LITTLE BOYS' – ROLF HARRIS

Open University was freely available, even in a backwater like Withingdean, so why was I bothering enrolling at Sussex University when I could do it at home? My dad said he'd give it twelve months when I put in my BA application, but in the end I only lasted six – in fact, I lasted about as long as Jim Morrison lasted in the bath. He perished in Paris in July, exactly one month after I perished in front of Professor Graham Hayes, head of the English department.

Graham Hayes had quite a few problems with me from the start. To begin with, I tried to pay my Student Union fees in old threepenny bits I'd been saving up in a jam jar, even though the rest of the country had long since gone decimal. Then I wrote an essay on Flaubert and called him a self-satisfied, nauseating example of self-deluding European white male supremacy – well, I think that's what I put in the first paragraph. I hadn't been to any of the lectures, of course, and Professor Hayes gave me three out of twenty-five and told me I was wasting my time, and his.

The last straw for Professor Hayes, though, was the night I ruined his charity concert. He and his wife Shirley had organized a student-teacher night at the Union bar, for 30p admission, in aid of Oxfam. Because Graham and Shirley had organized it, they were also *in* it. And for some unknown reason they had decided to perform 'Two Little Boys' by Rolf Harris. Graham had two coconuts to clop together, to make the appropriate battlefield horse sounds, because he couldn't sing. Shirley Hayes, who was in some housewife choir in Eastbourne, decided to raise Rolf's song by a dozen octaves and sing it a cappella. In perfect BBC English. They were also wearing identical leather plaited belts, I remember. Somebody told me Shirley's sister made them.

There were free drinks on a trestle table to encourage the students. But for most of my life, or until the age of twenty anyway, I had never drunk anything more expensive than cider. I knew its limits. With cider, the inside of your cheeks went squashy and tender at about two glasses, and by three you were talking to yourself in the mirror in the Ladies.

'God you look great in your navy blue clogs tonight, Linda.'

'Linda, what the hell are you doing with your life?'

And so on.

The problem was, although I had *heard* of some of the drinks they were offering at Graham Hayes's charity concert – rum punch, for example (a very posh drink), and mulled wine (très sophisticated, très Ye Olde English), – I had never actually imbibed any of them. They were drinks without known limits.

Where rum punch and mulled wine were concerned, it was like hearing about Aleksandr Solzhenitsyn but never actually reading him. Or someone telling you about Germaine Greer, or colour television – you just blithely assumed you knew what they were like, even though you didn't have a clue. And I suppose, at the age of twenty-one, I presumed I'd already drunk rum punch and mulled wine, even though my liver wasn't aware of it. All it had ever filtered in its entire life was Bovril, cider, weak tea, Lucozade, PLJ (when I was dieting) and Withingdean tap water.

The results went straight to my brain, then my bladder, then my mouth – in that order. I picked up the Oxfam donations bucket and shook it loudly, like a pair of Maracas, during Graham Hayes' speech about starving children. I used the mens' toilets, then came back and told everyone in the front row all about it. And then, fatally, I started heckling.

'This is a very special song,' said Graham Hayes.

'Gerroff!'

'By a very special singer—'

'Gerroff you bloody Rolf-loving Australians!'

Except Graham and his wife weren't Australian and I was so drunk I couldn't pronounce the word anyway. Osrayian? Ossyrawiyan? Any word with a t in it had become impossible at that point.

Clip-clop, clip-clop, went Professor Hayes's coconuts. The louder I yelled from the front row of the concert, the faster and more passionately he banged them together. Then I started singing about twenty octaves higher than Mrs Hayes, because I thought it was funny. Then suddenly I got bored and shouted 'Show us your wobbleboard!'

Then some pissed bloke in the middle joined in with me. 'Oi, where's Coogee Bear? What 'ave you done with Coogee Bear?'

At which point both me and the pissed bloke should have been dragged off. But nobody seemed to have the authority to do it.

'Bang a gong!' the pissed bloke yelled, gamely putting in a request for T-Rex which was unlikely to be satisfied.

And then suddenly I grabbed him and tried to put my arms around him – a trait often seen in the rum-punch-affected – and that was it. I threw up on him and he ran away. Professor Hayes banged his coconuts down on the floor, and Mrs Hayes was forced to finish the song early and disappear round the back.

I was still there after the concert had finished, sitting cross-legged on the floor in a puddle of sick. Nobody wanted to come near me. I smelled like Barbados. Like a medieval pub and Barbados.

That wasn't what got me kicked out of the university, though. It was cheating on my essays. I paid a girl called Heather Montgomery £2 to copy her essay on Turgenev. It was nothing really, we all did it, and Heather was saving up for a Mini, so she needed the cash. I was the only person Graham Hayes made sure he caught, though.

6. 'NEW ROSE' – THE DAMNED

My father knew something had gone wrong when I stopped ironing.

'You used to be a demon on the ironing board, Linda, now you never use the damn thing.'

Other signs that I had gone over to the dark side in 1976? Putting egg white in my hair then blow-drying it with my head hanging upside down over the end of the bed. And discovering that if I hung around the Brighton clock tower long enough in black tights with the feet cut out of them and my eyebrows drawn into V-shapes with a black Rimmel eye pencil, people who looked like me would come up and ask me for a cigarette. It was magic. Instant friends.

I had no idea what 'New Rose' was about, because I couldn't understand a word David Vanian was singing, but it didn't matter. Sometimes, when I was pissed, I thought the song might have been about me. I wanted to meet David. I wanted to meet

Brian James, I wanted to meet Captain Sensible (everyone did) and I even wanted to meet Rat Scabies, despite the rumours that he had started out drumming for a pantomime performance of *Puss In Boots*.

I'd been off music for years – everyone had. By 1976 it had lost its ability to addict and to excite. It didn't have the power to make me shoplift records in Hillage's; it didn't even have the power to make me change my hair or the way I dressed. I wouldn't have paid to listen to music before 1976, and I didn't. Genesis, the Doobie Brothers, Olivia Newton-John, Captain and Tennile and Neil Sedaka – no thanks. My poxy waitress salary – I was waiting on tables by then – went on other things instead. Like food.

The best thing about Punk, it still seems to me, was that you could express your love for it by hating all the things it wasn't. If you wanted Mick Jagger to die in a Learjet crash, then you were expressing your passion for Punk. It was exactly like loving England, which my dad did – expressing it was easy, you simply spent a lot of time and energy hating France, or better still, the Americans, or the ultimate object of loathing, the Germans.

'You can't hate the Germans, Dad, they like Bobby Charlton as much as we do.'

No reply from my father.

'You shouldn't call Americans bloody foreigners, Dad, they were in the war with us.'

More silence, and a long nose-blowing session into his handkerchief.

One day I copied a Punk I'd seen on Oxford Street and wrote 'ELTON JOHN' in felt-tip on my T-shirt, then crossed it out and wrote 'GO AWAY' above it.

'What if you run into Elton John in the Co-op?' David asked. 'What will you say to him then? I bet you'd get embarrassed and say sorry.'

When 'Anarchy In The UK' came out, and things got serious, and I got more serious too and started getting the train down to London with all the other girls in black tights with the feet cut out of them, David only ever said, 'Phone me when you need picking up from the station.'

We used to argue more when the Pistols arrived.

'Anarchy? You don't even vote, Linda. I mean, do any of them vote?'

'Well that's the point. Anarchy. Idiot. Get it?'

'A lot of little Punks at the Roxy like you, who can't be bothered voting Labour. Brilliant. You do realize the Tories are going to get in next time, don't you, because of *anarchists* like you?'

'No they're not.' My father had said they wouldn't, because their only hope was Margaret Thatcher and that was no hope at all.

'Enjoy London anyway. And keep 50p in your sock for emergencies.'

The key for me was going down Wardour Street with *girls*. We didn't even need our boyfriends. Some of us had men who were Punks like us, but if they came down on a different train, or didn't come down at all, it didn't matter. For the first time in my entire life I didn't need money, I didn't need a bloke, I didn't need to be good-looking, I didn't need a university degree, and I definitely didn't need a good job. Do you know how exciting that is? And can you remember what it felt like, hearing The Damned for the first time? I can, I can, I can.

7. 'WATERLOO SUNSET' – THE KINKS

Depression had to get me sooner or later, according to the psychiatrist. My mother had died of cancer, slowly, and I hadn't really reacted. And there were other things: knowing I was clever and not being able to do anything about it; hating the world for not giving someone like me a job to be brilliant in. All of that.

When the psychiatrist interviewed me, he asked me if I had trouble sleeping or eating.

'Yes.'

'Which?'

'Both.'

And did I take pleasure in things that used to give me pleasure? Tennis, for example, or my friends, or the TV? I had to think hard about that one. I've never played tennis in my life. Something clicked when he ran through his boring list though – picnics, nature walks, holidays, theatre – and finally

26

got to music. Music. Yes. Something was definitely ringing a bell there.

'I can't be bothered listening to The Kinks any more,' I told him.

'And you used to like listening to them?'

I barely had the energy to nod.

Which was an insult to Ray Davies, because if I hadn't been so, well, *depressed*, I would have clambered on top of the psychiatrist's desk to deliver some kind of ode to The Kinks. Did I used to like listening to them? There were times when I was so happy listening to their records, I would not only forget where I was, I would also forget what species I was supposed to be.

In the end, it was The Kinks who brought me back to the real world – or at least they were playing my song on the day I realized I was better. And it was 'Waterloo Sunset', which was fitting again, because I'd deliberately avoided it when it first came out. 'Waterloo Sunset' had appeared in the record shops when Mum was dying, and it had all those guitar chords that make you cry, no matter what the song is actually *about*. And the minute I heard it, on the radio driving back from the hospital, I knew two things, both about the song, and about myself. Firstly, I knew I would fall obsessively in love with it. Secondly, I knew bloody well it would make me sob for a week. So I banned it. Never listened to it.

After my first session with him, the psychiatrist medicated me. I slept a lot. I stared out of the window a lot. I ironed a lot. And then eventually I started eating a bit more – I think one of Mr Kipling's cakes broke the drought – and then one day I caught myself singing along to 'Waterloo Sunset' on a radio in a boutique in Soho, hearing it properly for the first time. I was still singing it to myself when I got home to Withingdean, which was such a shock it made my father put down his toast and forget to pick it up again. The depression had caught me unawares, like someone grabbing my foot. When I was released from it, it happened in much the same way – quickly, easily, when 'Waterloo Sunset' came onto someone's transistor radio in a smelly little Soho boutique. And before I knew what had happened, I was even enjoying tennis again. Ha.

8. 'WHAT A WASTE' – IAN DURY

I didn't actually realize that music was allowed to be poetry until I heard Ian Dury and the Blockheads singing 'What A Waste'. I've got this magazine from last year, with song lyrics in it, and it's interesting because there's stuff you expect from rock 'n' roll lyrics in there – inarticulate, moronic, pointless, clearly written on a truckload of drugs – and then there's Ian Dury, who is so articulate that his words ping off the page. I took Hazel to see him at the Hope and Anchor in London, and she even deemed him a tasty fella.

'Quite tasty in fact, Linda. But what happened to him?'

'Polio. He got it in Southend in a swimming pool when he was a kid.'

The more correct answer, though, would have been genius. Genius happened to Ian Dury. All the different bits of Punk and New Wave that later made up the unofficial manifesto – being clever, being funny, writing about real things, looking strange, being a bit ugly, acting different, being poor and cool at the same time – they were all him, and they'd probably been him for years, it's just that nobody ever understood it before 1976.

Ian Dury got me writing. I don't mean I suddenly enrolled in a course, because I'm not that stupid, and anyway, Professor Hayes and his plaited leather belt still give me nightmares. What Dury's stuff did was make me think I *could* write. I went round the back of the Hope and Anchor once, when his roadies were packing up in the rain after a gig, and I gave one of them a poem to pass on to him. They were nice to me, the Blockheads roadies. And no, they didn't even want to sleep with me. So after that I wrote more poems. And I showed some of them to David and Hazel, and they said they were good. And then I started writing a diary, and a few letters to *Melody Maker*, and now I'm even having a go at this. I'm never going to be the catalyst that sparks a revolution, but since Ian Dury, there is definitely more to me than there used to be.

9. 'SHEENA IS A PUNK ROCKER' – THE RAMONES

Gabba gabba hey. I saw them at the Roundhouse in 1976, while David waited outside to collect me.

'All the animals in London Zoo have gone mad, you know that?'
he said.

'Where? What?'

I was still deaf from the speakers, covered in sweat, and my spiky
hair was stuck to the side of my face, melted egg white dripping
down.

'Linda. Can you hear me? Down on Regent's Park,' David
shouted, 'the elephants and lions in the zoo, they've all gone mad
because of these bloody Ramones.'

'Oh shut up.'

'I could hear it as far away as Oxford Street.'

I gave him a look.

'So what were the other bands like anyway?'

'Oh, The Flaming Groovies, they were OK. But The Stranglers,
they were fantastic.'

'*Fantastic.*' David imitated me, turning his back and stomping off
to the car.

It's funny how many relationships begin or end in the front seat of
a car. On TV and in films, the big discussions always happen in
parks, or on yachts, or on clifftops, or in restaurants. For me, though,
it's always been David in the driver's seat and me in the passenger
seat, not looking at each other, with the engine running, my shoes
kicked off on the floor and the doors closed. You can say a lot of
things when you're sitting side by side which you'd never say if you
could see the whites of each other's eyes.

'Linda.'

'What?' (Pronounced *Wot?*)

'You said I only owned eight LPs the other day.'

'Well you do.'

'Yes, but it's not a character flaw.'

'It is when one of them's by Billy Joel.'

Pause. Oh God. This is the last thing I feel like doing, having a
talk. Especially after spending the whole night pogoing to 'Blitzkrieg
Bop'. But David's come to pick me up. He wants to talk. It has to be
done.

'I support Man United.'

'Yes, David. I know.'

'I'll probably stop one day. Or at least it won't be with the same kind of enthusiasm. Will that change me? I don't think so.'

'What does that mean?'

'Just that this is a phase. It's something you've picked up, and you'll put it down again just as fast when you're bored with it. I know you! I mean, Linda, what were you when I met you? A big Sweet fan.'

'Oh piss off.'

'I'm just saying, the fact that I only own eight albums, and one of them is by Billy Joel, means about as much, in the grand scheme of things, as the fact that you own about eight hundred, and half of them are by groups nobody's ever heard of. It's only music – and a few clothes. Life should be about something more permanent than that. And I think our life is. This Punk thing with you isn't going to last for ever, any more than I'm always going to be mad on Man United.'

'I can't marry you.'

There, I'd said it. Sometimes it's best just to say the unsayable.

'I'm not asking you to.'

'Good, well I'm going for a walk then.'

I pushed down the car door handle and got as far as sticking my leg out – toes poking out of sawn-off black tights – before he pulled me back in again.

'The thing is, people go away eventually. Unless you make a firm promise, they disappear. I don't want to be like that, but I will be, I know it.'

'You mean you'd leave me because I wouldn't marry you?'

'Open your eyes. How do you think the world actually works, Linda? At the end of the day, it's supply and demand. Same as everything else.'

The crowds were still pouring out of the Roundhouse. David wouldn't come tonight. Not that I really wanted him to anyway. That's the terrible truth. He would have looked all wrong. And he would have hated it.

'Can't we just live together or something?' This said in a rush, as if it was the first thing that had come into my head, though I'd been thinking about it for months.

'You're so bloody romantic, aren't you.'

He closed his eyes and leaned his head back on the car seat.

'Don't be angry. I want to live with you, David, I really do.'

He was still not opening his eyes.

'I feel too young to get hitched though.'

He opened his eyes then, and laughed. And I could definitely hear elephants trumpeting over the noise of the traffic, so maybe he was right about The Ramones' effect on London Zoo.

He lit a cigarette and wound the window down.

'I know girls your age who've had a couple of kids by now. It's only hanging around with this lot' – he jerked a thumb at the leather-jacketed masses outside – 'that makes you think you're different.'

Long silence. This time it was my turn to close my eyes.

'So will we live together or not?' I asked him.

'We'll talk about it later. All right?'

Another pause. Then he drove us back to his Auntie Sheila's flat in Bermondsey, where she'd agreed to let us have the fold-up bed for the night. We both knew it, though – we'd crossed the final frontier. A few days later he proposed to me. And I accepted. Gratefully, even.

10. 'CA PLANE POUR MOI' – PLASTIC BERTRAND

After we moved in together, David and I started to collect compromise objects. Bovril was one of them. We both liked it on our toast, and it became part of the overlapping section of the Venn diagram we were making together. Protein 21 shampoo became another part, because it suited both our hair. Eventually the Venn diagram also came to contain Morecambe and Wise, sheepskin car seat covers, Tate and Lyle's Golden Syrup and a mutual loathing for the Tories. Music was harder, though.

Those eight albums of David's in full—

A Night At The Opera – Queen
52nd Street – Billy Joel
War Of The Worlds – Various Artists (I really, really, really hate this one)
Rumours – Fleetwood Mac
Songs In The Key Of Life – Stevie Wonder

Atlantic Crossing – Rod Stewart
Blood On The Tracks – Bob Dylan
10CC – The Original Soundtrack

When Plastic Bertrand put out 'Ca Plane Pour Moi' last year, and we both dug into our shared jar of coins on top of the fridge to buy it, it seemed like we'd finally sorted the relationship. At last! A song that fitted into the Venn diagram. It even fitted into my father's Venn diagram of both of us, because it gave him a chance to make jokes about what bloody idiots the French were, even though Plastic Bertrand was (as an army of DJs was always telling us) Belgian.

Radio 1, any day, in 1978:

'But the interesting thing about Plastic Bertrand, you know, is that he's not French at all, he's actually Belgian.'

'Yes shut up, just put the frigging song *on*.'

David and I mis-learned the words off by heart, enjoying the fact that we were deliberately getting them wrong, and used to sing them in unison, making the obligatory pop-eyed, slack-jawed, stupid Plastic Bertrand face. He looked like he was rocketing off a trampoline in the film clip, but instead we just jumped up and down on our bed with stiff arms, as if we both had a bad case of tetanus.

I like to think I had learned enough about poetry by then to realize that 'Ca Plane Pour Moi', in its own cretinous way, was a kind of poem. David just liked to chant it whenever a plane went overhead – or, as he liked to remind me, pointing to the jumbo as it flew over, 'That plane's for me!'

How do you know when you've finally grown up and become part of a mature, adult relationship? When you both agree to spend good money on a Plastic Bertrand single.

Anyway, that's my ten songs.

No, get rid of that bit, you sound like a prat again.

THE END

So . . . fine.

The clock in the kitchen says it's 3.31 a.m. And

there's only one thing to do, as far as I can see. Gather all the paper together, fold it neatly, put the biro back in the drawer, put my coffee mug upside down on the draining board and – rip the whole thing up.

I can't quite bring myself to shred it somehow, but it's clear it's got to be destroyed. It's embarrassing. It's revealing. It's drivel. In a word, it's my diary all over again, but instead of keeping it under my bed, I'm sending chunks of it off to some man in London I've never even met. It's a diary dressed up as a job application, for the best job in England. The job I'm not going to get.

After the wodge of paper goes in the bin, in two neatly ripped pieces, a soggy tea-bag goes in after it, making a nice dirty brown splat, which more or less completes everything. When I go back up to bed again, David's wide awake, staring out of the window and smoking.

In summer he spends so much time in the sea down on Brighton beach that his hair goes yellow at the front. Right now, in the middle of winter, it's gone back to a funny sandy colour again. And so has his chest hair. Despite all our ups and downs, I think I'll always be addicted to his chest hair.

'Do your pyjama buttons up, David, you'll freeze.'

'I wish I could do what you do,' he says at last. 'Just write like that.'

'Well I've chucked it out anyway.'

'What?'

'I'm embarrassed about it. It's rubbish.'

He lights a cigarette for me and I climb into bed; we hold each other for a while, feeling apart and together at the same time, watching the rain begin to hit the windows.

'I'm sorry about just now,' I say at last. And I mean the sex that hasn't happened again.

'Not your fault,' David says. I know he hates talking about it.

'It'll get better,' I promise him as he passes the ashtray over. It's a stupid joke ashtray he bought for me in Blackpool once, when we had one of those days when we never stopped talking and couldn't keep our hands off each other. It seems like years ago. It *was* years ago.

'Stop worrying. Just go to sleep,' he says. And then we finish our cigarettes.

CHAPTER TWO

A few days later, everything happens at once. I discover an incredible new band called The Gang Of Four, Barry Andrews leaves XTC and David says he's leaving me as well.

We're in the kitchen, not the car, when he gives me the news. He's spreading Bovril on his toast, and he's almost crying – but not quite. I'm – I don't know. I've had so many shocks in my life, I've developed this thing where my mind races ahead of the event in question, in search of a solution that will make me feel better.

'I don't think this is working, Linda.'

Good. I can move to London now, I've wanted to for ages, plenty of restaurants there, they must be crying out for assistant cooks. There's a rumour that Stiff Little Fingers will be touring any minute, maybe I can get a stack of tickets and scalp some to pay my train fare.

'What do you think?' He looks at me, hard.

'Um. I dunno.'

'Well you must have been thinking about it too.'

'No, actually, I haven't. What, David? Do you want to break off the engagement?'

He stands up, puts his toast down, picks it up again, then sits down again. 'I read what you wrote.'

This takes some time to sink in. And then I get it. The stuff in the bin. He's always the one who takes out the rubbish. He must have picked it out and put the pieces back together.

'Well you shouldn't've.'

David shrugs. 'It just confirms some things. That's all.'

'Oh don't be so bloody stupid! Confirms what?'

'You don't really love me. Not properly.'

I stare at the wall, listening but not taking it in.

'Come on, be honest. You're not sure about me any more.'

'What? No!'

'And after I read that, I realized I hardly know you, Linda. I don't know you very well at all.'

I go over and put my arms around him. He doesn't move, and he feels so cold and stiff in his winter coat, it's like hugging a dummy in a shop window. My mind has stopped racing ahead to the future, neatly taking care of everything, and instead I'm feeling terrified. Desperate, even.

'The reason I ripped up what I wrote is because I thought it was tripe. So how can you possibly use any of it against me?'

'No, it was good.'

He gently pushes me to one side, finishes his toast and gives me a look. 'Linda it was really good.'

'Oh shut up.'

'I sent it in for you.'

'You didn't.'

'I stuck it together with Sellotape and sent it in. It'll probably work in your favour. Ripped up and covered in tea-bag stains, very Punk that.'

Now it's my turn to cry. 'We're engaged! We can't split up now!'

David gives me a look. 'Let's just have a break for a while. Have a bit of time away from each other, that's

36

all I'm asking. I need time to think, Linda. I'll move out for a while. Or you can go back to your dad's.'

'Oh God, I'm not doing that.'

'Well I'll move out then. I just need some time, all right?'

Anger is my thing. I have about five seconds of tears, then I go to anger. It was like that when Mum died, and it's like that now.

'WELL SOD *YOU* THEN!'

'Oh Linda.'

'AND HOW DARE YOU SEND MY PRIVATE WRITING TO THAT FUCKING MAGAZINE IN LONDON WHEN I CHUCKED IT IN THE BIN!'

'Linda, please.'

He's been hiding the letter to show me. And he gets it out now. It's from someone called Howard Baker, who is the publisher of *NWW*. I've got an interview. He thinks I could be what they're looking for, and he and Jon Whitten, who's the other journalist who works there, want to meet me. The piece was brilliantly raw, and I've got an interview, and they want to meet me in Wardour Street next Tuesday at 2.30 p.m.

I try to take this in. It's the best job in England. And they want to interview me for it. I'm brilliantly raw. *I'm brilliantly raw.*

'David. I can't believe it. Oh my God.'

'I'll drive you up to London if you want, I've got Tuesday afternoon off.'

'No don't, it's your free half day.'

Then something occurs to me.

'You're moving out. We're having a break. You can't give me lifts now.'

He shrugs. 'Suit yourself.'

And although now is probably the moment to throw my arms around him and go down on my knees and thank God that he got my letter out of the bin and sent it, I don't. I don't because I just *can't*. At exactly the same moment that I realize David has given me the biggest gift he could possibly give me, I also realize that there is now a life out there without him – because it's become suddenly and fantastically possible.

'I can read your mind,' he insists wryly as he watches me struggle with my conscience, 'can't I? You're thinking, wow, London. Lots of men with spiky hair and badges. Freedom at last. Good old David, he can wait for me while I get this out of my system.'

I shake my head.

'The thing is, Linda, you'll be getting things out of your system for the rest of your life. Because I'm the wrong person for you. And you're the wrong person for me. And that's why I'm leaving. Unless you can convince me otherwise, I've got no reason to stay.'

Against my better judgement, I start to cry. 'Oh God, David. No. It's not like that.'

But of course it is. And he can read my mind. He was doing it when I was smuggling 'Ballroom Blitz' up my bomber jacket six years ago in Rave At Hillage's, and he's doing it now. He watches me for a while, after this, waiting for me to say something, and when I don't, he gets up from his chair and leaves.

'David!'

But he's gone already, with a tight little smile that makes my stomach drop. And now my heart is doing its own kind of 'Ballroom Blitz'. It sounds just like Mick Tucker thumping a snare, produced by Chinn and Chapman with plenty of overdubs. Banga banga, banga banga, BOOM BOOM, banga banga.

David will be back, I know he'll be back. He's *got* to be back. Then I think, *My writing is raw.* I'm raw. Wow, I'm raw. *I'm raw, I'm raw, I'm raw!* Which takes over from everything else.

I go into the restaurant the next day and ask for Tuesday afternoon off, but they say no.

'Linda. You already turn up late as it is. We need you Tuesday. We've got fourteen frozen chickens need picking up.'

So I say sorry but I've got a job interview in London (I can't help myself, I've got to show off to someone). Whereupon they tell me they'll have to find someone else then and they might make it permanent. I can't even be bothered arguing, and as I leave, I know I've lost it. They were nice too. A Chinese family who had the difficult task of competing with both a Wimpy and a Kentucky Fried on the high street, and the local National Front skinheads who occasionally lobbed bricks through their window.

A few songs get me through the week. 'Alternative Ulster' by Stiff Little Fingers. 'Hong Kong Garden' by Siouxsie and the Banshees – which reminds me of the Chinese family at the restaurant – and 'Rock Lobster' by the B-52s. 'Rock Lobster' is another reminder of the job I've just left, because the lead singer Fred Schneider put down the El Dorado restaurant as the band's contact number on the back of the sleeve. I wonder if he's an assistant cook like me?

I have no idea what to wear for the interview with Howard Baker. To get the job at the Chinese restaurant, I wore an orange cotton dress and a white cardigan, but that was before 1976, in the days when I used to iron. Maybe I should just get an instant New Wave wardrobe by mail order from the back pages of *NME* instead: a German officer's tunic (£8.95 state chest size), US Army fatigue trousers with zips on the pockets (£7.95), a Blondie T-shirt (£2.50) and a gas mask (£4.95 + 70p postage and packing).

In the end I buy another pair of black tights from Marks & Spencer, cut the feet out with the kitchen scissors, and decide on my skinny black leather tie, my man's white shirt from Oxfam, my old red kilt, and some brown winkle-pickers that Hazel gave me because they gave her blisters. I dye the winkle-pickers turquoise, then think about going back to Marks to shoplift some thermal underwear, because it's still the Winter of bloody Discontent out there. Finally, I cut my hair back around my ears, making nice sawn-off V-shapes with the kitchen scissors, and dye it black again with a kit from the chemist.

Then, suddenly, it's Tuesday morning, and I find myself waking up in a bed which is big enough for two people, even though it has only one pillow. As I come to, I remember. It's a blur but somehow, in the middle of all this shoe-dyeing and hair-dyeing and preparation for the best job in England, David's moved out of our flat and into a house with his friend Jeff. We are, officially, *apart*. And one of these mornings I'll be able to wake up and ease into it, instead of opening my eyes, seeing a blank space beside me and going into mild shock.

David rings me at about 10 a.m. and checks to see if I want a lift with him to London for my interview. I don't know what to do, so I tell him I'll have to check my train timetable and call him back later.

'I might be out,' David says. 'And you'd better check the trains are running, with all the strikes.'

'OK,' I say.

Then I put the phone down and call Hazel.

'Don't do it to him, Linda.'

'We haven't split up, we're just not living together for a while. I can say yes to a lift if I want.'

'But you're using him, aren't you?'

Her voice sounds faintly sniffy and disapproving.

'No I'm not.'

'Look, Linda, I'm his friend as well as yours and I have to stick up for him. All right?'

'Yes, all right, all right.'

She goes on, 'Poor love, he's moved out and waited all this week just to call you, to *pretend* to offer you a

40

drive up to London. And you're going to take it just like that, and you don't even care about him, do you? He's got that post-dumping passion thingy and you haven't. Well that's cruel.'

'Well of course I haven't got the post-dumping passion thingy, because I'm the dumpee. *He's* the dumper. Honestly!'

'It happens all the time, you know,' she says sagely. 'They leave you and then they realize how much they miss you.'

Hazel's been in more relationships than I have, so I suppose I have to believe her.

'And what happens after that?' I ask.

'Oh I dunno, write to "Cathy and Claire",' she hurrumphs.

'So what should I do about this lift to London then?'

'Just tell him no,' Hazel insists. 'Call him back and tell him you'd rather get the train so you can have time to think before the interview. David deserves his half day off anyway. That bank is bloody murder. I went in there yesterday; it was full of pensioners.'

A pause.

'And I'll give you the train fare, Linda. Just give me double helpings of Chop Suey when I come into the restaurant.'

'I can't. They sacked me.'

She sighs.

'But what if you don't get this magazine job? How are you going to pay your rent on the flat?'

'Well David's covering it until the end of the month. Until I get someone new into the spare room.'

'Oh, not that horrible end room that smells of wee!'

'Someone will have it if I scrub it down,' I shrug.

'Oh well, I'll ask around at school, then.'

Hazel has a proper job, unlike me. She's a teacher in Haywards Heath. She also has proper hair, unlike me. Hers is permed and blonde, and she uses hairspray.

41

Mine has been so many colours it looks like a tortoise-shell cat.

'Hazel, if I get the job, I'll probably have to interview Bob Geldof. So I'll tell you what. I'll get his autograph. That'll make up for the train fare.'

This makes Hazel squeal. I know that Bob Geldof is easily the tastiest of all tasty fellas in her tasty-fella pantheon.

'Don't get his autograph unless it's on my boobs, please.'

'Well all right, I'll tell him to come down to Haywards Heath and do it. Happy now?'

In the end, I not only borrow my train fare from Hazel, I also borrow money for some aspirin from Boots because I've got a thumping headache, and enough coins for emergency phone calls, just in case *NWW* turns out to be a front for a white slave trade operation.

'Howard Baker and Jon Whitten,' Hazel mutters darkly, reading their letter. 'They sound well dodgy.'

After this, I call David, who's gone out, as he warned – either that or he's letting the phone ring off the hook to spite me – then dash out of the house. I finally make it up to London at 2.25 p.m., where a wild wind is blowing straight up the Berwick Street Market in Soho and all the way up my kilt. I didn't have any clean knickers so I'm wearing my old PE shorts under my tights.

Number 8A Wardour Street is above a shoe shop. The label on the buzzer says *NWW* in proper spiky New Wave writing, no biro rubbish, so I immediately feel this is A Good Sign. On the way up the stairs, which stink of cabbage, I can also hear X-Ray Spex playing 'Germ Free Adolescents'. Another Good Sign.

It's the best job in England and I'm not going to get it. It's the best job in England and I'm not going to get it.

About halfway up the stairs, the smell of cabbage is replaced by the smell of new wood – pine or something – and when I push open the door marked *NWW* I can see why. The entire office is crammed with antique pine furniture. There's a Welsh dresser on the back wall, but where old ladies normally stack china plates, there's a row of singles instead. The chimneypiece is pine. There's a pine bookcase, with both doors hanging wide open because it's crammed full of old copies of music magazines. Four pine cabinets are stacked on top of each other behind the door, and if there are human beings in this office I can't see them, because there are several huge pine wardrobes parked in the middle of the floor.

Impressively, a ticket for the Pistols this time last year, in Texas, is Sellotaped to one of the pine wardrobe doors. Below it, a teddy bear wearing a John Cooper Clarke badge is hanging from the wardrobe handle. He's also got a little paper hat on, like a paper boat, on which someone has written 'BOLLOCKS'. For some unknown reason there are also framed photographs of greyhounds at the racetrack, crossing the finishing line, on every single foot of wall space.

Finally, a pair of feet in brown suede Hush Puppies poke around the side of the wardrobe. When I look up, I see a man with bad teeth, holding a Benson & Hedges special filter in one hand and a scone in the other. It's got jam dropping off it.

'I'm Howard Baker. You *are* Linda, aren't you?'

He puts down the scone, but not the fag, so he can shake my hand. And I think, well it *is* 2.30 p.m. on Tuesday, and this is 1979, and I *have* been waiting my entire life for this moment, so I *must* be Linda, mustn't I?

Another man comes forward, edging gingerly past

43

the pine dresser in case he knocks something over, and I realize that although something stopped me from ordering all my clothes from the back pages of the *NME*, nothing has stopped him. This man is wearing a German officer's tunic, PVC jeans that come halfway up his ankles, a black V-neck woolly jumper, a string vest dyed black, woolly socks (odd colours) and Doc Martens.

'I'm Jon Whitten.'

No handshake. But then, he has a cigarette in each hand, so he can't. He's wearing cheap reproduction Elvis Costello glasses as well.

Howard gets up and moves two of the wardrobes flat against the wall, grunting with the effort. Then Jon wheels over a chair, from the kitchen on the landing.

'Have a seat.' He pushes it towards me.

When I sit down, though, I realize that a pine sideboard is now blocking my line of vision, so although I have a good view of Jon Whitten's ankles in the odd socks, I can only see the left side of his face. And Howard has disappeared from view completely.

Another pine wardrobe is moved.

'Sodding furniture,' Howard says. Jon smokes both his cigarettes, puffing on each in turn.

'Germ Free Adolescents' has stopped playing, and instead there is only the sound of someone doing things loudly with bits of paper. Then that also stops, and a short woman in skin-tight red Capri pants with fluffy pink mules and a long blonde ponytail shoots out of what looks like a broom cupboard tacked onto the side of the office.

'This is Cindy,' Jon explains. 'She works in the art department. Actually she *is* the art department. We knocked down a wall in the broom cupboard and invented it one day.'

Cindy smiles and asks me if I want a coffee. Or more specifically, a cawfee. She has bright pink lipstick, and talks like Debbeeee Harreeee, or maybe Pattiiii Smith.

'Yes please, thank you very much, one sugar.'

Yes please, thank you very much, one sugar? As David would say, that's not very Punk. That's not very *New Wave*.

But then, neither is Howard Baker, who pats his knee – where the hell did he get those tweed trousers, it's like sitting next to Evelyn Waugh – and motions for a King Charles spaniel to jump onto his lap. The dog, it turns out, has been sitting patiently inside one of the pine wardrobes, farting.

'Phew,' Howard says, fanning the wardrobe door backwards and forwards. 'No more soup bones for you, Mr Smelly.'

I smile, because I know he's doing all this jokey dog-farting stuff for my benefit, but I notice nobody else does. And I must admit, the smell is terrible – along with the pine.

'Cindy has the difficult job of making us all look good,' Howard explains as he eyeballs the blonde with the ponytail. 'And when she gets fed up, she just gets the glue out of the drawer and has a jolly good sniff, don't you, Cindy?'

Oh my God. I think Howard went to a posh school. Visions of the hard man in the leather jacket and studs, the man who could get Bob Geldof to autograph Hazel's boobs in Haywards Heath, suddenly vanish.

'Cindy's from Detroit,' Howard waves a hand at her backside which is bobbing up and down as she wobbles onto the landing in her mules, then goes through the complicated process of finding milk, coffee, sugar, cups, teaspoons, saucers and biscuits, all of which involves a lot of bending down and getting back up again. I count eight bobs in total, also closely watched by Jon in his big horn-rimmed glasses. Cindy, I gather, doesn't say much.

'Do you know the worst thing about publishing this sodding magazine *New Wave Weekly*?' Howard confronts me suddenly.

I don't. I shake my head and try to look sympathetic and intelligent. This is a job interview after all. I need him to like me.

'It's trying to pronounce it properly,' he sighs. 'I mean, I've put thousands of quid into this thing, and I can't even say it on the phone.'

'Too many Ws,' Jon says, sniffing.

'It's worse when you're drunk,' Howard informs me. And he says it experimentally to himself a few times: 'New Wave Weekly. New Wave Weekly. New-Wave-Weekly.'

He offers Jon and I cigarettes after that, and we both take them a bit too quickly. The ashtrays, I notice, are overflowing.

When I've finally had enough of looking at the photographs of greyhounds all over the walls while Howard smokes and twitters away to himself, trying to say the name of his own magazine, Cindy comes in with coffee and digestives on a tray. There is nowhere sensible to put the cups as there are so many pine wardrobes getting in the way of everything, so in the end she slaps them down on the floor, slopping coffee on the rug. Then she teeters back into the tiny art room in her mules. Jon watches her go, pushing his Elvis Costello glasses up his nose and crossing his legs in his shiny black PVC trousers which creak. Cindy and Jon look like two people who are sleeping together and trying to cover it up, and I suppose if I ever get this job I'll find out all about it.

Howard Baker waves a hand at his desk. 'I got the typewriters from a journalist friend of mine who was severely peed off with Fleet Street so we pinched the lot,' he explains while Jon hunts for another record to put on. Howard pats the spaniel. 'I'll tell you the worst thing about the music business, Linda, it's the cheese.'

'The cheese?'

'I went to the launch party for some dreadful little band last week. What were they called, Jon, The Sneaky Beavers? The Evil Weasels?'

There is no reply from behind the wardrobe, where The Stranglers are being put on the turntable. 'Anyway. Something to do with small animals,' Howard goes on, drawing breath. 'I knew, Linda, when I arrived, that there would be cheese and biscuits and beer at this event, and that's exactly what I got. Cheese and biscuits and beer. I've put on three stone since this bloody Punk business started.'

He looks at me for a moment. 'Do you have any questions? I suppose I should have asked you that first.'

'Yes. Why have you got all these wardrobes in here?'

He nods, as if this is an eminently sensible question. 'It's my other business. The Pine Palace. I have to do some of the storage in here. I was going to call it the Pine Mine, actually, but some other bugger in Fulham thought of it first.'

'And how come there are pictures of greyhounds everywhere?'

'Ah.' Howard nods again. 'This used to be the home of *British Racing Greyhound Gazette.*'

'Which he inherited from his uncle,' Jon interrupts. Howard gives him a look.

'I have to confess it's true. Uncle Walter died and left me the lot: filing cabinets, telephones, even the blinking telephone directories were still here.'

'Howard also imports two-in-one mini bidets,' Cindy informs me, appearing from the other side of the wardrobe.

'£14.90 with a thirty-day money back guarantee. Can't say fairer than that,' Howard says quickly.

47

'You'll see one if you ever use the loo in here,' Jon adds, 'though if I was you, I'd use the pub over the road.'

'I found a dead rat stuffed inside a loo roll in that plastic box we use for women's things,' Cindy drawled, 'and it wasn't pretty.'

Embarrassed at this sudden turn in the conversation, Howard lights another cigarette. 'And I manage some groups as well.'

'All of whom will, mysteriously enough, be featured prominently in *New Wave Weekly*,' Jon interrupts.

'I wanted to sign The Jam, you know.' Howard sighs. 'Three years ago, they were down here in Soho busking. *Busking!* They borrowed the electricity from some shop and just plugged themselves in. They had matching white shoes. I thought to myself, I want to sign that group with the matching white shoes.'

Howard gets up from his chair, regretfully shaking his head at lost opportunities and gently nudging the spaniel off his tweed trousers. 'I'm off to L'Escargot if anyone fancies some snails,' he says to nobody in particular. I notice that neither Cindy nor Jon make a move.

'Well come on then,' he says, directing the invitation at me. 'Celebrate your gainful employment by having some Brians with me.'

Brians, I realize, must be the snails, named after the character in *The Magic Roundabout*.

'And some Alsatian wine, *of course*,' Howard adds. 'Cindy, would you look after the pooch for me?'

She teeters out of her office and bobs down to pick up the dog, which immediately licks her face – something that Jon looks as if he'd like to do too.

It's only when I've squeezed past one of the pine wardrobes and made it onto the landing that I realize Howard's acting like I've got the job.

'I'm not very good at the chain-of-command thingy,' he explains, 'but do bear with me.'

'OK.'

'And I'm afraid it will be slightly less money than we thought,' Howard explains as I float down Wardour Street. But I'm so happy I don't even care when my kilt blows up over my black PE shorts.

'Probably more like £3,500 than £4,000,' Howard goes on, without seeming to notice either my happiness or my shorts. 'And I can't pay you overtime.' He coughs. 'For God's sake don't tell the NUJ.'

'That's all right,' I tell him. I don't even know what the NUJ is.

'Are you sure? You look distressed,' he says.

'It's just that I want to call someone and I don't know if I should,' I say, and it's the truth. The only problem is, it's David, and I have no idea if that's allowed yet. My need to call him is like some mad homing instinct, but what are the rules? Should I call, or should I not? I wish Hazel had explained that bit to me.

CHAPTER THREE

After Howard and I finish two bottles of Alsatian wine, and he eats a lot of Brians and I eat a lot of his bread rolls, he asks me about Withingdean.

'It's too boring, Howard. It's the most boring town in England. I just can't.'

'Have you got a boyfriend to make it more exciting?'

'No.' I can't bring myself to tell him about David.

'Oh well,' Howard lights another cigarette. 'Is Withingdean near Rottingdean by any chance? A friend of mine went to school there.'

'It's near Rottingdean, Ovingdean, Saltdean and all the other bloody boring Deans near Brighton.'

'And what do you do there?'

'Same things I've been doing since 1975. Having a bath on Sunday night. Watching my neighbour try to repair the heater in his VW. Going down the laundrette. Having an Aero and a packet of salt and vinegar crisps in front of a repeat of *The Onedin Line*. Cleaning guinea-pig wee out of my beanbag. There's not a lot going on in Withingdean.'

'You've got guinea pigs?'

'My neighbours do. They come in through a hole in the kitchen door and wee in my beanbag and then they shoot off again. It's the most exciting thing that happens in our town all week. It stops traffic.'

Howard turns the conversation back to *NWW*.

'I know it was a cheek asking for someone under thirty – I'm thirty-eight myself for God's sake – but Jon insisted.'

'Lucky for me.'

'Cindy liked the way you ripped your job application up, by the way, and made it look all grotty and stuck a tea-bag on it. She thought it was very inventive.'

'Thank you.'

Suddenly Howard leans forward over the table as if he's about to tell me a secret. 'Unfortunately, Linda, the magazine will have a slight *British Greyhound Racing Gazette* quality to it – in the initial stages anyway.'

'Why's that?'

'We're using all their old equipment. Can't afford new stuff. I mean, I want to get one of these word processors you hear about, where you can just stick a floppy disk in—'

'Floppy what?'

'But while we have this slight cashflow problem, I'm afraid we will just have to put up with the typewriters, and Cindy will just have to do the best she can. She's going to cut out letters from the headlines in *Woman's Own* and give us that sort of Sex Pistolly kidnap-letter bollocky look.'

'Hmm.'

'However, I'm afraid the overall appearance of *NWW* is still going to be a little bit . . .'

Howard searches for the words.

'A little bit *Greyhound Gazette*?' I suggest.

'Yes. A little bit *Greyhound Gazette*.'

The first issue comes out on Wednesday, 5 March, so we've got about a month to put it together.

'Jon's marvellous, of course,' Howard tells me. 'He just takes vast quantities of Black Beauties, or that

51

powder he likes, mixed up with Imperial Leather and Harpic, shoves it all up his nose and then puts five articles on your desk at the end of the day, just like that. No, I'm not at all concerned about the deadline,' Howard says, knocking back another glass of wine and crunching on a snail. Then he gives me a look.

'Linda, you're not nervous, are you?'

I tell him the truth.

'It's just that I've never written anything before. Apart from essays, anyway, and my diary, and some poems.'

'But you're so deliciously raw, that's why we want you on the magazine!' Howard cuts in before I can dribble on about any of my other insecurities.

And so deliciously cheap, I think to myself. I wonder how much he pays Cindy?

As the conversation goes on, though, and the waiter keeps pouring the wine, it appears there might be other reasons why I've been hired.

'You look as though you'll do a wonderful job on our crossword, Linda.'

'The crossword?'

'Actually, I've got the list of things we want you to do, if you want to accept the job, that is.'

'I sort of already have accepted. I mean, I really want to do it.'

'Oh good. Well anyway, here's the list.'

Howard gets a piece of paper out of his pocket, and then the waiter comes over to say he's got a telephone call, so he wanders off with his napkin in his hand, apologizing to both of us in that twittery way the English upper classes have.

The list is headed LINDA JOBS:

1. Do the crossword.
2. Write something about fashion, e.g. black plastic trousers.

3. Review records Jon doesn't like, e.g. popular.
4. Think of clever headings for things.
5. Do the hit parade.
6. Go and see concerts Jon doesn't want to review, e.g. Vibrant Thigh in Manchester and Nazareth on the Isle of Man.
7. Make up stories about groups press officers will not let us interview, e.g. The Sex Pistols.

When Howard comes back – 'Sorry about that, Linda, it was a Pine Palace call' – I realize I've drunk enough Alsatian wine to assert myself, so I try to shake the piece of paper at him and complain. In the end, though, the only thing I find myself brave enough to moan about is the fact that he's included Nazareth in the list.

'We can't have them in *NWW*,' I say, having difficulty pronouncing it.

'You see!' Howard says triumphantly, waving his wineglass around. 'The moment you consume any kind of alcohol, the name of the magazine becomes impossible to say!'

'Anyway, what I'm trying to say is, Nazareth aren't New Wave. We can't have a review of them.'

'But Jon told me they were cutting-edge Punks from the squats in Notting Hill.'

'I think he was having a joke, Howard.'

'Bastard!' Howard says.

I ask Howard about all the bands he manages, and he reels them off. 'Stiff Hamsters. The Rejected. Terminal Sausage. Pensioners On Acid. Mandy and the Mutants. Throw enough mud at a wall and some of it will stick, Linda. Though I must say, there's quite a buzz in Bristol about Terminal Sausage at the moment.'

'Well exactly.'

God, I must be drunk.

I look at the 'Linda Jobs' list again and feel confident

enough to ask Howard another question. 'Is it just the four of us then, working on *NWW*?'

'Tight little ship, yes.' Then Howard remembers something. 'Oh, Jon's cousin in Welwyn Garden City is going to sell some of the advertisements. Over the phone. It's an extra earner for him – I've already got him shifting some hatstands for the Pine Palace up there. And I'll sell the big advertisements, of course – to HMV and WH Smith and people like that. And we'll have freelancers in to do all the extra writing and photography and whatnot, so don't worry about any of that.'

'And what about editing it? Like, checking everything? Will you do that?' I ask him.

'Oh God no. I'll get Alan Jennings to do that.'

'And who's he?'

'Alan Jennings is former editor of the *British Racing Greyhound Gazette*. We're going to post him the pages, first class, to Surrey, and then he'll write his remarks on them in red pencil and his wife will post them back.'

It's all I can do not to laugh through my nose, but Howard's paying the bill, so I don't.

After he's tipped the waiter in one-pence pieces, we share a taxi back to his flat in Basil Street. He collects the nameless farting spaniel on the way, throwing bits of litter at the windows of the *NWW* office until Cindy yells that she's coming down. We then get back in the taxi, Howard cradling the dog like a baby so it won't do anything to upset the driver, and we crawl through the traffic at Piccadilly Circus, as the dog gently dribbles on his tweed jacket and the driver actively tries to ram all the tourists.

'You show them, my friend,' Howard encourages him. 'Bloody Swedes gawping at Eros!'

'If you get out here,' Howard says, when we finally arrive at Basil Street, 'you can leg it to Victoria Station in two shakes of a lamb's tail.'

I look up at his flat, which is something with white turrets that Bertie Wooster might have lived in, and at his wallet, which is bulging with ten-quid notes, and wonder why I have to get out and walk. But anyway.

When I get to Victoria, I find out that the Brighton train is delayed. What a surprise. There's also a puddle of sick in front of the ticket office, and a fat bloke with no pants on is trying to have a kip with half his body wedged inside a phone box.

I think about David again. I could call him right now, from the phone box, if it wasn't for the fat bloke. Then again the phone probably isn't working, and the one at Brighton Station certainly isn't. Allowing for a delayed train home and a missed bus, I'll probably walk back into the flat at – midnight? A reasonable time to call him, I think, in that very reasonable, drunken way you can only achieve after two bread rolls, no proper food and a bottle of wine. And he'll be up, after all, won't he – *missing me*.

In the end, when I finally walk back from the bus stop outside the Withingdean corner shop, kilt blowing up, arms crossed, teeth gritted – at midnight – the wine has worn off, I've got a headache, I'm freezing, I'm starving and the drunk but reasonable logic has vanished.

The flat looks depressingly empty without David's stuff, and it feels wrong without anyone home to call out to. And there's condensation on the kitchen window again, freezing from the inside. Needless to say, the landlord hasn't emptied the meter either, so I can't stuff any more money in there and turn on the fire. So I do what I always do and put my old fun fur coat on over the top of my fluffy dressing gown over the top of my clothes, and then pull on two pairs of socks under my slippers. It's always your feet which end up freezing, especially on the kitchen lino.

I'm making a mug of Horlicks when the phone rings,

and my heart jumps at the thought that it might be David, but it's Hazel.

'I'm dying to know what happened,' she hisses down the line. I suppose she doesn't want to wake her flatmate up.

'Oh. Well I think I've got it.'

'Oh my God, Linda! So you're going to take it?'

'No, I'm going back to the Chinese restaurant to make Special Fried Rice. Of course I'm going to take it.'

There's a sniffy silence after this, and I have to apologize for being tired and having drunk too much.

'Where will you live?'

'God knows.'

'And you can afford it on the salary?'

'What are you, my dad? Anyway, it's £3,500 a year. It's more than I'm bloody getting now.'

This reminds her of something. 'I saw your dad today by the way.'

'Oh, did you?'

'He asked me if I knew whether you and David were coming round for tea on Sunday night.'

'Oh bugger.'

'And someone had to tell him, so I did.'

'I bet Dad didn't say anything,' I tell her as I lean against the kitchen wall, glancing at one of the very few things David didn't take with him – a coffee percolator we ordered together from a catalogue. The only thing is, neither of us ever worked out how to use it.

'You're right,' Hazel says. 'He didn't say a word.'

'Did you tell him about the job interview as well?'

'It seemed too much to throw at him. Broken engagement, moving to London, you interviewing Bob Geldof.'

I laugh. 'More like doing the bloody crossword. By the way,' I remember something. 'It's not a broken engagement. It's a trial separation.'

'Is it?'

'Don't go telling everyone in Withingdean the engagement is off. I mean, I've still got my ring.' I look at it for a minute, on my finger, for reassurance.

'Well let's just say it's the *risk* of a broken engagement then,' she argues. Hazel hates being wrong. 'After all, David's not there, is he?'

I light a cigarette and exhale into the phone, which I know annoys her. Hazel and I have been friends since we were thirteen years old, and after that amount of time you know almost everything about someone, including how to irritate them in expert ways.

'Of course there's the *risk* of a broken engagement, Hazel, but if David goes out and gets knocked down by a bus tomorrow, that's a risk as well, isn't it? I mean, there's a risk of me finding a dead mouse in this packet of Smash potatoes as well, isn't there?'

Another thing David has deigned to leave behind – an old packet of Cadbury's Smash, propped up next to the kettle, so I can have all the instant mash my heart desires.

'You know what I mean,' Hazel tuts, and I smoke into the phone again.

While I think of something else to say, I stare mindlessly through the kitchen doors and into the living room – not that there's much to look at. David and I used to have a Salvador Dali poster above the fireplace, with a silver frame and a tiny crack in the glass. Gone. We used to have a coffee table with cork coasters that David's mother had given us. Gone. He's left the TV set, but that's about it. No orange shagpile rug, no Monopoly set, no big green glass ashtray.

'It's not hard to see who had the salary in this relationship, Hazel,' I tell her. 'I haven't really looked at the flat properly since he's gone, but honestly, there's nothing left in here. You should see it.'

On the other end of the phone, Hazel sighs.

'Regarding the job again ... and David. Well. I just don't want you to make a mistake,' she says at last.

'You're sounding like my dad again.'

'I bet you really love him deep down, don't you?'

'Well he obviously doesn't think so.'

'Well, he must love you deep down anyway.'

'Yeah, Hazel, that's why he suddenly decided to move out.'

After that, neither of us can think of anything to say. David's taken the trendy digital clock from the kitchen wall – of course he has, I gave it to him for his birthday – but I'm guessing it's something like 1 a.m.

'I don't feel I'm getting anywhere with you,' Hazel says.

'I didn't ask you to.'

'Nyah nyah, Linda. We're not thirteen any more.'

'Well stop acting like it. You're bossing me around again, just like you always do.'

I remember us as teenagers for a minute. We had a really hot summer the year after Mum died, and I was burnt to a crisp after Hazel told me to put olive oil and vinegar on my legs and sunbathe in the garden. She'd read it in a magazine. Silly cow.

'Someone has to make you think, Linda. You were just going to come straight back home, wake up tomorrow and make an instant decision, weren't you?'

'I already have, so it's even more instant than you thought.'

'David won't put up with it, Linda. If you move up to London, he really will break off the engagement. Or you'll get fed up and break it off yourself. At the moment you've still got a chance. I just don't want to see you throw it away, that's all. I'm friends with both of you, remember.'

I smoke into the phone again, saying nothing.

I think back to this afternoon or rather, to yesterday, as I'm sure it's tomorrow morning now. I think about

Howard Baker and his snails, and his pine wardrobes and his bidets. And Cindy and her long blond pony-tail. The Sex Pistols ticket stuck to the wardrobe. The farting spaniel asleep in the wardrobe. The fashion column I'm supposed to write. And Jon Whitten.

Then I come back to Hazel's voice, talking on and on about my dad, and then about David.

'It must be the true mark of a music obsessive,' I say at last.

'What?'

'I can't even get upset about any of these things you're talking about. All I can hear is the new Ramones single in my head.' To prove it, I hum a few bars to her.

'Who are these Ramones when they're at home then?'

'You know exactly who they are.'

'If they're not on *Top of the Pops*, then I don't know who they are,' she sniffs.

I roll my eyes. We've had this kind of stand-off before.

I'm not lying to Hazel. 'I Wanna Be Sedated'. It's all I can think about at the moment, and it's certainly all I can hear in my head.

'Anyway, I've said my piece,' she finishes. 'I can tell you've already made your mind up.'

'Yeah.'

'You know as well as I do that if you trained to be a teacher like me you'd end up being on much more money than £3,500 a year.'

'Yeah.'

'And David's a catch, you know. If you let him go, someone else will snap him up.'

'Yeah.' Then I give up and put the phone down, and skid across the kitchen lino in my two pairs of socks, shuffling towards the bedroom.

David and I paid for our double bed together, but he left it here because he said it was too heavy to move –

although I expect he was being kind, as usual. Tonight, though, I'm glad it's still here. He's sleeping on a blow-up mattress at Jeff's place. Rather him than me, in this weather.

When I go into the bedroom, I notice the smell of Omo and wet clothes – it's like being in a mouldy laundrette. My pyjama bottoms obviously haven't dried. I washed them this morning and left them on the radiator, and nothing's happened. They're damp, frozen into weird leg shapes, and hanging pointlessly from a slab of cold metal on the wall that's heating precisely nothing, thanks to the landlord and his stuffed meter. Great.

I read somewhere that if you wear your tights to bed you'll get thrush, but at this point I'm so cold I couldn't care less, so I take my fun fur coat off, and my dressing gown, and my job interview clothes, and jump around with my teeth chattering, before I quickly hoist the tights up to my waist, put tracksuit bottoms on over the top and jump under the blankets.

All I can think of as I burrow into the pillow is Dad. For a while there it was me and Hazel versus Dad, but as we've grown older, it seems to be her, David and Dad all together against me. The voices of reason in Withingdean against my own little voice of unreason.

When Mum died, Dad expected me to cook for him. He gave me housekeeping money, from his salary as a bus driver, and he got Grandma and various other women in the family to show me how to cook, and then I was just expected to get on with it. He wanted me to take over where Mum had left off, even though I was only thirteen.

There were a couple of other girls at school who cooked for their families, because their mothers were ill or had run off, but I was the only one who was expected to do her homework and come up with meat and three veg for her father, followed by pudding, followed by the washing up, finished by the ironing. Other girls at school smelled of Avon eau de cologne. I just stank of Stork margarine.

Dad never formally asked me to take over from Mum, he just assumed I would, and he did a lot of grunting when I didn't. So at sixteen I was practically dead on my feet at school, falling asleep in maths, yawning my way through English, until the magical day when I walked into Tesco's and discovered Vesta instant dinners. All you had to do was add water and stir. And then, miraculously, you could take care of Monday (Chow Mein), Tuesday (Beef Curry), Wednesday (Chicken Supreme), Thursday (Paella), Friday (Chicken Curry) and Saturday (Beef Risotto).

And it might have worked, and even changed my life, except for the fact that Dad hated Vesta dinners and threw the Paella at the wall, then made me pay a fiver for all the housekeeping money I'd wasted on lazy instant foreign muck. Hazel's mother made her come round after school and help me cook dinner after that, so we both smelled of Stork all the time.

Then, after I turned seventeen, Hazel just came and got me. She made me pack my bags and she got her father to have a serious talk with my father, and soon after that I was out of there for ever. Sharing a place with her and another girl above the chemist. Liberated. Free of the smell of Stork, and the piles of shirts in the ironing basket on a Sunday night.

If it was warm enough in here, I'd probably allow myself some tears, not only about the near-fight I've just had with Hazel, but also about those long-gone fights with Dad and the way I've let him down again. I suppose I should pick up the phone and talk to him about it, but I just can't.

Not long after that, I fall asleep, shivering in my tights and tracksuit, with my arms folded and The Ramones going round my head.

Later on, something wakes me up, and I realize it's a full moon, so I pull open the curtains to have a better look. I rub my hand across the left side of the bed, where David always slept. It still smells of him, because I haven't washed the sheets since he left. I look around the room at his Jack Higgins books which aren't there any more, and the big Crombie coat which isn't on the back of the door any more, and the photo of us last Christmas which makes me look like I've got an enormous nose – it made him look so handsome, though, that I've always had it propped up next to my side of the bed.

I've already taken off my engagement ring a few times this week, to look at my finger naked, then fully clothed. It's a platinum ring which I know David took out a loan for. Then I put it on the bedside table, just to see how it feels to go to sleep without any guarantees. As I fully expect, it feels horrible. But I sleep anyway, with the full moon hanging over my neighbour's VW in the street outside.

CHAPTER FOUR

Howard rings a few days later and suggests I have a trial day at *NWW* before I start there officially. 'Can you come up to London tomorrow?' he asks.

'Well I could. But can I sleep on someone's floor?'

There's a pause, then Howard obviously thinks it might be not very Punk to refuse me, because he gives in.

'I'll boot the dog off the sofa in Basil Street, so you can sleep on that. Don't worry,' he says quickly, 'it's not made out of pine. In fact, it's rather comfortable.'

'And there's something else, Howard.'

Howard makes a little sharp breathing sound, and I realize he's expecting a money question. Maybe all his phone calls are like that.

'There's this band called The Pretenders that everyone's talking about. And if I'm going to be in London tomorrow night . . .'

'Yes?'

'Can you get me in for nothing?'

'Oh Christ, is that all, how many people do you want on the guest list?'

'Just one. Wow. Howard, do you know how much I've always wanted to do this?'

'What, get into things without paying? Good grief, woman, one year from now you'll be trying to get *out* of them.' Then Howard pauses, and I can hear him wrestling with the spaniel as well as the telephone. 'I don't suppose you'd review something called John The Postman next week, would you? In Manchester?'

'I'd love to.'

'And The Not Sensibles? Also in Manchester?'

'I can do that.'

Howard pauses. 'What about Crispy Ambulance?'

'Let me guess, in Manchester?'

Howard pauses again. 'And Linda, just a teensy favour, The Smellies are possibly on a double bill with Terminal Sausage at the London School of Economics if someone else cancels. Could you go along and say something nice about them?'

'It's all right, Howard, I read the list, anything Jon Whitten doesn't want to do, I'll do it.'

Before I can even get to London, though – or Manchester for that matter – everything goes pear-shaped. The radio says Sid Vicious has found a stash of heroin in his mother's purse and taken the lot. I never cried when Elvis died, but I cry all over the washing-up when My Way comes on the radio. And then I start to laugh at the song. It is *Sid* after all.

David rings some time after this, breaking the stalemate.

'I thought I'd better call you, because of this Sid Vicious disaster,' he says, 'this suicide.' From the sound of the old lady in the background, I can tell he's calling from the bank.

'It wasn't a *disaster*,' I say, finding anything about the Pistols impossible to explain to David. 'And we don't know it's a suicide yet.'

'So how's things?'

'Has Hazel told you anything?'

'Haven't seen her,' he says.

'Well I got the job.'

'I knew you would.'

'I'm going down tomorrow, for a day. Just to see.'

'So will you move there?'

I tell the truth. 'Probably.'

'And where does that leave us then?'

'It's not the moon, David. It's London. We can still see each other.'

'If we want to,' he says.

'Yeah, if we want to.'

'And do you want to?' he asks me, but just then the old lady interrupts him, and I hear him sigh and say he'll have to call me back.

When I get into the office, Howard and Jon are talking about Sid, while Cindy sits on top of a pine dresser, leopard skin skirt hitched up her thighs, swinging her feet in their fluffy black mules and nodding.

'It's typical of Sid,' says Jon, 'to die on the wrong day.'

I ask him what he means.

'Too late for our deadline,' Jon explains. 'That's what I mean. It's just bloody perversity.'

'I heard someone's already bringing out a record,' Howard says, 'with Sid's voice on it. Someone who used to work with them.'

'Yeah, well, they're already taking orders for T-shirts down the Kings Road, aren't they?' Jon adds.

I sit still for a minute, among the forest of pine, and think about Sid. I remember an issue of *Sniffing Glue* where Steve from The Banshees said Malcolm McLaren would put out Johnny Rotten dolls one day. The Pistols were never supposed to be about money, but in the end that's all they were about. And I think we can safely call it the end of them now.

'The night I saw Sid at the Screen,' Jon remembers, 'I never saw any bass player try so hard. His fingers were almost bleeding.'

'Poor old him, with the padlock round his neck and the awful spots,' Howard interrupts.

'We're not going to do anything in the magazine, Howard. Or are we?' Jon asks.

But Cindy has already trotted out some ancient photographs from one of the filing cabinets in her office. She slaps them down, and there is Sid, snapped from year to year by some unknown photographer. ''Sevenny-six, 'sevenny-seven, 'sevenny-eight,' she says in her drawly voice. 'Nobody else has these.'

'This is clearly not a man who ever ate free record company cheese,' Howard observes, flipping the photographs of Sid over and looking at his pale, skinny ribs. 'No matter how many times EMI and Virgin must have dragged out the Cabernet Sauvignon and the cheddar, I can safely say that here is one fellow human being who appears never to have touched it.'

'Red Leicester,' Jon says, smirking and sloping away with the photos. 'So much better than smack, innit.'

I've already worked out my drug profile of Jon Whitten, of course. It's not hard to do. He's clearly a man who does speed for the gigs, and dope for the album reviews, and occasionally, I would guess, dabbles with something harder. You can see it in his writing. In the magazines and newspapers he wrote for before *NWW*, the names change – his bylines range from Terry Torpid to Mick Misfit – but the style is always the same.

Here's Jon on 'Killing An Arab' by The Cure:

Minimalist darkness made by moody men in mascara, with darkly threatening overtones and a throbbing, relentless bass line that could kill an Arab at ten paces all by itself. Brooding, magnificent, brilliantly ironic.* * * * *

And Jon on Adam and the Ants at the Marquee last year:

The last death throes of pure pop passion expertly captured by the last of the princelings of Punkdom with plastic-consuming proles prepared to pogo to the painful bitter end.

When Jon's on a diet of talcum powder, toilet cleaner and amphetamine sulphate, there's usually a lot of alliteration. And the punctuation disappears as well.

Today Jon is coming down from Thursday night. 'UK Subs,' he explains, rubbing his headache away at his desk.

For some reason, even more pine furniture has been shifted into the office since I was last here. There are lamp stands now, and hatstands as well.

'Some of that will go soon,' Howard promises vaguely, waving a hand at the pine pyramid now blocking the door.

Tactfully ignoring what is obviously the biggest lie she's heard all day, Cindy sashays into her art room in her Capri pants and shuts the door.

'There she goes,' Howard says, 'our little mystery woman.'

Jon gives him a fierce look, but Howard ignores it.

'You know, it's nice to have a brunette in the office,' Howard says, looking pointedly at me.

Jon takes his glasses off, rubs his eyes and says nothing.

'Cindy's all very well,' Howard continues, 'but one does tire of her constant blondness. Anyway,' he leaps up, lighting a cigarette, 'I'm off to chat to a bloke in Kensington about some portable bidets. If some odious little band manager rings up asking us to reserve the front cover for The Snivelling Toads, or whatever they're called, you know what to tell him, and where he can put it.'

'Orright,' says Jon.

And now it's just the two of us. Me, the assistant cook from Withingdean, and him, Jon Whitten, king of drug-fuelled purple prose, the brilliant biro-wielding black-leather baron of Buzzcocks B-sides, born in Brixton and brought up on Brian Eno.

'Oh fuck, here comes a publicist,' Jon says, leaning out of the window and peering into the street below. 'Get in the wardrobe.'

I watch him do it first, amazed at the way he manages to get himself in, then drag in the folds of his army greatcoat after him, carefully closing the door with a click.

'It's dangerous to do that,' I say automatically. 'You should never shut yourself in a wardrobe.'

'Cindy will get us out,' says a muffled voice. 'Just get in!'

So I do, finding my own sizeable wardrobe on the other side of the office, and it must be the same one that Howard's dog sleeps in because the smell of spaniel flatulence is overwhelming.

'It's either get in the wardrobe and hide,' Jon says in a muffled voice from across the room, 'or die a long death as some boring bint waves four hundred records in your face for two hours and tries to convince you to write about them.'

After this I hear someone creaking up the stairs, and then the creaking stops, on the landing. Then there's a knock – which Cindy, tucked away in the art room, is pretending not to hear. After that there's a bit of puffing – whoever it is seems to be squeezing her way between every last hatstand and dressing table from the door to Jon's desk – and a throaty, feminine, cough. And then there's a papery rustling sound, more footsteps and more creaking on the stairs, fading away to silence.

Jon starts rapping on the inside of his wardrobe a few minutes later. 'Cindy! Get us out of here!'

I start laughing, then realize what I must sound like, cackling away inside a pine wardrobe, and that makes me laugh even more.

'CINDY!'

Eventually she teeters in on clacking heels and lets both of us out, the same expressionless look on her face as she has for everything. Then she shuffles back into her art room and closes the door again.

I think she and Jon might have been fighting lately. Not that I can ask Cindy about it, of course. She's like the sphinx in pink winkle-pickers.

'Oh for God's sake,' Jon says, ripping open the brown paper bag the anonymous publicist has just left on his chair. 'An exciting new band called Heinz and the Haemorrhoids from Bristol. Geniuses who have just discovered Post-Punk apparently. And, oh what a surprise. There's a can of baked beans in the bag too – what a brilliantly original promotional concept.'

He hurls the offending single across the office and then kicks the beans into a hatstand. The can dents, then even more records go flying across the office like frisbees.

'Crap, crap, crap and crap, with no stars,' Jon rates them.

I get a funny feeling that these are the records I'm supposed to review.

Then the phone rings.

'Probably The Snivelling Toads,' Jon sighs, but a few seconds into the call his face drops. It's like watching someone receive really bad news – so he must be. There seems to be a lot of talking on the other end, with bits of Jon starting to say things then sighing and giving up, and then a lot of double cigarette-lighting from his end of the phone.

He puts the receiver down and takes off his big

horn-rimmed glasses. And then slowly but surely he starts to cry.

'Oh God,' he moans. 'What have I done?'

Too many drugs, appears to be the correct answer, but there's no point in telling him that.

'Oh my God! Oh my God!' Jon cries.

Seeing one of the wardrobe doors still open, he gets in, sitting inside it sideways so that his knees are pulled up to his chest, and his long legs in black leather pants stretch out on the floorboards. His blue suede brothel creepers make his feet look enormous.

'What?' I say. 'What?'

But he won't talk.

'Get Cindy for me,' Jon pleads. 'Please, please just get Cindy for me. Tell her I need help. Tell her I'm sorry for everything.'

But Cindy won't come out, no matter how hard I try. Instead, she covers her ears with her hands, perched on her little stool in the art room, looking like a monkey in a tea-bag advertisement trying to hear no evil, see no evil and say no evil, shaking her head from side to side.

'Please Cindy,' I say. 'I don't know what to do. Jon's asking for you.'

She's having none of it, though. 'No, no, no,' she mews, so I give up, close the door and go back to the wardrobe.

'I slagged off this Heavy Metal band in Amsterdam,' Jon begins to explain, 'and now they want to kill me.'

'Who wants to kill you?'

'The Dutch chapter of the Hell's Angels. I've insulted their favourite band apparently.'

'Was that them on the phone?'

'They say they're in a phone box down there,' Jon waves a hand at the window, looking pale.

'What, out there in Wardour Street?'

'Yes. They know what I look like, and when they

find me they say they're going to destroy both my face and my genitals with a crowbar.'

'Really? Both of them? That's a bit unfair. I would have thought one or the other.'

Jon sticks his head out of the wardrobe and gives me a terrified look. 'Howard's going to have to give me protection money. He'd better sell some more mini bidets – and fast.'

It's hard to say how much of this is about Jon, and how much of it is about last night's drug intake, but in the end I feel sorry for him – enough to make him a cup of tea and bring it back to the wardrobe anyway. Then I look out of the window, to see if there are any Hell's Angels lurking in the phone box outside, but it's quite empty. And there's nobody in the street either.

Eventually, like an old stoat emerging from its lair, Jon is chivvied out.

'Thanks,' he says, taking the tea and blowing his nose hard on some horrible hankie which has fossilized in the pocket of his army greatcoat.

'Howard told me I could have a ticket to see this new band The Pretenders,' I say to take his mind off the Dutch Hell's Angels.

'Oh yes. This week's next big thing. I give them until Christmas.'

'Don't you want to go?'

'Not a question of wanting to go, I *have* to go. The *NME* are in love with them. Whenever that happens, we all have to play along.' He snorts to himself as the tears stop. 'I'd rather go and see Feral Beryl. Now *there*'s a woman singer who'll still be around in twenty years' time.'

Pins and needles finally drive Jon out of the wardrobe, and I notice that his hands tremble when he tries to light a cigarette. He also appears to have shredded skin, instead of fingernails.

'Whenever you get that peeling bit around your nails, that's lack of nutrition,' I tell him.

'The shock of that information could very well kill me,' Jon says. Then he gives me a look. 'You've got a ring on.'

'I'm engaged,' I reply. 'Or anyway, I think I am. He moved out.'

'Left you?'

'Not really. I don't know.'

Jon watches my face while I watch his hands shake.

'There's this Australian bloke you should meet.'

'Yeah?'

'Photographer. Born-again Mod. Women really like him. He's coming out with us tonight to The Pretenders.'

Then Jon gets back in the wardrobe, tells me he's looking for Narnia, and sobs himself to sleep.

Shortly after this, Cindy stalks out of the art room, tossing her blond ponytail and sniffing a lot.

'Is he orright?' she asks me.

I nod. 'I think he's just paranoid.'

'Yeah, his middle name is paranoid,' she says. And then she turns on her spiky heels and goes back into the art room, shutting the door in case I should make the mistake of thinking that I'll ever be invited in for a sociable chat.

CHAPTER FIVE

I go to The Pretenders gig at the Moonlight with
Howard, who spends the whole time sitting in the car
with his dog; Jon, whose hands are still shaking; and
the Australian photographer who's good with women.
I can't work out if he's called Evan, Eddie or Ivan,
because of his weird, twangy accent. And I'm not even
sure they ever had Mods in Australia, but he's dressed
in the full kit: an oversized khaki parka, stripy lace-up
shoes, and his hair looks like the Small Faces cut it on
the back of a Lambretta, in one of the wing mirrors.
He's every Paul Weller fantasy I ever had, but he says
'G'day' as well. Weird.

When the support band are on, Jon and Evan both
disappear into the toilets, so I go into the street, find
the car and talk to Howard because I don't want to
hang around the club by myself.

'So what's this Australian photographer actually
called then?' I ask him. 'I can't understand a word he
says.'

'His name is Evan. I suppose you want to sleep
with him, don't you? Oh mercy me, everyone wants
to sleep with Evan,' Howard says, shaking his head.
Howard has a tartan rug on his knee; the dog is peace-
fully asleep on the back seat wearing a little woolly
white coat.

'I didn't say I wanted to sleep with him, Howard. I was just asking you what his name was.'

'Evan takes terrible photos. Dreadful. Always out of focus. And Cindy keeps buying them. With my money. Why? Because she's fed up with Jon and wants to have a *grand amour* with Evan, like every other man, woman and beast in London.' Howard pauses, and pours himself a cup of tea from a Thermos on the floor.

'I think she and Jon had a fight the other day,' I tell him.

'The other day? Linda, they never *stop* fighting. It's the only way either of them can work up anything resembling passion.'

As I walk away from the car, I try to pinpoint what Howard's been playing on the car radio and realize it's an Agatha Christie play. Someone should tell him that his dog's been asleep on a pile of posters advertising Terminal Sausage.

Inside the club someone tells me this is only the fifth time The Pretenders have played. It's hard to believe. The lead singer – her name is Chrissie – doesn't seem to be nervous at all. Which is weird, considering how thoroughly she's being scrutinized by all the record company men standing to the side of the speakers. I can't even imagine what it would be like to have so many strangers sizing up your voice, your playing, your band, your songs, your make-up, and – let's face it – your arse. Amazingly, the singer looks like she couldn't care less. Maybe she already knows it's the A&R men who are part of the cattle call, not her. She's singing like a woman who expects to have the right to choose. Even if Jon only gives her band until Christmas.

When I was a kid my mum let me adopt a cat from the local shelter. There were plenty of the usual chocolate-box fluffy tabby kittens, but in the end we both liked this sleek black tomcat best. No matter how much we sized him up, and no matter how many people poked and prodded him in the cage, he looked as if he couldn't care whether he was chosen or not, even though rejection would probably have meant that he died. We took him home and named him Kipper. Chrissie, the lead singer of The Pretenders, reminds me of Kipper. And just in case I have to end up writing anything about tonight, I scribble it down on a piece of paper in my coat pocket: 'CHRISSIE, PRETENDERS – LIKE KIPPER'.

Jon comes back with a drink at that moment and catches me in the act of writing this down.

'Oh God, no, not proper *rock* journalism, anything but that,' he says. Then he reads what I've written. 'Chrissie Hynde is like a kipper. Yes, that's brilliant, Linda. What penetrating insight.'

He barks with laughter.

'Load of bollocks, The Pretenders are,' he says, and various friends of his nod, standing in a little circle around him. Like Jon, they all have grey raincoats with little badges on.

Judging by the fact that half of these nodding heads also have funny Elvis Costello glasses, and that so many are scribbling on what look like black policemen's notepads, I gather they must be music writers too. And that's the most terrifying thought I've had all week. Howard might have given me a job, but in my mind I'm still taking orders for two Beef and Black Bean sauce with Fried Rice in Withingdean.

Evan, who had wandered away with his camera, comes back again. 'My bloody Nikon's not working,' he tells me.

'Serves you right. It's your own fault for nicking it from someone you don't know,' Jon tells him.

Evan chooses not to explain. He's shedding hair, I notice. Short, blond hairs are falling off his head and onto the shoulders of his green parka at the rate of knots. He must dye it. That's what always happens to me, anyway. I've gone from brown to black to red to blond and back to black again, and each time great handfuls of my hair end up in the plughole.

'Do you want a drink?' Evan asks me but not the others. I ask for a beer and he vanishes again. People make way for him as he passes, I notice, and some of them nod at him like they know him or want to know him.

While people push past us and tread on my feet, Jon tells the story about being threatened by the Dutch Hell's Angels. Amazingly, it doesn't include the fact that it left him crying inside a pine wardrobe.

The other journalists laugh, and one of them catches my eye because I'm laughing at the same things too, but I don't fancy him. It's partly down to Evan, I suppose. In the space of half an hour, general standards of male attractiveness in this particular dark corner of the club have shot up.

Evan could almost fit into one of those Mod bands, like The Chords or The Purple Hearts, but he looks younger and stranger and rougher, because his nose is a bit bent, and his weird Australian accent makes him seem more interesting, somehow, than most of the blokes standing around me. It's a bit Rolf Harris, a bit 'Two Little Boys', a bit Skippy. Or am I thinking complete bollocks as usual?

Since David moved out, I've played with the idea of fancying Jon (and dismissed it immediately), I've vaguely entertained the thought of Howard (if he lost a few stone and didn't remind me so much of Evelyn Waugh, and if there was a nuclear war and we were the last ones left alive), and this week I've also had passionate dreams about Adam Ant, Gary Numan and Lene Lovich, which must mean I'm secretly bisexual as well.

Finally Evan squeezes back with the beer. He's not the only one wearing a sludge-green parka, I notice – there are a lot of them around, and some people have painted the names of their favourite groups on the back, in white house paint. A few people are wearing hacked-off kilts, like mine, and there are plenty of black leggings and winkle-pickers about. People seem to be growing their eyebrows back, though – that's a new thing. Then I see a girl in the crowd in a tomato-red leather jacket with zips, and I want it immediately. So does Evan, by the look of it, because he can't stop looking at her and nearly spills the beer.

While everyone else in our little circle gossips about Stiff Little Fingers' new album – it's out this week – Evan and I drink our beer in long gulps, him looking at me, me not looking at him. I want to find a phone box and call David. There are too many new things going on here, I've decided. New prices for everything. New people, who I don't know very well. Even the beer doesn't taste the same as it does at home. And now there's this other new thing, called freedom. It's like that time I ran away from home and got on the train to London by myself and ended up crying in Green Park. Or the time Hazel came and got me, after the Vesta curry revolution. It's terrifying. 'Can you mind my beer?' I ask Evan, then I go off to find a phone.

One day they'll invent some new *Star Trek*-type telephone that you carry around in your handbag, but until then the only choice I've got is to do laps of London until I find a box that a) hasn't been pissed in, b) hasn't been knocked over and c) hasn't had the phone wrenched out.

When I do find one, though – next to an Indian take-away not far from the club – David's not home. And the machine swallows my change as well. Typical. Maybe it's a sign from God I think as I wander back to the music and the crowds. A sort of 'Yes, my child, go ahead and snog Evan the Mod' sign, and let's face it, it can't hurt – he'll go back to Australia any minute, won't he? And besides, he looks like one of those bumblebee men who stop at every flower they see. Maybe it's time I was a bit more like that, given that I'm half a free woman now.

Back inside the gig, people are actually sweating. This is a hard thing to do in February, but it's also a good sign. I wonder what Jon is scribbling in his notepad, other than 'The Pretenders won't last beyond Christmas.'

Evan brings over my beer and says something in my ear. I nod and smile. I have no idea what he's talking about. Then he frowns and shouts something else. Instantly I stop smiling and nodding and start frowning instead. Then he just laughs in my face and walks away. I haven't got a clue what he was trying to say. It happens all the time at gigs. God knows how many relationships haven't started, how many deals haven't been done, how many babies haven't been born, all because the mix is too bloody loud.

I finish the beer, and then Jon offers to sell me some speed.

'Come on, Linda, help me to supplement Howard's poxy salary.'

'I can't afford it.'

'Have it on hire purchase then.'

'God, you are desperate, aren't you.'

Jon shakes his head, like a horse tossing its mane, and I notice his dandruff for the first time. Then he shoulders his way into the crowd, shoving his notebook in his pocket and joining all the other heaving bodies in the front row.

I made the mistake of taking David to a gig like this once. I can't even remember the band – it might have been The Human League, or The Tourists. One of those bands anyway. He sat through it in silence while I drank myself stupid; then, on the way home, I got a two-hour monologue on everything that was wrong with it. Everything that didn't make sense.

'Like, any other form of entertainment, Linda—'

'Yes, David.'

'Well, there has to be some structure. Some order to it. You pay a fair price to get in, and you expect a certain level of entertainment. Usually, in my book, a concert has a beginning, a middle and an end.'

'Don't call it a concert.'

'The trouble with tonight was you didn't know where the start was, and there was nobody to give you any indication when the bloody thing would stop. I mean, when was the ending exactly?'

By this stage, I remember, I was just staring out of the car window.

'The encore wasn't real, Linda, nobody wanted it, the guitarist had already made up his mind to get back on stage, no matter what anyone thought of his playing.'

'Shut up about the playing. Nobody cares how you play.'

'Well that's not music then, is it?'

That should be David's epitaph. *That's not music then, is it?* The number of times I've heard that, from the time I brought home The Sex Pistols' first bootleg, to the tricky day I came home with a copy of 'Stretcher Case Baby' by The Damned (they were giving them away free). The record sleeve had a picture of a Victorian woman at a bureau looking in a mirror, but at a distance the picture turned into a skull. The label said, 'Special snob collector's artifact of no historical/cultural value. Throw it away.' I thought it was really clever. David didn't.

'That's not music then, is it? What do they mean, throw it away?'

I want to call David more than ever now, but it's going to take me a few more drinks to pluck up the courage to face the cold and find the phone box again. My father was right. I should wear thermal underwear and a sensible coat on nights like this. Being New Wave is all very well, but it prevents you from doing other things, like being able to walk.

Out of the corner of my eye I notice the woman in the leather jacket the colour of tomatoes, snogging someone against the wall. Then I realize it's Evan. Annoyingly, Jon chooses this moment to come back and notice me noticing.

'He moves fast for an Australian,' he says.

'It's probably your bloody drugs. Did you sell him any?'

Jon laughs. 'Evan throws up on them.'

The Pretenders are playing brilliantly – I know it's special and seductive and people will be talking about this gig for months, but at the same time that my music head is taking it in, my Withingdean head is thinking of too many other things.

'Get up there,' Jon elbows me in the ribs, nodding at the front row.

'I can't, I've got to call someone.'

I leave Jon jostling for space and push my way through the crowd, spiking people's Doc Martens with my heels and saying 'Sorry, sorry, sorry,' like a mantra – not that anybody notices or cares.

Outside there are girls sitting two by two in the gutter – getting stoned, gossiping about boys, eating hotdogs from the nearby stand. I could kill for something to eat, especially with the smell of fried onions all around me, but I'm flat broke.

For a minute I think about finding Howard in his car, braving the Agatha Christie and asking him for an advance on my first week's salary, but maybe that's not the best start to my new professional life. I'm sleeping on his sofa, for a start. I might be pushing it too far.

Then suddenly something cheers me up. Howard Baker's fridge. Imagine the glories that probably contains. All the cheese he scoops into his pockets from record company parties, and probably a few grouse and stuffed pheasants as well.

I step out into the street, thinking about the food to come, and my foot goes straight through the thin sheet of ice covering a puddle.

'Shit.'

When I step forward, though, there's nowhere else to step, except onto more ice. So I can either take off my shoes and carry them in my hand, and suffer temporary agony but dry feet later, or give in and slosh ahead.

'Hey, what are you doing?' someone calls behind me.

I turn and look, still up to my ankles in freezing slush, and see Evan, holding hands with the girl in the red leather jacket.

'It's a puddle,' I say stupidly. Then Evan pulls out a camera. It's not his broken Nikon – it looks like some cheap thing you give to kids for their birthday – but he clicks three or four shots of me anyway.

'You look fantastic!' he says, walking up to me as the girl in the red jacket moves away and lights a cigarette.

'Please don't do anything with those photos, Evan,' I bleat.

He shakes his head. 'They're just for me. And for you, if you want a copy.'

'I must look really pathetic.'

'You look . . .'

Instead of finishing the sentence, Evan turns around to see how close the red leather jacket girl is standing, and then winks at me.

'I'm just off to call my fiancé anyway,' I tell him. 'I said I would.'

'Did you?' Evan challenges me. I can tell he's not one of those people it's particularly easy to lie to. Maybe it's all that close-up study of the human face through a lens.

He scribbles something down and I realize it's his phone number. There's not much point in giving him mine – I can't see Evan ever coming to Withingdean. A little way away, the girl in the jacket is blowing cold breath and smoke rings into the air.

'I'll see you,' Evan says, holding out his hand to help me out of the puddle.

Like a madwoman, I shake it. As if we are part of some top-level music industry negotiation, for God's sake. And then I watch him walk away with the girl; I notice that he declines a cigarette before she leans in close and they both start laughing.

I find myself making a list in my head of pros and cons for David, as if it will help me sort out my confusion. Instead, it makes things worse. This is the man who sewed the end of my jeans back together once, after I borrowed his bicycle and the denim got shredded in his bicycle chain. I was wearing flares then – that's how long ago that was. But it's also the same man who had a serious conversation with me about how much housekeeping money I'd get from him once we were married. Just like Dad all over again. Just like your worst nightmare, in fact.

The ticks and crosses keep coming. I remember the night I had a 'Ban The Bomb' badge on in the pub, and some bloke came over and told me I was a silly bitch because if we banned the bomb, we wouldn't have peace in Europe, and David punched him. That's a tick. Then I remember the wool safari jacket David wore to a schoolfriend's wedding, with big blue and yellow checks all over it that made him look like a cross between Rupert Bear and Noddy. A cross, a definite cross. More crosses: the night he spent in the pub

82

ignoring me and playing a stupid tennis game called Pong when we should have been celebrating our first moving-in anniversary. The horrible Christmas when he decided his present to me was going to be a twin-tub washing machine on hire purchase. More ticks: me thinking there was an IRA bomb inside a pillar-box in Withingdean, and him throwing himself on top of me in the street to protect me. And the first time he kissed me, by backing me straight into a holly bush – that's a *huge* tick, even if I did get scratched to pieces. And then there's the last time we snogged in public, at a funfair on Brighton seafront, when we went on the Whip, the Big Dipper, the Big Wheel and the Wall of Death, and he held my hand while I screamed. It seems like a long time ago now, but I suppose it was only last July.

In the end, though, none of this is helping, because, like every other decision in my life, waving goodbye to David is going to be a case of all heart and no head.

CHAPTER SIX

It would be nice to report, after all this, that when I finally crawl home to Withingdean the next day, David is waiting for me on the doorstep with a bunch of flowers, helping me to make up my mind, reminding me who I am, where I belong and who I'm supposed to be with. It would be joyous to have him make those decisions for me so my feelings could be pulled into some kind of shape. But of course he doesn't. Do men ever do anything resembling a grand gesture, except in films? Especially when you really, really need one?

There are so many moments like this in my life. Vacancies instead of things actually happening. Boring, predictable, disappointing gaps instead of nice chunky events. My life is as full of fantasies as it is of big flat puddles of nothing. When I was at school someone told me The Kinks would be driving past the gates in a special bus at lunchtime. I stood there, that lunchtime and every one after it – for a week, hanging around the gates getting ready to wave at Ray Davies – waiting and wishing and believing. The absence of flowers from David now – in fact the absence of anything at all, even a note shoved under the door – is like every Kinks no-show moment I've ever had.

It's Valentine's Day on Wednesday. Meanwhile, the

papers are full of The Sex Pistols, now that Sid and Nancy are both dead. Sid's last wish was to be cremated and have his ashes put next to hers, apparently, but Jon told me that her family won't tell his family where they've buried her. How romantic. Meanwhile, the shops are full of white teddy bears holding up balloons.

Just as I'm settling down to watch the news, David calls.

'I've got you a place in London if you want it,' is the first thing he says. 'It's a bedsit, but it's cheap.'

'What bedsit? What?'

'Only for a few months, but it's £25 a week. It was a squat before. They've kicked the people out and now it needs looking after. Mostly so rats don't eat the place alive, I think. One of my clients told me about it.'

I'd forgotten how David likes to call people with bank accounts *clients*.

'Wow.'

'It's got a bit of rising damp as well.'

'Well that's not going to kill me.'

'And there's no bath, just a sink.'

'I've washed my hair in a sink before.'

He gives me the man's phone number and I take it down.

'So when am I going to see you?' I say after all this, suddenly wanting him and missing him more than I have for days.

David pauses then, on the other end of the phone. 'What do you mean, see me?'

'Well I haven't seen you for so long. I miss you. And I've got so much to thank you for, haven't I. God. Why am I talking to you like this? Why are you *making* me talk to you like this, David?'

Silence.

'I'll give you a call to say a proper goodbye, if you like,' David says at last. And at that moment it feels as though someone has just jacked all the ice off the window ledge and shoved it straight down the back of my jumper.

'What do you mean, give me a call to say a proper goodbye?'

'I haven't said anything to you before, Linda, but—'

I interrupt him then, getting in quick before he can tell me something horrible. 'WHAT DO YOU MEAN, GIVE ME A FUCKING CALL TO SAY A FUCKING PROPER GOODBYE?'

More silence from him after that. And then it all comes out in a rush.

'To be honest with you, there's someone else. She won't be interested, of course, because she's a good friend to you, but in time I'm hoping she might be.'

My mind races. 'Who?'

'Hazel.'

'What? Are you *mad*?'

Several scenes go through my head. Hazel and David going off to see *Jaws* together, years ago, because I was too frightened to go. All of us playing Spin the Bottle and Postman's Knock at a party when we were pissed, and David taking Hazel out into the corridor. Just as David and I have always had Venn diagrams of things we both like, like Protein 21 shampoo and Morecambe and Wise, we've also had a subset of mutual friends for most of our relationship. And Hazel's been the biggest part of that subset. But maybe she's an even bigger part of it than I thought.

I slam the phone down and take it off the hook. Then I take my engagement ring off my finger and chuck it across the room. That's not satisfying enough though, so I get down on my hands and knees, hunting for it in the filthy brown carpet so I can do something really nasty with it. If David and I had ever been able to afford a place with a sink disposal unit, that would be the obvious option. Or I could chuck it in the loo, I suppose. But it's platinum – it would probably sink to the bottom and sit there for years, refusing to flush.

I find the ring at last and hold it in my hand. David gave it to me on the beach in the rain at Newhaven, and it would be very easy if I could look at it and call it a cheap and meaningless piece of shit, but the fact is, he had to go cap in hand to the bank just to get the money to pay for it.

I should hate him. *Hazel*, for God's sake! The friend in the subset of friends in our Venn diagram of life. But instead I find myself suddenly and desperately needing him, and it's all I can do to stop myself picking up the phone again. He's found me a flat, he bought me this ring, he posted my job application. He's put up with my moods for years, he's lent me money and he's been the best mate I ever had, if I'm going to be honest about it.

He got me through my mother's birthday last year, when I cried all morning and had to take the day off work. He got me through depression; he held my hand when I got chucked out of university, and he's sat through all the films that I liked and he hated.

I rub my hands over my face, trying to see straight. David's right and I'm wrong. Music is exactly like supporting Manchester United. In a few years, football will be off his agenda, the way music will be off mine. And *NWW* won't matter by then, and neither will The Ramones, or Lene Lovich, or whatever else it is that I'm obsessed by at the moment. My obsession with music is not something that defines my personality. I use it as an excuse to mark out the gulf between us, but it's just a pile of vinyl.

Then I think, sod it, and put on 'I Wanna Be Sedated' at full volume. And suddenly, my compass bearings come back.

I wonder what David's been up to with Hazel. I can just imagine it, because I can still remember how he started with me. A friendly lift in his car while she's waiting at the bus stop. The brush of his hand against hers while he's offering her some of his chips. It's enough to make you sick. David probably thinks he's Withingdean's answer to John bleeding Travolta at the moment.

After The Ramones, I put on Siouxsie Sioux, The Clash, The Jam and Elvis Costello, one after the other at full volume. And then I wind down the window and chuck the ring straight out into the street. The way things are around here, someone will take it straight down to the pawn shop and I'll never get it back. And you know what? I hope he sees it, gleaming in the front window. And he can piss off with his London flat as well. I'll find my own rat-infested basement to live in.

By Sunday, though, when I've combed all the week-end papers' classified advertisements, I've found nothing that's anywhere near as cheap. Even a bedsit in Plaistow is going to ruin me, and that's after I've trimmed back the groceries to bread, margarine and some of Howard's free cheese.

Then, some time after this, Hazel calls. And within minutes I realize she's clueless. If David has been developing a secret passion for her this winter it's obviously passed her by, because her primary interest in life is still a) teaching b) shopping and c) getting her boobs signed by Bob Geldof.

'So have you seen David at all?' I ask her, trying to sound casual.

'No. I don't want to be the piggy in the middle between you two.'

'So you haven't spoken to him then?'

'Relax, Linda. No, I haven't spoken to him.'

I tell her that David's called it off, but I don't tell her about the other bit. Then I let her know that I've chucked my engagement ring into the street.

She sounds as if she's going to cry. 'Oh, Linda!'

But I've been waiting for this. I'll get it from Dad, and I'll get it from everyone in Withingdean, so I may as well practise my speech on Hazel first.

'He said goodbye and that's that. He says he's got his reasons, so fine, goodbye it is. I had a mad moment of panic when I really missed him, but I soon got over it.'

'Yeah, and you chucked your ring into the street. God, Linda!'

'It made me feel better, if you must know.'

'But you've been together all this time!'

Not, 'You're made for each other', not 'But you love each other', not 'But he's your soulmate'. Just that we've got longevity. That just about sums it up. In Withingdean it's permanence that's the thing, not passion.

I can hear Hazel having a little weep on the other end of the phone after this.

'What?' I bark at her. She's irritating me now. I mean *I* haven't even cried properly yet.

'It's just so sad,' she tells me. But that's the problem. I don't think it is. Some losses in my life have been sad – Mum, primarily, because it was a stupid waste and it nearly destroyed my dad. In fact, it helped to turn him into the old bugger that he is today. But this? This isn't a tragedy. It feels more like an inevitability.

'David's such a good man, Linda; are you sure? I mean, are you really sure?'

'But that's just it. I don't think he is a good man. Not any more.'

She returns to her tears. 'I think David keeps you stable, Linda. I think you need him.'

'What, so I'll go off the rails without him? Is that it?'

'That's not what I said.'

'Yes it is.'

'No it's not.'

We're getting dangerously close to nyah-nyah

territory now, and suddenly I'm reminded of the day when I bet her I could win a goldfish on the coconut shy at the Withingdean church fête, and I didn't, and she laughed at me until I was forced to shove her into the side of the tea tent.

'Hazel, believe me, he's not right for me. And I can't tell you why, I just know it.'

She sighs into the receiver. 'Well I think you're being a coward. I think you're throwing it away. How long do you think this job in London is going to last anyway? You should try harder with him, Linda. I don't think you're bothering at all.'

Then a silence – until I can't stand listening to her disapproval any longer and I tell her I'll see her tomorrow, for a cup of tea.

'A cup of tea's not going to solve anything,' she says stupidly. Then she realizes how idiotic this sounds and gives a half laugh, half snort, and I do too, and that's our cue to hang up the phone.

And the laughter doesn't stop, really, for the next few days. On Valentine's Day I go to the front door mat to look for . . . nothing. In other years David has sent red roses in plastic cylinders, and big stupid cards and even a box of Black Magic once. Today there's just a hairy brown doormat and a leaflet from the local dry-cleaners. Very funny. Most enervating, as Howard would say.

And it gets even better after that, when Hazel calls to say she's had a mystery Valentine, with no signature, and it was hand delivered as well. I think that's the point at which my hysterical laughter becomes quite uncontrollable, if you must know. Of course it's David. Stupid git. It's exactly the kind of thing he would do.

I try to think of what might be attracting him to Hazel, and I fail. Usually, with love, there's mystery. That's what makes you fall for someone – the guessing, the imagining, the not knowing. But David has known

Hazel for ever, thanks to me. He's seen her sulk at Monopoly and throw her metal battleship on the floor. He's seen her being sick in a car park. He's seen her swimming at Eastbourne and losing her bikini top in a freak wave. In short, her romantic appeal should be in minus figures, but clearly it's not.

On Friday Howard calls, getting me out of bed at 7 p.m. I don't know what to do with myself in the evenings at the moment, apart from getting into bed fully clothed and trying to read.

'What are you doing?' he asks me.

'Reading Jackie Collins and eating cold spaghetti hoops out of the can with a fork, if you must know.'

'I've just been listening to a very interesting group called Fish Turned Human, from Cambridge. It's a song called "Here Come The Nuns". I thought I might have a go at reviewing it actually. Jon says I should call myself Howard Hacksaw.'

I laugh.

'Anyway, I was ringing to say that if you need hospitality at Chez Howard again this week, the offer remains warm and, indeed, firm.'

He's forgiven me for breaking into his fridge and stealing all his cheese after The Pretenders then.

'Actually I've found somewhere. Well, my ex-fiancé found me somewhere.' Something makes me want to tell Howard the truth now. And after Hazel, he must be the first person I've told.

'Ex-fiancé, now *there*'s a category.'

'He's a stupid bastard but he's good at practical things. I mean, I owe him a lot,' I tell him. Then to my horror, I feel a tear coming.

'Since when has he been your ex-fiancé?' Howard asks.

'Doesn't matter.' I trap the tear and hold it down. 'Anyway, it's supposed to be a place up the back of Kentish Town.'

'Near Jon. That's nice. You can walk to work together in the summer.'

'Is he actually capable of walking before lunchtime?' I manage to say.

Howard laughs at that, and then we talk about Jon's review of The Pretenders, which Howard's already decided he can't use.

'You write something for us, Linda. Jon's so rude about people.'

'I'd like to write about them. I really like them. Chrissie Hynde reminds me of Kipper, my cat. Can I write about that?'

'This is a Post-modernist, Post-Punk magazine, my dear Linda, you can write about anything,' he says. 'Compare her to a halibut, if you wish.'

On Saturday I finally force myself to go round to Dad's and tell him the news about David. We're sitting at the kitchen table, me peeling more Formica off the edges, him drinking his tea, when I break it to him.

'You say there are rats in this place in London?' is all he can manage. Then when Kipper suddenly comes past, mewing for food, Dad scoops him up and puts him on the table, like he's at a cat show. I know then that something's wrong, and so does Kipper, for that matter. In all the years he's lived in this house, he's never once been allowed up on the kitchen table.

'You've made your mind up then?' Dad says at last, stroking the cat.

'David and I have grown apart.'

'Well that's very sad news.'

I can tell he's thinking about Mum and what she would have said or done. Or am I making things up, as usual? For all I know, as he's staring out of the kitchen window he could be thinking about next week's episode of *Coronation Street*.

I look around the kitchen, at the horrible Formica

with the glittery silver sprinkles in it, and the frilly curtains that Mum made on her sewing machine, from material with brown onions all over it. Dad and I have had so many stand-offs in here. I'm sure there are still bits of Vesta Paella dotted all over the walls.

I feel like revealing that David has suddenly decided he wants Hazel, just in case Dad makes the mistake of thinking he's a really nice bloke and it's me who's being unreasonable. But Dad doesn't need things like that in his head, not when he's driving a bus up and down Brighton sea front. He's an old bugger, but he also happens to be an old bugger I feel sorry for these days.

The cat stands on the table, still stunned by its new freedom.

'He's good with vermin,' Dad says, looking at Kipper. 'Maybe you should borrow him for your bedsit.'

'If he's good with vermin I should set him onto David,' I say, trying to make a joke, but it comes out wrong and sinks into our conversation like a Christmas pudding lined with concrete. I'd forgotten that David came round here once and asked my dad for permission to propose. David said he was moved to tears. But all I could think of was the humiliation of being handed from one man to another.

'How are you getting up to London then?' Dad calls as I walk down the street backwards, waving goodbye and trying to leg it at the same time.

'Don't know.'

'Can't David drive you?'

I give up. It's as if nothing has penetrated his brain at all.

'I have got other friends, you know!' I yell back. 'Friends with cars!'

But he can't hear me in the howling wind, and he finally gives up waving, disappearing inside the house as a gale threatens to push him back over the front doorstep.

The arguments between us stopped a long time ago, and now we just say as little as possible. I don't mind it. It's more peaceful. And in any case, there's no alternative. Real life isn't like TV shows, where you have a heart-to-heart every five minutes. You just put up with things and get on with your life, and as far as I'm concerned, the less fuss there is, the better.

Later on, I take the number David gave me and ring up the bloke who owns the bedsit – some smooth operator in Hove – and tell him I'll take it. He makes me pay in advance, asking for four weeks' rent, and gives me an address to send it to. He asks whether I want to inspect it and I say I don't. Then he asks me for a referee, so I give him David, of course. Instantly it becomes a done deal. He tells me that as soon as he gets the cheque he'll leave the key for me under the bins. Not under a pot plant, under the bins. I suppose nothing grows there except rubbish.

After this, I ring up one of the old Punks from my Brighton clock tower days and tell her I'll swap some free records if she gives me a lift to London. Her name is Annie, and she's got an Austin with purple nylon fur all over the dashboard. I think it might be stolen, but I've never asked.

Driving down the motorway with her, I feel more compass points returning.

'I'm going to boycott the film', she says proudly, 'in honour of Sid.'

She means *The Great Rock 'n' Roll Swindle*, of course. That's what I like about Annie, she just picks up where my brain left off the day before.

I nod. 'Me too. Though I'll probably have to see it for work.' There. A little boast. Directed at a person who'll see the point of it too – I think I can be forgiven for that one.

94

Annie shakes her head, dangly earrings flying. 'You just got the best job in bloody England. I bet everyone applied for it.'

I feel myself smirking on the inside then. Thank God for Annie.

'And what's that Jon Whitten really like?' she asks as we try to overtake a truck.

'I wouldn't recommend him,' I reply, and now it's Annie's turn for a little secret smile. She works as a cleaner at a pub in Rottingdean, and I've just made her feel like a contender for the key to Jon Whitten's underpants. Well, it's the least I can do. Besides, I'm telling the truth. Jon Whitten would crawl into bed with her tomorrow. A car with purple fur on the dashboard? She's *in*.

When she drops me off at the address in Kentish Town, with my boxes of records and clothes, and the single setting of plastic picnic cutlery she's lent me, Annie offers to stay the night to help me settle in, but I shoo her away.

'At least the electricity's on,' she says, testing the lightbulb dangling above the sink.

'And there's all the rat shit under the sink, as promised,' I say. 'Lucky I paid in advance, isn't it.'

'How did you find it?' Annie asks.

'My boring ex-fiancé,' I say, and she nods, checking my face to see if it's OK to laugh.

'Is that the one in the bank?'

'Oh yes. One of his *clients* told him about it. You know, Annie, one of his very important *clients*.'

She laughs again, then she jumps up and down on my fold-up single bed, testing it for staying power.

'There's supposed to be this fantastic new band in Liverpool called Teardrop Explodes,' she says when she has stopped jumping and is finally ready to drive back to Brighton. 'Do you want to go up some time and see them?'

'I can get you free tickets probably,' I say. I can feel the smirk coming back again. I'll have to stop that.

But Annie is happy, though, happier than I've seen her for ages. People get girls like me and Annie wrong a lot of the time. They think we're angry, but we're not. A lot of the time it's just boredom covered up with a bit of spare energy. It's something I'm still thinking about when I fall asleep on the fold-out single bed and the rats start having a disco under the sink.

CHAPTER SEVEN

On Monday morning Howard organizes what he calls a Planning Meeting, except there are two problems – Cindy, who isn't there, and Jon, who is sitting on the floorboards stoned out of his mind reading the *Dandy*.

Howard has taped eight sheets of butchers' paper to the back of one of the wardrobes, and drawn eight squares on each of the sheets, numbered one to sixty-four.

'It could be Bingo,' drawls Jon, waving a joint in the air, 'but I think it might be our first issue. And it's only due in two weeks' time, isn't that nice, Linda?'

I can see my name on some of the squares. 'Hit Parade – Linda'. 'Fashion – Linda'. 'Crossword – Linda'. 'I Nearly Married A Human – Linda'.

'What's all that about then?' I ask Howard.

'It's a record I want you to write about. Because you like him . . .' Howard frowns in deep concentration, trying to remember the singer's name. 'You like him because you told me you had an erotic dream about him once. Oh God.' Howard tuts in frustration. 'What the hell is his name, Jon?'

'Gary Numan.'

'Oh yes, the man who looks like he's covered himself in self-raising flour. Well, that's his record. "I Nearly Married A Human".'

I keep scanning the big sheets of butchers' paper. It's quite exciting seeing my name everywhere. My name is also pencilled in next to 'Cartoon' – which I hope I'm not drawing – and then three groups I've got to profile, who I've never heard of, which must mean they're managed by Howard, and . . . The Sex Pistols.

'Don't get too excited,' slurs Jon, watching me staring with wide eyes at all the bits of paper. 'You're not going to meet any of them. He just wants you to beat something up.'

'Beat something up?'

'Make it up,' Jon says impatiently.

'And then there are some live reviews,' interrupts Howard, trying to jolly me along. 'For example, you can do The Pretenders.'

'Load of rubbish,' Jon mutters.

'And then we need you to go out and see, er—' Howard looks at a list of names written in biro all the way up his arm so he can remember them. 'Wreckless Eric at Chelsea College, Psychedelic Furs at the Music Machine, and Lene Lovich at Kings College—'

'Ooh, be still my beating heart,' Jon lisps in the corner. 'Lene Lovich is the other one she's been having erotic dreams about, apparently. Did you know that, Howard?'

'Is all of that all right with you?' Howard asks, ignoring him.

I notice quite a few blank spaces, filled in with big green felt-tip question marks, and wonder aloud what those are for.

'Advertisements,' Howard says. 'Naturally, there's already one for Pine Palace in there, but we do have another twenty-two pages to fill, and that's not including the back cover. Still, I feel we can rely on your cousin in Welwyn Garden City,' he tells Jon.

You have to admire Howard. If he's feeling nervous

about the challenge ahead, he's not showing it.

I look at the sheets of paper again, and see that Jon's pencilled in to interview The Buzzcocks, Squeeze, Tom Robinson Band, Alternative TV, Sham 69 and The Specials. Basically everyone I want to meet in the entire world. And the rest of the juicy stuff – Joy Division, Elvis Costello, The Damned – seems to have been pencilled in for freelancers.

The freelancer who seems to get most of the work at *NWW* is a bloke called Mark Oggers who has a shaved head, a pointy nose like a ferret, no fixed address and a habit of delivering his interviews on the inside of Cornflakes packets, written in biro in CAPITAL LETTERS. Everyone thinks Mark Oggers is a genius. Cindy sent him down to the corner shop to get a jar of instant coffee once, and he didn't come back for six days; and I even heard him having a conversation with Jon about how he couldn't work out how to put 5p in the chocolate machines on Victoria Station. When Mark Oggers swaggers into a gig in his black leather pants, though, grown men and women genuflect.

'And if you wouldn't mind taking a few classifieds when people ring in,' Howard tells me while I'm thinking about the genius Mark Oggers. 'Just people wanting penfriends and ads for Genesis T-shirts, things like that.'

'I thought it was *New Wave Weekly*,' I reply. 'What are ads for Genesis T-shirts doing in the back?'

Jon laughs then, so hard that he has to blow his nose.

'Howard thinks they're Punks!' He yelps with laughter, covering his face with the *Dandy*.

Howard gives him a withering look.

'No I don't. I'm not completely stupid. I just want to make some money. Is that all right with you?

'Linda, dear,' Howard suddenly addresses me. 'Do you know who bankrolls The Stranglers, that extraordinarily street-cred group that Jon enjoys so much?'

I shake my head.

'Shirley Bassey. She's the cash cow at their record label. You don't think songs about Leon Trotsky make them any money, do you?'

And with that, Howard leaves the room, dodging a pine hatstand, in about as much of a tiff as I'll probably ever see.

Over in the corner Jon is still laughing and smoking his joint. Even from this distance I can see his eyes are both bloodshot. Then, at last, Cindy shuffles in. For some strange reason she's gone nautical today. She's wearing a jaunty blue beret, a stripy blue and white fisherman's jumper and little navy blue deck shoes. Perhaps it's the stripes, but after lifting his head off the floorboards for just one look, Jon flops down again with his hands over his face. All of which must mean their relationship has hit another interesting phase. If interesting is the right word.

Cindy looks the sheets of butchers' paper up and down, as blank-faced as ever. We haven't really made friends yet. All that stuff about the sisterhood is bollocks. If you've got nothing in common with someone, it doesn't matter whether they're the same gender, you're still not going to be able to think of anything to say to each other, especially at half past nine in the morning. Especially with a stroppy cow like Cindy.

'Can I have that Pistols piece by the end of today?' she says in her cup-of-cawfeee accent.

I nod dumbly.

'It's the historeee of the band. You're gonna make it all up, right?'

I nod again. I have no idea. However, she seems to be the only one who knows what's going on.

Cindy nods back at me, then waddles off in her tight navy blue pants to the tiny art room while Jon turns himself over on his back so he can keep breathing. I'm glad he's done it. I really didn't want the responsibility.

'Can you tell me how this beat-up thing works again?' I ask him.

'You take little tiny pieces of everyone else's stuff that's already been printed, and then you put it all together to make it look like your own, and if you're very clever, it might even look as if you've actually *spoken* to the band.' Jon makes little-tiny-piece gestures with his fingers to illustrate the point.

'Won't people find out?'

Jon shakes his head from side to side. 'No they won't. Not if you're subtle about it. Anyway,' he rubs his eyes hard for several minutes, 'everyone else does it. And face it. Sid's dead, the album's out any minute, what do you think everyone's going to want to read two weeks from now? There's only one thing that's going to sell this magazine, and that's the scent of a fresh Punk rock corpse.'

With that, Jon indicates a pile of old newspapers and music magazines in the corner and tells me to get on with it.

'And here's a tip,' he says, breathing dope fumes over me as he leans on me for support on his way to the toilet. 'Go down the Golden Lion or somewhere and get some vox pops.'

I'm buggered if I'm going to admit I don't know what they are.

'And use Howard's typewriter,' is Jon's last piece of advice before he lurches onto the landing. 'The F key's stuck on yours.'

So. My first ever piece of writing, on my first ever proper day at work, in the first issue of a magazine that's got Genesis T-shirt ads in the back and pine furniture ads in the front. I wish I could say I was going to turn out a masterpiece, but I'm not.

Cindy shimmies out, looking for something on Howard's desk, then sees my face and reads my mind.

'Glamorous job, huh?' she says, and then she pops back inside her room again.

I feed a blank sheet of paper into Howard's typewriter, moving things off his desk – brochures for bidets mostly, and copies of *Private Eye* and jars of half-eaten marmalade – and start thinking about The Sex Pistols.

Howard comes back into the room, sees me sitting at his desk, stops, then realizes there's paper in the typewriter and grins at me like a maniac. Annoyingly, he also stands on tiptoe and peers over the top of the typewriter to see what I've written . . . nothing. Not a bloody word.

'Cindy's asked me to get on with the Sex Pistols history thing,' I tell him.

'Good, good.' He looks across the room. 'I'll sit at your desk, Linda, how about that?'

'Jon's in the toilet.'

'Yes, I heard him,' Howard tells me. Then he thinks of something. Scrabbling around in one of the drawers of an antique pine dresser he finds what looks like a hundred copies of various old music papers and newspapers all stuck together.

'Plenty more stuff in here, give you something to write about,' he says.

But what I find, in the end, is probably nothing that anybody else would be interested in. There's a letter from someone in Lancashire three years ago, which says that he'd seen the Pistols live and decided to hate Punk for ever, until he'd seen some big stadium band at Earl's Court that he had to watch on a screen and pay loads of money for, and then when he realized they were tax exiles as well, he decided he hated them so much he became a Punk the next day.

Then there are other little things. A picture of Sid

with his teeth sticking out and his hair sticking up, looking like a twelve-year-old on his first day at school. And Keith Moon saying, 'If any of them Punk rockers gets near my drum kit I shall kick 'em square in the knackers.' And then something in a Pistols gig review by Neil Spencer, the editor of *NME*, where someone in the band talks to him afterwards and says they're not into music, they're into chaos.

After half an hour Howard wanders up to my desk to look over my shoulder again and see if I'm making progress.

'Sod it,' is all I can say.

'Oh come on, Linda, you can do it.'

'But I can't.' Weirdly – it must be tiredness, or worry, or rats under the sink or something – I feel tears pricking at my eyes. I feel like I'm back at university, about to fail an essay for Graham Hayes.

'Sorry. Am I getting in the way?' Howard suddenly shuffles off again, his corduroy trousers making a whistling sound as they rub at the knees.

'The thing is,' I say as Jon walks back in the room, 'I'm not qualified to do this. A few weeks ago I was putting on the Chop Suey at a Chinese restaurant in Withingdean. Know what I mean? And I only saw the Pistols once. It was a children's Christmas party in Huddersfield. I only got in because my friend babysat one of the kids.'

'Eh?' Jon says.

'They had bottles of pop and a big cake and it started at 3 p.m. They were all firemen's kids, or the kids of workers who'd been laid off. It was the Pistols' Christmas treat.'

'Well write about that then,' Jon says. 'Because nobody else bloody will.' Then he puts on Throbbing Gristle very loud.

Over the top of the music, I can hear Howard on the phone to a company called High There in East

Grinstead, which sells solid silver pendants in the shape of cannabis leaves.

'I've bought them for all my nieces,' Howard lies cheerfully into the phone, 'they're absolutely marvellous – tasteful, witty and original, and I congratulate you on your creativity.'

It's interesting listening to Howard negotiate. First he offers the drug jewellery people a full page ad for a few hundred, then he offers them the spot opposite the crossword for slightly more – but less space – and then he seems to be angling for a fifty quid box above an advertisement for gas masks. I'd love to know who's buying the gas masks. I must have been to thirty-five gigs in the last three months and I haven't seen anyone wearing one yet. Maybe I should write about it in my new fashion column.

'Oh hello Evan,' Cindy says, psychically shooting out of the art room just as a familiar blond-haired man in a parka walks into the room. Evan, I notice, doesn't bump into any of the pine furniture. Instead, he seems to glide around it, giving me even more proof that he doesn't inhabit the same planet as the rest of us.

'Hi Linda, hi Cindy, hi Howard, hi JON.' Evan shouts this last name above the sound of Throbbing Gristle, who Jon has cranked up to full volume on the record player. Swivelling in his Doc Martens, Evan suddenly clicks the Nikon camera in front of his face and points it at me, sitting at the typewriter.

'That won't come out,' I say.

'Let me be the judge of that,' Evan replies, sounding even more Australian than he did the other night.

I try to concentrate on the paper in my typewriter, but it's no good. Evan has X-ray eyes.

'Do you want to go down the pub, Linda?' he asks me at last.

'I can't. I've got to write this,' I say.

'Write what?'

'About Sid dying and everything. And the new film.'

I am now, for no apparent reason I can think of, going red. Burning with humiliation. Feeling more publicly stupid than I have for quite some time.

'That photo of you I took the other night', Evan continues, apparently not noticing, 'is a beauty.'

I try not to look at him and stare at the paper – still blank – in my typewriter.

'Tell him', Evan jerks a thumb at Howard, 'to put it in the paper.'

And then he leaves, picking up a white envelope from Howard on the way, which could either be drugs or money, but as Jon's already told me Evan throws up on speed, I assume it's a few of Howard's prize ten pound notes instead.

After this Jon begins scribbling furiously. Then Howard gets back on the phone, trying to persuade the HMV Shop to take out an ad on the bottom of page fifty-two. And I suppose I should be concentrating on Sid and Nancy, and Johnny and Malcolm, but I can't. I just can't. I mean, does Evan's entry into a room have this effect on everyone? Plus the phone on my desk seems to be ringing constantly, mostly with enquiries for *British Racing Greyhound Gazette*.

Then a very different kind of call comes through. It's Hazel, calling from a phone box outside her school, at eleven o'clock in the morning.

'I feel sorry for you,' is the first thing she says, in a voice that's so tight, so angry, I can only just make out that it's her.

'What? Why?'

'I've been talking to David. And he told me what you did.'

'Told you what, for God's sake? Look. Hazel. I'm at work. Can't you call me at home?'

'You haven't got a phone at home, remember. You're in that poxy bedsit.'

'Yeah, well thanks for reminding me.'

'I'm really disgusted with you, Linda. In fact, I think you're disgusting.'

'Hazel! What the hell are you talking about?'

But she's hung up. And when I finally find her work number scribbled in the back of my old address book, the school secretary tells me she's in a staff meeting.

'Staff meeting,' I say out loud. 'Bollocks.'

Howard looks up. 'People being difficult, my dear?'

'Yes. Not music people. Other people.'

'Can I help?'

I shake my head and go back to the blank piece of paper that's still stuck in my typewriter. Jon puts on another record. At full volume – again.

'Turn it down!' I yell, across the wardrobes, and the hatstands, and the bookcases.

But he either can't or won't hear me, and after that I rip the paper out of the typewriter, give Howard a look, nearly tread on his spaniel and push my way out of the office.

There's a patch of park near here, which I spotted on the day I went for the interview – if you can call it that. I find it, dodging dog shit, beggars and tourists to get there, and sit down on a park bench covered in graffiti next to an old alcoholic who's falling sideways into a bin crammed full of rubbish.

There are a few things David could tell Hazel about me. But none I can think of that would make her pick up the phone and scream at me. Unless there really has been some dedicated hand-brushing going on and a few lifts to and from the bus stop, and suddenly her view of me has become *his* view of me.

It's an old tactic, but a good tactic. If you fancy someone, the first thing you do is have a good moan about your ex while the someone nods sympathetically at you from across the table. Even if she has been your ex's friend since the age of thirteen.

I'd feel sick about Hazel's phone call even if the alcoholic sitting next to me didn't stink so much. What is it about tramps that they always smell of home perms and French cheese?

I can't go back to work just yet. I'll probably pick up my typewriter and hurl it at someone if I do. But I do have to tackle the Hazel thing. Maybe tonight, from the phone box outside the flat. Unlike most things in my life at the moment, it actually seems to be working.

CHAPTER EIGHT

I already know what's disgusted Hazel so much, of course. David's told her that I stopped him from buying the house of his dreams. Worse, he's probably told her that I went behind his back and sabotaged him. For what it's worth, both statements are true.

The dream home was a funny old house around the corner from the seafront at Brighton. He wanted it for two reasons, firstly, because we could fall asleep listening to the sea, and secondly, because he thought it was a good investment. 'Brighton will go up in value one day,' David said to me on the Pier, getting all excited about it, although I couldn't.

The dream home eventually became something quite different, though, mainly because my only contribution to the mortgage was half a Kit Kat, which I snapped off and gave to David while he was doing his sums on the back of an envelope. All David could manage to save up for in the end wasn't a house in Brighton but a horrible semi-detached at 119 Waverly Crescent, Withingdean. It was so bloody ordinary. Pebble dash on the outside, a garden with some dead tomato plants, and a wonky driveway that was crazy paving gone wrong.

What made David salivate, though, was the fact that 119 Waverly Crescent belonged to a little old lady whose time was up with the bank.

'It's an FTS job,' he told me.

'What's that then?'

'Forced to sell.'

'And you're the only one who knows about it, I suppose, is that it?'

He smiled then, the broad smile of a man who is about to become the first ever male in the entire history of his family to own his own home.

'Guess how much,' David said.

'Oh, don't ask me. What? £50,000?'

'God Linda. You've got no idea, have you. £12,000. Maybe less, if I can point out all the rising damp to the bank.'

'So are you going to buy it then?'

I remember how I felt when I asked him, as though it was nothing to do with me, when in fact it should have been everything to do with me.

'It'll be our place,' David said. '119 Waverly Crescent.'

'Oh good.' Still, I felt nothing. In fact, I felt more for the old lady.

'Our place, no rent to worry about and we can paint it how we like.'

'Great. A pink toilet at last.'

'And I've got that nice juicy low interest rate from the bank as well,' David finished up, practically drooling. '119 Waverly Crescent. It's practically ours. Can you just see us there Linda, or what?'

And I nodded. Like a total hypocrite.

I went round to look at it after that of course. And if there was an old lady in there, she was either asleep or hiding under the bed with the lights off. The house looked small and dark, and, if you must know, like every other boring house in Waverly Crescent.

A posh letter from the bank arrived in the post some time after that, signed by David's manager, which I thought was the most stupid thing I'd ever seen, given that he could have reached across a couple of desks and handed it to him at work.

'Procedures,' David said, trying to give their stupid little bank routines a James Bond air of mystery.

We went out and got moderately pissed to celebrate – David even made me leave my handbag bottle of port at home – and then we split some fish and chips between us on the way back to the flat.

'It doesn't even seem like a proper home now, does it?' David asked me, looking around our old bedroom.

'Why, because it's rented?'

He nodded. 'It cheapens the experience when you know. When you *realize*.'

At which point I also realized something: I couldn't go along with his dream. But I didn't have the heart to tell him to his face.

The next day I asked the Chinese restaurant to give me fifteen minutes off and I legged it to R. H. Nesbitt, which, as anyone in Withingdean knows, is the only real estate agent to see if you really want to get a good deal and rip off your fellow man.

The woman at the desk gave me a look that most women of a certain age give me – in Boots, at the bus stop, in Tesco's. I'm used to it now. I wasn't so used to it then.

'Can I help?' she said, looking at my ripped tights and not wanting to help at all.

'I'm not after a rental,' I said, getting in before her.

She kept staring.

'It's just that I heard a property might be on the market. Not officially, of course. But I thought you might know about it.'

I told her the address, and I said I'd heard that someone was already trying to buy it cheap, and I told her about the little old lady who was being forced into a quick sale by her bank.

After that, 119 Waverly Crescent sold for more – a lot more – than David could afford. It was his best chance of buying a house, if not the only chance he had at that stage of his life, and that's no doubt why Hazel rang me up this morning, screaming at me and calling me disgusting.

Well she's right. In the Withingdean scheme of things, I probably am disgusting.

I had to confess to David, in the end, I couldn't stand the guilt. We were on the end of Brighton Pier when I did it, and for half a second I imagined he was going to push me off, into the water. He couldn't even look at me, never mind speak to me. And I suppose we still haven't spoken about it to this day.

When I finally get home, pulling the Tesco's shopping bag off my head (it's all the rage, everyone's wearing them when it rains) and shaking the water off my coat, I look around my new bedsit. I look at the plastic picnic cup on the plastic picnic plate, and the fold-up single bed, and the rat shit still under the sink, and then I think about 119 Waverly Crescent. It's not even a case of dreams versus realities, really. Just realities versus realities.

I switch on the radio; there's some disco crap playing so I switch it off again. Why, whenever I have the radio on, do I never hear The Buzzcocks?

As David probably explained to Hazel, he comes from a family that has almost nothing. After three generations of unemployment, not to mention the deaths of a few crucial males in a couple of world wars, they've ended up like a bad Monty Python sketch. So poor they can't afford cardboard boxes, that kind of thing.

David's family is all about bad luck and bad management, so of course the first thing he and his brother did when they left school was make a beeline for jobs at the bank. And David's always been good with money.

111

He saved everything he ever had from his first job, which was picking cherries, and the second, which was cleaning windows, and the third, which was the part-time gig as a security guard at Hillage's.

Money isn't just money to him. And owning a home is much, much more than it appears.

By the time David had been promoted at the bank from junior underling to slightly less junior underling, he'd saved up more money than I thought possible. He showed me his bank statement more than once, and every time the amount just seemed unreal to me.

'How did you get it all?' I asked him once.

'Through honest graft, Linda; how do you think I got it?'

'If you divide all that by the weeks you've been alive, for the whole of your working life, it's like . . .' I couldn't think of a word for it. 'It's like some kind of self-punishment. I mean, how have you *lived* all these years, David?'

Dosh. I never think about it. And is that such an awful sin? I remember David shaking his head, looking at me stashing a cheap bottle of port in my handbag one Saturday night, asking me if I was ever going to grow up and buy my drinks like everyone else did.

That's always been the key to my weekends, though. For the same money everyone else might blow on an album, I can take myself from Friday afternoon through to Monday morning, no problem. It's always been how I've lived – running in the back entrance to gigs, pushing past security. Blagging my way into big concerts. Getting my port bottle out in the ladies' toilets. Jumping the barriers at Brighton Station. Begging cigarettes. For me, the important thing has always been that being broke shouldn't get in the way of your freedom. For David, I don't think the word freedom has ever entered into *anything*.

I try to remember David the way he was when he

112

was in places that didn't remind him of money, or work, or being married, or saving for a house, or anything else. Stonehenge was one of those places. It had such a big effect on him he even ended up lying down in the grass with me and singing Beatles songs. Hastings was another one. We went there once on a freezing cold day in April and ended up playing crazy golf, cackling like idiots and nearly killing each other with our bad shots. *That*'s the sort of memory I feel I want around me now.

Or there's our first date. Our fantastically romantic first date, when I was so excited that I marked it in my diary five days before it happened. 'Date with David tonight' it said under 12 February, and I even drew a love heart next to it, with three exclamation marks and three question marks. In the end, though, I had a cold, so he came round to my house and we played Mastermind while he made me cup after cup of Lemsip. He let me win, and then he kissed me for the first time at the front door. Despite my cold, he kissed me. I still remember that. I'd been longing for it all night.

It was my first chance to see the Steve McQueen chest hair close up, not to mention the tasty fella sideburns, and I think I might even have stopped breathing for a few seconds too.

There are men who are so artless in the game of love that everything is obvious from the start. There's no mystery, no suspense, no energy and no surprises.

From first arrest to first, heart-stopping screw, all I ever felt with David at the start was a kind of wildness. And that's what makes it so sad now, really. It all got obvious. There was a time when I never knew what might happen with David, until the day came when we both knew *everything* that was going to happen, all the bloody time.

I look at the fold-up bed. What would it be like to

have Evan in there, clamped onto me, under the tartan blankets and the cheap nylon sheets? The gigantic leap of imagination required to slot some hotshot peroxided photographer from Australia into this bedsit is more than my head can stand though. Evan would have exotic art prints and photographs on his walls. I've got nothing. Just a Police poster, which I'm rapidly going off.

I turn the radio on, then turn it off again, praying for some great song to come on, but it doesn't. Linda Ronstadt followed by Earth, Wind and Fire. I can't listen to that.

I put the kettle on, and realize there are no tea bags. And no, I still haven't typed out my historeeee of The Sex Pistols for Cindy, either.

CHAPTER NINE

By the time the second issue of *NWW* has come out, and I have written two crosswords (4 Across: Plastic Bertrand's real name, 11 letters), one fashion feature about gas masks and twenty-four record reviews, including 'Warrior in Woolworths' by X-Ray Spex, my shameful history of The Sex Pistols no longer bothers me. In fact, if you must know, I can't even remember what I wrote.

I've worked out that Howard's only managed to sell an average of eight pages of advertisements in each issue, which means the rest of the blank pages have been filled up entirely by me, and Jon, and the genius freelancer Mark Oggers, who has taken to sleeping in his smelly Mini outside the front door of the office just so he can nab Howard on the way in and make sure he gets paid. I always tell Howard that people like him should get paid less if they can't type, but he still gets his ten quid per Cornflakes box anyway. What I'd give to be a male literary genius in a raincoat.

Instead, I am just me – wonderfully raw me – until I buy a second-hand thesaurus down the market, anyway.

Then the combat trousers in my fashion column go from being dead cool, to being brawny, durable, hardy, hearty, robust, substantial and vigorous – at least until Howard tells me to stop.

And what words I find for the latest Boney M single! Base, degrading, loathsome, contemptible and sickening. Stentorian, lurid, ostentatious and vulgar.

And then there's Abba. 'Banal, boring, buttock-heavy. Listen to their new single and you'll wish you'd never been bjorn.' In the end, I start making ashtrays out of all the singles – especially the disco ones. I pinch the three-bar radiator from under Howard's desk, switch it on high, and hold the latest Donna Summer crap against the metal grille until it starts to warp and melt, satisfyingly, in my hands. 'If you twish the melting vinyl into shapes while it's still warm, you really can produce some very decorative ashtrays,' I tell Howard's spaniel, in a silly Blue Peter voice. 'And look at this Barbra Streisand album! What a fine fruit bowl this will make, once it's reached the right faren-heit!' It's only when I finish work one day and realize that I have made fourteen ashtrays and four fruit bowls in one afternoon, that I think my new life as a music journalist might be getting to me.

Jon survives our deadlines by taking huge quantities of speed, drinking Cindy's black coffee, smoking two cigarettes at once and playing The Fall at full volume. Howard survives by polishing his pine furniture, massaging his spaniel and retreating to L'Escargot for business meetings about bidets. Cindy survives by keeping the art room door permanently closed. And me?

Well it's simple really. I discover the incredible thrill of selling review copies of every single and album that I haven't melted to a man called Tony down at Camden Market. In one way it's sad. When I listen to Jon interviewing the bands whose vinyl I'm flogging, their ultimate destination (as a £1 bargain buy for Tony, who's also selling woolly hats and candles) seems wrong. All that angst. All that artistic struggle. All those long words they look up and save specially for Jon Whitten's feature articles . . . but anyway.

Perhaps it's David's influence on me over all these years, but I find myself doing calculations. If I get twelve records to review, every fortnight, and I flog them for between one and two pounds a time, and I work at *NWW* for at least two more years, I could save up enough money to . . . yeah, buy even more records.

There are some I haven't sold, of course, because I can't get them out of my head. *Cool for Cats*, for example.

'Squeeze,' Jon mutters, from behind a wardrobe. 'I give them until Christmas. And I'd give that bloody Cats song zero out of five if I was you, no idiot's going to buy that.'

I think one of the reasons the song sticks in my head so much is, it reminds me of David. I can just see him at some Brighton disco now he's single, posing and asking Hazel lots of questions as she's hanging onto a wall. It's like Glenn Tilbrook and Chris Difford have been following David round all the clubs on Brighton seafront with binoculars or something. Hazel, of course, hasn't rung me back since she told me I was disgusting. And he hasn't been in touch at all.

'I'm very sorry to hear that about your chap,' Howard says when I tell him, but I can tell his heart's not in it. He has, after all, got enough problems of his own.

After two issues, it seems we've only sold half the issues of *NWW* that were printed, so he's already had to cut back the copies, and sack Alan Jennings, our retired *British Racing Greyhound Gazette* editor.

'From now on I'll proof-read everything myself,' Howard declares one morning when Jon's been flogging The Fall on the record player and we're all feeling particularly depressed.

'Yeah, well you can start with *her* stuff on the Banshees,' Jon shouts over the top of Mark E Smith wailing plaintively out of one speaker.

'*She*'s the cat's mother,' I shout back. 'And don't be so bloody rude.'

'Now, now,' Howard says, patting his spaniel and eating a spoonful of Cooper's Oxford Marmalade from the jar on his desk.

'You don't spell Siouxsie and the Banshees without the X!' Jon yells at me.

'Well maybe I wouldn't make silly mistakes if you kept the buggerdy-bugger music turned down!' I scream back.

The volume, however, remains the same. So after that I take matters into my own hands, squeeze round the side of the two pine wardrobes that separate my desk from Jon's and pull the record player plug out of the wall. Suddenly, *Live At The Witch Trials* scrapes to a halt.

'You've just scratched the record, you stupid bitch,' Jon half mutters.

'What?'

'I *said* . . .' Jon begins.

But instead of saying anything at all, he storms silently over to Howard's desk, seizes the teaspoon from his marmalade jar and attacks my copy of *Cool For Cats* with it, scraping it backwards and forwards, leaving bits of sticky orange peel all over the vinyl.

Stunned silence in the *NWW* office.

After this, Jon gets inside the wardrobe closest to his desk, closes the door and sobs like a child, until Cindy hears the noise and comes out to see what's going on.

'This is nuts,' she says, glaring at Howard while she lets Jon out.

'He attacked Linda's record with a teaspoon,' Howard says.

'There'll be a homicide round here any minute,'

Cindy declares. Then she goes back into her office and slams the door.

'It's sexual frustration, old man. I know, I know,' Howard says, putting his hand on Jon's shoulder.

'No it's bloody not. I can sleep with Cindy any time I bloody want to,' Jon glares. 'It's just that this week she doesn't want to. All right?'

I try not to look too shocked by this sudden burst of information about Jon's private life and carefully wipe the marmalade off my copy of *Cool For Cats* with a tissue.

'Sorry,' Jon says to me at last.

'It's all right,' I say. He has almost no fingernails left at the moment. And his dandruff's got worse.

'I'm having a nervous breakdown,' Jon adds, forcing all the hair back from his forehead with his hands, looking skull-like and mad. 'Do you realize how many bands I've interviewed in the last four weeks? Do you understand how many shitty gigs I've reviewed?'

Howard nods. 'I know, I know. You've been working so terribly hard. We've *all* been working so terribly hard.'

Jon smiles at him. 'And you know the worst thing of all?'

Anticipating a joke, Howard smiles back, and says no, he doesn't.

'The worst thing, Howard, is trying to work on a music paper in the middle of the FUCKING PINE PALACE!'

And it's then that the first hatstand goes out of the window, landing with a crunch as it splinters into pieces in the street below.

'Christ, Jon, what are you doing?' Howard shouts, trying to stop him.

'Bye-bye!' Jon yells as he puts his shoulder against the side of the nearest wardrobe and heaves it out, so that it's balancing on the window ledge like Laurel, or perhaps Hardy, in one of those old black and white films.

'Don't do that, you lunatic, someone might get killed!' Howard bellows. But it's too late. With a grunt, Jon heaves the wardrobe beyond the point of no return and it crashes down into Wardour Street.

'I've got some good news for you,' Jon tells me with unnatural calm as he skids across the floor in his Doc Martens and shoves a bookcase under the window.

'What's that?' I try to humour him while Howard blinks at us, paralysed in his chair, the spaniel in his arms.

'You're going to interview a band called Altered Images,' Jon grunts, edging the bookcase towards the ledge. 'They're from Scotland. The singer's a girl called Clare Grogan.'

'Wow. Brilliant. Thanks Jon.'

Crash! Wallop! Another hatstand gets pitched, ahead of the bookcase.

'Yeah, she's from Glasgow,' he continues, as if nothing is happening. 'They're going to be huge apparently. I'd love to meet her.'

'Well, you can. I mean, why aren't you doing the interview, Jon?'

'Because', he gasps for breath, staggering under the full weight of the bookcase, 'I'm going to be in jail. For chucking all this fucking furniture out of the window.'

Suddenly Cindy comes out of the art room. 'Leave the bookcase Jon,' she says mildly. 'There's way too much of that Olde Rustic English junk in the street now as it is.'

And then the miracle arrives. Just as Jon is eyeing the pine kitchen dresser in the corner, the postman staggers up the stairs with a telegram for Howard.

'Oh thank God!' Howard roars, holding the telegram up to the light then kissing it.

'What?' I ask. 'What? What?'

'We're quids in,' Howard says. 'I've just sold all the furniture to a chap in Provence.'

Minus the various wardrobes, hatstands and book-cases Jon has just hurled into the street, that still means Howard can pay his printers' bills. To celebrate, we all head down the pub. Jon's episode with the furniture even seems to have aroused some passion in Cindy, and she shoves her hand in his back jeans pocket as the four of us wander down Wardour Street.

Once inside the pub, Jon and Howard have four pints in rapid succession, and then when Cindy has gone to the loo to do her face, they decide to tell me the abridged version of their life stories.

'I started out writing the captions in *Princess Tina*,' Jon confesses.

'My father wanted me to be a barrister, but I was thrown out of Lancing College for sleeping in the nude,' Howard reveals.

'Well you know all about me, I was making Chicken Chow Mein for a living,' I tell them.

'And Cindy was a part-time coke dealer, of course,' Jon informs us, five seconds before she comes back to the table with another round of drinks.

CHAPTER TEN

Just before our third issue – which we manage to produce faster than usual, thanks to the lack of pine furniture tripping us up – Hazel telephones me.

'I'm coming up to London,' she says. 'I need to get something for Mum's birthday. Shall we have a cup of tea somewhere? On Oxford Street?'

I say yes, then realize she's waiting for me to suggest somewhere, because I'm a Londoner now – but I can't think of anywhere except Wimpy.

'Very sophisticated, Linda.'

There is no mention of her yelling down the phone at me the other day, and certainly no mention of David.

'How's work?' she asks.

'The new issue's out tomorrow. I've written a story on this group called Echo and the Bunnymen.'

'Echo and the what?'

I knew that would make her laugh. Jon Whitten, of course, takes the Bunnymen *extremely* seriously, and he's even started dressing like them, in white socks, baggy trousers, school shoes and a raincoat. He's also growing his hair like some tropical bird in a David Attenborough documentary.

'And how's your love life?' Hazel asks.

'Nothing doing. And how's yours?' I reply, a little bit too quickly.

'Oh, you know. Still not seeing anyone. But Eric called me the other day. He wants to go to Bath with me. Of course I thought he was asking me to have a bath with him and so I started talking about bringing the Badedas over, which got him all confused.'

I laugh. Eric and Hazel have been playing games with each other for ever, and nothing ever happens. When I finally put the phone down, I feel as though I've crossed a bridge with Hazel. A shaky and precarious bridge that could collapse at any time, but nevertheless, I've made it to the other side. For the moment anyway.

I know David hasn't made a move on her. I just know it. Hazel's not capable of that kind of subterfuge. So finally, perhaps, I have permission to relax, and maybe even have a Badedas bath myself – in the sink.

When I get into bed that night, I find myself daydreaming about Evan, and I think about the girl in the red leather jacket. She wasn't *that* good-looking. And I'm the one he's been taking photographs of, I comfort myself. It must be the effects of sleeping on what's basically a child's bed: you regress to the mental age of a twelve-year-old nursing her first crush. What next, buying little tubes of Love Hearts and reading the messages as if they mean something? I've never been dumped before. Not seriously. Is this what happens, this backwards and forwards, to and fro business? Some days it's all about David, when I forget to stop hating him and start needing him again. Other days it's all about Evan. Or Feargal Sharkey. Or the drummer out of Blondie. I wonder if I should see a psychiatrist?

Normally I would have told Hazel about someone like Evan. Not for any purpose, because there's no solution – well, nothing she could provide anyway. It's more that conversational grooming thing you read about. Instead of Hazel picking nits out of my fur, she listens to my pointless, rambling conversations about men. And I do the same thing for her, whenever men like Eric crop up.

Lately, around this time of night, once any mad ideas about Evan have faded away, I find myself aching for David. My head is furious with him, and my heart wants him. It's like the ache you get for sugar, or cigarettes, or songs you're addicted to. It's like a cat going back for his Whiskas, or maybe some rock star going back for his heroin. Mostly, it's a mindless kind of craving that calls out for long baths and sad songs, but unfortunately my only option in this place is to sit in the sink with my legs hanging over the edge, listening to The Cramps.

Each night the confusion gets worse. It feels like trying to make sense of all the scattered bits in the end of a kaleidoscope, while some invisible force keeps shaking it. Do I feel this bad, I think, because I've lost the comfort of my home town and my old flat rather than David? Do I feel this miserable because there are rats under my sink and no bath or TV set? Is it insecurity because he says he prefers Hazel to me?

Then the kaleidoscope gets shaken again. For the first time in years I feel free. My new life excites me, and excitement is a feeling I only ever vaguely associate with daytime. Without David I can eat what I want and listen to what I want. Without David I can go to bed when I like and get up when I like. Because I'm single, I can go to the pub after work, stay there until closing time and fall face-down in the Ladies' toilets if I want to. Because I'm single, I can go to any gig I like and end up in bed with anyone who drifts under my nose.

Without David I also seem to have found my voice. All the writing I'm doing, even if it is about bands like Terminal Sausage and bad and obvious crossword clues, seems to have released something in me. A few readers have even written in to the Letters Page. They say they like what I've said. *They like what I've said!*

When I think back to David, all I can remember is short stops and interruptions. I could never finish a sentence with him, at least not the way I wanted to.

I start dreaming about Evan again. The perfect boyfriend for my soon-to-be-perfect life. One day – not now, but one day – I'll share a flat with him, with a proper bathroom and a TV, and I'll be interviewing all the people Jon gets to interview, and *NWW* will beat *Sounds* and *Melody Maker* and even *NME* in sales, and everyone will want to know me. And Evan and I will have a leopard skin rug on the bed in our flat, just like the one I saw in the *Sunday Times* last week. And he will take wonderful black and white photographs of me and our glamorous, brilliant children, who will all have the kind of mad names they would never allow in Withingdean, like Byron, Anastasia or Iggy. They will be better-looking versions of me, with dark hair, blue eyes, a few freckles, and very straight noses.

Back in bed, the dreams become more elaborate and ambitious. *Elvis Costello.* Without his glasses, I imagine he's probably quite sexy. I might marry him, when I've finally become the editor of *NWW*. Then there's Sting. Not out of the question, if I get my hair dyed at a hairdressers rather than out of a bottle from the chemist – and, of course, if someone is nice enough to introduce us. Jon knows where he lives. He went round his house to interview him.

Shake, shake, shake goes the kaleidoscope in my head again. David was the best thing that ever happened to me. He's a saint and I never, ever deserved him. Nobody will ever make sacrifices for me again, the way he made sacrifices for me. He had a soft touch with me, without ever being soft, and that's hard to find. I've thrown away a six-year relationship, not to mention an engagement ring, for something I can never have. And so it goes. All the way from 11 p.m. to 2 a.m. And lately it's been like that every night.

* * *

On Saturday, Hazel meets me on the dot of one, at the Wimpy bar on Oxford Street. To my horror, I see she has two copies of *NWW* under her arm, and she's wearing a poncho and culottes as well. Falcon Stuart, the unbearably cool manager of X-Ray Spex, is sitting at the back of the restaurant as well, and he's spotted me. Oh, the horror.

'You can't get *NWW* at home,' Hazel says, 'so I thought I'd get two copies here. One for me, and one to take back.'

'Take back to who?'

'Oh, maybe your dad. I don't know. I'm sure David would like to see a copy at some stage.' She catches my eye to see my reaction.

'Yeah, we have to talk about David,' I say as we sit down at an uncleared table and look for our cigarettes.

She nods, then she nervously shows me a revolting soap-on-a-rope in the shape of a pelican that she's bought for her mother.

'It's so annoying that you have to come all the way to London to find things like this,' she says.

'About David,' she continues after a pause, and my heart jumps.

'Well go on then,' I say. 'Tell me.'

'He was with someone the other day,' she says quickly.

My heart jumps again. 'What do you mean, *with* someone?'

The dirty plates get taken away, and at last Hazel looks at me properly. She looks tired.

'I think she might be his new girlfriend.'

Shake, shake, shake. In all the confusing patterns made in my late night kaleidoscope of love and life, this is the only one I've never managed to see until now.

'I'm sorry,' Hazel says after a long silence, with both of us staring stupidly at the menu.

'Tell me everything then,' I hear myself saying. 'Tell me the lot.'

'She's in the Labour Party,' Hazel says.

'Typical!' I spit before I can stop myself. Though what should be so typical about David and someone in the Labour Party, I have no idea.

'She's got a "Vote Labour" sticker in her car window anyway,' Hazel adds. 'And he told me they were off to a meeting together.'

'What sort of car has she got?'

'Nice. A Vauxhall Victor. It's orange. And she's sort of nice looking. Not like you – quite different – but she's not ugly, Linda, put it that way.'

The waitress arrives to take our order and I manage to say one word: 'Tea', while Hazel manages two: 'Plain hamburger'. Then we spend several minutes letting all the various explosions in the conversation settle, ready for the salvage work.

'You're in shock. I can see I've shocked you,' Hazel says at last. 'Better put more sugar in your tea.'

'The thing is,' I stumble, 'he said he fancied you. That's what I was going to talk to you about.'

'What?' Now it's Hazel's turn to look shocked. 'When did he tell you that?' she asks.

'Ages ago. When he got me the bedsit in London and told me it was finally over.'

'Oh my God.' She shakes her head. 'Well I don't think you can have heard him right,' she says finally.

I shrug. My heart, true to form, is doing banga-banga-booma-banga Sweet drumbeats. David and a girl from the Labour Party. With a nice car. Nice looking too. More of a threat than Hazel then. *Shit, shit, shit.*

'Anything else about this woman?' I ask her above the sound of Radio 1 and screaming kids.

'She wasn't wearing a bra.'

'She wasn't wearing a *bra*?'

In an instant my mental picture changes. I have gone from a freckled, pretty girl with an earnest face and buck teeth to a kind of sexy Germaine Greer type, but younger, in a transparent cheesecloth shirt. In my head, she is leaning out of the window of her orange Vauxhall Victor, waving at David and smiling.

'Oh, and she likes that funny music,' Hazel adds.

'What?'

'Reggae.'

I sigh.

After that, there is nothing more that Hazel and I can talk about, it seems, and we don't. She has known me for long enough to understand when I just need to sit there, stirring my tea, gently being upset. So that's what she does, until she thinks I'm ready to hear more.

'I should tell you something else,' she says at last.

'What?'

'You can get soap-on-a-rope like this at home in Boots. I didn't have to come all the way to London to get it. Sorry. I hate telling lies. But I had to see you. I couldn't tell you all this on the telephone.'

'Did David ask you to come here?' I ask her. 'Tell me the truth?'

Hazel shakes her head. 'Don't be stupid, Linda. Anyway, I'm on your side, not his.'

And that, for the next few seconds anyway, is the one thing that promises to get me through the rest of the day. She's on my side. Nobody else seems to be, but Hazel is my friend, not his, and my current twelve-year-old self is well pleased by this fact.

'Did you mean it when you rang up the other day? When you said I was disgusting?' I ask her.

She looks down at her hands. 'Yes, I did. But I was so *angry* with you, Linda.'

'So what did he tell you? And when did he tell you it?'

'It was a couple of days after you'd driven up to London with that girl.'

'Annie.' All my old Punk friends are nameless to Hazel, as if they don't really matter.

'Anyway,' Hazel goes on, 'David rang me and he had a bit of a cry actually.'

'He cried?'

'I think it was shock. It was starting to sink in – what had happened between you two. Anyway, there was a piece of paper stuck up in the newsagent's front window saying your ring had been found in the street.'

'Oh no.'

'So he rang me, and he was all upset, and then he told me about the house.'

I nod, finishing my tea. I'd like more, but the waitress in here is impossible to catch.

Hazel gives me a look. 'How could you do it to him, Linda? How could you have gone behind his back like that?'

I shake my head. 'It's complicated. I'm not even sure it makes total sense to me.'

'But you do regret it, don't you?'

I sigh. 'That's just it, I *don't*. I mean, I regret being so underhand and pathetic about it, but what he was doing was wrong as well.'

I check her face, to see if she understands. She doesn't. I knew she wouldn't.

'All he wanted was to make you happy, Linda, and you ruined it all for him. You know that house was his dream house. And he'll never get another one at that price now.'

'Oh for God's sake, he'll buy a house one day. Why does everything have to come down to money?' I stare her down for a few seconds, and then Hazel does a most un-Hazel-like thing. She stands up, puts a few pounds down on the table, reaches for her bags and turns her back on me.

She starts to walk away, then turns around. 'I teach kids who are more mature than you,' she says in a funny, teary voice. 'And whatever you say about

David, remember he's my friend as well as yours. And I'm a very loyal person.'

And then she's gone. My twelve-year-old self immediately wants to blow a raspberry and give her the finger.

'Well stick it up your bum and set fire to it then,' I mutter under my breath, and that, of course, is the exact moment the Wimpy waitress chooses to appear by the table and overhear me.

Later, much later, after a day of window-shopping for stupid things I don't want and can't afford, I ring David, trying to catch him at his mate's place. It's not easy. Jeff keeps answering and taking messages, which is embarrassing. Alternatively, the phone just rings off the hook, making me visualize all kinds of ugly things happening across town, involving David, the Labour Party, reggae and a woman with no bra in an orange car.

Finally, I catch him late on Sunday night.

'Well it didn't take you long,' are my opening words.

'Linda. What's going on? I've got four separate messages here from you.'

'We were together for six years and it's taken you about six weeks to forget me.'

A pause. I can hear Jeff now, hovering in the background, and I can also sense David willing him to go away.

'David, are you listening to me?'

'Yes.'

'First you tell me you've fallen for Hazel, and now she tells me you're madly in love with some bird from the Labour Party. What's wrong with you, David?'

'That's a bit of an overdramatization,' David says at last, when Jeff is out of earshot.

'What is?'

'Saying I'm madly in love with her. How would you know what I'm feeling? She's a friend.'

'Oh piss off. And what was all that stuff about fancying Hazel? What a load of bollocks. Did the freedom suddenly go to your head or something? Who will it be next week, David; will you suddenly realize you're in love with Margaret Thatcher?'

I slam the phone down, then pick it up again and ring back.

'That's not what I meant . . .' I manage to say, then I start to cry, which annoys me beyond belief because it means my brain's stopped working and at the very moment I need it most.

'Who have you been talking to?' he asks. 'Hazel?'

'Who else would come all the way up to London to tell me?'

'I've made some new friends in the Labour Party. And I've got involved with the Labour Party because there's an election on.'

'Yes, I *had* realized, David.'

'Yes, well, I'll let that one go.'

'Stop patronizing me, you bastard!'

'Hazel saw me with a friend, that's all. She's just a friend. She gives me a lift home sometimes.'

'In her beautiful Vauxhall Victor. Yeah.'

I start crying again, and try to think of Debbie Harry and Chrissie Hynde, and Siouxsie Sioux and Ari Up, and all those other women with black eyeliner and bad attitudes I should be imitating.

'Are you sleeping with her?' I hear myself whine. 'I mean, now that you've got over me and gone off your secret passion for Hazel too, are you sleeping with this Labour Party woman?'

'Oh, Linda. Pull yourself together. What kind of conversation is this?' Then, a pause. 'And by the way, someone found your ring. In the road. I've got it in an envelope in the drawer – if you want it.'

Shake, shake, shake. The kaleidoscope changes yet again. And still, the picture makes no sense.

'I'm so confused, David. I don't know what to do. I feel as if I'm drowning.'

'Drowning in snot more like it. Blow your nose.'

So I do.

'Do you miss me?' I ask him.

'Yes. Of course I do.'

'What, like you miss your Grandmother when you say goodbye at Christmas?'

'Exactly,' he says, catching me off guard. Then he laughs.

'Don't fucking laugh at me.'

'And you stop swearing. It's ugly.'

I think back to *NWW* and my life there, with Jon and I hurling obscenities at each other, and our typewriters and the telephones ringing every ten minutes of the day.

'Hazel's got a copy of *NWW* to show you,' I tell him, once I've blown my nose again.

'Will I understand any of it?' he says.

'Well there's no Billy Joel in there, if that's what you mean.'

'What about good old Plastic Bertrand then?'

'Oh yes! Yes there is something about him! I put him into the crossword!' God, I sound like a schoolgirl again. One shared piece of our relationship Venn diagram has come into the conversation and I'm almost beside myself.

'I've got to go now, Linda,' David says gently before I can tell him any more.

'Don't you want to hear about the job you got me? And oh my God, wait until I tell you about the bedsit!'

'Another time. I'll call you next week,' he says.

'Why? Why have you got to go all of a sudden?'

'I'm tired,' he says simply. 'I want to go to bed.'

I tut into the other end of the phone, like a twelve-year-old again. 'I remember a time when you would have taken the phone to bed with you and stretched the cord round the bedroom door,' I tell him.

'So do I,' he says flatly.

And I think then, When the hell was that? And although I'd like to believe it was one or two years ago, I realize it was more like four or five.

David says goodbye then and hangs up, leaving me in a blur of tears and, as he rightly guessed, snot. I go back into the bedsit but there's nothing to blow your nose on, apart from thin toilet paper. Mainly because everything that's in it has to be provided by me. And so far I haven't even managed to find my local supermarket.

The next day, the new issue of *NWW* is out, which cheers me up. Even though I always take a copy home on Friday night, I still can't stop picking it out of the racks at the newsagent's on Monday mornings and holding it in my hands. I can't get used to seeing my name in print either. Even the pseudonyms give me a thrill. Record reviews by Pamela Piranha. Crossword by Becky Biro. Fashion by Suzie Skrewdriver. Howard makes me change my name, so it looks like we've got more staff working on the paper. But I do what I always do when I pick up the magazine on Oxford Street: I shove it under my coat and take it round the corner into the nearest quiet street so I can look at all my different names in print and silently squeak inside.

We have a new rule in the office. Ever since Jon went mad and threw all the furniture into the street, we now have Wednesday mornings off, once a fortnight on publication day. Howard says we need to have at least some time every two weeks for eating and sleeping so we don't all go barking mad. It's a rule I'm learning to love.

Because I don't have to be in the office until after

lunch, I mooch about at home, putting records on and then taking them off again, and picking up Jackie Collins and putting her down again, then fantasizing about ringing Evan, but doing nothing about it because *Cosmopolitan* tells you girls shouldn't be pushy, and even though I think *Cosmopolitan* is crap, I'm still worried that they might be right.

I think about Hazel's job as a school teacher, and realize that, like all teachers in my experience, she has a special gift for making me feel guilty. 'All he wanted was to make you happy, Linda, and you threw it all away for him . . .'

But I said it was complicated, and it is. And I knew Hazel wouldn't understand, and she didn't. The fact is, David's like a juggernaut when he wants something. Particularly if it's money, or something solid, like a car, or something valuable, like my engagement ring.

I know what it took for him to get that engagement ring. He pushed, and he prodded, and he dug his heels in, and he pressured, and he bullied, until the man who owned the little jewellery shop in The Lanes practically begged him to take it away for the price David was offering him. No wonder he cried when he realized I'd chucked it into the street. And no, I don't want it back. Not now.

When it came to that poxy house in Withingdean – the one that Hazel insists was his dream, as if it really mattered or something – David became like an armoured tank. He decided that it would make us happy because he just *knew* that deep down I really wanted it, didn't he, and so he barged his way through everything – my feelings, even a little old lady's feelings – so he could get to it.

And then I screwed it up for him. Right royally screwed it up, in fact.

So why does it still feel so bad then? And does the guilt after the end of a relationship ever get any better?

The answer to that, I suspect, is one that David's already found out. There really is only one option now, and that's to screw my way out of misery, fear, loathing and regret.

I check the gig guide in *NWW* – the gig guide that I put together – and see that a couple of Mod bands are on tonight, at Bridge House. That's the kind of thing Evan and I could do a story on, if Howard was willing. And I'm sure he would be, if I was mean enough to ring him up at home now and disturb his Agatha Christie, or his opera or whatever it is that he's pre-occupied with at the moment. In the end I find Evan's phone number – on the milk crate I'm using for a bed-side table – and go outside to the phone box to ring him. Sod it. This is the 1970s, not the bloody nineteenth century.

CHAPTER ELEVEN

You can encourage a crush if you want to, and bring it on – the way you can bring on the flu by waiting in the rain at bus stops and forgetting to eat oranges. I'm doing it with Evan now as we watch Secret Affair finish their set, and a few die-hard fans with Fred Perry shirts hang around the speakers, waiting to buy the band their drinks. A review is already forming in my head. 'Secret Affair are the Small Faces but with bigger ambitions.' Something like that, anyway. Evan takes a few shots from the side of the stage, and people stare, and I think, like an idiot, *I know him.* See, I'm still an assistant cook from Withingdean really.

Evan is even better looking side-on than he is front-on, I decide after he's passed me a few glasses of Scotch. And don't ask me how I know that it's going to happen tonight, but it's going to happen. We go for a coffee afterwards, in a little Italian café that's full of mirrors, and full of Evan's sideburns and broken nose, repeated endlessly down the length of the table.

I'm well aware that he's faking it, of course. From the dyed spiky white-blond hair to the camera round his neck to the way he asks for a cappuccino, there is nothing real about Evan. I wonder what he looked like in Australia, where he comes from and what his last job was. I bet his name's not Evan either; it's probably something like Bruce.

'Stop thinking so hard,' he says, lighting a cigarette. Then he gets up to go to the loo.

For a minute I think he's about to go into the Ladies' by mistake, then I realize my vision's so bad I'm reading the sign wrong. It's all the typing and reading I'm doing at work: I'm slowly becoming as blind as a bat.

I could get to the real Evan, I suppose; it would be easy enough through careful interrogation. But why bugger up my own happy fantasy? I like this version of himself he's created. I like the Scotch he buys instead of beer, and I like the music in this café – he's picked the only place in London where they have ska on the jukebox. I like his dyed blond hair, and the silver ring with the anchor on it, which he wears on his little finger, and the tight grey pants with the sharp creases down the front.

Part of the fantasy I'm weaving now is also the idea that Evan might be interested in me, and only me, and that all the other women in his life have suddenly been eliminated from his agenda. It's the hardest illusion to take on board, but I do it anyway. I've always felt that fooling yourself is a small price to pay for bliss.

When we finally leave the café, just after eleven, it's pouring down and the rain soaks my hair, then gets into my eyes.

'London rain stings,' I say, rubbing my eyes furiously as we walk down the street.

'Mind your mascara,' Evan says, and I realize I must have panda eyes. He finds a spotless handkerchief in his parka pocket and wipes first my left eye, then my right, and then he takes his arm out of the sleeve and makes a tent for both of us, pulling me under.

So different to David, I think, as we walk quickly up Tottenham Court Road.

'I live with some other Australians,' Evan says, 'near Olympia.'

'What are they like then?' I ask him.

'Tragic disco bunnies, but I don't have to pay rent.'

I nod. The inside of his parka smells of damp, and a bit of sweat and something like my mother's old hairspray; and the smell of him and his coat up so close is gently drugging me.

'Have you read any Colin MacInnes?' Evan asks me as we walk, faster and faster, as the rain falls harder and harder.

'No. But Jon has.'

'You should read *Absolute Beginners*.'

And that's what I feel like, I think, as we zigzag across wet black roads. Not just an absolute beginner but a totally clueless ignoramus beginner. I've only ever been with David, since 1973. I've only ever really known one pair of lips, one side of the sheets, one familiar kind of noise in the bed, one way of doing it.

'I can hardly see,' I say as the rain keeps falling into my eyes.

'Close your eyes then and I'll walk you,' he says, holding my arm.

And so I half shut my eyes then, and that's the way I find my way back to his house, like someone being helped along by a Labrador in a harness.

When we finally get inside his house, it's dark and silent, and the hallway smells of fried potatoes.

'They always go to bed early,' Evan says, not bothering to whisper.

He shakes the parka hard, out of the front door, and then hangs it on a hook in the hallway, next to a lot of striped scarves.

'Football scarves,' he says, looking at them, 'but Australian Rules Football. The colours are weirder.'

You can usually tell who dominates a shared household by the way the bedrooms are doled out. I wonder whether Evan's got the top front room, overlooking the street, and of course he does.

As we squelch up the stairs, I see a poster of John Travolta on the landing. I see what he means about the disco bunnies.

'Is Australia like America?' I ask him, trying to make conversation. 'A lot of people tell me it is.'

Evan shakes his head and smiles, and I realize I should probably just shut up.

Evan peels off his suit. The beautiful white shirt with the button-down collars is transparent, and I can see his rib cage through it. My tights are so soggy, they might have come straight out of the washing machine at the laundrette. My fingers are wrinkled. His blond hair is sticking up in wet spikes. My arms are pink and dotted with raindrops. We're soaked, and cold.

'Why is your bedroom covered in chiffon?' I ask him. There are great sheets of it in pale whites and greys, stuck with drawing pins in the ceiling, dangling from the window to the door.

'Something I'm trying,' he says.

There's nothing else in here. No alarm clock. Nothing sensible, like a lamp or a dressing-gown or a bedside table. A black and white postcard of Audrey Hepburn is wedged in the corner of a mirror on the wall, and there are dead cigarettes in a tin Union Jack ashtray, but that's it.

He puts on *This Is The Modern World*.

'Do you know anything about birds?' he asks.

'What, as in women?'

'No, birds birds,' Evan yawns, taking off the rest of his clothes and leaving his pants on, while he helps me off with mine.

'Leopard skin,' I say, pointing out the obvious. I've never seen David in anything but white Y-fronts from Marks & Spencer, so Evan's jungle underpants are a bit of a shock.

'I got them in Oz,' he yawns again.

Suddenly I realize I'm freezing. And I realize we haven't even kissed yet. 'What sort of birds did you mean anyway?' I ask as he fiddles with my bra.

'There are nine thousand bird species and 97 per cent of them don't have a penis,' he tells me.

'Yeah?'

I get under the blankets, partly because I don't like being looked at – and Evan is staring – and partly because it's pneumonia conditions in this big, empty freezing room at the top of the house.

'Bigger birds have them, like ducks and geese, and ostriches and swans,' he tells me.

I brush away a hanging sheet of chiffon as it drifts towards us. 'Well even I knew that,' I say.

'In fact, the Australian blue duck has a penis so large that after copulation it has to stuff it back into its cloaca,' Evan informs me.

'What's a cloaca then?'

Evan leans over me suddenly, and I see how pale his back is, and he finds a candle and some matches. Then he turns the light off.

'Mind that chiffon doesn't catch alight,' I say, then I realize I must sound like the most boring twat in the world.

'It's never caught alight yet,' he tells me, and suddenly I have a vision of the red-leather jacket woman in here, and maybe Cindy as well, and possibly half of the girls who were at the gig tonight.

In the candlelight we both look strange, not like real human beings at all. 'Sometimes it works and some- times it doesn't,' Evan says quickly.

'What works? What doesn't?' Then I realize he means the contents of his leopard skin underpants. 'You don't need to have conversations about Australian ducks and penises to tell me you can't get it up, Evan,' I say quickly.

'Well,' he says, sounding embarrassed. 'That's all right then.'

'I'm used to it anyway,' I lie to make him feel better.

'Are you?'

'I had the same boyfriend for six years. It's no big deal. It happens.'

If David could hear me now he'd kill me, of course. Because whatever else was wrong with him, impotence wasn't one of his problems. If anything, David was the Thomas the Tank Engine of sex.

'Nuh,' Evan sighs after I stick my hand down the leopard skin underpants. 'It's no good. Sorry. It's not happening.'

'That's all right,' I say, lighting a cigarette. Then I wonder if I should put it out. I've never had to deal with this kind of situation before. I mean, what do you do next? Is there a chapter in *The Joy of Sex* about this?

Evan takes a drag on my cigarette, then holds it away from him while he kisses me. And all the time I wonder how long it's going to take for us to get somewhere. Of all the things I might have imagined going wrong with Evan, this is the absolute last on my list. And although cigarettes are OK for about ten minutes, we can't just chain-smoke our way through the night.

I stick my hand down the front of his underpants again, but he pulls away.

'Have you seen anyone about this, Evan?'

'Nuh.'

I should have known. Men never want to ask anyone about anything.

'On the plus side, though, Linda,' he says, holding my face in his hands, 'my nipples are sensitive like you wouldn't believe.'

Thank God. A set of instructions. A map in the jungle.

141

'The worst thing is, I think it must be me,' I say lamely suddenly feeling inadequate.

'Don't be stupid. I could have Debbie Harry in here and nothing would be happening at the moment.'

'Tell me what to do then.'

Evan sighs and shakes his head.

'Am I talking too much?'

He sighs again. Then suddenly he gets up and changes the record.

'Let me test this theory about sensitive nipples,' I tell him, diving into his chest when he comes back.

Despite myself, I remember how different it was with David in the good old days. He didn't make any noise. He just got on with it. At the moment Evan is making a lot of noise and not getting on with anything at all.

Some time later we have wriggled around the bed so much, and slid so far down the sheets, that we are now almost on the floor, reflected in a mirror. And we still haven't got anywhere.

I suddenly realize The Jam have long since finished on the record player, but I have no idea what time it is.

'Look at us. We look good, don't we?' Evan asks. But I'm too tired to speak.

'When it gets light,' he asks me, 'can I take some photographs?'

'If you want. Why do you want to?'

'Would you believe me if I tell you that it might help?'

He pulls out a shoebox then, from under his bed, and I see dozens of black and white shots of women, some taken in here – I can recognize the wallpaper – and some in other rooms in other houses.

'I've got this feeling I'm going to recognize someone I know in here,' I tell him.

He smiles.

'Well they're good,' I say, despite myself. And they are. Misty, grainy, dreamy images of women who look more like mermaids than real people. Blonde Punks, brunette Punks, bald Punks, pretty Punks, fat Punks.

'I put Vaseline on the lens,' he says. 'That's why they look like that.'

Evan goes to the loo, and I pull the blankets up to my chin, wondering what time it might be, and whether I can get any sleep at all before I have to go to the office. There is evidence that the real world is out there somewhere, because even though it's still dark there are dogs being walked and cars are just starting to come up the street.

When he comes back, he does so with two mugs of hot water with cinnamon in them.

'No tea bags,' he apologizes.

Later on, as more light comes into the room, I realize the wallpaper is pale pink and the sheets of chiffon which I thought were white are actually pale yellow.

'Normally, when the sun comes up, it breaks the spell,' I tell him.

He nods.

'This is like a never-ending spell, though. I mean, I know the milkman will be round any minute, but it's like nothing touches this room.'

He rolls me over then, and rubs his hands together quickly, and I realize from the smell that he's found the jar of Vaseline.

'I lived in Thailand for a while,' he says.

'Did you?'

'I got taught massage by this Thai hooker. She was fantastic.'

And then he gets to work on my back, slowly moving down my body with his hands as more cars start in the street outside and the pigeons begin to warm up with the sun, and then ... I just pass out. It's not even like normal sleep, just a heaviness that's impossible to fight, and then oblivion.

When I wake up again, it's after ten o'clock and I can hear a bath being filled across the landing. The room smells of candle smoke and the sticky Vaseline on my skin, and the sunlight is streaming into my eyes so that when I turn away again there are patches of floating navy blue in front of my eyes.

Evan is smoking, sitting on the carpet, wrapped in a blanket and reading an art book.

'I don't know what you did to my back but I feel fantastic,' I tell him.

'Yeah, but the idea wasn't to make you fall asleep,' he says, half smiling.

'Sorry. It's just, we were up all night.'

'My idea of a good time.'

'Oh well. Of course.' God, when am I going to stop sounding so English?

Evan laughs. 'I'm running a bath,' he says. 'I decided to get the rest of the cinnamon and put it in.'

'Is anyone else home?' I ask.

'Just us.'

I wrap myself in a blanket as well, and we go to the bathroom, passing John Travolta on the way.

'His eyes follow you round the room, don't they,' Evan says. 'Like the Mona Lisa.'

As I get into the bath – all cinnamon and steam – Evan pads out again, then comes back in with his camera.

'Won't the lens fog up?' I ask him.

'That's the point,' he says.

And I do know Cindy was in the shoebox full of photographs, because on one of his trips to the loo I slid it across to my side of the bed and looked. He'd photographed her wrapped up in some of the chiffon sheets, gazing into the middle distance in a way that made her look more like some Renaissance painting than a blonde with a ponytail and mad shoes.

144

While Evan clicks, I sink further into the water. I wonder vaguely if he's drugged me during the night, because suddenly I seem to be slipping into his photographs, and his desires, as if I've lost all will power.

'If they could see me now', I say with a straight face, 'in Withingdean.'

Evan ignores me, switching cameras and trying every angle.

'There was a painter in Australia called Norman Lindsay, and you remind me of the girls in his paintings,' he says in his twangy accent, with his blanket tucked around his waist like a native skirt.

'I bet you say that to all the chicks.'

'Can you go right under the water for me?'

'Maybe.'

But when I do – I don't think I've tried to submerge myself in a bath since I was a kid – the cinnamon gets into my eyes and I come up blind and choking. He quickly puts a towel into my hands.

'This is someone else's towel, isn't it?' I say, smelling it and making a face.

'Flatmate's.' Evan shrugs. He wanders out again, trailing his blanket behind him, and comes back with a clean one, folded up.

'I've got this urge to read *Absolute Beginners* to you in the bath,' he says.

'Well what could possibly be stopping you?'

Because I'm not behaving like myself, I'm also not talking like myself. This strange chunk of time with Evan, and the chiffon, and the cinnamon, and the art books, is like being slotted into someone else's film. I try to check myself and think of normal things, like work – Howard will be wondering where I am – and Hazel, and what I'm going to have for dinner.

When Evan comes back, the bath water is going cold, so he lets some drain and turns the hot tap on again. As he does this, his blanket slips, and I try hard not to stare.

Evan reads, perched on the side of the bath, and I listen – to Colin MacInnes.

'He was Australian, did you know that?' he asks when he has finished reading to me aloud, in his twangy voice.

When the hot water has taken the water level almost up to my nose, Evan gets in next to me, flooding the floor.

'That will teach them to take their *Reader's Digest*s in here,' he says, watching as piles of magazines next to the toilet go soggy.

We lie in the water for a while and eventually hear the post come through the letterbox downstairs. Evan pours some of his flatmate's bubble bath into the water and starts churning it up with his hands; we sit for a while as the sun streams in through the net curtains and lights up the row of shampoo bottles on the edge of the bath.

'Everyone in this house smells of fruit,' Evan tells me. 'Apple shampoo, banana conditioner, peach shampoo . . . and I do as well, because I borrow all theirs.'

'No you don't,' I say. 'You smell of something quite different.'

It's at this point that I realize I'm half obsessed with him already. And that's lethal. Dangerous. Bad news all round. Perhaps it's because he's washing my hair. Perhaps it's because of the way he's been using his mouth on me. Or maybe I'm just off my head on cinnamon fumes.

Evan puts his hand in the water, sliding it down my body and then underneath me, and pulls out the plug.

'You're beautiful, Linda,' he says, 'but it's time to get out.' He hauls himself out, raising himself up on his arms on the sides of the bath like a gymnast.

After that he gives me one of his flatmate's skirts to wear, and a big V-neck jumper of his, and I find some tights to borrow. My shoes are so waterlogged they are beyond hope, but I can put up with them temporarily.

'Hang on,' Evan says as I pull up the tights. He pulls me towards him and pulls down the zip of his jeans and goes inside me.

'Now?' I ask.

He nods. Then he takes me down on the floor, and a few minutes later – three minutes? four? – it's all over.

'I've gone off the pill since David,' I think out loud.

Evan shakes his head, panting hard. 'You'll be fine,' he says. 'Trust me. I never get anyone pregnant.'

'Can I call work?' I ask before he can ask how it was for me. I suppose the correct answer to that would be, not like anything you're supposed to enjoy in *Cosmopolitan*, but I did anyway.

'Don't call work,' Evan shakes his head. 'It'll make them appreciate you more if you're a bit elusive.'

Evan has a huge bowl of goldfish downstairs, and I watch them swimming around their fake underwater fairy castle while he throws fish flakes into the bowl.

'Are you excited by coming to London?' he asks me.

'I suppose so. There's more food to choose from in the supermarkets. Sorry, is that a crap boring thing to say?'

'London, for me,' Evan informs me, 'is like sticking my finger in a live electrical socket.'

He talks about his work for a while, but I'm not listening. Instead, I'm trying to stop myself falling in love. Being with him would involve a lot of sacrifices, my common sense tells me. I'd have to enter Evan World, and leave mine behind – and I'm not sure I want to do that. He doesn't treat women like you're supposed to, he doesn't have sex like you're supposed to, and I'm not even sure he's human.

'Stop thinking so much,' he says as he puts something

classical on the record player. Then he asks me more about my writing, and my obsession with bands, and the endless power struggles between me and Jon, and how I put up with my horrible bedsit, and the rats under the sink, and all the rest of it.

'I'd like to keep this clean between us,' he says when the record has finished.

'What do you mean, clean?'

'I'd like us to keep everything and everybody else out. I'd like it to be just for us. Our secret.'

'I bet you say that to all the Punks,' I joke.

We listen to the other side of the record, and Evan teaches me some yoga breathing thing he learned in Thailand, where you have to shut one of your nostrils. Slowly, gradually, I manage to slip back to the real world.

Outside, the rain has started again, and it would be nicer to stay here and maybe even wander back to bed again, but I remind myself that if I skip any more time at work, Jon will nick all the best records to review and I'll be left with the dross as usual – none of which Tony at Camden Market wants to buy from me.

'Bye then,' I say on the front doorstep. Behind me, thunder rolls across the outskirts of London. I hover for a minute, waiting for the lightning to follow.

'You're breaking the spell, you know that, don't you?' Evan asks.

I nod, and then I wince as I see a dead cat in the gutter. 'Oh God, I hate it when cats get run over.'

Evan laughs. 'You're looking at a hessian sack,' he says. 'Get some glasses, woman.'

We kiss then, but eventually I manage to tear myself away, and somehow get out of his street, and up to the main road, and onto a bus.

Stop fantasizing, I tell myself, as I find a seat. Stop obsessing. And stop thinking you'll be able to change him.

I've got Vaseline on my shoulders, cinnamon on the backs of my hands, and – I can feel it – a love bite on the side of my neck. No wonder nobody wants to sit next to me – and it's a crowded bus as well.

If I was still with David, living in Withingdean, I'd be having elevenses and getting ready for work at the restaurant. Breakfast would have been three hours ago and it would have been Cornflakes, milk and sugar and a slice of toast after a night of no candles, no chiffon, no cinnamon, no camera and no bath. I remember we looked at candles once in some gift shop in Brighton, and David said no.

'It's a waste of money, Linda. They only burn down.'

Evan's sure to be a waste of energy. I might need glasses, but even I can see that. Even *Cindy* can probably see that. And the red leather jacket woman. And everyone else who's in the shoebox, in black and white and out of focus.

I finally make it up the stairs at Wardour Street at a quarter past two. One look at what I'm wearing, of course – some Australian shiftworker's very ordinary work clothes – and both Jon and Howard know something's up. Cindy, fortunately, is locked in her art room, so she can't see me.

'You might have *rung*, Linda,' Howard says. I suppose that's as stern as he gets.

'What was it you saw last night? Mod bands?' Jon asks.

'Yeah. I went with Evan.'

A meaningful office silence follows, and I ignore it.

I wade through a pile of press releases and readers' letters, and as the afternoon goes on the night that's just passed seems further and further away.

When I finally go back to the bedsit, though – I work on past seven o'clock because I feel guilty about turning up late – there's an envelope under my door. Inside is a large black and white photograph of me, already developed, and I'm looking not like me at all but more like some Victorian maiden lying in a lily pond. You can see Evan's arm, and his camera, reflected in the bath water, and it's hard to see where his arm ends and my leg begins.

There's no note. And when I open the front door, there's nobody there waiting for me.

I'd give anything for a normal life right now. It's like choosing between two different species, never mind two different men. Evan is not a man who would ever ask my father for my hand in marriage. David is, and more to the point, he did. David's dreams are all about money and houses. Evan's dreams are all about photographs, and paintings. Evan gets excited about London. David gets excited about braless members of the Labour Party. There aren't even shades of grey there, it's all black and white. One of them is as sexually predictable as a steam train on the way to Scotland. The other comes and goes like the tube in rush hour after an apology for a delay.

I get rid of the last of the cinnamon and the dried sweat under my arms and the Vaseline by flannelling myself in the sink. Then I switch the radio on, hear Pink Floyd, groan and switch it off again.

CHAPTER TWELVE

On Wednesday we get a sixteen-year-old schoolboy in to do work experience and he asks me to help him lose his virginity.

His name is Kelvin Collins and he brings cold shepherd's pie in a Tupperware container for his lunch, given to him by his mum. He has been given a week off school to learn how to be a music journalist, although the only jobs Howard has given him so far are answering the phone, going to the post office to get stamps, and cutting up the Swiss roll for afternoon tea.

'Linda,' Kelvin asks me at lunchtime, 'can you show me how you have sex?'

This should probably be the cue for a clip round the earhole, as they say in Withingdean, but Kelvin seems so serious, so sincere and anxious about his virginity that I have to hear him out.

First of all, though, I choke on my bread and butter.

We are in the Wimpy bar on Oxford Street, when Kelvin suddenly leans forward over his cup of tea and propositions me.

'Linda, I'd rather have sex with you first than anyone else in the office,' he goes on. 'Would you consider it?'

I think about it for a moment. This must mean that he asked Cindy first and she said no.

'I'll consider it, yes, but I'm probably not going to do it.'

'Why not? I think I know how to do it. I've been reading all about it. And the thing is, I don't think I can be a proper rock writer unless I've done it. Know what I mean?'

I look at Kelvin Collins for a minute. He has blackheads on his blackheads, and a Sham 69 badge on his green V-neck jumper. His favourite film is *Star Wars* and he's got a *Smash Hits* free sticker on his spiral-bound notebook. Even if it was the professional thing to do I wouldn't. Even if I fancied him, I wouldn't. And even if I was sixteen, like him, I still wouldn't.

'Why do you want to lose your virginity anyway, Kelvin? You're only young. You can wait a couple of years, can't you?'

'But Jon's sending me to Solihull to interview Gastric Reflux. I'm getting a free coach ticket and I'm even staying in a hotel and it's free.' He sounds extremely excited.

'Jon is making you go to Solihull?'

'I thought there might be some groupies there. I want to know what to do with them.'

'Great. So you want me to have sex with you so you can have sex with women from Solihull who want to shag Gastric Reflux.'

'That's it in a nutshell,' Kelvin agrees.

Later, I tell Jon off for making Kelvin go to Solihull on the coach by himself. 'Just because you can't be arsed doing it, there's no reason to send the work-experience boy.'

'Kelvin can manage. He wrote some great record reviews earlier. Much better than anything you've ever done.'

'Go screw yourself.'

'Stop using Cindy's terms of abuse. They don't suit you.'

Jon puts The Ramones on the record-player, extremely loud, leans back in his chair and closes his eyes, nodding fast to the music.

'Twat!' I say loudly, but as usual he pretends not to hear.

After work, Howard and I go to the pub and then I tell him that Kelvin has just propositioned me. Shortly after this, though, Howard has four pints and does exactly the same thing.

'You look so pretty in that top with your bra showing over the edge, Linda. Like a cuddly Audrey Hepburn.'

Instantly I yank my shrunken long-sleeved T-shirt back into place.

'Come to Provence with me, let's forget about work. My parents have a cottage there. We can spend the summer. It's never too early to think about summer, is it?'

'And what do you see us doing in this cottage, Howard?'

'Taking it to the edge,' he replies, holding back a belch.

'Taking what to the edge?'

'You know.' Howard stares hard into my eyes, and licks his lips. Howard has incredibly thick lips. I'd never really noticed them before.

'You know you should never have an office affair,' I say lamely, because I can't think of anything else to say.

'Bollocks. Look at Jon and Cindy.'

'Well exactly.'

'Come on, Linda. Think of it. I bet you've never even been to France, have you?'

'Yes I have,' I say. 'A day trip to Dieppe on the ferry and very nice it was too.'

Later on, when Howard has had two more pints and decides he's starving and needs some Kentucky Fried

Chicken, I make my excuses and leave. As I walk back across Oxford Street towards home, I see a couple up ahead of me in the rain. He is giving her most of his umbrella, and they can't keep their hands off each other. From where I'm looking, under the cover of another plastic shopping bag, they seem happier than I'll ever be – or maybe happier than I've ever actually been.

Single life. A sexually unpredictable photographer who sleeps with every woman in London, an over-enthusiastic schoolboy, and a pissed boss on the rampage. Things are so fantastic at the moment they can hardly get any better.

CHAPTER THIRTEEN

When I go into work on Tuesday Howard rushes up to
me. For a moment I worry that he's going to start bang-
ing on about my bra again, or the house in Provence,
but fortunately he seems to have forgotten his alcohol-
fuelled lust of last week.

'Now that we've got you lined up to interview Clare
Grogan, we'd like you to interview The Raincoats as
well.'

The Raincoats is something Palmolive started when
she left The Slits. A girl called Vicky plays violin and
guitar, and there are two other women, Ana and Gina,
in the band.

'When?' I ask him. I'm knackered. The Members are
on tonight at the Moonlight, and I'm supposed to
review them as well.

'As soon as possible.'

Something occurs to me. 'Am I only going to get
women to interview because I'm a woman?'

'No, not at all,' Howard says quickly. But I can see
his embarrassment and Jon is smirking in the
background.

Annoyed, I feel like Emmeline Pankhurst. There are
endless tedious magazine and newspaper articles
appearing at the moment asking whether women
really have become men's equals in the music

155

business, whether feminism has really triumphed at last. A lot of them are written by men like Jon Whitten, who wouldn't have a clue. I think about the way he looks at Cindy's arse all the time, and the way he asks her to make him coffee but never really talks to her.

Later in the morning I decide to tackle Jon about the way the interviews are being farmed out. Howard has gone to Clapham to talk to some of his bidet people.

'I'm not interviewing The Raincoats, all right?'

'Why? Have you had a fight with one of them?' he asks, smoking two cigarettes at once and putting 'Sunday Girl' on the record player.

'No, I'm just fed up with always being given women to interview.'

Jon pushes his glasses up his nose and gives me a lopsided smile. 'You've got Clare Grogan lined up and you're maybe going to talk to Palmolive if you're lucky. And you call that always being given women to interview. It's a grand total of two, Linda.'

Annoyingly, I go bright red. What is it about my face? Two layers of foundation and concealer, and I still find that most emotions – anger, sadness, desire – manage to break through as nasty blushes. Jon notices, and suddenly the lopsided smile becomes a real smile. In that moment I decide I want to kill him.

'It's not *sexism*, Linda, it's just the way the stories have panned out. I'm not free to do The Raincoats and neither is anyone else. You just happen to have scored two women in a row first up. It's a coincidence.'

'No it's not.'

I keep on blushing, higher and hotter, from my jaw up to my cheekbones.

'What's your real problem then?' Jon sniffs, stubbing out one of his cigarettes, which has burned shorter than the other.

'I haven't got a real problem. You've got a real problem.'

Slowly and deliberately. Jon turns up the volume on the record player, and then addresses the wall, not me, in a voice that precisely matches the sound and volume of Debbie Harry, who's now blaring out of the speakers. 'Three months ago you were cooking Chicken Chop Suey in Withingdean By Sea. I think we can be forgiven for not sending you out to write an in-depth interview with The Clash.'

That's when I throw my typewriter at the wall, mainly because I'm not quite brave enough to chuck it at his head.

'Shit!' Jon yelps, flinching as the Olivetti hits the bricks.

'Stick it up your arse, Jon.'

'Calm down, for God's sake!'

I pick the typewriter up, put it back on my desk, tap away at it experimentally, and then discover that I've damaged the E key. I decide to write Howard a note about Jon anyway.

'*D-ar Howard,*' I type, my heart still pounding. The adrenaline rush of throwing the typewriter at the wall feels incredible.

D-ar Howard,

For th- n-xt f-w days I will b- writing articl-s without any -s in th-m. This is Jon Whitt-n's fault for b-ing a s-xist wank-r so pl-as- s-nd him th- r-pair bill, not m-. If I wasn't forc-d to work with stupid toss-rs lik- Whitt-n the-r- wouldn't b- a probl-m.

Moments after I leave it on Howard's desk, he breezes in, throwing open the office door, marches straight over to me, grabs me and starts kissing me.

'Linda! We've sold out!'

I stare at him at close range. He smells of garlic.

'Jon!' he whirls around. 'We've sold out every single copy of yesterday's issue!

'We're all going to L'Escargot for dinner tonight, on

157

me,' Howard burbles. 'This is extraordinary news. Cindy, come out of there and listen to this. We literally have no copies of the magazine left from Brixton to Birmingham!'

'Yeah, well congratulations,' I mutter. Then I walk out of the office and into the street. My hand still hurts from where I chucked the typewriter.

Outside, the rain is starting to fall on Soho, turning white paper bags soggy and cigarette butts into orange mush. There is something fantastic about Soho in a storm. It wouldn't have half the impact if it was clean and tidy. Endless rubbish strikes have left a legacy of all kinds of shit stuck to the pavement – including shit – but now the rain is washing everything away. As the water rips down the gutters on Dean Street, you can see bits of the *Sun*, plastic straws, old puddles of sick and even the occasional black sock, all being swept away. Just looking at it all being cleaned up makes me feel better.

Just then somebody behind me calls my name. It's Howard with the dog under his arm, obscured beneath a big red tartan umbrella.

'Linda, what are you doing in the rain? Come and have a cup of tea with me at least.'

'I like the rain. I'd rather be in it, than not.'

'Well come and have a cup of tea and then go back in it, for God's sake.'

I realize he must have read my note and probably seen the damaged typewriter as well.

Howard puts his hand in the crook of my arm and manages the umbrella and the dog with his other hand. It's like being taken for a stroll by the vicar in a Jane Austen novel. I suppose that's what they teach them at those big, expensive schools that people like Howard go to. Maybe they even have special English gentleman strolling classes.

We end up at a noisy Irish pub on Berners Street,

with a leaky roof and a plastic bucket in the corner to collect the drips.

'Do you realize everything in this country is like that at the moment?' Howard moans, watching each drip.

'Going to rack and ruin.'

'Crumbling in front of our eyes.'

Howard shakes his head, looking sad. 'Do you know, I saw a dead cocker spaniel in the gutter in Sloane Street this morning? And someone had put a copy of the *Beano* over its head. Linda, I nearly wept.'

Howard orders a toasted cheese sandwich at the bar but I can't eat anything. In the end, he forces me to have a Guinness.

'I'll say one thing about the Guinness in here, Linda, it's the real thing.'

I nod and take a sip. It's just what I feel like.

'About your note,' he begins.

'Sorry. I just got so frustrated.'

'Forget about it. And forget about the typewriter too. I'll get you a new one,' he says.

'And what about the way the interviews are being doled out?'

'I'll sort it out with Jon, I promise. Oh God, I'm so bad at keeping everybody happy.' Howard sighs. 'It's so much easier dealing with pine dressers and portable bidets.'

Both of us sit in silence for a minute, drinking our beer.

'Are you going to vote?' he asks suddenly. The election's on in a week.

I shake my head. 'They're all rubbish.'

Howard nods as if he's used to hearing people like me tell him things like that.

'I think we're in for a Labour government again,' he says. 'Which my family would kill me for saying, but there you are.'

'Are they Tories?' As if I need to ask.

159

'My mother has just made and frozen a blue sponge cake to hand out to the village on election day. The cake itself is a pale blue, and the icing will be a dark navy. And before she put it in the freezer, my father took a photograph of it. I think that gives you some indication of where my family stands.'

'Mrs Thatcher needs more than blue sponge cake, Howard. She's a woman. No man in this country's going to vote for her.'

The dog slobbers against Howard's leg until he gives in and drops a piece of cheese sandwich on the floor. I stare out of the window at the rain, and for no reason I suddenly picture Evan in his leopard skin underpants.

'A bit happier now?' Howard asks, catching me smiling to myself.

'Look. About throwing the typewriter,' I start again.

'Please forget it.'

'No, I need to explain something to you. It's not really the interview situation, Howard, and it's not even Jon, although he's a prat and I hate him.' Howard brushes this away, as if he hears it from people all the time, which he probably does. 'The reason I'm so uptight is that I found out the bloke I was engaged to is with someone new. He says she's a friend. Of course. And if you must know, I haven't been sleeping too well the last few days.'

There's something about Howard's earnest face, stuck behind a cheese sandwich, which makes me feel I can tell him anything.

'And you've been in touch with him to talk about it?' he says, looking worried for me.

'No, not really.'

'Well go and ring him up at once,' Howard pushes me.

I shake my head. 'I can't. It's not fair to her. The new girl.'

Howard rolls his eyes as if I'm out of my mind. 'What do you mean, not fair? Good grief, Linda, she's absconded with your intended!'

'But he isn't my intended. We ended it before she came along.'

'Rubbish,' he says, fishing pickled onions out of the jar on the table. 'Get on with it. Call him up. Get him back. Who is she anyway?'

It's wonderful, really, to have Howard on my side like this, even though he doesn't know what he's talking about.

'She doesn't wear a bra. She's in the Labour Party.'

A pickled onion almost shoots out of Howard's nose at this, he laughs so hard. He laughs so rarely in the office I've forgotten what it's like, but when it does happen it's like something out of a cartoon. His mouth hangs open, his eyes squeeze tightly shut, he leans forward and then he leans backwards, and sometimes he even shuffles his feet on the floor as if the agony of being amused is killing him. Anyone walking past this pub now and looking in would probably think he was having some kind of attack.

'Good grief,' he says at last, 'is there any chance of this braless Labour bird handing out "How to Vote" cards in our village this Thursday? My mother would have *enormous* fun with her.'

And now that the laughter has broken the ice I can talk about something else as well. So I do.

'Howard, I don't want you to make any more moves on me.'

'Understood,' he says quickly. 'Understood, absolutely. I must apologize to you. Four pints and the goggles of lust do tend to go on. My dog hates me for it.'

He picks up his nameless farting spaniel and makes a fuss of him, and then I realize I've embarrassed him so much that I really should go. So I do. And Howard

161

mutters something about a man in Hammersmith with a big bidet order for a hotel chain.

I can't face going back into the office to use the type-writer without an E key, so in the end I just give up and wander home early. It's still raining, but most people seem to have given in to it. From Soho to Kentish Town there are dead umbrellas pointing the wrong way out of rubbish bins, and soaked children carrying their raincoats under their arms, and wet cats padding up and down the street, not even bothering to look for shelter.

I find the right change – and, more importantly, a phone box that works – and call David.

'I just thought I'd ring and wish you luck for this Thursday,' I say, realizing what utter bollocks this is as soon as it's out of my mouth. It's almost as stupid as when David rang me to commiserate about Sid Vicious.

'No you didn't,' he says. 'I'm surprised you even know there's an election on.'

'Is it going well, then, with your friend?'

'Yes, thank you very much.'

'So it's sorted then? You're a couple?' That's the question I really wanted to ask, I guess.

'And what about your love life, Linda?' David interrupts. I knew he would. I've never been able to finish half the sentences I start with him.

'It's OK,' I say, thinking about Evan and my high hopes for his leopard skin underpants.

'Well then.'

'So that's it, is it, we'll just never see each other again?'

David puts on his reasonable voice. 'Any time you like, Linda, any time you like. I go up to London some-times. You're going to come back home now and then, aren't you, to see your dad?'

'Oh, to see Dad, yes, and to see Hazel, I expect,' I say

– and I let this last piece of information hang, hoping to make him feel guilty.

'Yes,' he says after a short pause. 'You really should see your dad.'

'Oh shut up. You know what it's like.'

'I saw him the other day. The way he sees it, you just upped and left.'

'Yeah, well that's bollocks. I hope you told him what really happened.'

'I'm just saying you can't forget about him, that's all.'

'Oh, who are you, the bloody Pope, David? Stop being so sanctimonious.'

After that, we just breathe down the phone for a while, and I realize I have pins and needles in my leg.

'Well, we can catch up for a coffee, can't we?' David says at last.

'Maybe.'

'Oh for God's sake, Linda.'

'So tell me, you're definitely off Hazel now, are you, and you're on with this other bird?'

A pause then.

'Just grow up, will you.'

'You're the one who should grow up. First you get some secret crush on one of my friends, and now you're off getting involved in politics because some woman goes around without her bra on.'

'What?'

'And your lot aren't going to win this election any-way, so what's the point?'

David sighs. I can tell, though, that this cut-and-thrust thing, this silly verbal fencing thing, is helping to do the trick. It always has. Our passion always did run on arguments, and when there wasn't something real to fight about we'd bring it on anyway, just to light the indoor fireworks. It has never been this serious before because we've never gone all the way and split up before, but still, it's there.

'All I can say to you, Linda, is that if you come down here, or I go up there, we should make a point of getting together to have a coffee. All right?'

'I slept with someone the other night,' I tell him. 'And he's lovely. He's a photographer and he wears leopard skin underpants.'

He hangs up then, and by the time I've found more change to call him back, he's left his phone off the hook.

CHAPTER FOURTEEN

The Jam are on at the Rainbow, and I thought Evan might take me, but in the end there's no word from him, and I'm too down on myself to ring him, so I go by myself. Paul Weller sings 'It's Too Bad' and I have to take two aspirins and suck hard on a Polo mint so I won't cry, and then I just give in and let my eyes well up anyway. Or should that be Weller up? Oh God help me, I'm even beginning to *think* like a sodding music journalist.

You know a band is approaching greatness when their fans are prepared to suffer for *their* art. Some of them are squashed up against the front of the stage – accidentally spat on by Weller, as he barks into the microphone, then shovelled up by bouncers.

Then there are the four little Mod girls hopping around their handbags right in front of the speakers. Their ears will be bleeding later, and they might lose their hearing tomorrow, but the look on their faces says it all. They just don't want to be anywhere else.

I see Jon in the crowd in the street afterwards. He asks me what I thought of the band, and I tell him they were fantastic. I suppose that means the air's been cleared between us.

Naturally, after that, he feels compelled to tell me that Paul Weller will be finished by Christmas. The gaggle of young Mod girls tagging along with him are open-mouthed at this revelation.

'So Paul Weller's doomed, along with The Pretenders then?' I ask him.

'Yeah.'

'What about Sting? Not long for this world?'

'I give him until next year.'

'What about Elvis Costello? Flash in the pan?'

'The way he's going, he'll be around for even less time than Thatcher.'

'And Thatcher?'

'Oh God, what is this? The Withingdean inquisition?' he spits. But Jon being Jon, he can't help himself. When asked for his opinion on anything, he just has to give it. 'Margaret Thatcher will be our Prime Minister for about as long as The Cure get more than eight people at their gigs,' he sniggers. 'In other words, not very long.'

'But I though you liked The Cure?' I say, thinking of his review of *Killing An Arab*.

'They've sold out, Linda, in case you hadn't noticed. So Robert Smith might as well get down the dole office right now. Hey, if you're going to flag down a cab, can you get one for us as well?'

I realize 'us' in this context means Jon, the two weird freelance writers with badges he always hangs around with and the four Mod girls in black tights and white winkle-pickers who are stalking them, hoping for a snog.

'I'm getting the tube,' I tell him. And I do, with Bruce Foxton's guitar still jangling in my head and a plastic bag over my hair to keep the rain off. It's been pissing down for about nine hours now, but luckily London's overflowing rubbish bins are always full of free Tesco's carrier bag rain hats.

When I go into work on Friday, it seems that Mrs

Thatcher's election victory has made a difference to Howard's life as follows: his parents seem to be on some kind of unnatural high and are consequently prepared to give him loads of money. In fact, Howard's mother has even lent him her charge account at Fortnum & Mason, so when he comes in, he's swinging two plastic bags full of tea and biscuits.

I've been listening to the results all morning, of course, so I'm completely sick of hearing about Thatcher by now. It's funny how people are already dividing into two camps – those who call her by her surname, as if it's an insult, and those who call her Mrs T, or even worse, Our New PM.

'My mother's gone quite mad since she heard the news,' he says, rubbing his hands together. 'She seems to think she and Dad will be quids in now that the Conservatives have taken over.'

The office is empty because both Jon and Cindy have come down with filthy colds and rung in sick.

'So can I come round to yours and eat caviar then?' I ask him.

'Not exactly, but you can come and see Terminal Sausage play and eat very fine salami.'

'Fantastic.'

'I've ordered a selection from the butchers at Fortnum & Mason, to attract the A&R men along. I've asked for venison and port sausages – I don't think that's too extravagant, do you? It's theme night. I do hope they appreciate it,' he says. Then he looks worried. 'Linda, you do think the A&R men will actually get the connection between all this salami and the name of the band, don't you?'

'Not necessarily. Remember, it was an A&R man who signed The Smurfs.'

'Oh well,' he rolls his eyes.

'When's the gig?' I ask him.

'Thursday night. I've hired Mickey's.'

'God. That's not cheap either.'

'And neither is Terminal Sausage. I want at least a £100,000 for them. And wild rumours in Wardour Street confirm that at least two major record companies are willing to pay.'

Poor Howard, I think, as I wrestle with the crossword. Not only is he never going to sell Terminal Sausage to EMI or Polydor for £100,000, he's also wasting his money on The Stiff Hamsters as well. And The Rejected. And Mandy and the Mutants, and all the rest. I've heard his entire roster of talent and I'd rather listen to a washing machine going round at the launderette.

'Then again,' Jon tells Howard the next day, 'Virgin have just signed The Human League, so anything's possible. I can see it now. The Stiff Hamsters with a six-album deal and a support gig with Blondie at Christmas.'

At the end of the day Jon and I do one of our trade-offs. He says he'll go to the Terminal Sausage gig, to support Howard – and more importantly, to steal some salami for me – if I review the new Patrik Fitzgerald album, which I am supposed to be nice about because Polydor have bought an ad on our next back cover.

'You've got to go and see his gig as well, though,' Jon says.

'Why?'

'No live review, no salami.'

'What am I suddenly, the Patrik Fitzgerald expert?'

'Well at least he's a *man*,' Jon smirks, 'so your feminist principles aren't being compromised.'

'Yeah, but how come I never get to do Joe Strummer, though?'

On Thursday night, whilst Jon and Howard go to see Terminal Sausage, I lie in bed listening to John Peel, enjoying my freedom. The Cure are on, with a song called 'Desperate Journalist In Ongoing Meaningful

Review Situation', and I wonder for a minute if it's been written about Jon, or that wanker Oggers who can't operate a chocolate machine, and then I go red and wonder if it's about me.

The next day I go into the office early because I've been dreaming about Fortnum & Mason salami all night and Jon said he'd bring the precious booty in first thing. It gets even better than that, though, because when I arrive Howard say's he's taking us out to Claridge's for breakfast.

'Why? What?' I ask, but somehow I already know.

'Howard didn't quite get £100,000, but he's still going to make a pile,' Jon informs me.

'Fifty thousand smackers, if you must know,' Howard grins, and pats his dog hard, repetitively, until it finally makes a yarping sound and jumps away. 'Oh God, sorry,' Howard apologizes vaguely.

'And here's your share of last night's sausage selection,' says Jon, finding a big lump of silver foil in the pocket of his army greatcoat.

'Yuh, eat that and it rilly will be terminal,' says Cindy, blowing her nose. She and Jon have matching cold sores, I notice.

CHAPTER FIFTEEN

The Ramones have a double live album out, which is the kind of thing that we're supposed to hate at *NWW*, because it sounds a bit too much like Emerson, Lake and Palmer doing a concept album about a mechanized armadillo. Because it's da bruvvas Ramone, though, even Jon manages to agree with me that I should automatically give it five stars.

'Before you've even listened to it?' asks Howard, stunned at this rare moment of unity in the office.

'It's that gig they did at the Rainbow,' Jon tells him, as if this needs no further explanation.

'But won't it sound horrible if it's live, full of people oohing and aahing in the middle of it? And people coughing and sneezing all over the place?'

Jon shakes his head and shares a 'Howard-is-hopeless' look with me. He's being a bit nicer to me lately, even giving me The Ramones album to take home, so maybe things are changing. Maybe he's found a way to get rid of his dandruff, or his drug problem, or whatever it is that ails him.

Since I've been working on *NWW* – over three months now – I've developed a technique all my own for record reviewing. I sit on the end of my fold-up bed at home with a phone book on my knee to give me something to lean on, and I drink half a bottle of

vodka, extremely fast, while I write down the first
things that come into my head.

IT'S ALIVE, THE RAMONES (SIRE RECORDS)
Reviewed by Linda Tyler

The Ramones aren't Punk rockers, they're mathematicians.
They allow forty seconds in between each song, which lasts,
on average, two minutes. The songs are counted in by Dee Dee
Ramone yelling, 'One, two, three, four.' On stage, Joey Ramone
then proceeds to kick himself with his own right leg about
thirty times a minute, like a human metronome. For every 120
seconds you hear about eight hooks and four power chords,
and on this album, which is twenty-eight tracks for £4.99, each
song costs you 17.821428 pence. There's nothing faster or
cheaper this year. Someone told me Tommy and Johnny
worked out that if they played more rapidly than usual at their
London gig they'd get to fly back to New York quicker. So
they did, and that's why they sound like a chopper mating with
a chainsaw on this album, but who cares! There's a rumour that
da bruvvas fight between songs, backstage. Someone told me
that Tommy Ramone reckons they go straight back on and play
even *better* after the fisticuffs. Which means faster, shorter,
tighter, louder, etc. etc., in case you were wondering. If you
don't like one song, The Ramones will try another one two
minutes later, just to stop you getting restless. So try
'Rockaway Beach', 'Teenage Lobotomy', 'Blitzkrieg Bop',
'Sheena Is A Punk Rocker', 'Cretin Hop', 'Pinhead', 'Now I
Wanna Sniff Some Glue' and 'We're A Happy Family' for
starters – that little lot will have cost you around £1.40 on this
record, in almost the same time as it took Rick Wakeman to get
started on the first wife in *The Six Wives of Henry VIII*. Now,
do you need any more convincing? * * * * * Let's go!

Reading my review back now I think it's crap, which
is usual, so I let it go. Howard will do what he always
does, which is smile and tell me it's very good, even

though he hasn't read it, and Jon will do what he always does, which is tell me if there are any spelling mistakes and if I got the track listing wrong. Cindy will worry that it's too short and her photos aren't big enough, and one mentally ill reader in Nottingham will write me a letter about it, which goes on for ten pages and tells me he's been talking to Satan about my review and they both agree it's rubbish. No real Ramones fans will bother writing in about it of course, though they might look at the stars bit at the end and moan if there aren't enough. And if they agree with me, I'll never know about it, and if they disagree, I'll never know about it either. And as for Joey Ramone ever reading this? Forget it.

I would give almost anything to be able to articulate even a part of what I feel when 'Cretin Hop' booms out of the speakers. That's the whole problem with Punk, though. You just can't translate it. How do you get that fantastic, cool, clever, noisy, furious, great big addictive sound onto a sheet of paper?

I hand the review in the next day and make a change in my diary for the fourth time as my interview with Clare Grogan gets postponed again.

'We'll have room for it later in the summer,' Howard says, trying to be kind. 'But I'm afraid, for the moment, Terminal Sausage has to come first. Business is business, Linda. By the way, I've just sold a half-page advertisement to some people in Bolton who do these funny little round blue sunglasses – you know, the kind that make you look like you've had terrible eye injuries in the First World War. They're hoping they'll be the next big thing. I don't suppose you'd write it up nicely in your fashion column, would you, Linda?'

Then, just after lunch, David rings.

'You said if I was ever in London to call, so I am,' he tells me.

'What, are you here now?'

'Tomorrow. I've got some business in the city.'

He's trying to make his life with the poxy bank sound like a James Bond film again, and failing. But despite that, the sound of his voice makes me stop everything that I've been thinking, and everything that I've been doing. We agree to meet after I finish work tomorrow, and go down the pub. Then Cindy calls me into the art room and tells me to make The Ramones review shorter because Joey's legs are too long in the photo.

When David turns up, he's got a new coat on. I'm used to the old Crombie, and even his horrible blue parka – left over from security guard days – but this is a funny brown tweedy number. We walk down to the Sterling, at the top of Poland Street, and he buys himself a beer and me a Scotch. He raises his eyebrows when I ask for it, but the private memory of this very Evan-like drink somehow helps to make it easier to deal with David's new tweed coat. I know that braless woman helped buy the new coat. I just *know* she did.

'You don't normally drink Scotch,' David says.

'Well I do now,' I say smugly.

He folds his arms and looks at a stain on the table.

'So what are you going to do now that the Tories are in?' I ask him. 'Are you going to drop this Labour thing, or what?'

He gives me a look. 'What you really mean is, am I going to drop my new friends.'

And that's when I lost it. 'New friends? Oh come off it, David. There's only one bloody friend you've got out of the Labour Party, and she's not a friend at all, she's your new girlfriend.'

I realize I've been spitting as I've been talking, and I might have accidentally spat on his leg. How extremely Punk of me.

'Jeannie's not my girlfriend.'

Oh my God. Jeannie. *I Dream of Jeannie*, and 'I

173

Dream of Jeannie With The Light Brown Hair', and 'The Jean Genie'. What kind of Jeannie is she?

'You took our bed back,' I argue. 'So it would make sense for you to have someone else in it. Don't tell me you're not sleeping with her, I know you are.'

David takes his coat off then and hangs it over the back of the chair.

'What's with the new coat?'

He shrugs. 'It was in a sale so I bought it. Is there a law against that?'

I try to make the Scotch last. I can afford to buy us another round, but then that's it, I don't even have enough money for a bus home.

'You're acting like a stranger, David. You're being strange. You're not the same.'

He smiles into his beer and shakes his head.

'What? What?' I ask.

'Snap.'

'Well how am I being strange? I haven't changed.' As soon as the words are out of my mouth, though, I realize how wrong they sound.

'You've got spots on your chin for a start,' he says.

'It's the food.'

'You're more nervous. You can hardly sit still, look at you.'

'I've been at work. And London makes me like this.'

'Excited.'

'Yeah, and just so *wired*. When I wake up now, David, the radio's all about London weather and London traffic, and I think, I'm actually *here*, getting wet in the rain they're talking about, and being stuck in the traffic they're telling us about. And the songs they play on the radio – they're the same songs I've just written about in the magazine. You know?'

He peers at me as if I'm something under a microscope. 'You must be too excited to sleep as well – you've got bags under your eyes,' he says, and drinks the rest of his beer. Then he pauses. 'Are you doing speed, Linda?'

I shrug, and he looks away at the wall.

I take a deep breath then, and say the things which have just struggled up from my rib cage. 'You said to me once if I didn't marry you you'd just drift away, because that's what people do.'

He nods.

'Well, do you realize that if you don't work out what you want soon, whether it's this Jeannie woman or me, I'll just drift away as well? I mean, you can't just keep me hanging on, David.'

'But I'm not.'

'Here we are having a drink with each other. You're the one who says we should still see each other. Stop dangling me!'

David sighs. 'Jeannie's not my girlfriend and I'm not dangling you. Stop being so dramatic.'

'I can't get over that new bloody coat either. You look like Steptoe and Son in it.'

'And you've got ruder the more time you've spent on that magazine. Did you realize that?'

'So would you be,' I shoot back, 'if you had to work with Jon Whitten all day.'

I have a good moan about Jon then, and because he's exactly the kind of man David loves to hate, I can tell he's completely on my side, and he cranes in to listen, so I can see his eyes properly again under his fringe, and there's a moment when I have to snap myself back to reality and remember we're not actually together any more.

'What's the attraction with Jeannie anyway? I mean, is she more sorted than me? Is she better looking than me? Is she *nicer* than me?' I ask him after a while.

'Oh get off it, Linda. It's like me asking you what's the difference between . . .' He gropes for an example, and I can tell he's trying to think of bands, but he's not getting anywhere. He is, after all, Mr Eight Albums.

'You mean, it's like asking me what the difference is between Talking Heads and XTC,' I tell him.

'Yes, those two, whatever that means to you.'

'Well, I have to disagree with you. I mean, I just plain, totally disagree.'

I can't think of anything to say after that, but I know we've reached that tit-for-tat, nyah-nyah stage we always get to just before it all ends up in bed – or used to.

'You haven't asked me about my life,' I say.

He shrugs. 'Is there one? Apart from your work?'

'Anyway, my round,' I say, trying to be mysterious, dangling my handbag and walking to the bar. I've gone to massive effort for him tonight, using conditioner – which isn't easy when you've only got a sink – and wearing my highest spike-heeled boots and my shortest school uniform skirt. Consequently, even if David's not watching me as I wait for the drinks, I can tell other men in the pub are. Good. *Good.* I hope he can see it.

'You're the one who'd better work out what she really wants,' he says when I bring back his beer.

'And how can I tell, when you've got this Jeannie woman hanging around?' I try to think of the right word. 'It obfuscates the picture, David. Obscufates it. Whatever. It confuses me.'

'You want me to tell Jeannie to go away so that you can stop being confused?' He makes a little movement with his shoulders that annoys me, a kind of mock-amusement signal.

'Oh sod it, David, I can't talk to you.'

'Well write to me then,' he says, still with a forced smile on his face. 'You're the one with the typewriter. Why don't you write to me if you've got something to say?'

'I can't,' I tell him, 'the E's broken.'

When we've finished our drinks he gets his coat and leaves. The someone really makes my night and puts bloody Boney M on the jukebox.

Later on at home, I get out of bed after midnight because I can't sleep, and I put my coat on over my pyjamas, then pad out in my slippers to the phone box. David picks up the telephone just as it's about to ring out.

'Hello?'

'It's Linda.'

'Oh.'

'One thing I want to know, just one thing.'

'Yes?' he sighs.

'What did you see in me? You were so distant tonight. I mean, we had six years. At least do me the favour of telling me what kept you there for all that time.'

A silence.

'Snap.'

'What do you mean?'

'When I read what you wrote for your job on the paper I thought the same thing. What the hell have you ever seen in me?'

'But David, you were my boyfriend for six years.'

'That's not an answer.'

'And anyway, I'm asking *you*. Did you ever love anything about me, really? Other than the fact that I was there? I mean, what made it work for you for all those years? What made you want us to get married?'

He pauses, and then he tells me it was my eyelashes.

'Not good enough.'

'OK then, I felt sorry for you.'

'Oh, great.'

'And you've got huge tits, of course.'

'Very funny.'

'The bottle of port in your handbag,' David goes on. 'The way you laugh in your sleep. The way you sing in the bath and make all the guitar and drum sounds as well. The way you always used to bring me the leftovers home from the Chinese restaurant. The way you cheat at Mastermind. The fact that you've left me all your records in your will even though I don't want any of them, and even though it's not a proper will.'

'Yes it is.'

'It's on stationery with little bunnies all over it, Linda; that's not a bloody will.'

It's freezing in the phone box, but I can feel a semblance of heat. He can too – I just know he can. I wonder if Jeannie's there listening, and I deliberately try to stretch the conversation out longer.

'So you weren't just faking it then. You did love me once,' I say lightly.

'Go to bed. You're mad. It's the middle of the night and you're standing in a phone box.'

'OK then,' I finish, although my heart is hammering. 'Thanks. Bye.'

And I put the phone down, just as one of the neighbours turns their front light on to see what's going on.

When I go to sleep a few hours later, I dream about my mother. She looks pretty, with her hair curled under at the side, and pale pink lipstick, and a blue jacket and skirt she used to wear for parties.

'Hello, Linda.'

'Hello, Mum.'

We're at the seaside, and it could be Brighton or it might be Eastbourne, I'm not sure. The sun's shining, and we're both in deckchairs, looking at the view.

'I'm sorry about David,' she says.

'Yeah.'

'He's right though. You'd better work out what you want.'

'Oh God, how can I?'

'Well, you know the things that are precious to you, don't you?'

I nod.

'Your music. And your freedom. Well, concentrate on that, then you'll know.'

I sigh and think my mother is probably the only person in the world who understands me, even if she is dead.

'Linda, listen to me. It's not him choosing between you and another girl, it's a matter of you choosing between him and the other things that matter to you. One of them has to be sacrificed. You can't have both. And you have to know exactly what you're doing this time.'

At last, I think. Something that makes sense.

'Give this new life a go,' she says. 'Make more of it.'

'All right.'

'And by the way, Linda. The rats will be gone soon. Your landlord will do something about them.'

And then Mum's gone suddenly, and I wake up and breathe out. Then I breathe out one more time. I feel as though something has just been lifted from my shoulders. Isn't it ridiculous, how you can go through all those nights of confusion, fear and loathing, and your mother can sort the whole thing out for you in a dream in ten minutes? Even when she's been dead since 1967.

After that, I make a cup of tea and think about what she's said. Enough of missing David and hating Jeannie. It's time I was grateful for the other things that have happened lately. My sudden dose of freedom, for a start.

It's not the first time I've had advice from Mum in my dreams, though I've never told Dad about it. It first happened in the days when Dad and I were fighting over the ironing and the Vesta ready-meals. Even now I can still smell her old perfume sometimes – I did the day Howard interviewed me for the job, and on the day David told me he fancied Hazel. It's not

179

something I give much thought to normally, but this morning it's all I can think about.

At quarter-past nine there's a knock on my door. The pest control people are here – the landlord's sent them – and they want permission to come in and inspect the rat's nest under the sink. They say the rats will be gone by Friday.

CHAPTER SIXTEEN

I understand nothing about politics, but I think I'm getting away with it. The man on the other end of the phone at the Brighton and Hove branch of the Labour Party seems to suspect nothing, even though I've already got Michael Foot's name wrong and called him Michael Feet.

'So you're aware of our manifesto then?' he asks.

'Oh yes.'

The only manifesto I know about is the Roxy Music album, but I try to go along with him.

'It's nice that you want to join up,' he says. 'Since last month we've actually found more people leaving.'

'Well I think it's like football: you can't just give up on your team because they're losing,' I say.

He laughs, but he doesn't sound very happy. 'We like to encourage women to join, Linda. So you've come to the right place, let me assure you.'

'You mean I won't be the only one?'

'Far from it.'

'Actually,' I decided to push my luck, 'is there anyone called Jeannie in your branch?'

'Yes, there is. Jeannie Sheridan. Do you know her?'

'Is that the only Jeannie?'

'Yes it is.'

'Oh it must be her then. No, I don't know her. I think

she might have gone to school with someone I used to know.'

We talk for a while longer, about my decision to join Labour. I tell him that ever since Jeremy Thorpe I can't support the Liberals, and I make a joke about not liking dogs, so I can't see the point of Auberon Waugh's Dog Lovers' Party.

'Next thing you'll be telling me you're one of those girls who vote Labour because you look good in red!' he jokes back.

'Ha ha ha!' I laugh.

I'm so excited by this small victory – finding out Jeannie's second name – that when I put the phone down I immediately have to call Hazel and tell her.

'Oh for crying out loud,' she says when I ring.

'What? What's wrong with that?'

'Are you going to come here and stalk her? Are you going to hang around and spy on them?'

'No, nothing like that.'

'You are, aren't you. I can hear it in your voice. You're mad, Linda. Can't you just leave David alone for a while? He needs to find himself as much as you do, you know.'

'God, Hazel,' I complain, 'has anyone ever told you that you sound like someone on American television? In a minute we're going to get back to "I'm his friend as well as yours" stuff, and I don't think I can stand it'.

'Don't get obsessive about Jeannie and David,' she warns as we wind the conversation up.

'I'm not really, I just need to know,' I tell her.

'Know what?'

'Things like her second name. I feel I've got a right.'

'It won't make you feel any better,' she cautions me, and then she tells me she's got to go and the call must be costing me money, and she hangs up.

Actually, the call is costing Howard money, but he doesn't seem to mind. Personal phone calls and long tea breaks are becoming part of daily life now that Terminal Sausage have been signed to a record company and he's feeling more relaxed about the magazine.

In the afternoon, the drummer in Terminal Sausage comes in for a meeting. She looks strangely like Howard, with his round cheeks, big blue eyes and pink and white face. She's the same shape as him too, which makes her, in her long black coat and lacy black gloves, look a bit like a Victorian great-aunt in mourning.

'This is Julie,' Howard introduces her.

I thought Cindy was quiet, but Julie is practically silent. All the meeting seems to consist of is Howard doing a lot of talking about units and the American market, and her sitting there going, 'Mmm,' and crossing her legs.

Then something extraordinary happens. Howard has a long, knowledgeable conversation about Joy Division. 'I'd like you to have this advance copy of the album,' he tells her, pushing *Unknown Pleasures* over the desk. 'This cover illustration, you know,' Howard points to it, 'is an astronomical drawing of the intergalactic scream of a dying star.'

'Oooh,' says Julie.

'This isn't a record, it's an *enigma*,' Howard pronounces.

'Oooh,' she says again.

'What I like about this new album is the way Hooke's bass and Morris's drums are right at the front of the mix,' Howard tells Julie. 'I'd like to do that with you. Where the Sausage is concerned, your drumming should dominate the whole sound.'

Shortly after this, when Julie has left, there is a stunned silence in the office.

'I love her little black fingerless gloves,' Howard half whispers.

183

'I love the way you gave her *my* album, you bloody twat,' Jon says.

'I got carried away,' Howard replies, looking ashamed.

'You gave away my only advance copy of the album of the year to some fat female drummer from Tooting Bec in a black headscarf.' Jon shakes his head. 'I can't believe it.'

We go down the pub after that, and when Jon gets up to change the jukebox, Howard asks me how things are with David.

'I'm jealous,' I tell him.

'Jealous of this woman without the bra?'

'I joined the Labour Party today just so I could get to see her.'

Howard makes a whistling sound. 'My God, you have got it bad.'

Jon comes back, moaning that a pack of heavy-metal fans are drinking round the other side of the bar, and that Motorhead will be on the jukebox for the next twenty-five minutes at least.

'You need to get drunk,' Howard tells me. 'Come on, let's both of us get drunk and then I can bore you about Julie and you can bore me about David.'

We both realize, at the same instant, that Jon doesn't have anyone. I never really think about his love life – it seems to consist of vague couplings with female *NWW* readers at gigs and the occasional lunge at Cindy in the art room – but there's something about him that's almost asexual. It's like Ian Curtis in Joy Division. He doesn't eat enough bacon or something. It's hard to imagine that he's got it in him.

'So what's in it for Julie then?' Jon asks Howard suddenly.

'Nothing,' Howard shrugs.

'She just likes him,' I tell Jon, 'that's all.'

'Rubbish. You've got nothing in common with her, Howard. How could she possibly fancy you?'

'We have a certain something,' Howard protests, and then he realizes he can't think of anything else to say.

After that, he just keeps drinking, and I keep him company, until I realize I have to go to the toilet or I'll explode all over the carpet.

Jon follows me as I wrong-foot my way on the stairs, then manage to stumble into the long narrow corridor that leads to the Ladies'. Typically, this doesn't lead me to the right place at all – it leads to the Men's instead, but Jon's not going there either. Then, in a drunken second, it suddenly occurs to me that he's deliberately going exactly where I am.

'Linda,' he says, propping his arm up on the wall.

'What?'

'Linda, do you want a Quick one?'

'No.' I manage to say it so fast it's actually ahead of my brain and my body. It's incredible really how survival reactions can kick in, despite the fact that you've had four pints.

'Are you sure you don't want a Quick one?'

'Yes.'

'You must do. Come on. Let's go round the back.'

'No.'

Listening to myself, I must say I'm impressed with how serious and rational I sound. From the tone of my voice you'd think I was answering a telephone survey on detergent.

'Come on, Linda.'

'Um, no.'

Jon gives up then and stumbles off up the corridor.

Maybe it's Howard and Julie, I think. Maybe their presence in the office has done something to the droplets in the atmosphere. Isn't it hormone droplets in the air that make everyone want to have sex? I look in the toilet mirror, over the sink, and say the word experimentally.

'Droplets.'

It's fun to say. I must be pissed, so I say it again. 'Droplets.'

A woman comes into the toilets and gives me a funny look, so I shut up and wend my way back to the table. With any luck, Jon will have gone home.

Annoyingly, though, he's still there – talking to Howard as if nothing has happened. And then he chats to me about some Manchester band called The Frantic Elevators – 'The singer's called Mick Hucknall. I give him six months.'

Something occurs to me halfway through the next pint. Disturbingly, it's the similarity between Jon Whitten and Gregory Bannerman.

'I used to know someone like you,' I slur, 'and he thought sex was like washing up or putting the kettle on. It meant that much to him.'

'So what?' Jon says, drumming his fingers on the table. I can tell he's annoyed that Howard and I are more pissed than he is.

'Just an observation,' I tell him. But I can't say it properly, it comes out wrong, and I'm reminded of my attempts to pronounce obfuscate, to David.

'Jeannie is obfuscating my love life,' I tell Howard later when Jon has finally gone home and I've had a few more drinks.

'Julie would make a good mother for my children, don't you think?' Howard asks in reply.

When I finally stagger home, just after 2 a.m. – Howard's been feeding me Fortnum & Mason food from his fridge at home – I try to call David so I can tell him what a shit he is and how I've joined the Brighton and Hove branch of the Labour Party to scare Jeannie. When I look in my purse, though, all I can find is a bus ticket, a piece of Juicy Fruit and a one-pence piece. After that, I give up, throw up, and go to bed.

CHAPTER SEVENTEEN

I'm standing at the sink, doing the washing up when I see my mother standing behind me in the mirror.

'You're a free spirit, Linda. Don't forget.'

Then she's gone and it's hard to say whether she was really there or not.

Mum gave me a choice when she visited me in my dream the other night. David or the chance of a new life.

So I start with her money, because it seems like the sensible place to begin. David never knew, but I've got £2,000 stashed away in the bank, which Mum left to me when she died.

Mum's £2,000 has always seemed like special money, and even Dad never asked about it. It didn't seem to be the kind of money you could spend. I suppose if I had ever bothered to check any of the bank statements I chucked out, I'd probably have seen that it'd increased as well. I lived with David long enough to learn about interest rates.

If I was still engaged to David the money would stay where it was. Partly because I know he'd try to force me to put it into some house like 119 Waverly Crescent, or at least invest it with his bank.

Being by myself changes everything, though. The money's been invisible for years. But now it seems visible, close enough to touch and definitely close enough to spend.

Is the price of freedom about £2,000? I'd say so.

I can buy candles, for a start. And twenty boxes of Black Magic chocolates to keep next to the bed. I can go up Oxford Street and buy three pairs of patent leather boots with buckles on them, in red, black and white. I can buy a T-shirt from Vivienne Westwood. I can travel anywhere I like. Mexico, Manila, the Andes. I can probably afford to go to Antarctica too – and I would, if there was any evidence they'd latched onto The Damned.

I think about Evan for a minute. I could go to Australia with *him*. Well, couldn't I? After that it takes me about five seconds to find some change and walk outside to the phone box and ring him.

'Linda, I've just woken up. Sorry.'

Evan sounds groggy, as if he's talking under water.

'Listen. I've had an idea. Do you want to go to Australia with me, just for a holiday? I'll pay for the tickets.'

There's a pause and I can hear my own heart thudding. Now that I've made the offer, I feel like 5,000 volts have just gone through me. Is this what freedom really feels like?

Evan sighs. 'Linda, if you have enough money to fly two people to Australia I think you should fly yourself first. Use the rest of the cash on something else.'

'Oh.'

'Maybe at a different time in my life, this would be fine. In fact, it would be the finest offer of the hour. But I'd rather you blew the money on other things. I feel like I'm turning away from the smorgasbord of life here by turning you down, but I'm also enough of a saint—'

'Of course you are,' I interrupt him.

'Enough of a saint to martyr myself in your interests. Don't waste your money on me.'

I think for a minute. 'Look, I know you're scared of relationships, but this isn't a relationship, Evan.' I hear him light a cigarette, next to the phone. 'I mean, I know you're terrified of anything that approaches a promise between you and me. Or you and anyone else for that matter.'

'Right.'

'So do me a favour and trust me. I mean, I know what you're like. Even more amazing, Evan, I can allow you to be like that.'

Another pause.

'OK. Thanks.'

Evan goes off to find his address book then, and when he comes back he gives me his sister's number in Sydney.

'Her name's Penny. She's my twin. If you go, she'll look after you. You can stay with her. Go to gigs. All that kind of stuff.'

'God. Does she look like you?'

'Me in a frock.'

'Well at least I'll know what to look out for if she meets me at the airport.'

He goes quiet for a minute. I can tell he's fantasizing about going back to Australia, even though he's just turned me down.

'There are some great bands at home.' He sighs. 'Go to a place called the Crystal Ballroom in Melbourne, and see the Boys Next Door. If you make it to Brisbane, go down to the Curry Shop and see the Go-Betweens. Make sure you hear Mental As Anything in Sydney – they're my sister's favourite band. And if you go to Perth, check out The Scientists. Oh God, it's such a tragedy for you The Saints have broken up, Linda.'

I try to change the subject, before he gets weepy. 'The only thing is I don't even know where half these

189

places are, Evan. Perth and Brisbane and things like that.'

'Penny will show you. If you want to go. You just get on a bus and hit the highway.'

'Anything else I should know? If I do decide to fly out there, that is.'

'Oh you're going,' Evan says. 'I can hear it in your voice. Even without me. You've already decided.'

I can hear him taking a deep breath. 'God, Linda. What can I tell you about Australia? Go to Whaley for a swim, then go to Palmy for a surf – Whale Beach and Palm Beach. Then when you've done that, travel around a bit and go up north to a proper beach, like Hungry Head. The water's like blue glass.'

Evan sounds as though he's salivating at the thought of the salt water.

'You're not homesick by any chance, are you?' I ask.

He can't speak.

'I mean, you don't miss it all?' I say again.

'Oh shit, Linda, I'll come with you. I mean it. I've changed my mind. I'm coming.'

When Evan gets off the phone, I find some more spare change and ring a travel agent and book two tickets to Australia.

Getting the money out of my account to pay for all this is not quite as easy as I thought, though. In fact, it's even harder work than booking the trip. In the end it takes me a week of faffing around, trying to prove I'm really me, just to get my hands on it. 'It's Mum's money,' I tell the woman behind the counter in Camden. 'It's her money, and she died of cancer, and she gave it to me in her will to do what I liked with, and it's even spent most of the last ten years earning interest, so now I want it. So why can't I just get it off the bank, right now?'

She smiles at me and gives me a look.

Getting the first few hundred out seems to change

things, though. After that, the woman at the bank in Camden knows who I am, and then I take out another hundred and spend Saturday afternoon down the markets, buying whatever I want. The more forbidden it seems, the more exciting it is when I hand over the pound notes and get back another plastic bag.

'Is it someone's birthday?' asks a stallholder when I shell out ten pounds on lots of glittery diamanté jewellery.

'Yeah, mine. In a couple of weeks,' I tell him. 'I'm treating myself.'

I go on spending. Markets are the easiest thing to start with, because I know them, but then I think sod it, and go up west to Liberty's. Maybe it's just the name. I pick up some soap, turn it upside down and look at the price, put it back down again, pick it up again, and then buy three bars of it. The rush is incredible. Is this what it feels like to be rich?

Then I wander round the King's Road area for hours, buying men's business shirts from Oxfam, and old Harris tweed jackets, and a black studded belt, and black lipstick, and ten pairs of fishnets, and some army surplus combat pants, and five bottles of black dye to attack the men's business shirts with. Then I find a second-hand pair of bondage trousers from Seditionaries, with a fly zip that goes under my bum and zips down the back of each leg, a bondage strap and a clip-on towelling nappy. Perfect for sitting in the gutter after a gig.

It's only when I sit down for a coffee in a snack bar (oh the luxury of being able to order a plate of spaghetti bolognaise as well) that I realize something vital. I no longer own a washing machine to dye any shirts in.

My dad has different terms for money. He calls it filthy lucre or funny money. Because it's always caused problems for him, he can't bring himself to talk

191

about it properly or even take it seriously. He calls fivers Lady Godivas, and he never does his tax. Perhaps because of him, I've never seen the point of money either, but right now, with plastic bags going up both arms, I'm beginning to see what all the fuss is about.

I'm getting the British economy going again all by myself. And it makes me feel, well, almost as excited as the first time I heard Iggy Pop. The five pound notes will run out eventually, I know, but until then I just don't care. And David would have a screaming fit, of course, but perhaps that's the whole point.

CHAPTER EIGHTEEN

All the time that I was engaged to David, I always woke up when he did, even when the alarm went off at 7.30 a.m. I've always had Cornflakes with milk and sugar for breakfast. We always had one bowl each too, though of course he used to get more Cornflakes than me, because he's a man.

On Thursday I get rid of my alarm clock, wake up at ten, and chuck the Cornflakes in the bin. I don't even know why I eat them. I'm sick to death of that big red and green Kellogg's rooster on the front of the packet. I seem to have been staring at it for twenty-five years, along with the thiamin and niacin content on the side of the box.

Annie meets me in the pub that night. She's come up from Brighton and we're having a drink for my birthday tomorrow.

'You look different,' she says, waving her cigarette around.

'Good.'

'You've got earrings on I haven't seen before. And new boots.'

'It's the money that Mum left me when she died,' I explain. 'I've finally decided to spend it. And I think I'm going to Australia as well. With that Mod photographer Evan.'

She gives me a look. It's as if I've just announced I'm taking a space shuttle to Mars with Adam Ant.

Then Annie makes a joke about how I could give some of the money to her, so I do.

'Shit, Linda, you can't give me that,' she says as I put twenty quid in her hand.

'You've been going on about wanting to see The Cramps in Manchester tomorrow. Well now you can.'

'What?' She gives me the kind of look that suggests she thinks I'm losing my marbles.

'Go on. Go and see The Cramps.'

The next day the morning post brings a birthday card from Dad, which is exactly the same as every other card I've had for the last ten years – a furry animal on the front and no message inside, just a signature – and absolutely nothing from David. Perhaps it's just the slowness of the Brighton post, but I surprise myself by bursting into tears anyway.

'For God's sake, Linda,' I tell the mirror. But maybe this is what the aftermath of being dumped is like. Just when you think you're in control you start to unravel again.

To make up for it, the postman also brings some brochures from the travel agent, and I sit on the bed, enjoying the luxury of flicking through endless exotic options. The names in Australia are so strange. Woy Woy, Wagga Wagga, Wangaratta. Sunshine, Emerald, Coober Pedy. Half the names in the brochure sound like limericks you try to say for a dare when you're pissed in the pub.

Later that night, when I'm lying on my fold-up bed dreaming about what it would have been like to see The Saints before they split up, a note is shoved under my door. By the time I run over and open the front door, the person who left the note is gone. Still, it's not hard to guess.

Evan has left it in half a puddle, so his purple ink

(of course he uses purple ink) is running, but I can see all I need to see. He's changed his mind again. He says he doesn't want the burden of feeling he owes me anything. I can only just decipher his last line: 'Australia will look after you, and so will my sister.'

Oh great. Brilliant. Bloody *great*, Evan. What a birthday this is turning out to be.

Outside it's beginning to rain, even though summer's supposed to be coming, and I can hear a drunk shouting to himself in the street. I couldn't feel further away from Australia if I tried. So, tomorrow morning, I'm going to do two things. I'm going to get a phone for this place at last, so Evan can ring me up on it instead of shoving notes under my door and running away, and I'm going to get my money back from his ticket and buy myself a proper double bed, with pink pillows and a pink rug for the floor, just like I've always wanted. And *then* I'm going to go to bloody Australia.

To celebrate this new sense of purpose, I go out and get some Chinese – by myself. It's a weird thrill ordering the food that I used to cook for other people. Lemon Chicken. Special Fried Rice. Prawn Crackers.

'Ten minutes,' says the young Chinese girl behind the counter, pointing to the window ledge for me to sit on. I flick two dead flies out of the way and sit down.

After that, someone who looks vaguely familiar comes in. It takes me a few minutes of checking and cross-checking to get it, but in the end I realize it's definitely *him*. Fatter and without a beard, but nonetheless, it's . . .

'Gregory Bannerman?' I ask.

And he smiles, revealing a jaw full of brown teeth.

'Linda!' he seems genuinely pleased to see me. 'Wow. Why here? Why now?'

'Well, I live round the corner,' I tell him, amazed

that he still talks like something out of *The Myths And Legends Of King Arthur*.

'So do I,' he grins, and then I realize any minute now he'll be asking for my phone number.

'So what are you doing with yourself?' he asks.

'I'm a music journalist,' I say, although I've never called myself that before.

'Wow,' says Gregory. 'Who for?'

'*NWW*,' I tell him, and I can see he's never heard of it.

Banging sounds come from the kitchen, and I pray that the deep-fat frier is working as fast as it possibly can. I can see a tuft of hair sticking out of the top of Gregory Bannerman's holey V-neck jumper, and it seems to be the same tuft I might have had close contact with at the age of seventeen. It's making me feel slightly sick just thinking about it.

'I'm married now,' Gregory tells me, and I try not to fall off the window ledge in shock.

'Nice,' I say.

'We have three daughters and a parrot.'

I nod.

'And what do you do now?' I ask him.

'Oh,' he shrugs, 'Music. Poetry. Life. A little bit of filing in the Marks & Spencer stockroom.'

'Oh, right.'

'No ring on your finger then,' Gregory says, peering at my hand.

'I did have,' I say too quickly, then wish I hadn't.

'I highly recommend marriage,' he says as if he's suddenly got one up on me.

I smile politely.

Then he tells me I'll have to come round some time, and I nod a bit more, and then leap up like a lunatic as soon as a white plastic bag is dumped on the counter.

'There's my Lemon Chicken,' I tell Gregory.

'Well, give me a ring,' Gregory says, and he tells me

his number, and he says it's easy to remember because it's got two nines in it.

'Lovely,' I say.

'Nine's a magic number. Do you remember, we did it to "Revolution Number 9" once', he adds as one of my legs is out the door.

'Yeah,' I say, kicking the door behind me. 'I wrote about it in my job application.' And then I walk, very fast, across the street, taking a strange zigzag route to get home, just in case he's staring at me from the windows of the Chinese restaurant and trying to work out where I live.

They never tell you that the cure for a humiliating sexual experience is the ecstatic revenge of a brilliant career, do they? If only I'd know that at seventeen, while he was chucking his underpants on the lamp-shade and treating me like another hippie damsel on his personal production line of love.

'I'm a music journalist and he works in Marks & Sparks,' I sing to myself, as I dodge down an alleyway to get home. 'Tra la la la la, stick it up your arse, Gregoreeee Bannerman.' I can't wait until I get home to eat the Lemon Chicken, so I sit down on a milk crate on the pavement and dig in with my fingers.

CHAPTER NINETEEN

The travel agent seems to enjoy himself when I cancel the second ticket to Australia.

'Has he changed his mind then?' he asks, sounding smug.

I suppose it must make you miserable sitting in a glass box on the high street in Kentish Town all day, watching the clouds go over the sun every ten minutes while everyone else is booking tickets so they can bugger off to hotter and more interesting places.

'I'll tell you what, rather than go through all the refund business, we can do a deal on a Laker fare to New York instead,' he says.

'What, go to New York as well as Australia?'

'You might as well,' the travel agent says. 'It's cheap enough if you do both. It's a special offer.'

'So what does Freddie Laker charge then?'

'You'll never get to New York this cheaply again.'

I look at the brochure. I can just about afford the New York bit, if I stop there and then fly all the way to Sydney as the next stop.

New York. *Noo Yawk*! CBGB's, The Ramones, Blondie, Talking Heads, Television, hot dogs, hamburgers. I don't know a soul. I literally don't know one person in the whole place. But I've also never felt this excited about anything. I try not to stop breathing, and get my chequebook out, signing it quickly before I change my mind.

Devo have a new song out called 'Pink Pussycat' and it runs through my head as I take another wad of Mum's cash and go shopping in C&A for pink pillowcases, pink sheets, pink towels and a pink rug.

The weather's getting warmer and the people on the streets are pink as well, as their shins start fading from red to lobster after last Sunday's roasting session in the park. 'Rock Lobster' is on the radio, and that makes the world change colour too. London doesn't seem like London when the B52s are shrieking in the background. England doesn't seem like England. Then I realize something. I can *see* them. I'm going to New York. I can see the B52s. Wow. Eating hot dogs sideways and jigging around to Fred Schneider.

After that the day just gets better, and with some of Jon's speed in my bloodstream, a little faster as well. I wonder where you can buy a pink telephone from in London? I'm sure the B52s have got one in their flat in New York. In the end I settle for a green telephone instead – standard issue bloody boring British sludge green – but I drag home four cans of pink paint to make up for it.

I don't think I've ever had the right to choose the colour of the room where I sleep. Right from the time I was little, I've never chosen the curtains, I've never chosen the bed, I've never chosen the lights. In fact, I've never been able to do anything except put up Siouxsie and the Banshees posters on the walls to cover the stains. And there was even trouble with that when I lived with David.

'Can't we have some proper musicians on the wall?'

'What do you mean, proper musicians?'

'People who can play their instruments and sing.

Guitarists who know more than three chords.'

I used to have fights like that with Dad too. In fact, my teenage bedroom was as much of a battlefield as the kitchen.

'Who said you could put stickers on your lamp-shade, Linda?'

'I did.'

'What's that silly red lightbulb doing in the light socket? You can't read with that on.'

'Yes I can.'

While I think about this, standing on a milk crate, painting the first wall, my new double bed arrives.

'Where do you want it, love?' the delivery man asks.

'You'll have to put it outside,' I tell him, 'there's no room in here yet.'

'Does your landlord know you're doing this?' he asks, watching me turn the walls from dirty yellow to sugar-mouse pink.

I shrug.

'There's a chest of drawers in the back here,' he offers. 'Someone put their foot through the back of it. Do you want it? You could paint that pink as well.'

'I can put my records in that,' I tell the delivery man when he brings it in for inspection. 'It doesn't matter about the back.'

'Is that all you care about then, your records?' he asks.

'Yeah,' I tell him. And I suppose I'm telling the truth. Then he finally drives off, because he's got a dining table to deliver to Chalk Farm.

Soon, everything is pink. The radio — I got a few splodges on the aerial so I decided to just give in and paint the whole thing — and me as well. I have pink paint in my hair, and in my mouth, and on my shoes. It's like living inside a giant marshmallow. David would hate it. David and Jeannie from the Brighton and Hove Labour Party would absolutely hate it.

The vodka I use for reviewing records is standing on the floor, looking conspicuous now that it's not hidden under the fold-up bed, which has been shunted into the street. So I finish off the bottle and, not surprisingly, that seems to make the painting go even faster, along with the speed still zipping around my blood cells.

I put on the new Buzzcocks single 'Harmony In My Head', then I play it about fifteen times, and the walls are finished in no time at all.

Because it's sunny outside, a few kids start playing cricket in the street, and to drown The Buzzcocks out, the man next door starts washing his car to Electric Light Orchestra played very loud. So now it's 'Harmony In My Head' versus 'Mr Blue Sky', and the more annoyed I get by ELO, the louder I sing along with Pete Shelley, trying to roar over the top of Jeff Lynne, and the faster my paintbrush moves across the walls.

By the time it gets dark I have decided to paint the floor as well because the lino's so crappy, and there's no point in having nice walls when the floor's a disgrace. So I move every last object I own out into the street and kneel down to paint. Before long, my knees are pink and my back's killing me, but I keep going.

The last of the vodka goes into the fourth paint can, because I want to see what patterns alcohol makes in paint, and then I chuck in the bottle of perfume Hazel gave me last Christmas as well, for good measure. I've never liked Cachet. It's *exactly* the bleeding same on every woman who wears it, no matter what the ad says.

Finally, when the whole floor has been painted pink, complete with streaks of vodka and perfume, I back out of the front door and take a proper look at the whole thing from a distance.

I'm sure about it, but I'm *not* sure about it. I'm

drunk, it's pink. It's pink, I'm drunk. That's about all I can sort out at the moment. Then someone walks past and I ask them the time. It's after ten o'clock at night. I've been painting for over six hours.

Have you ever slept under the stars in London? It's a weird thing to do, because it's so dirty and built-up, there are almost no stars to sleep under. That's where I collapse for the night, though, in my fold-up bed in Kentish Town, stuck out on the street, tucked behind a brick wall and a long hedge, covered in piles of blankets and stinking of paint.

I have the best dreams of all time. A reversing truck wakes me up just after Sting has been personally piercing my ears. I fall asleep again almost immediately and I am swimming in Australia with David, who's kissing me passionately after Jeannie has been taken by a shark. Two cats having sex interrupt the next dream which, satisfyingly, is about Gary Numan and Joe Strummer both telling me how fantastic and beautiful I am. And finally, as the milkman screeches around the corner and the sun comes up, I am in Evan's bath, with cinnamon floating in the water and his arms tightly around me. He's inside me for ages in this dream, and then we both seem to have an extended orgasm that lasts for fifteen minutes. When I wake up a stray dog is trying to hump the corner of my fold-up bed.

CHAPTER TWENTY

It's Monday and the world has gone mad. They're playing the Boomtown Rats on normal family radio stations. Even Howard's mother loves 'I Don't Like Mondays'. What next? Low-flying pigs over Heathrow?

'Bob Geldof,' Jon mutters behind his desk. 'He'll never get anywhere.'

Now that my flat has gone pink and the weather is hotter, I spend lunchtime leafing through magazines, wondering if I should buy some new pink clothes as well.

'What should I wear if I'm going to Australia?' I ask Howard and Cindy and Jon, as a way of breaking it to them.

'A Rolf Harris deterrent,' Jon says.

'Oh God, don't go to Australia, you'll never come back', Howard moans.

Cindy says nothing, but smiles politely.

'Oh, and I'm going to New York as well,' I say clumsily. I've been wondering how I can fit that into my confession to Howard and Jon without sounding like a wanker; but no, I find I've said it and I *definitely* sound like a wanker.

'New York?' says Cindy. 'You should go see my friend Karen Emmanuel.'

'OK,' I nod, picturing a carbon copy of Cindy in fluffy mules and clam-digger pants.

'Karen is a great writer,' Cindy says, 'and she knows everyone. Here.' She scribbles on a piece of paper and pushes a ridiculously long phone number at me.

'Thanks, Cindy.'

'No problem.'

Then she sashays into the art room again and closes the door, as Jon licks his lips lustfully.

Howard sighs and stretches out his legs on the floor. 'Oh God, don't resign, Linda,' he says. 'Please, please don't resign and move to New York. I'll give you a pay rise.'

'It's all right Howard. I'm not going anywhere.'

'But you're going halfway round the world!'

'Two weeks. I'm just away for two weeks. On my summer holidays, that's all. Mum left me some money.'

I can see from his face that Howard has never really thought about me having a mother, or not having a mother.

'Well, before you go, you must interview Clare Grogan for us,' he insists.

'Oh, it's finally happening, is it?'

'She's coming up to London to do a session with that man who looks like Lenin.'

'John Peel,' Jon says helpfully.

'Yes, him. And remember, the key thing is, find out if Altered Images need a manager. I've heard they're going to be big. And drop my name into it a few times. Tell this Grogan schoolgirl what spectacular results I've had with the Sausage.'

Howard is obsessed with Terminal Sausage at the moment, not only because of his infatuation with Julie but also because there's talk that their first single could be a hit.

'The Wombles have had hits, Australian nuns have

had hits, dead people have had hits – anything's possible I suppose,' Jon shrugs.

In the end, Clare Grogan rings up and leaves a message to say she'll meet me on Saturday at the Black Cat café on Berwick Street. Which is all very well, I suppose, except I haven't got a bloody clue what I'm going to say to her.

'You can borrow Jon's tape recorder,' Howard suggests.

But from the look Jon gives me, I'm not entirely sure I can. I suppose he thinks I'll drop it, or throw it against a wall.

When I go home, I find a pile of magazines, including damp old copies of *Jackie* and *Princess Tina*, as well as *NME* and *Sounds*, and try to find some proper interviews so I can see how everybody else does it. It occurs to me that I've read several thousand of them in my life, but I've never actually worked out how it's done.

After exhaustive research and some more vodka from the corner shop, I get the idea. First, the interview subject always needs to be eating something and pondering something in the first sentence. So, for example:

A. Gary Numan
B. Hugh Cornwell
C. Andy Partridge

consumes

A. Raw meat
B. Cheese sandwiches
C. Duck à l'orange

while pondering:

A. The long overdue consolidation of creative impulses first tentatively explored on the last album.

B. His band's connection to the Zeitgeist, along with the crippling commercial constraints of the biz.
C. The fact that every critic in town thought their last record was pig swill.

After that, there needs to be a brief mention of the music:

A. Mellow, sensitive, raw and painstakingly fragile vocal lines woven with slashing guitar solos.
B. Criminally underrated drumming, backing a rousing wave of throbbing bass and keyboards.
C. They can't play but who cares?

And then so on, for another 3,000 words, throwing in as many references to the artist's ever-changing facial expressions as possible, for good measure – grimacing is good but concerned frowning is even better.

After reading some more music papers I manage to work out my opening sentence for Clare Grogan, and it's going to involve her eating a Knickerbocker Glory – even if she doesn't want to. Then I think I'll describe Altered Images as quirky, uplifting, post-Punk and future-shock pop.

Unfortunately, I have only managed to work out two questions for her so far. 'What's your favourite record of all time?' And the devastating, 'So, Clare, where do you get your inspiration?'

It's no good, of course, but then I don't know what else to do. Tony Parsons asks people about dropping acid and trying bondage in his interviews, but unless Clare's school in Scotland is unusually advanced, I can't do that.

Finally I find a copy of *Jackie* from two years ago, where they interviewed some bloke from Smokie. Or at least, they put questions in and left a space, and he wrote the answers down in very bad handwriting.

My idea of beauty:	A plate of beans on toast
My favourite place:	Bradford
My favourite amusement:	Growing parsnips in my garden
My favourite hero/heroine in real life:	Dunno
My motto:	Plod on

Why do I get the feeling that my interview with Clare Grogan is going to be exactly like this? Me coming up with deep and meaningful questions and her saying things like 'beans on toast', 'Dunno' and 'Plod on'.

In the end, I decide there's only one thing to do on Saturday morning to get rid of my galloping nerves. So I take more money out of my new pink chest of drawers and go down Oxford Street to get some new clothes. Proper new clothes to interview a proper new pop star in.

I should go into Boots as well and get something for my throat – it's sore and dry from inhaling paint fumes – but just now it seems like more fun to take five pairs of jeans into the changing-rooms in C&A, try them on, then chuck them all on the floor.

You can get blouses from Oxfam and cut them up with scissors. You can get tights from Marks & Spencer and rip the feet out with a kitchen knife. You can get old school ties for 10p at jumble sales and wrap them round your head, and you can get your boots from army surplus shops. You can get your winkle-pickers from rubbish left out by old ladies on the street, and you can get your make-up by doing some subtle shoplifting in Woolworth's, but – and this is a big but – when it comes to jeans, I know for a fact that even the most diehard Punk is always forced to shop at C&A.

I look in the changing-room mirror, make a stupid

pouty face and turn my leg sideways, which is what I always do when I look in the mirror. I wonder what Clare Grogan will be wearing? I've already heard Jon go on about her, so I'm expecting some porridge-eating bombshell in a school uniform who'll make me wish I'd tried harder. I try more clothes on. Bright pink T-shirts so I'll disappear nicely into the walls of my flat, and then black baggy trousers with braces and a white string vest. Then I think about shoes, and then I wonder about fingerless gloves, and then I catch sight of the clock in the shoe department and swear, because I'm already ten minutes late for the interview.

I pelt down Oxford Street, running along the yellow stripes in the gutter so I don't have to push against the crowds. Then, when I finally get to the Black Cat in Berwick Street and see a young, pretty, short-haired girl sitting in the window by herself, looking bored, I realize something else has happened. I've lost my voice.

Clare Grogan is tiny, and possibly about three years old.

'Hello,' I croak. But it comes out as the letter H, and a long hoarse whisper, and nothing more.

She smiles sympathetically.

I try again.

I sound like John Wayne gargling sand. It's horrible and it hurts.

'Never mind,' Clare smiles. 'Have you got a sore throat?'

I nod.

'That happens to me sometimes', she says, 'when I've been singing too much.'

Because I am sitting there with my mouth opening and closing like a fish, she suddenly realizes the only sensible thing she can do is talk to the waitress, so she does.

'Can we have two glasses of water and a pot of tea

please?' she asks, sounding unreasonably Scots and mature. 'And would you mind turning the radio down, because this lady's trying to talk over the top of it with a sore throat.'

I manage to find a pen, although there's no paper in my bag.

'Paper?' Clare guesses. I'm reduced to miming now, like Marcel Marceau walking against the wind. 'Here,' she pushes over a pile of paper napkins.

'How about you just write the questions and I'll write the answers for you. I can see you can't talk.'

The first thing I have to do is make her order a Knickerbocker Glory. I have to. It's in my opening sentence. I point to the menu, then to the waitress, then to Clare and back to the menu again.

'I think she wants a Knickerbocker Glory,' Clare says.

I shake my head violently.

'No, she's changed her mind,' she says.

I nod like a nodding dog on speed.

'Whoops,' Clare says to the waitress. 'Back again. She does want it. Sorry about that.'

Rolling her eyes, the waitress puts her pencil back in her pocket and stomps off to the kitchen.

It's possibly the biggest humiliation of my professional life to end up being the object of a schoolgirl's pity but then I have no choice. It's either be pitied or face the wrath of Jon when I return to the office without a story.

I write the first question on a napkin.

'Tell me about John Peel.'

Clare finds a pen of her own in her bag, which like all good schoolgirl biros is chewed to bits, and writes on the other side of the napkin.

'I'm doing a session at the BBC studio in Maida Vale for his Radio 1 show.'

And that seems to be it, really, as far as answers go.

But I can't blame her. There's only so much napkin to go around, and the waitress already appears to be insulted at the fact that we're using them as notepads.

The next question is for Howard, so I get it out of the way.

'Can my boss Howard manage you? He looks after a band called Terminal Sausage.'

Clare laughs at that and makes a face, then writes back.

'Sorry, no. The bass player Johnny's big brother Gerry looks after us, and he won't let me out of his sight in London in case my mum and dad kill him.'

Then, amazingly, I manage to think of another question.

'How did Peel discover you?'

And back comes the scribble on the other side of the napkin.

'At Leeds Futurama. We played alongside all our heroes – Echo and the Bunnymen, Siouxsie and the Banshees, Simple Minds.'

I mime a frock to Clare, to try to convey that I need to know what she was wearing. Amazingly, she gets it – they must play a lot of charades in Glasgow.

'I borrowed a flapper dress from the school drama club. Usually I wear 1950s floral swimsuits with rain-coats over the top. And white tights and ballet pumps.'

We have now filled one napkin. One down, four to go. So there's only one thing for it: the Smokie questions in *Jackie*. I start writing them down fast, while the scowling waitress brings over the Knickerbocker Glory.

'Here you are,' Clare says, pushing it across the table at me.

I push it back, trying to gesticulate that I want her to have it.

'You're a bit bothered about this Knickerbocker Glory, aren't you?' She sighs.

And then for some mad reason I push it towards her, knock the sugar bowl over, and send the whole thing flying into her lap.

'Sorry', I write on the napkin, turning bright red while the waitress comes back with a cloth. Clare Grogan's lap is now filled with dodgy-looking strawberries, cream, jelly and chocolate.

'That's OK,' she scrawls back politely. And an embarrassing nonwriting silence follows, until I finally remember the next question.

'What's your favourite record?'

' "Hong Kong Garden" by Siouxsie and the Banshees', Clare replies, pushing the second napkin across the table. Then she takes it back and adds, 'I even carry a copy around with me just in case I get to someone's house and they don't have it.'

We keep scribbling, despite the filthy looks from the waitress.

It goes on. Clare's idea of beauty is Debbie Harry in a bin bag. And if she could change her name to anything, she'd change it to Tallulah Gosh. And it seems that Altered Images got their name off the back of a Buzzcocks single, and she thinks Punk will never die, and she also wants to marry Johnny Rotten. Finally I just give up and hand her the rest of the napkins, and she drinks tea and writes for ten minutes without stopping. I suppose it's just like doing school exams in Scotland, really, being interviewed by me.

'Have you heard the new Monochrome Set album?' Clare asks, when she's finished. Because I still can't speak, I nod enthusiastically instead, like a brain-damaged carthorse who wants more oats.

Clare looks at her watch, says she's got to catch a train, gets up, shakes my hand and says she hopes I get my voice back soon. Then she hands over a pile of neatly folded paper napkins which I stuff into my handbag. I try not to look at her skirt. After the

211

Knickerbocker Glory incident, it's an absolute mess.

Later, much later – when I've gargled tap water in a public toilet and crawled back to the office on the top of a 73 bus – I read the paper napkins back. Instinctively she's given me everything I need. Thank God.

She hopes the band gets a record deal soon so they can go on *Top of the Pops*. And she loves Glasgow, and the bands, but she thinks London's too big and she keeps getting lost. She just had her first McDonalds today – they don't have one in Glasgow – and she had a cheeseburger and a strawberry milkshake, and it was amazing. And she loves Simple Minds, and they were supposed to play with them last week at Glasgow University Students' Union, but they wouldn't let Altered Images play because they were under eighteen. Nevertheless, Jim Kerr's still promised them a gig somewhere else. And she loves Tequila Sunrise. And the rest of the band drinks tea. And she'd never vote for Mrs Thatcher, even if she was over eighteen, which she's not, and she loves Hercules, her goldfish, and she'd like a dog one day, as well.

And that's it – my attempt to be Lester Bangs crossed with Julie Burchill, without a voice or a tape-recorder, and with questions stolen out of *Jackie*. I try not to wince when Jon shakes with laughter as he watches me typing up my paper napkins at my desk.

'I suppose you're going to write about the fact that she had a cheeseburger in the first sentence,' he sneers.

'She sounds rather nice,' Howard says, leaning over my shoulder to look at Clare's quotes, as I type them up. 'A shame about the bass-player's brother managing them. I think I could do a lot with a young lady like that.'

Howard sends me home in a taxi soon after that, because even though my voice is slowly coming back, I still sound like I should be in hospital. It's one of those infections where you can feel the spots growing on the back of your throat.

As I lurch through the front door, I hear my new green phone ringing.

I run to pick it up before it rings out. It's David. And Jeannie. How the hell did they get my new number?

'Linda, it's David. Look, I've got my friend Jeannie here, and she's a bit upset.'

'Why? What?' I croak.

'You've joined the Labour Party, haven't you?'

'No I haven't.' I sound as dry and hoarse as an old man in a nursing home.

Suddenly, it's Jeannie on the other end, taking over the receiver. 'Linda, your name's on the list. I saw it.'

'It's a mistake!' I shout-whisper.

I suppose David got my number off Hazel. I wish she hadn't given it to him.

David takes the phone again. 'Linda, I don't think you understand how angry we are about this, so you might as well tell us the truth. Why did you join? I mean, why can't you just leave us alone?'

'What do you mean *us*? What do you mean, us, us, *us*?' I croak. And then I burst into tears.

I can't speak, because of my sore throat, and somehow that forces me into crying. It's my only voice option really. And then the thought of humiliating myself like this, in front of braless Jeannie Sheridan, like a little *kid* for God's sake, makes me want to die.

I slam the phone down, and take it off the hook.

How many more days till I leave for Australia?

CHAPTER TWENTY-ONE

'So you're ready for your in-depth exclusive with David Bowie now, are you?' Jon jeers when I get back into the office on Monday morning. I suppose my reputation will never survive the paper napkin and Knickerbocker Glory incident.

The radio is playing 'I Don't Like Mondays' again, and it's dedicated to all the women who work in a canteen in Colchester, 'because they don't like Mondays, ha ha ha'. There are some days when you'd think every DJ in England has had three quarters of his brain removed and put in a jar of pickled onions.

'One day I'm going to chuck that radio out of the window,' I say to Jon. He always has it on first thing on a Monday morning, even though he knows I hate it. He says he has to have it on to gauge the Zeitgeist. I say he puts it on because he knows it annoys me.

'Yes, *mein commandant*,' he says, in a stupid *Fawlty Towers* German accent.

'I've had a shit weekend, Jon. So shut up, will you?'

'Let me sell you some acid, that'll cheer you up.'

'I'd rather have a Jaffa cake than your acid. What's it made out of anyway, Imperial Leather talc?'

Start as you mean to go on. It's that kind of day.

Jon puts on Patti Smith's new single, 'Dancing Barefoot'. I fall in love with it straightaway. I ask him

214

if I can take it home and tape it on my new tape-recorder – another weekend purchase. He says no. I throw a stapler at his head, willing it to staple him and do some serious damage. I miss, and the stapler hits Howard's dog instead, asleep in the corner.

'Steady on, Linda,' Howard says. 'My God, you still sound dreadful. You really shouldn't be shouting at Jon like that, it will just make it worse.' Then Howard goes back to reading his Japanese phrasebook. He's just heard about some invention called a Sony Walkman, which means you can play tapes on headphones from a machine clipped on your belt, and he's trying to do a distribution deal with the men in Tokyo who make them.

Jon sniffs disapprovingly. '*Walkman*. I can't see that lasting.'

Then, against all hope, Evan walks in. A vision from heaven in a white Fred Perry shirt, arms still brown from long-gone Australian summers, and hair that is whiter and spikier than ever.

He doesn't look at me. Instead he jumps into the chair in front of Howard's desk and starts talking to him about money. Jon puts on Ian Dury singing 'Reasons To Be Cheerful (Part 3)' and turns the volume up, looking at Evan, then looking at me, then looking at Evan again. Once more I find myself wondering, does Jon know? Has Evan told him? Then I think, even if he does, I couldn't give a toss. I'm not at bloody school any more.

There's a smell of cinnamon in the air, and I have a sudden vivid memory of my fantastic fifteen-minute orgasm dream. Then I instantly think of Cindy and the shoebox full of photographs, but she's gone for the day – she's taking her summer holidays ahead of the rest of us.

Jon slopes out when Ian Dury has finished telling us all his reasons to be cheerful, and says he's off down the pub. This is usually Howard's cue to join him, and I pray silently that he does. Instead, though, the conversation between Howard and Evan goes on – and on. Evan can't fancy me any more, I think, or he'd have stopped by now, or at least looked at me.

Then Howard gets up to go to the loo, and Evan pushes his chair away, walks over and kisses me so hard I almost fall over.

'Funny way to say hello,' I manage as I come up for air.

'Let's go back to mine,' he says. 'I need to talk to you about Australia. And New York. And I need to do a few other things to you as well.'

'Oh yes?'

'Yeah. I want to make up for last time.'

Evan hovers by my desk, taking his camera out and checking it, and rechecking it, until Howard returns.

'Is a cheque all right?' Howard asks, fishing his Barclay's chequebook out of his top pocket. He's in his summer kit today – a pink gingham shirt and a pair of trousers in the style the British probably wore when they ruled India.

Evan nods.

'I'm off up the pub then,' Howard says, trying not to look as if he minds about the money. 'Care to join us in the beer garden? It's a beautiful day.'

Evan shakes his head. 'I said I'd give Linda some advice on Australia,' he drawls.

Howard gives me a look and waggles his eyebrows. 'Well that's a piece of luck for you then, Linda. So, I'll leave you to it, shall I?'

Yes, please leave me to it, I think as I watch him disappear down the stairs, followed by his spaniel. Leave me to it, Howard, for as long as the planets rotate in the heavens.

Evan finds a towel in his bag. 'Let's go for a swim in the Serpentine,' he says.

'I haven't got my swimming costume.'

'Just go in your undies.'

A lot of Evan's words get shortened like that. If he's ill he's having a sickie, and if he's cooking vegetables he's having veggies. I'd forgotten that about him, and now it's coming back to me. It's like the smell of cinnamon, and the little Fred Perry logo on his shirt, and his black Doc Martens with white socks. I haven't really missed him at all since the night we were together. But now, being confronted with him, he's taking me over like a wave.

As we walk down the stairs and out into the Soho sunshine, I tell him that I nearly lost my voice interviewing Clare Grogan. 'So I really shouldn't be swimming at all,' I croak. 'I'm not well.'

'Best thing for it, having a swim,' Evan says, stopping to kiss me again.

I think about what I have to do today. A story about the Tom Robinson Band splitting up. A fashion story about two-tone, and how black and white checks are about to take over the world. And the crossword – more black and white checks.

'I've got to be back in an hour or I'll never get everything done,' I tell him as we stride past Green Park, where people have collapsed in deckchairs, and make our way towards Hyde Park.

As I walk, in my nicely ripped new C&A jeans, Evan snaps away, playing with the lens.

'What I like best about your photos is that they never look like me,' I say.

'They always look like you,' Evan tells me as the traffic roars past, 'it's just that you've forgotten how to see yourself properly.'

We walk faster and faster, dodging tourists who are also trying to take photographs of each other.

'I often wonder about all the background people,' Evan muses as we pass Sloane Street.

'What do you mean?'

'Those people who are accidentally in the background of your photographs,' he explains. 'I mean, what happens to them all?'

We reach Hyde Park and zigzag our way across it, our shoes in our hands and our bare feet in the sticky grass, until we see the Serpentine.

'The water in Australia is so clear in the rivers, you can see trout swimming up to your ankles,' he says. 'Not like this. Just look at it. What does the Queen do, chuck her tea bags in it?'

'Australia is paradise, isn't it. People keep telling me. God, why don't you just come with me, Evan? And New York, think of that!'

I hold my hand up against the sun and gaze across the park. I can see secretaries in white nylon bras and skirts, and businessmen with their ties off, sweltering, and Arabs being Arabs and taking nothing off at all.

Evan pulls me into a secluded patch of trees. 'Let's get changed here.'

He makes me stand in front of him, then pulls off his shirt, his trousers and finally his underpants, and puts on his swimming costume.

'New bra?' he asks, approving of the hot pink number I bought on Saturday.

'And new pants,' I show him.

'You must have known I was coming into work today.' Evan nudges me, and after that we forget about the swim altogether, and he throws me back on the grass, so that when I finally get up about half an hour later, I have bark in my back and those funny criss-cross creases of skin on my legs where the grass has pressed in.

We get into the water quickly after that, with our stuff on the bank so that we can keep an eye on it.

'In Australia,' Evan says, 'nobody nicks your gear.

You should try it. Go to Bells and leave your gear on a sand dune – it'll still be there by sundown.'

We splash around for a bit, and he bites me again, on the other side of my neck.

'Evan, for God's sake, you know I have to go back to work.'

'Howard and Jon will be in the pub for hours. You know that. Getting pissed. Talking to girls. Getting some sun.'

He's right, of course.

He dives under the water and pulls my leg, then pulls me under. I open my eyes and see a flash of green murk and floating black lines in front of my eyes, before they sting so badly I have to come up again. Evan keeps swimming, submerged, like a fish on the bottom of the ocean.

'That's all you need to pack for Australia,' he says, gasping, as he comes up.

'What, my bra and pants? Isn't Sydney supposed to be having its winter in August?'

Evan towels his head, which makes him look more like a blond porcupine than ever. I look at his tanned, muscled stomach and feel a wave of lust, which I quickly get rid of.

'I wish that sending me to your twin sister in Sydney was some kind of sacrifice for you,' I say suddenly, then want to bite my lip as soon as the words are out. 'I wish you'd miss me or something.'

'Why, because you think love always has to involve a sacrifice?' he asks, sitting down to put on his socks.

We don't talk after that – my sore throat is coming back, and I think he's shocked himself by using the word love – but I find myself thinking about what he's said, all the way back to Soho.

Maybe I *do* always think love means having to give up, or give in. Not that Evan is anywhere near loving me, of course. And it's so obvious, really, when you

219

watch him winding his way up Piccadilly, gazing at every pair of legs that walks his way, every breast that's moving in a T-shirt, every pair of eyes that meets his. It's not even as if he wants any of them, it's just a declaration of freedom.

Next minute he's off, with his camera round his neck, moving ahead of me in the crowd and snapping away, as if I'm some rock star and he's on assignment. People stare, then look away, irritated, when they see the damp bra patches showing through my shirt, and my stringy wet hair, and realize I'm just a nobody after all.

'Come to my house tonight,' he says as we walk past Eros.

'You'll only vanish in a puff of smoke afterwards,' I say.

'But don't you have much better dreams since you met me?' he asks. And I realize he's serious. So I have to give him a serious answer.

'Well, weirdly – yes.'

'Sex is often better when you dream it,' Evan concludes as we kiss for the last time and he pats his camera to make sure it's safe.

I wonder about his sister Penny again, and what she's really like. And I wonder about Australia again, and give up. I always get as far as picturing kangaroos bouncing up the street and then it all seems too stupid, and I have to stop. And as for New York – it's just a cartoon in my head, of The Ramones eating hamburgers.

'I still wish you'd come with me,' I say, as Evan leaves me to get the tube home.

'You'd only have me in your power if I did,' he smiles.

'You've already got me in yours anyway,' I say to myself, quietly.

As he disappears down the stairs into Piccadilly

Underground and out of my life, I think that of all the men in London who have the least to offer me, he's probably the reigning champion. And yet, knowing that doesn't stop a thousand buckletloads of hormones pumping through my system.

With a few good plays of the new B52s album, though, I should be over this Evan madness by dinnertime. I've done it before. I can do it again. I can crush-proof myself, hope-proof myself, dream-proof myself and, most importantly, love-proof myself. It just takes will power. And anyway, it will be good practice for the rest of my life, and no doubt for the rest of the men to come.

When I walk into the office it's deserted. Evan was right. The sun and the booze, and the local temp typists have all proved too much for Howard and Jon.

My hair is still wet from the Serpentine, then I remember that Cindy has a hairdryer. She uses it to dry the glue on the layout pages. It seems wrong, somehow, to go into her domain when she's not here. But then I think about it for a minute, and realize I'm going to anyway.

The room smells of her strange, sticky, patchouli oil scent, and it's as neat and coordinated as Cindy herself, from the rows of coloured pencils in jam jars, to the expertly filed photographs in the cabinet. The hairdryer is a cheap purple plastic job, and it's usually on the shelves underneath her lightbox. Today, though, it isn't there. I wonder for a minute if she's packed it with her to take on holiday, then I pull out the top drawer of the filing cabinet just to check.

Something's stuck to the sole of my shoe – an incredible live shot of Echo and the Bunnymen, which I've never seen before, so I do Cindy a favour and peel it off, then find the E file so I can put it back. And that's where I find the photo of Evan, which is also incredible – because he's stark naked. Cindy's turned a light on him, to make it obvious. And I can tell she's the photographer because she's initialled the corner of the frame.

I manage to shove the filing cabinet drawer back, get out of the art room, close the door and be back in my seat seconds before Howard's plodding feet get to the top of the landing and he crashes back inside.

CHAPTER TWENTY-TWO

On Friday, my last day at work and the day before I fly to New York, Howard tries to tell me what to expect from the journey. I suppose I have to believe him, because he's done this trip before and I haven't. But I wish he wasn't making me so nervous.

We sip instant coffee while he waves his hand in the air showing big sweat patches under his arms, and tries to explain the mysteries of international travel to me. The unmistakable smell of Hai Karate aftershave wafts around the stifling summer air.

'It's Julie's flatmate's stuff,' he apologizes. 'I forgot to pack my own last night.'

'Nice one, Howard,' I tell him. I'm glad summer is bringing him his fair share of lust.

'Anyway. About your grand expedition to America,' he continues.

'Yes.'

'As soon as the plane grinds to a halt,' Howard says, 'you'll want to run off immediately, Linda, because you'll be so excited – but for Christ's sake, don't.'

'Why not?'

'The plane might tip over.'

I have some more coffee.

'Another thing about flying with Laker,' Howard warns me, 'is that they won't feed you much. So buy as many egg sandwiches as you can now and put them in a plastic bag.'

'Howard, can't you just come with me to the airport and tell me what to do?'

'Sorry, Linda, I'm busy. I've got a bidet client barbecue in Chelsea all day.'

'Oh God.'

'No, don't be nervous.' Howard waves his arms around again.

'You know I haven't done this before. I mean, do you just get on the plane when you walk in? Is it like catching a bus, or what?'

'Tell you what,' Howard says, tapping the side of his nose like George Cole in a St Trinian's film, 'the best thing for you is to look for a lone Japanese schoolgirl.'

'Really?'

'Yes, lone Japanese schoolgirls are continually taking expensive transatlantic flights, with nice air hostesses as their chaperones. When you see a pair of them, just sneak up behind them and follow their every move.'

'Yeah, but I don't look like a Japanese schoolgirl, Howard. I'm not going to blend in very well.'

In the end, though, a kind man at the Laker desk helps me navigate my way through the queues, and the security guards, and all the confusing numbered signs. I had no idea Heathrow was so big. My heart hammers the whole time, and I feel as if I'm going to be sick. Every time I go through another door or gate I think I'm suddenly going to see the plane, but I never do. In the end, I'm so rattled I can't even organize myself enough to buy a Jackie Collins from WH Smith.

After more queues, more gentle perspiring and a few heart-thumping moments of panic – I think I'm in the wrong part of the airport at least twice – I finally shuffle onto the plane with the rest of the Laker passengers.

Once we are on board, I close my eyes until some-one starts making announcements about our arrival time, which sounds exciting, and then I realize noth-ing's going to happen for ages, and shut them again. I want David to be here with me now. I don't want Evan and his mad promises. I want David. He's safe. He's warm. And it's him who should be sitting next to me now on my grand adventure, not some old woman with evil-smelling cough drops who keeps clearing her throat. Oh God, I wish I could be as certain about David all the time as I feel about him right now. He's the only thing in my head, in this world, and certainly on this plane that feels like home. And I could kill myself for feeling this, but I miss him. I miss him, I miss him, I miss him.

As the hours crawl past I tuck myself into the foetal position and clench my fingers together under my aeroplane blanket, praying to the Statue of Liberty to send me miracles. I'm absolutely starving now, and I wish I'd done what Howard advised and packed some egg sandwiches.

'Dear Statue of Liberty, please send me some magic. And some Maltesers. And some music,' I mutter under the blanket, in the dark. I have the number of Cindy's friend Karen Emmanuel in my purse, but that's all. And somehow I think I'm going to need more than that to survive the next few days.

We get into New York just after 11 p.m. local time and I realize that if I was in London now, I would have been asleep for at least six hours. No wonder my eyes are watering. I look for signs of Americanness at the airport, but there are none at all. The grunting man who takes my passport looks pale and sweaty, and he might as well be English. There's a photograph of the President, which is weird – do you see a picture of Margaret Thatcher flying into Heathrow? No you don't – and Stars and Stripes flags everywhere, but that's it. I've read about airports being all the same, but here's the living proof. I might as well be back at Heathrow.

In the taxi into Manhattan, we pass huge billboard ads for weird brands of cigarettes and perfume I've never heard of. The excitement is starting to hit me now, and I can't stop gawping out of the window.

'CBGB's please,' I tell the driver.

'I sort of wanted to go straight there,' I explain. 'To see a gig.'

He doesn't react.

'It's where The Ramones started out,' I add before I give up on polite conversation altogether. Then, about half an hour later, he stops the cab and jerks a thumb at a run-down building to the left of us. 'CBGB,' he says. The queue to get in is winding around the corner, and it doesn't look as if anyone's being allowed inside.

I join the end of the queue with my wheelie suitcase, because I'm so tired I don't know what else to do.

'Are you with the band?' a woman with a black leather jacket and long red plaits asks me.

I shake my head. I can't even see who the band is, because the queue is blocking out the posters.

'Did you just get here?' the woman with red plaits asks. She's got that talkative, ultrafriendly air that can only come from an interesting combination of drugs.

'I just flew in from London,' I tell her. 'I'm a music journalist.'

'Wow!' the plaits woman shrieks. 'Get out of here, you should be at the front of the queue.' Then she gives me a pleading look, and grabs my arm. 'Can I come in with you? Is your name on the door?'

A tall, skinny, pale man in black leather trousers and a black biker jacket – with matching jet-black hair – comes up behind her in the queue. He's holding two hot dogs. Instantly I realize how hungry I am.

'Hi, I'm Joe,' he says, 'want a bite of my hot dog?'

I do, taking far more than I should, so that the onions and tomato sauce squelch over my chin.

'Joe's my baby,' says the red plaits woman, who tells me her name is Alana. A conversation follows about how an English music journalist like me should be at the front of the queue, and then Joe grabs my arm.

'Come on.'

'No, I can't.'

'Come on, don't be shy, let's go see the doorman. Are you famous?'

I shake my head. 'No. No. Not famous.'

'Doesn't matter. You look famous. Come on, Alana.'

His girlfriend follows as we leave our place in the queue and march past the waiting hordes, getting filthy looks along the way.

'Got a problem?' says the bouncer at the entrance.

'This lady is from London, England, and she's a famous music writer,' says Joe. 'Look, she's even got her suitcase with her. She just got off the plane. From Heathrow,' he says, reading the label.

I'm so embarrassed I can't look at anyone. Maybe I should fluff my hair up into a mad puffball, though, just in case the man on the door thinks I'm Julie Burchill.

The bouncer jerks his thumb to the back of the queue.

'What's your name?' Alana asks quickly.

I say it out loud, feeling like a twat, but the bouncer doesn't even blink.

'She's famous,' Alana says. 'You're gonna regret this.'

While we have been arguing with the doorman, about twenty more people have joined the back of the queue, something that Joe and Alana now realize simultaneously.

'Oh fuck it, Joe,' Alana whines.

'Where did you get those hot dogs from?' I ask them,

because my stomach realizes it has missed dinner and is not too far away from breakfast.

But the black-clad couple aren't interested in hot dogs. Instead, they suddenly seem to be more interested in each other, and I look away as Joe shoves his hand up Alana's T-shirt, and they explore the back of each other's throats.

'Phew!' Joe says when he comes up for air. 'Wanna come home with us?'

I shrug.

'Come on,' Alana encourages me. 'Come home with us. There's food and there's a bed.'

'Just round the corner,' Joe says, pushing black spiky hair out of his eyes.

'Come on. We'll have a drink and watch the tube. It's better than standing around here while some arsehole does his Nazi act.'

Meekly, I follow them up the road, trailing my wheelie suitcase behind me. In no time at all it's covered in old chewing gum, and the wheels are sticking.

'I'll carry it,' Joe says, though he's so skinny, I can't see how he's even going to raise it above his knees.

Finally, after snogging stops for them and suitcase crisis stops for me, I find myself in Joe and Alana's apartment. A plastic picture of some puppies and kittens is stuck inside the front door, beneath a row of Christmas lights which look like they might have fused in the early seventies.

'Here, have some food,' Alana says, opening the fridge and handing me a block of Parmesan cheese. There's nothing else in there. Then she takes me by the hand and leads me into the bedroom, while Joe strips down to his very baggy, very khaki, underpants.

'He wears army issue underwear,' Alana says proudly and gets into bed, wriggling off her T-shirt to reveal a spectacular pink bra that's much better than anything I could find in London.

228

'Get naked and get in, or get out,' Joe grins, and uses the remote control to switch on the TV.

'Do you get *The Dukes of Hazzard* in Eng-er-land?' Alana asks as I modestly take off one layer and crawl into bed with them. I only manage to hear the opening theme tune, though, before I black out.

'She's pretty fat for an English girl,' is the last thing I hear from Joe before the sweet relief of sleep takes me away.

The next day I wake up to an empty bed and open curtains. The sun is streaming in, revealing a flat that is so filthy it looks like a performance art piece. Fag ends are stubbed out in mouldy coffee mugs. Mouldy coffee mugs are balanced on records, out of their sleeves. The TV is still blaring, and I realize I have fallen asleep holding the block of Parmesan cheese in my hand. Someone has kindly left me a note, though. It says 'THANKS 4 THE 3-SOME', and there is a row of kisses after it. It's probably Alana, I guess. I'm not sure Joe can even hold a biro.

I chuck the Parmesan in the bin and think about it. Thanks for the threesome? Was there a threesome? Like an idiot, I immediately check to see if my pants are still on, but they are. I suppose it's New York humour. Yes, that's what it is. I didn't really have sex with Joe and/or Alana in my sleep. Please tell me I didn't.

Amazingly, the phone works. Given the fact that a cat has wandered into the flat and is pulling a blood-stained plastic bag out of the bin, and there is a large Johnny Thunders poster lying in a soggy mess in the bath, it probably shouldn't, but perhaps this is more New Yorkishness. They can't survive without their telephones, even if they do live in a tip. I find Karen Emmanuel's number in my bag and call her.

'Oh, you're Cindy's friend,' she says when I ring.

'She said you were coming. Where are you?'

'I don't know. Somewhere near CBGB. There's a cat eating a plastic bag.'

'Well here's my address. I'm stuck living in this dopey apartment on the Upper East Side. If you are near CBGB just hop on the number 6 train at Astor Place. The party starts in about an hour, so your timing is perfect.'

'What time is it?'

'Three o'clock. It's an afternoon party. And if you're hungry, don't worry, there'll be plenty of ice-cream.'

She hangs up, and I try to wash myself in the bath with the soggy Johnny Thunders poster, before Joe and Alana get back and drag me into bed with them again. I don't even want to think about the state of the sheets.

My English soap and shampoo with their Boots price stickers look comfortably familiar, even if the hot water tap splutters and the cold water tap delivers, at best, a trickle. I use last night's jumper to dry myself and my hair, rub some foundation over my face without even looking in the mirror, get changed into a 1950s frock I found at Camden Market, grab the wheelie suitcase – which is covered in dog shit as well as old chewing gum – and bump the suitcase down four flights of stairs into the street outside, where, by a miracle, I find a taxi. The thought of using the subway is just too much.

When I get to the address, a woman in a 1950s frock like mine is standing outside her apartment, shouting and waving her arms around, trying to get rid of a queue of gatecrashers while the doorman looks on.

'GET OUT!' she shouts, and I realize this must be Karen. 'I'VE HAD ENOUGH GATECRASHERS TO SEE ME THROUGH TO NEXT CENTURY!' she tells them. Then she sees me and my wheelie suitcase. 'You weren't actually thinking of staying here, were you?' she croaks, looking for a cigarette in her pocket. 'I mean, my God, I can barely take the freeloaders trying to get to the fruit punch, never mind the British moving in with suitcases. No offence or anything.'

'Sorry,' I say, feeling very English and embarrassed all of a sudden.

'It's OK. My crazy flatmate's not here. You can have her bed. You look like you need a rest.'

And she invites me up, carrying my suitcase for me. She's certainly stronger than Joe.

Once inside, I see a flat that's not unlike the kind of place I'd like to have – if I ever had any proper money. Knowing that Karen wears dresses like mine, and likes the same kind of furniture as me, somehow makes me feel less strange about being here.

'I won't even bother to introduce you,' she says, waving a hand at the people bobbing around to the B52s. A lot of the women are wearing cat's-eye sunglasses, even though they're indoors, but they look so good I realize I'm going to have to get some.

Karen offers me a cigarette, and we smoke in the sunshine, out on the balcony. Then I realize lots of people are smoking something else altogether. It makes English dope smell like weak tea.

'I was growing dill in these nice empty beer barrels on my balcony,' Karen tells me. 'Or at least I thought I was growing dill. So much dope got dropped in the soil from people's party joints, I'm now apparently growing some extremely healthy marijuana plants. One call to the cops and I'm living on the street with the bums, let me tell you. And I've got Lester Bangs in here as well.'

I stare at her. 'Lester Bangs who interviewed The Clash?'

'Yup. Lester Bangs who interviewed The Clash.'

'Oh my God.' I remember my prayer to the Statue of Liberty on the plane. Music. Magic. Miracles.

'How do you know about Lester and The Clash?' Karen asks.

'He's famous in London.'

'Hey, you want to interview Fred Schneider from the B52s?' Karen asks suddenly. 'He's upstairs in the kitchen with a lei round his neck. That'll wow them in London.'

'Shit. Yes! Or no. I don't know. I'm not very good at interviews. Unless they're written on paper napkins.'

Karen snorts with laughter. 'As I said, you can stay here if you want,' she says, looking at my case. 'You're never going to find a hotel now. And you want something to eat, right?'

'Right.' I like the way Americans say right instead of yes. 'Sure' and 'right'. Good words. Strong words. Words you'll never hear used in Withingdean in a million years.

'And maybe you want to use the bathroom?' Karen offers, staring down at the gatecrashers who are still hoping to get in.

'Oh God, yes please. I'm busting.'

'Well go on,' Karen says. 'Freshen up.'

'I sort of prayed for this,' I confess as the B52s' 'Rock Lobster' blasts out of the upstairs window for the third time in a row. 'I prayed to the Statue of Liberty on the plane.'

'Prayer answered then,' she says lightly. 'They usually work, in my experience.'

I follow her up the stairs.

'Lester Bangs is my mentor,' she says. 'I'm a writer.'

'You're so lucky,' I tell her. 'So am I, but I don't have a mentor.'

'Do you know a band called Pylon?' Karen asks, pushing open another door at the top of the stairs, and stepping casually over a half-naked man with his head stuck in a chandelier.

I shake my head.

'They're from Athens, Georgia. Vanessa Briscoe, the

lead singer, is a good friend of mine. We go to the Mudd Club a lot.'

I duck, as someone throws a bunch of grapes through the air. The party is hot and sweaty, and it stinks of dope and perfume.

'I've heard of the Mudd Club,' I tell Karen as she lugs my suitcase obligingly into a spare bedroom.

'The bathroom is unisex, and everyone shoots up there. And there are no doors on the stalls and everyone's too fucked up to care. But honestly – what's your name again?'

'Linda.'

'Linda you're just going to hafta go. It's way downtown and it's scary, but I'm telling you. You just *hafta*. And go to Dave's Luncheonette on the corner of Canal Street first, for an egg cream. If you're going to get drunk in New York, I totally recommend one of Dave's egg creams.'

I nod.

Then a tired-looking man in an overcoat wanders in, complaining that there's nothing to eat.

'Of course there is,' Karen says. 'Ice-cream and cake. Go in the kitchen and grind yourself some ice-cream. That's what the machine's for.'

She waves a hand after him. 'Wearing an overcoat on a hot summer's day,' she says, 'how crazy is that?'

'Who's he?' I ask.

'Michael Stipe,' she says, lighting a cigarette. 'Just another struggling musician.'

CHAPTER TWENTY-THREE

New York with Karen lasts a week, but it feels like one endless twenty-four-hour day. On my last night we get a bottle of vodka and lie down on the fire escape, in the heat, talking about the rest of our lives.

'I plan to marry Richard Hell, and have The Voidoids as my bridal party,' she says. 'Na, only kidding.'

'I plan not to marry at all,' I tell her.

'Oh get out.'

'No really,' I tell her. 'I was engaged and he left me, and I've sort of gone off it now.'

'And what about this guy you were telling me about? The guy who can't commit?'

I shake my head. 'Not even him. It would be like marrying a mirage anyway. Blink and he'd be gone.'

'So how's your love life been, since you got dumped?' she asks me.

'Oh, pretty typical. The work experience boy asked me to have sex with him, because he needed to lose his virginity in order to hump some groupies from Solihull who were following a band called Gastric Reflux.'

Karen snorts with laughter.

'And my boss asked me to go to France with him, so we could take things to the edge. I'm still trying to work out what that means. And then there's the threesome last night with Joe and Alana and the Parmesan cheese.'

'The cheese makes it a foursome,' Karen smiles. 'I think you'd better change your story.'

I swish the vodka around my mouth and stare down at New York through the fire escape railings.

'The teeth are better here,' I tell Karen.

'What?'

'Sorry. I'm just trying to compare New York to London. Oh, I'll tell you the other thing I like—'

'What's that?'

'Chopped liver bagels. When I first saw them advertised, I thought it sounded like medieval torture, but I'm addicted to them now.'

Karen laughs and stretches her arms out to catch more sun.

'And what else will you miss?' she asks.

'Oh, the subway. It sounds so much more glamorous than the tube. And episodes of M*A*S*H I haven't seen. And those mad men you see jogging in Central Park with bare chests and five dogs on a lead running behind them . . .'

Then I fall asleep.

On Saturday morning I say goodbye and Karen promises she'll ask Lester Bangs for interviewing tips so I no longer have to run my career on the back of paper napkins, and then I head for JFK airport in another yellow taxi. Annoyingly, the theme song from *The Dukes of Hazzard* is going around my head all the time at the moment.

'Australia?' says the check-in woman at the airport. 'Good luck. That's one looooong flight.' New Yorkers are onomatopoeic, I decide. Long is never long, it's always loooooong. Good is never good, it's gooooood. Similarly, bad is always baaaaaad. The local language is like the city itself – it has to have ten times more life squeezed into it than normal.

In the end, thanks to sleeping pills given to me by one of Karen's friends, I pass out for most of the flight to Sydney, waking up long enough to sleepwalk through a change at LA, where I buy mad chocolate called Hershey's and read a newspaper that seems to think America is the only country in the world which exists.

When, at long last, we land in Australia, the man sitting next to me has to poke me in the arm. The sleeping pills must have been designed to knock out zoo animals. I feel as if I'm made of rubber, and I must have been out for at least thirteen hours.

The queue off the plane takes for ever, and then I realize something incredible. I've just woken up. And what's more, I feel free. Perhaps it's the seagulls soaring over the runway, or the fact that nobody in Australia knows me, but it's finally happened. An overwhelming sense of freedom I never knew was possible.

Australians have twangy voices, and it's hard to understand their accent until you realize it's cockney slowed down because of the heat. Even though it's six o'clock in the morning, they all seem to be smiling. Someone in New York told me that Australia is called the lucky country. Maybe that's why. You don't see lazy smiles like that on the Northern Line.

The biggest smile I see is Penny's, though. And I recognize her instantly, waving at me in the arrivals hall. She's not quite Evan in a dress, but she's still got his slightly bent nose, sharp blue eyes, and long, long, legs.

Suddenly, the world seems very light, and far too bright.

'Welcome to Sydney,' she says, taking my case and slamming it onto a trolley.

'I love it,' I say, feeling as if I'm still stoned on Karen Emmanuel's dope.

'Wow, and you haven't even left the airport.' Penny

laughs. 'You'll feel even better after you've had a shower.' I don't tell her I've never had one before.

'Oh my God, I'm in *Australia*,' I say, looking around me as we get into her beaten-up car. And that's another weird thing about foreign countries – the cars are all different shapes. This one has pointy bits sticking up above the headlights. The birds are different too. None of the dirty, oversexed pigeons or boring, weeny brown sparrows you see in London: this airport car park flock is quite different. Seagulls that look big enough to put in a pie and eat. And weird, brown hopping things with black hats and yellow beaks. Even the sounds Australian birds make are different.

Penny's car smells of old bananas and petrol. There's mad Australian money, too, with pictures of animals all over it, lying on the floor. And when Penny pulls open the glovebox to look for a set of house keys for me, about a hundred more coins fall out.

I realize I don't know what she does for a living.

'I'm a hairdresser,' she says. 'I used to want to be something much brainier than that, honestly, but I couldn't be buggered doing the exams.'

'Does it pay well?'

'Well I sort of ended up owning the salon, so yeah, it does,' she shrugs.

I try not to show it, but I'm impressed. No wonder she can afford to live in a house by herself.

I stare out of the window as Sydney rushes past me, and Penny tells me she lives in a place called Darlinghurst, which sounds quaint and romantic – as if the people who live there call each other 'darling' a lot – so it's a surprise when she tells me that half the people walking up and down the road are prostitutes.

'They must be cold in those miniskirts,' is all I can think of to say.

That's another thing Evan's got wrong. Even though

237

I'm sure the summers are boiling, it's bloody freezing at the moment. The wind is howling down the street outside like a Brighton gale.

'How long are you here for?' Penny asks.

'Well, I wondered if I could stay here until the end of the week,' I hear myself saying, feeling English and embarrassed again.

'You can stay as long as you like,' she reassures me.

It's odd, hearing her voice, because it's like listening to Evan again, but a few octaves higher.

Eventually we pull up outside a house with a balcony and wait until a rubbish van has moved away so Penny can park.

'What are you thinking?' she asks.

'How clean it is,' I tell her, dragging the words out of myself because I'm so exhausted. 'We've just had all these strikes in England. The rubbish was up to your waist.'

'Oh I know,' Penny shudders. 'We saw it on the news. And all those dead people they couldn't bury.'

Another reply forms in my mind about that, and then the yawning takes it away. I'm trying, I really am trying, but I've never been so tired in the whole of my bloody life. Thankfully the freedom feeling hasn't gone away, and I'm hanging on to it desperately.

In a blur, as Penny takes my case into the house, I realize something. English birds sound like Julie Andrews. The birds here sound like Joe Strummer.

'Punk birds,' I mutter, to myself.

Penny overhears me, and laughs. 'Wait until you hear the crows. All they ever say is faaaark.'

'And it smells of disinfectant here.'

'Oh, that'll be our garbos.'

I suppose a garbo is something to do with garbage. Like Evan, she chops off all her words.

'No, it's like a medicine smell,' I tell her. 'Not in the house, I mean outside, in the street.'

'Gum trees?'

I shake my head. 'I don't know.' And then, magically, I make it up the stairs of her house, and a
bedroom door is opened, three pillows are produced,
and then everything just goes black. Just like the time
I passed out in Alana and Joe's bed with the Parmesan
cheese.

When I wake up again, the prostitutes have stopped
marching up and down the street in their miniskirts
and high heels, and been replaced by a tramp, who is
shouting about the Bible. It's also getting dark. I look at
the clock next to my bed – it's just after five o'clock.
I've slept for an entire day.

My bedroom is tiny, but you can see into a back
garden, and there is a round thing down there which
looks like a spaceship, though I suppose it's a barbecue,
and the strangest clothes line I've ever seen – more
like an instrument of torture than something to dry
your clothes on.

The pictures in the room remind me of Evan. There
are lots of postcards from art galleries, and a few hand-
painted pieces. There are records too, piled up
between two house bricks on a wooden plank, and I
stagger over to have a look. Nobody told me about
swaying on your feet. Every time I try to stand up, I
feel as if I'm going to fall down.

Penny owns all the right records, and I instantly feel
less strange about being in this room, in this house, in
this country. She's got Ian Dury's 'New Boots And
Panties', and The Buzzcocks' 'Orgasm Addict', and yes,
even good old Plastic Bertrand, which makes me think
of David. He doesn't just seem far away geographically,
he seems light years away in time as well. I remember
my panicky need for him on the plane from London to
New York, and tell myself it must have been the jetlag.

I decide to have a bath. I need something normal,

and something deeply English, to get me feeling human again.

As I pad towards the bedroom door, swaying, I realize there's a note under it from Penny. Maybe notes are a family trait. She can't spell – Jon Whitten would have a fit – but it's a note that instantly makes me feel better. There are crumpets in the fridge, she tells me (crumpits in the frig), and I can use her Badedas (Badidas) bath stuff, and if I'm too cold, I can even throw some of her tweed (twede) coats on the bed.

You can tell a lot about a woman from the coats she wears. As soon as I see a girl in a nice second-hand tweed job in London – the kind my grandmother might have saved up her ration coupons for – I know we're going to be friends. So when I push my way into Penny's bedroom, next door, and see a whole wardrobe full of fake fur collars, and red patent leather macs, and rugged tweed greatcoats, and pale pink checked capes, I immediately feel reassured. Penny's guessed right. I am bloody freezing. So I take as many coats as I can hold in my arms, stagger back to my room and get back under the blankets again, this time covered in her wardrobe, as if I've been buried alive in the coat room at a party. Then I strip down to my pants under the mountain of bedclothes and throw my clothes on the floor.

When I wake up again, I remember two things: I needed to go to the loo, and I didn't, and I meant to have a bath, and I didn't. I also realize someone is sitting on the floor, watching me. It's Penny.

'You poor thing,' she tuts, patting me on the arm.

'What time is it?' I ask. I feel wide awake suddenly, and I'm starving.

'Midnight.'

'Oh shit. Howard said you're not supposed to do that.'

'Is that Howard your boss?'

240

I nod.

'Evan told me all about him. He takes ages to pay, doesn't he?'

I wriggle around under the blankets and her coats, realizing that my bladder has passed the point of no return.

'I have to get up,' I tell her.

But Penny shows no sign of going.

'Um, can you pass me one of those coats?' I say, realizing that my bra is somewhere on the bedroom floor.

She does, but she still shows no signs of going. Maybe it's an Australian thing, feeling comfortable about being naked. Then I look at Penny again and realize she is staring at me the way Evan sometimes does.

She helps me wriggle into the pale pink checked cape, like Superwoman.

'God, you're so *white*,' she says.

'I haven't been on holiday for a while. I mean, this is my holiday.'

'Go up north. That's where the sun is this time of year.'

'Is that where those beaches are? Emerald, and Hungry Head?'

'You just like the names, don't you,' Penny laughs. Then she pads off to the bathroom, ahead of me.

'You have to turn the hot tap right round at first, then let it warm up, then turn the cold tap on,' she says, explaining the shower.

I look at her again, and realize she's still not going away. 'Evan and I had a fling,' I tell her, suddenly feeling this might be a useful piece of information for her to know.

'I know.'

'Oh.'

'Evan's lousy with women,' she says conversationally.

'Yeah, I realized.'

241

'He's like a great single, though. You can't get enough for the first fifty plays, and then you want to replace it with something else.'

'Really?'

'That's what my girlfriends over here used to say. And that's why he keeps moving, Linda. He likes to replace you before you get a chance to replace him. Simple.'

She holds the shower curtain out for me, as if she's introducing me on stage at Shaftesbury Avenue, and I lose the cape and climb in.

'That's better, isn't it,' she says, sitting on the edge of the loo seat.

So this is what a shower feels like. It's like rain, only hotter and more concentrated. It's the most amazing physical sensation I've had since Evan rubbed half a jar of Vaseline into my back. 'I've only got a sink at home,' I tell Penny, realizing that the steam is fogging up the shower curtain, so my privacy has been restored.

'You poor girl.'

'I don't suppose I could have one of those crumpets you were talking about, after this, could I?' I shout through the noise of the water.

Then Penny pushes the shower curtain aside, giving me a very Evan-like look. I'd know that lopsided smirk anywhere.

'You fancy some crumpet?' she barks, winking at me like Benny Hill and attempting a ridiculous northern English accent.

Then she sashays out of the bathroom – she seems to be wearing some tight red velvet dress made out of a curtain, completely covered in her customers' hair – and leaves me alone at last. Her own hair, of course, is spectacular. I wish I could dye mine the way she dyes hers.

A few minutes later I am dry and wrapped in her

cape, and not even caring that she can see me half naked as I eat one crumpet after another on my bedroom floor.

'What's this brown stuff on it?' I ask.

'Vegemite.'

The clock on the bedside table says it's after 1 a.m.

'Evan said you broke up with a guy before he met you.'

I nod.

'He only had eight records and they were all crap,' I say. And we laugh then, because Penny is one of those women who will laugh at anything, and because I am so tired that the most stupid things seem funny.

'Let me give you a neck massage,' she says a few crumpets later, 'then you'll sleep better.'

'No, it's OK.'

'What about I make you some more tea then?'

'No, it's OK.'

'Do you want a joint?'

'Um. Not really.'

'Shall I put The Saints on?'

'No really, I'm fine.'

'You English,' she tuts, 'so polite. What about if I just piss off back to bed then?'

I laugh. 'Yes. That would be very nice, thank you awfully.'

She laughs then too, and does just that, but leaving my bedroom door slightly open.

Later, much later, when I think she's gone to sleep, I close it. When I wake up the next morning, though – at 11 a.m. for God's sake – there's another note, this time on the pillow next to mine, in a scrawl that could be Evan's, as well as hers.

'DEAR LINDA,' the note says, 'COME TO SEE MY FAVORIT GROUP TONIGHT, MENTAL AS ANYTHING. LOVE PENNY XXX'

243

I've heard about Mental As Anything from Evan. And as I wander through Darlinghurst and into the city, I see some posters advertising the gig.

Most people in Sydney look the way people in London did a couple of years ago. The women have hair that's flicked back at the sides, and the men have bald bits at the front and long hair at the back. I think I've only seen one woman so far who doesn't look like she's trying to be Olivia Newton-John.

I get as far as Town Hall, which is hilariously like an English town hall, then I start swaying again, and feel my eyelids drooping. So I hail a taxi – the driver is wearing long woollen socks and shorts, like a Boy Scout master – and go straight back to Penny's house again.

So this is jet lag. More blankets. More of Penny's coats lying on top of me. Then a strange dream about Penny also lying on top of me. Then suddenly I'm being stroked gently on the arm by her, and she's telling me it's time to go and see Mental As Anything.

'Wake up, Linda. It's nine o'clock.'

'It can't be.'

'You've got terrible jet lag, haven't you?' Penny sympathizes. My arm hairs are standing up in goose bumps where she's been stroking me. This time, though, when I get out of bed, at least I'm still fully clothed.

We get dressed up in the two coats which haven't ended up on the bed, and tights with the feet ripped out of them, and old grannies' shoes.

'We can put our make-up on in the loo,' Penny says. 'We're going to a place called the Civic. You can grab a feed there if you want. They give you this kind of slush on paper plates – they have to, because of the licensing laws. You can't get pissed unless you eat the slush.'

When Penny and I arrive at the Civic, it's heaving

with people. It's cold outside, but inside it feels like a sweaty midsummer night. There are bodies squashed into corridors, bodies queuing for the toilets, and bodies crammed into the doorways that lead into the street outside. It smells of beer and sweat and cheap aftershave, and suddenly I could be at the Hope and Anchor in Islington rather than upside down and several million miles away.

There seem to be about three hundred people wedged into a space meant for half that number, while an outrageously tall blond man in a paisley woman's pantsuit wanders around, talking to people.

'That's Greedy Smith, he plays the keyboards,' Penny explains. 'And the pantsuit is polyester nylon, believe me, I've felt it.'

Then she spots another man, in a skinny tie and pointy shoes, and waves frantically.

'G'day Reg,' she says, 'I like your new haircut.'

He grins in reply.

'Reg plays mean slide guitar,' Penny bawls into my ear as the two men disappear and the band starts to take its place on stage. I can see why – he's got a piece of cut-off copper piping on his thumb.

Greedy Smith puts on a Stetson and an apron with pockets for his harmonica, and picks up a beer. With his free hand, he starts playing the organ, and what looks like the entire art school population of Sydney starts jigging around in front of the stage.

'"The Nips Are Getting Bigger",' Penny squeals, squeezing my arm. 'I love this song!'

'Who's the guy singing it?'

'Martin Plaza.'

'Isn't that a place in Sydney though?' I ask her, remembering something from a street map.

'Yeah, isn't he *great*?' she asks me without expecting an answer.

She points out other people in the crowd as the

band moves from one addictive, weird, retro-sounding song to another. Jon Whitten would love these songs. 'Talk To Baby Jesus', 'Egypt', and they even cover 'I'm A Believer'.

'That guy over there at the side of the stage is called Modern Michael,' Penny explains, 'because he's just so incredibly modern.' Then she disappears to the bar, and comes back with two cans of beer.

'This is Tooheys', she explains when I ask her, 'and I guarantee you'll get pissed on just two cans if you scull it fast enough.'

I coast from beer to beer, and song to song. And perhaps because I haven't written a word for over a week, I suddenly long for a pen and a notepad.

'I've going to review them,' I slur.

'Fab!' Penny says.

'All of England must know about this band,' I declare. 'They're brilliant. They're art with amplifiers. They're the future.'

The beer is metallic, and so is my mouth, so I can't even pronounce *amplifiers* properly, but it doesn't seem to matter.

Then suddenly the gig is over. Because Penny knows Reg – his second name is Mombassa – she hangs around, swapping jokes and cigarettes with him at the front of the stage. I'm introduced to a guy called Richard, who mixes the band.

'What is it about Australian men wearing women's pantsuits?' I ask him, and he shakes his head and smiles.

'You love it here, don't you,' Penny breathes into my ear as we stagger down the stairs, following the band. Reg disappears into a weird white car which he tells me is a Valiant and says he's going somewhere called Glebe, whatever or wherever that is.

'I do love Australia,' I say, feeling pleasantly drunk.

'Good,' Penny declares. 'Because I want you to move

here.' Then she staggers into the road and finds us both a taxi as bats flap past us in the night sky towards the park.

The days speed by in Sydney after that, just as they did in New York, and I try desperately to get a sense of where I am, while trying to cling to everything I know about England, just to get my bearings back.

It's funny listening to the local radio station, 2JJ, which Penny plays every morning, because each song I hear, and each piece of music gossip they pass on, make me realize how small the world is, but also how distant Australia and England really are. It seems wrong, somehow, to be listening to the new Madness single and hearing some Australian DJ call it nutty, when he can't even say the word properly.

'Why? Why isn't he saying it properly?' Penny demands one evening as we try to tape 'The Prince' off the radio.

'You don't say the "t" in nutty. It's more like' – I try to imitate Jon Whitten – 'nuh-ee. Sort of, nuh-ee, know wot I mean?'

Penny likes this and mimics me like a parrot. 'Nuh-ee.'

Then she makes more crumpets, from her endless supply in the fridge, and lies on the carpet with her chin in her hands, propped up on her elbows, gazing at me as if I'm the most fascinating creature she's ever seen.

'When I come to England,' she says, 'can I stay with you?'

'Of course,' I tell her, because it would be rude not to, 'but wouldn't you rather stay with Evan?'

She gives me a look.

'I mean, he's got more room than me. I live in a pink pantry. That's what it is. Enough room for a few tins of baked beans and that's it.'

Penny shakes her head. 'That's two depressing

247

things I've heard this week,' she says. 'X-Ray Spex are breaking up, and you won't let me stay with you when I come to London.'

'It's not that,' I tell her.

'God I'm so in love with Poly Styrene,' Penny says, changing the subject. 'She looks exactly like my last girlfriend.'

So there it is. Out of the bag. Or out of Pandora's Box. I suppose I've been waiting for something like this.

'Let me see you off at the airport,' Penny says sadly, after I've let her words hang for a while.

'That would be nice.'

'Evan's my twin, you know.'

'I know.'

'So at least you can say goodbye to one twin, and say hello to the other one when you land.'

'Oh, I don't think he'll pick me up from the airport, somehow.'

Penny shakes her head.

'Think how simple life would be, Linda,' Penny sighs, 'if you were with me instead of Evan. Men are such idiots.'

My departure date arrives far too soon, and I realize I never did go up to the mysterious beach called Emerald, I never did see the ocean looking like blue glass, and I never did have intimate contact with a koala. Instead, it's been a week of beer, of gossiping to Penny and replaying Mental As Anything songs in my head, of mooching around Sydney, wondering at the strangeness of a whole other civilization busily getting on with life at the very end of the world.

Part of me thinks I'm insane not to stay longer, but the other part of me likes the intensity of Sydney in concentrated form. It's like the concentrated orange juice you get here – Penny uses the bottles as bongs after she's washed them up.

I like the Lime Spiders as well, and the sweets shaped like mint leaves, and the Polo mints that have turned themselves into the far more egalitarian Lifesavers.

Crows that say 'faark', a lot of water in every direction you look, taxi drivers in schoolboy shorts and very, very old episodes of *Are You Being Served?* on the television . . . I'm going to miss Sydney, even if I only remember this much about it.

When a taxi driver takes Penny and me to the airport – (she doesn't want to drive because we've shared four farewell vodkas) – she is moist-eyed from the last set of traffic lights in Darlinghurst to the last row of cars at Sydney airport car park.

Under another tweed coat rescued from my bed, Penny is wearing an old 1960s shirt-dress, in wavy red patterns, and black tights, with winkle-pickers. Her mascara is running all over her face. I'm still in the pink cape – she won't let me give it back to her.

'Souvenir of Australia,' she says gloomily as we look up at the departures board for my flight number. 'Or at least it's a souvenir of me anyway.'

And then she kisses me. It had to happen. *She's just like Evan*, I catch myself thinking, *but softer.*

I open my eyes, just in case people are watching and we should stop. And people are watching, of course, but she doesn't.

'Well, I felt something,' she says, when she pulls herself away. 'Did you?'

I can't answer her. Because either way I'm going to hurt her feelings.

Penny walks away then, because she says she can't bear to stay. And I'm left with a trolley and a few curious onlookers, waiting for two more long hours before my plane is due to take off.

So, did I feel anything? Well of course I did. And it

surprised me. But the fact is, she lives on the other side of the world, and I live in Kentish Town. And The Buzzcocks have a new album out today, which I have to review for Monday.

CHAPTER TWENTY-FOUR

Terminal Sausage have a new single out, and on Monday morning Howard proudly lets us know it's been picked up by forty-eight radio stations.

'Picked up and put straight back down again,' Jon sniffs.

I laugh, despite myself. It's like I've never been away.

It doesn't take me long to readjust to the office. Evan hasn't rung, or even left a note, despite the fact that I've been staying with his sister. I knew he'd let me down and he has. And there's no call from David either. So it's business as usual in my love life. Meanwhile, Jon is listening to The Fall and trying to review their new single.

'What in God's name is it about?' Howard wonders aloud as a sound like gerbils gargling comes through the speakers.

'Valium and speed,' Jon informs him, and turns up the volume.

From all the phone calls crossing Howard's desk, I gather there's a Mod gig on tonight at Vespa's. I know Evan will go, but so what?

It's interesting to speculate how much Evan's powers of attraction would fade if he was freely available. It's like this horrible chocolate yoghurt they put out when

I was a kid. There was never enough chocolate or sugar in it, so it just used to taste faintly of sick. But because you could hardly ever get it, everyone in my class used to beg for it, and slowly but surely the cheap chocolate yoghurt became hot property at school. It's like Evan's sex drive: it's rationed out, like the wins you get on a fruit machine at the pub. So you keep playing, and you keep hoping, no matter if you're actually losing.

'What are you thinking about, Linda?' Howard interrupts me, and I shake myself upright in my chair. I've been miles away. Remembering Penny, thinking about Australian beer and its nutty, wooden taste; longing for New York again.

Howard's developed a new business since I've been away – imported Spanish hammocks – so there are a few of them strung up around the office and several dozen of them knotted together in a cardboard box in the corner.

'You'll never sell hammocks while Thatcher's in power, Howard,' Jon warns him.

'Why not?'

'It's not a slumping kind of political climate. It's more like, stand up straight and take it like a man.'

'Oh come on. I think my hammocks will do very well if we have an Indian summer.'

'The other thing is, Howard, what about liability insurance? I mean, what if some really fat geezer gets in one of your hammocks and it snaps?'

Howard tries to stare Jon down then, but he doesn't have Jon's pinprick amphetamine pupils, so he fails.

'Imagine Hattie Jacques getting into one of your hammocks!' Jon shouts, throwing me a look.

'Shut up, Jon,' I reply. 'The bottom's obviously fallen out of the bidet market; how else is Howard going to finance *NWW*?'

He nods seriously. 'Yes, Linda. We can't survive on Sausage alone.'

Then the phone on my desk rings, and it's David, and I stop breathing for half a minute.

'Just to let you know we're voting you out of the Labour Party,' he says, diving straight in.

'What?'

'We thought we'd better do it before you actually started coming down here and making trouble. There's been a meeting, and it's been recommended that you be barred from local membership.'

Suddenly, despite myself, I can't think of anything to say.

'Linda, did you hear me?'

'Yes. I did. I mean, big deal. Really. I couldn't give a flying—'

'Jeannie and I have spoken to them about it,' David interrupts. 'I mean, it's a joke, Linda. You should never have been allowed to apply in the first place.'

'Some socialists you are.'

'What's that supposed to mean then?'

'Oh sod it. I don't care. Just – I don't know, just fuck off, David, will you?'

I slam the phone down hard. I feel shaky. Then suddenly I realize why. In all the years David and I were together, I've never, ever, in the history of our entire relationship, told him to fuck off.

I pick up the phone again. And I know Jon and Howard are listening, and Cindy too, rustling away in the art room, but I don't care. Instantly, David picks up the call.

'Yes?'

'I've been to New York and Sydney for my summer holidays, David. Where have you and Jeannie been?'

Silence.

I hate it when he does this to me, when he just listens and lets the silence hang, so it sounds like I'm ranting.

'I said, I've just been to New York and Sydney.'

'Well congratulations. You've joined the jet set, have you?'

'Yeah, and I used the money Mum left me. You didn't know about that, did you? And it's almost all gone.'

'Well good for you, Linda.'

Then I slam the phone down again, while Jon puts 'The Lord's Prayer' on the record player.

CHAPTER TWENTY-FIVE

I get a long-distance call from Australia on Saturday afternoon, and it's Penny, drunk, ringing from a phone box in somewhere called Toukley.

'I've just seen the best band in Australia and you have to come and see them!' she shrieks. Then she remembers something. 'Oh my God, Linda, what time is it there?'

'About three o'clock in the afternoon.'

'Oh. Anyway, they're called INXS and I am totally in love with them!' she squeals.

I try to picture Penny, in her big woollen granny coat and her pointy shoes, standing in a phone box in the middle of some Australian country town, underneath the black night sky.

'Have you heard from Evan?' I ask her as my voice echoes thousands of miles away.

'Nuh,' she says, and I realize she's annoyed that I have changed the subject to her brother.

'I've been meaning to send you something in the post, to say thank you for having me,' I try to explain.

'Can't you just send you?' Penny slurs. And I wonder how many cans of nutty-tasting Tooheys she's had.

The beeps start, and I laugh my way out of the conversation, send her my love and put the phone down, then stare at the wall. Staring at the wall is something I've become really good at lately.

Of course the time after a holiday is always the worst, and that's no doubt why I feel this bad. I've spent all of Mum's money, and I'll probably never get back to Australia again this century, or New York for that matter. The next time I see Penny, she'll probably be sixty-five years old.

The next day I get the tube to Brixton and walk down to Brockwell Park to see Stiff Little Fingers play an afternoon gig. I'm not here to write about them, I just want to see them.

Couples are wandering along, holding hands, like zoo animals let loose from Noah's Ark. When I find myself thinking that, I feel ashamed. For all the years I was part of a couple, I don't think I ever realized how that would make single people around me feel. And now I know – it makes you feel cynical. And there, I've admitted it. I'm single. By myself. Totally alone in the world.

Hardly anybody writes songs about being by yourself, except Gilbert O'Sullivan, and you can't count him. If you like music – sorry, if you're totally obsessed with music – then you're doomed to a lifetime of subtle brainwashing, hearing stuff about holding hands and meeting someone new, and falling in love again, and knowing this time it's for real, and threatening to die if anyone ever leaves you, and making love in the back row of the cinema.

Nobody's got it right. Nobody. Where are all the songs about men who can't get it up and are terrified of relationships? Where are all the songs about their lesbian twin sisters, or weird couples in New York who want to take you home to bed and eat Parmesan cheese with you? And why doesn't someone write a song about people like David and Jeannie, whose desire for each other seems to be based heavily on the fact that they both feel moral outrage against me? Maybe I should start writing lyrics myself.

Most of all, there are no songs about being single. Well, nothing that doesn't sound like a suicide note anyway. 'Alone Again Naturally', 'All By Myself'. Sod off, the lot of you.

Watching the Stiff Little Fingers fans stream towards Brockwell Park, I realize that even the ugliest of their most ugly male fans have got equally ugly girlfriends to hold their hands. For my part, I'm being followed by a stray dog without a collar, which is running along with the crowd in case someone accidentally drops a hamburger.

The Selecter are playing in Brixton today, too, so the crowd is black as well as white. And there are girls holding hands, which reminds me of Penny again.

Single isn't really the word for what I am, I think, as I squash past even more couples, of all colours, genders and sexual preferences. It's more like being an alien. It doesn't get much edgier than this, being on the very edge of the edgiest section of society. How much of an outsider can you possibly be, when you can't even fit in with the bloody fringe dwellers? Everyone is holding hands. Even the skinheads. Even the Hare Krishnas. Even the cooler-than-thou Mods.

I can see Stiff Little Fingers any time, I tell myself as beggars try to stop me walking past the front door of Woolworth's, and I decide to go home instead.

In the end, I catch the tube all the way to Victoria – Victoria Station, the mecca I ran away to, when I was a child, in the days when I wanted nothing more than to bump into The Kinks, running up the Mall in their elastic-sided boots and paisley shirts.

If I could believe that all the women accompanying the men streaming through the station were in- tensively farmed wives or battery-hen brides, I'd feel better about my life. But the truth is, there are plenty of couples wandering past the Victoria ticket office, sharing crisps and jokes and holding each other tightly, who are just madly in love. They are madly in love in the same way that David and I were, once, or maybe as David and Jeannie are now. I bet some of them have been like this for years, the lucky bastards. And I wonder how that would feel? And I wonder if it will ever happen to me again.

I could get the tube to Charing Cross and change for Kentish Town, but instead I decide to walk home to the flat. Ever since I was a kid, walking's got things out of my system.

'It's spitting,' a man in a raincoat says to his wife, in the archway outside the tube station.

And it really is, too, like a kind of a heavenly gobbing session, meant for human heads – particularly mine. I used to have a daft plastic pixie hood when I was a kid. My mother always used to make me carry it in my pocket so I could whip it out and stick it on my head in emergencies.

I wish I had my pixie hood now. And I wish I had my mother. But instead it just keeps on spitting, all the way from Kentish Town Station to my flat, where I pick up the phone an hour later, and hear from David that he's been made redundant by the bank, and he's walked out on Jeannie.

CHAPTER TWENTY-SIX

Without thinking too much about it, I offer to get the train down to Brighton and meet David in a pub near the station. He sounds in shock.

'I'll stay at Dad's or something,' I tell him.

'Well that'll be fun for you both.'

'It's an emergency, isn't it? Strange things happen in emergencies.'

'Well, thank you for seeing my life as an emergency.'

'I'm not joking, David. I'm worried about you.'

'No, it's OK.' He sounds grateful. 'I'm glad you're offering. I mean, I'm glad you're coming down. But do me a favour, don't stay with your dad. Just stay on my sofa.'

'Don't be daft. Maybe I won't need to stay anywhere. I'll just get the train back tonight. I don't have to be at work until ten, maybe half past ten.'

A pause. I can tell this intensely practical and boring conversation about trains and sofas is helping to calm David down.

'Thanks Linda,' he says.

'That's all right.'

'I'm sorry,' he says.

'Don't worry. I'll just be on the train. I'll see you in the pub near Brighton station at about seven, all right?'

On the train journey down, I'm almost alone in the

carriage, so I have time and space to think as the train rattles past Haywards Heath and rain starts to fall in fits and starts – it will pour down later, I can tell.

A bunch of skinheads push their way into my carriage, pissed, leaving the door hanging open and singing some football chant. I look the other way. There are so many NF idiots around these days, it's getting scary.

'Got a light, love?' one of them asks me. He looks about sixteen. I have, but I shake my head. He stares at me for a minute, and then he and his mates boot open the door to the next compartment.

With any luck, I won't have to see them again until we reach Brighton. And then I'll leg it to the pub, just in case they decide to follow me.

When we finally arrive at the station, though, the skinheads have vanished, and I walk to the pub alone, crossing the road against the lights and pulling my coat tighter across my chest as the wind screams around the corner. When the rain finally breaks, it's probably going to flood the streets.

Inside, I find David stuck at the back, next to the window, in a little cubicle where we used to drink together during the summer. He always used to say that seat was better for people-watching, although there are no people in here on a wet, cold Sunday night.

Another memory comes, unbidden, into my head. David buying me beer after beer in here, one miserable night when the Chinese restaurant had forgotten my wages, and I was down to my last 20p and half a cheese sandwich in the fridge. He let me cry inside his coat, because everything in my life was so shit, and then I fell asleep on his shoulder until the bell clanged for closing time.

'Linda,' David brings me back to the present.

'Well I said I'd come,' I say stupidly, 'so here I am.'

Silence.

Then we both race each other to offer to buy the drinks.

'I'll get them,' I insist, but he stops me as I get up.

'Don't buy me a drink, everyone's been buying me a drink. I'm not a bloody charity case just because I've been laid off.'

'Well all right then.'

'On the dole for a couple of weeks, and I've already got my brother behaving as if I'm on the poverty line.' David's brother has often been a thorn in his side. 'He's kept his job, of course.'

'How come?'

David's talking a lot, I notice. It's as if he hasn't talked to anyone at all for the last few days.

'He works in a different branch of the bank,' he tells me, 'so he survived. But I dunno, maybe they just kept him on because he's better than me.' He sighs, and stares out of the window. 'They laid five people off on the Friday, and there was no warning, no nothing. They said they were sorry to have to let me go. Can you bloody believe it, after all I've done for them?' He gives me a look, and I realize that for almost the first time in his life he looks desperate.

I go to get the drinks whilst he's distracted.

When I come back, I can see the strain on his face, even in the dim yellow light of the pub.

'You've had a shock,' I say, although suddenly the shock feels like it's all mine.

'I can't believe you've come all the way down here, Linda,' he says, and he reaches for my hand.

That's a shock, too, like a few volts of electricity going through me, but I can't pull myself away. I can't do it to him. And for once I feel I have to put him first.

'What about Jeannie?' I say at last.

'I didn't love her. I worked it all out one day, going for a walk on the beach. I didn't love her. I'll never love her. And I've had enough of faking it in my life. I thought I should just get out.'

Instantly I wonder if he means he was faking it with me too, and instantly it hurts. Even now, after all these months, and a trip to the other side of the world, it still hurts.

David drinks his beer in long gulps while I sit on my glass of Scotch. I usually get drunk faster than him, but I can't afford to tonight.

'I didn't mean with you, of course,' he says out of the blue.

'Didn't mean me with what?'

'I never faked it with you. I loved you.'

One of the great things about being with someone for years is that they can read your mind. I'd almost forgotten the luxury of having magically synchronized conversations with David. And then I do it to him. Immediately, I think about his way of showing me how much he loved me – which was to try and buy us a marital home in Withingdean – and seconds later, he's talking about real estate.

'The thing that really hurts about the bank getting rid of me is the house I saw,' he explains. 'I found this beautiful big place down near the seafront at Saltdean; it would have been a walk to the beach in summer, and it had been passed on at auction, then knocked down again, so it was anybody's really.'

'Oh God,' I say. 'Another dream house. David, you're going to make me feel guilty again.'

'No,' he looks at me wide-eyed. 'No, I don't mean to make you feel guilty. Nothing like that.'

'Well I'm sorry anyway,' I say. 'About that house, and about the other house too. The one I shafted you on.'

He shakes his head then, and looks down at his drink. 'That old lady died in the end, did anyone tell you?'

'No.'

'At least she got a bit of money before she went.

262

Thanks to you. More money that if I'd beaten her down on the price. So you were right, in a way. Or at least God was on your side.'

'But about this other house you saw,' I prompt him. Then I wish I hadn't. It's horrible to watch someone's face when they're telling you about their dreams going down the toilet.

'I had the deposit, and I was all ready to buy it. Jeannie thought it was a great idea.'

I nod and try not to flinch at the mention of her name.

'And the bank wouldn't talk to me about it, though I kept pestering them. It was always just whispers, whenever I'd come round the corner. Now I know why. Nobody's going to sell you a house when you're collecting your dole cheque.'

I look at him for a minute. 'Did Jeannie want the house more than you? Was that part of it?'

He nods. 'She didn't love me, she just loved the things about me. And that's when I realized we were playing snap. I was as guilty as she was. I loved the fact that she was in the Labour Party, I loved the fact that she had a decent salary and a nice car; she loved the fact that I had a decent salary, she loved the fact that I could buy myself a house – beyond that, there was nothing.'

'And you both loved the fact that you could gang up against me, I'll bet,' I add.

David looks at an invisible spot on the wall.

'What does she do again?' I ask.

'She works on the council,' David says.

I take another gulp of Scotch and then think about what losing his job at the bank has done to David's life, and then I think about all the other men who are losing their pay packets, and their pensions, and their dignity, and their dreams. Suddenly the skinheads on the train flash into my mind.

'It's getting nastier out there, isn't it, David.'

'What do you mean, nastier?'

'Just around us. People seem harder than they did before.'

'Thatcher. It's the Up Yours government isn't it. Up Yours if you've lost your job, or if you can't get welfare any more. Here's a sleeping bag, here's a nice spot in the doorway at WH Smith's. Now get on with it.'

'I don't think that's it. I mean, you would say that, but I don't think that's the only reason.'

'Well, what then?'

'I don't know. It's just that people in Australia seem so much happier.'

'It's the weather.'

I shrug. 'I've noticed it's more vicious here now, that's all. I never noticed it before. It doesn't seem like England any more.'

The pub door opens and two women push their way in out of the cold, laughing and talking at full speed.

'That was another little dream I had, which I never told you about,' David says.

'What?'

'Australia. There are so many opportunities over there. I've seen some good jobs in *The Times* going in Australia. And in Canada as well. Even for a cretin like me.'

'You're not a cretin, David. Shut up. The bank gave you a good reference, didn't they?'

He shrugs.

'They're economizing!' I go on, trying to shake him out of it. 'They made you redundant because they couldn't afford the staff. It's happening all over England. Everywhere's closing down. God, I'll probably lose my job next and end up back at the Chinese restaurant.'

I finish my Scotch then, in one gulp, and David goes to the bar to get me another – his beer went ages ago.

'The relationship with Jeannie was weird,' he says at last, when we're facing one another again, across the table. In the background, one of the noisy, giggling women puts a disco record on the jukebox.

'I don't want to know about Jeannie,' I tell him.

'Well what about yours then?'

'What, Evan?'

David makes a face. 'He has to have a poncy name doesn't he. Bloody wanker.'

'He's not poncy at all. And he's not a wanker. He's an Australian experimental photographer.'

There's a pause, and then we both laugh.

We sit and drink in silence for a while.

'I still can't believe you chucked your bloody engagement ring out of the window,' David says eventually.

I ignore him.

David makes a face, and knocks back more beer.

'I think breaking up with me was good for you. And I think breaking up with Jeannie's been good for you too,' I say jokily, trying to keep the distance between us across the table. It's shrinking at the moment, as he leans in closer towards me, and that's not something I want to let happen tonight.

'How can she have been good for me?' David asks.

'You need to change. You never change, you're always fighting it, digging your heels in. Even if it takes two mad women in a row to get you out of your rut, then that's got to be a good thing. Doesn't it?'

'Mad women,' he smiles. 'You've got it in one.'

'And I'll tell you something else. Since I've been by myself, I've been getting madder.'

He shrugs. 'Doesn't matter, I still love you.'

And there it is. He's said it again. And annoyingly, I can feel tears starting in my eyes.

'You can't say that,' I tell him. 'That's well out of order.'

265

'Well I just said it.'

On the jukebox the disco record has finished and Bob Marley has taken over.

'We had lightning over Withingdean one night,' David tells me. 'It was raining worse than this, and I was lying in bed watching the storm coming in, and I just *realized*. I realized, and I even had Jeannie in bed with me at the time. And I surprised myself, if you must know.'

'So when was this storm? When did you realize?' I ask.

'Back in June. And it was that Police song as well; it was driving me mad, I couldn't get it out of my head.'

'"Can't Stand Losing You".'

'Yeah, that. It kept reminding me of you.'

'But you hate The Police. And besides, *you left me*, you tosser.'

He smiles.

'And what other rules have you broken in your life, then, apart from suddenly liking The Police?' I ask him.

'I don't have Cornflakes for breakfast every bloody morning.'

I gasp, and laugh at myself. 'Neither do I, David.'

'See, we're the same,' he jokes back.

He lights a cigarette and offers me one. 'If we'd never got engaged, Linda, we'd still be all right, just the way we were.'

'Oh don't start.'

'No, I've been thinking about it. Give me the benefit of the doubt.'

More people come into the pub, pouring off another London train. The skinheads aren't with them, luckily, but a stray terrier is, and the barman waves him in. It's autumn outside, but it already feels like winter.

'Come here, pooch,' David calls the dog over and says he's going to the bar to buy him some crisps. He's always been mad about dogs. I'd forgotten that.

When he comes back, the terrier has jumped up on his seat, and David plonks him on his lap. The dog has got a funny face, as if someone's come along and covered him in soot.

'Good boy.'

The terrier wolfs down the crisps and then looks for more, so David goes back to the bar again, while I stare out of the window, wondering if I should run to a phone box and call Dad before the rain gets too heavy. I can tell we're going to be here until closing time. And I can tell, the way this is going, that David will offer me the sofa at Jeff's place, and that's the last place I should be sleeping tonight.

'Come and stay at ours tonight,' David says quickly when he returns with more crisps, and thunder booms across Brighton. 'Your dad will hate it if you ring up now, out of the blue.'

'No, he'll be OK.'

'Linda!' He gives me a warning look.

'Best not stay with you,' I tell him. 'Not after this conversation.'

'Come on. You've come all this way.'

'No, I'll give Dad a ring.'

'Do it for me then?'

Something in his voice makes me look properly at him, and I realize how tired he looks, and how sad.

'I've been knocked back for a few jobs since they laid me off,' he says. 'So I was wondering if you could help me a bit. You're the genius with the job applications, after all.'

I give him a look.

'You can have my bed, I'll take the couch,' he adds.

'No,' I stop him, 'I'll have the couch, and you have your bed. And is that dog coming as well?'

The dog jumps down on the floor and looks at both of us, like Greyfriars Bobby doing relationship guidance counselling.

'The only reason I got the job with *NWW* was because they wanted someone they wouldn't have to pay much,' I tell him. 'So don't think I'm some genius with job applications.' But part of me wants to hear his praise as well. There hasn't been a lot of it around in my life lately.

'As soon as I heard you come back to bed that night, I knew you'd thrown your application in the bin,' he says, drawing patterns on the table with his fingers.

'Did you?'

Outside, the rain pours down, and the thunder rolls on.

'I know you so well, Linda,' he says. 'That's the problem.'

'Yeah, well that's *my* problem too.'

I drink more of the Scotch he's put on the table, and clink the ice around in my mouth. The taste of it reminds me of summer, although summer's dead and buried now.

'It was brilliant, what you wrote,' he says. 'That's why they hired you.'

'They hired me to write the crosswords.'

'I read it every fortnight it comes out. It's good that you can get it down here now. I used to get it from the newsagent next to the chippie. It used to drive Jeannie mad.'

I snort with laughter, despite myself. 'I interviewed Clare Grogan from Altered Images,' I say.

'I know. It was funny. Much better than anything else in there.'

'Well, she made it funny.'

'Kiss me,' David says suddenly.

In my head I do a beer count, and realize he's put three away by now, probably more if he'd been drinking before I turned up. I half smile at him and then turn my head away, so I can bend down to pat the dog.

'I'm going to adopt that dog,' David says.

'You should.'

'I'm going to adopt him as an act of faith. He's my guarantee I'm going to get another job.'

'You'll be OK.'

But right now he looks scared, and tired.

'I'm not like you, Linda, I can't just make up my life as I go along. I'm fucked, if you must know.'

David picks the dog up, swinging him in the air, and says he's going to get another round.

'No more for me,' I say.

'Boring. You never used to be like that. Come on, drink with me.'

I look at his face and give in.

Annoyingly, I realize, I also fancy him. *Again*. But then I'm drunk, and we've been apart, and that's exactly what's happened every other time we've fought and got back together again. I take a deep breath. I'm not giving in. Not again. Not this time.

'You can live on that house deposit you saved up,' I tell him when he comes back. 'Being unemployed isn't the end of the world.'

'Yeah, but doing that would be the end of a *dream*. My parents always said, if you can get yourself a house, you can get yourself freedom. And you can get your children freedom as well. And their children. How else do you think it works in this country?'

I can see his parents in my mind's eye. His mother, who sits in a chair all day coughing in front of the TV; and his father, who gets old jigsaw puzzles from jumble sales and puts them together on the kitchen table.

'Nobody in my family has ever owned anything,' he says. 'Never.'

I nod.

'When I have kids, I want it to be different for them. I'm fed up. I've had enough. It's the only way me and my kind are ever going to escape the system, if you must know.'

I nod again.

'Sorry. Labour Party bullshit,' he slurs before he knocks back his beer again.

I get up to put some songs on the jukebox.

'Oh my God, someone get her off the jukebox!' David yells across the pub, and the other customers stare.

I smirk, and see my smiling reflection in the glass. Ever since David's known me, I've been going into pubs, marching over to the jukebox and taking over the programming because nobody else in the place has a clue about music. And for six years David has been yelling at me every time I do it.

It's a couple thing, I suppose. A stupid couple thing. And I like it, I realize. I miss it. It's the Scotch talking, of course, but I want it back now.

Predictably, the pub has crap music, so in the end I struggle with the best of a bad bunch and come up with old Motown stuff and 'Bohemian Rhapsody'.

'My favourite,' David says, throwing more crisps to the dog. 'Thank you, Linda. You're a martyr. I know you hate it.'

'I don't hate it. That's the thing, David, you never remember what music I like or don't like. You're always getting it wrong. You think because Queen are a bit like Emerson, Lake and Palmer that I must hate them, but I don't, because Emerson, Lake and Palmer are Emerson, Lake and Palmer, and Queen are Queen.'

'Sure you're not pissed yet?' David asks.

I smile at him.

He pats the dog for a while, and then he blows his nose. 'Two things,' he says. 'First, I'm getting a cold, so we need to go home. Second, it feels like we're still a couple. Am I imagining it, or am I right?'

'You're imagining it,' I tell him. He's not getting away with it that easily.

'OK, it's my little hallucination then,' he says. 'But how does it feel to you now? Good? Or not good?

Because if it's not good, then I'll shut up and crawl into a hole, with this dog. But if it's good – well . . .'

I think about it. I think about fleeing back home, before the Stiff Little Fingers concert, and I think of the photos of all the women in Evan's shoebox, and I think about all the rest of it.

'It's good, David. You're right, it's good. I'll give you that much. Even if you are hallucinating.'

We stay sitting there, talking rubbish about the TV for a while, until the bell starts clanging for closing time, and the dog starts looking for a table leg to wee against.

'Come on then,' David says, holding my coat out for me. I stand on tiptoe to get myself into it, just as I always have, and he pulls the arms on too roughly, just as he always does.

I give him a shove then, and we're out of the door, in the rain, with the dog in David's arms.

'Harry Kakoulli is out of Squeeze,' I say, thinking about stories I'll have to write for the paper tomorrow.

'Poor old Harry,' David says.

'You don't know who the hell I'm talking about, do you?' I ask him.

He shakes his head and smiles. Then suddenly, for no apparent reason, he drunkenly kisses the dog on the head.

'You can be called Harry if you like,' he tells it. 'I think that's a good name for you. And', he adds, 'I think I'll call myself Harry as well. We can both be Harry this year.'

I laugh, despite myself, and walk ahead of David and the dog, with my hands in my pockets, all the way to the bus stop.

CHAPTER TWENTY-SEVEN

Blondie have a new song out called 'Dreaming' and I'm happily addicted. Jon hates it, and I love it, so it's agreed that I can take the new Blondie album home to review, and in return he'll get the new Stranglers album with the 3D picture of a raven on the front.

He and I seem to have called a truce these days, so that even though he still gets to review most of the great records – unless he develops some strange antipathy to them – when he's finished with them, he gives them to me, so I can take them home and tape them. This has upped my music collection by about 400 per cent, with the result being that I can go straight home from work, switch the radio on and blot out most of the hours from 6 p.m. until midnight with nothing but music.

And that's how I spend the next two weeks, curled up with Wire and The Selecter, Joe Jackson and The Police, and The Buzzcocks and The Undertones.

There are two other songs I can't stop obsessing over. 'The Bed's Too Big Without You', and 'You've Got My Number (Why Don't You Use It)'. I go to bed singing them in my head, and when I wake up the next morning, they're what I'm humming when I put the kettle on.

David hasn't rung at all since the night I spent on the

couch at his place. I thought he might, the following day, but then, as Annie reminds me, he's a man. They never ring. Especially after they scare themselves by getting too close. And even when they do, I might add, they never stay on the phone for bloody long enough.

After this, though, Evan calls me at home on Saturday morning and blows that theory to pieces. By the time we've stopped talking, we've been on the line for over an hour.

'The Lambrettas are on at the Marquee tonight, if you fancy coming,' he says towards the end.

'I'm going out,' I lie.

'Well that's a shame,' he says.

'Yeah, I'm going out to the cinema,' I say.

'Who with?'

'Um. Annie.'

'What are you seeing?' he persists.

'Um . . .' I can't think of anything, I'm a hopeless liar, but he lets it go.

Evan says that Penny's going to send him a copy of the new Mental As Anything album when it comes out, and I ask to borrow it so I can make a tape.

'Even if we didn't have music in common we'd still be friends,' Evan says apropos of nothing.

'Friends. I love the way men call it friends,' I reply.

'What does that mean?'

'You're all such cowards. You act like you love us in bed, and then suddenly it's like we're your mates down the pub, or something. It's just labels, Evan. Stop running away from yourself.'

'Well that's not very *friendly*,' Evan says, then he stops, almost as if he's trying to tune into my thoughts.

'What?' I demand.

'You poor girl,' he says, which is the last thing I expect to hear.

'Why am I a poor girl?'

'You're crying inside, I can tell. Do you want your old boyfriend back?'

'Oh sod off, Evan.'

He laughs. 'OK then, lovely Linda, I'll sod off. But if you change your mind about The Lambrettas, you know the number.'

'Yeah, well thanks,' I say, gracelessly.

'Think about it,' he finishes.

As I put the phone down, I remember another piece of legendary advice from Hazel. 'You can't fall out of love with one of them until you fall in love with another one to replace the first one.'

She's right, of course, and the fact is, now that Evan is on the way out, David is on the way in. I didn't plan it that way, it's just how it's panned out.

'I can't believe it,' Hazel says when I ring her.

'I know,' I tell her. 'He's a pretty irresistible choice, isn't he? First he dumped me, then he fancied you, then he went off with some weirdo without a bra, and now he's lost his job and he's back sponging off his mum and dad, who are living on the poverty line. You can see my logic, can't you?'

She laughs.

'I'm going to give it until Christmas,' I tell her. 'To be sure. I can't make any more mistakes.'

'Well that's a good idea,' she says.

'I'm going to be sensible about my love life for a change. No more heart. It's going to be head from now on.'

'Yeah, right,' she jokes.

'And how is it with you and Eric?' I ask.

'Oh, we're still planning our trip to Bath,' she says. 'But there's a married man down the bingo who fancies me, so it's not all bad news.'

When I put the phone down, I sit and think for a while. There is something in me that wants to find out more about love, to take it one step further. David called me a martyr the other night, but it's not playing old Queen singles that turns you into a saint, it's the capacity to love somebody else more than you love yourself, no matter what they've done, or who they've done it with, or how much of a mess they've left behind. All my life I've needed David, often without realizing it. Now, for the first time, he seems to need me. So it's my turn. A few minutes later I call his number.

When I ring, though, it's Jeff who answers, and he tells me that he's thrown him out.

'I gave him twenty quid for my share of the gas bill. A bloke turned up the other day to cut the gas off. When I asked David about my twenty quid, he said he'd spent it.'

'Oh shit.' That is most un-David-like behaviour.

'I know he's lost his job, but enough is enough. He had got that dog in here all the time as well. I had to give him the boot.'

'So did he leave a number?' I ask. Jeff sounds – as Penny would say – ropeable.

'Dunno,' he says. 'Try his mum and dad. I can't think of anywhere else he would have gone.'

When I ring, though, the phone's been disconnected. That happens from time to time, with his parents. I suppose they get to the end of their pension and start working out what has to go first. More often than not, it's the telephone.

I am at home on Thursday night, listening to Orchestral Manoeuvres In The Dark playing 'Electricity', when two things happen at once. First of all, the lights fuse. And secondly, David bashes on my front door, calling out my name.

'Hang on,' I yell. 'It's a power cut.'

He waits while I fumble around in the dark, looking for one of my pink candles.

'You always said these were a waste of money,' I say,

275

taking matches from him to light them, 'but now look.'

At that moment, though, the lights come back on again, and the tape player jumps into life, making both of us jump. Then Harry the dog runs in and leaps straight onto my pink eiderdown.

'It looks great,' David says, looking around the flat.

'You can't be serious.'

'No really, I love the way you've painted it all pink,' he says.

He looks grim, I think. Paler, and thinner, and just . . . grim. Longer hair, longer face. And yet I still want him. *I want him, I want him, I want him.* And I'm stone cold sober, not like last time. I suppose he must have got the train down tonight, just to see me.

David smiles and closes his eyes as he flops onto the bed. He looks exhausted.

'I've been staying at Mum and Dad's,' he says, 'but they've had the phone cut off again. And no bloody phone box around there works. And when you do find one that does, there's always a queue. So that's why you've not heard from me. Any time I've managed to call you at work, you've always been engaged, or that Jon Whitten wanker tells me to call back later.'

Silently I curse Jon for not passing on any messages.

'Jeff said you owed him money,' I say.

'I paid him back. The bank finally gave me my redundancy cheque on Tuesday. And all my savings as well. I'm taking it to Barclays instead; the bank can shove it up their arse.'

'So you're quids in then?'

'I am. And I'm not going to touch a penny either. Because of that song.'

'What song?'

'That "Dreaming" song.'

Our eyes meet, and something clicks inside me.

'I've been playing it all week, David.'

'I knew you would be. So have I.'

'So what's this all about then?' I say.

'I'm not giving up my dream. I want to have a house, and I want us to live in it. I'm not giving up, Linda, I'm not.' He looks at me. 'And you can paint it pink, and if you bugger off to Australia, I'll just stay at home and talk to Harry. And we're not getting engaged again, I've thought about it.'

'Hang on. You've thought about us *not* getting engaged again?'

'Yes. That's the key, you see. Not getting engaged. But I do know what will work, and that's us being together.'

'So you've worked it all out then,' I say.

'I've done a lot of walking on the Downs, and a lot of thinking,' he says. Then he notices my feet and laughs. 'Pink socks as well,' he observes. 'God almighty. You've got a pink flat, and pink socks.'

He walks over to me, bends down and takes one sock off, so he can kiss the top of my foot. 'And pink nail polish too,' he says.

David pulls the other sock off.

'My life has gone wrong without you,' he says.

I cuddle into his side, against the wall, with the dog between us.

'But even so, I know I'll never be safe and sound with you,' he adds.

'Why's that?'

'I just feel it in my bones. Life with you will always be like going round on a big dipper.'

'Being sick and screaming.'

He laughs.

'You're like that experiment at the Science Museum, Linda. The one where you stick your finger in a slot and you get an electric shock. The trouble is, you never know when the next shock's going to be.'

'But you keep sticking your finger in anyway,' I say.

He looks around the flat. 'It must be hard living here, even if it is pink.'

'I hate it.'

'There are so many opportunities in Australia, Linda. I mean, you must have seen it when you were out there.'

'The girl I stayed with had her own place. And her own hairdressing salon.'

'Who was she then?' he asks.

'She kissed me goodbye at the airport. You never know, David, she might have been my first lesbian affair,' I say, and then realize I've done the equivalent of giving his finger another electric shock at the Science Museum.

'I'd like us to be more honest next time round,' he says after a moment. 'Even with things like that. I mean, I'm glad you told me about that.'

'So you've got it all worked out, have you?' I reply. 'We're definitely getting back together in a nonengaged way?'

'I want to tell you the truth,' he sighs. 'Why cover it up? I think we should try again. I still love you. You're the one-off limited edition single, Linda. Everyone else looks boring. Or they all look the same.'

'Do they?'

'Come on, you want someone to dream about,' he says, 'don't you? Well give it a go. Try dreaming about me. Gloss over the rough bits, and just try dreaming, for God's sake.'

I remember a photo of him which I had stuck in my wallet for ages. It was taken when the sun was shining in his eyes, and sunlight flared around the edge of the photograph; he looked half real, like some prince in a fairy tale. I loved that photo, when we were first going out.

We get into bed after that and I feel myself giving in.

'It's like being thrown in the deep end,' I say afterwards when he's lighting a cigarette.

'What do you mean?'

'It's like someone's thrown me in the deep end of a swimming pool and I'm drowning, but I'm enjoying it as well. You know those stories about sailors who get high when they start to lose their oxygen?'

David gives me a look. 'Shut up, will you, Linda?'

The I fall asleep in his arms.

When we wake up the next morning, I can hear him splashing around in the sink. I get out of bed, with Harry following, and find him with his head submerged in a basin full of water.

'You can see tropical fish in there if you look hard enough,' I say.

David pulls his head out and gropes for a towel, blindly. 'I'm going to find a job today,' he says. 'I've washed my hair, and I've had a shave, and I'm going to find a job.'

'And what then?'

'I'm going to get you out of here and get us somewhere nice. Or leave you here, but get me into somewhere nice, and then you can visit. I'm not staying with my parents any more. It was bloody lucky they had the room, but enough is enough.'

'Well,' I say, hearing the words fall out of my mouth, 'stay here if you like. In the meantime. Stay with me until you get the job.'

He kisses me.

I light a cigarette and change the subject. 'There's this band called Wire I've got to write a story on.'

'Sounds interesting.'

'It's funny, I wake up and think of going to work and I still get excited,' I say. I can tell he's never heard of Wire, but I need to get him used to the way my life is now. Because if we're going to start dreaming together, he's got to begin with my new life.

'What else is on at work today then?' he asks.

'Oh, I'm going to do a story on those suits Joe Jackson is wearing. Not that I know sod all about fashion, but I've got to write the stuff so Howard can flog his T-shirt ads on the opposite page.'

David nods.

'And Jon keeps tempting me by saying I can interview The Buzzcocks if I promise to update the gig guide for him, so maybe that'll happen.'

'You love them, don't you.'

I smile. Then I brush my teeth and gargle with tap water, as I always do.

'One of the stupid things I thought about when I wondered if we could get back together was you brushing your teeth,' David says.

'How's that?'

'Well, you always used to moan at me for squeezing the toothpaste up the top,' he says. 'So I thought, when we're back together again I'll get two tubes of toothpaste, to fix the problem. And then we could be happy.'

I laugh.

'I just want to show you how bad things got for me,' he says seriously.

And this, more than anything else, makes me feel sufficiently sorry for him to forgive the fact that he's just marched back into my life and taken over again.

It's not that easy, you see. If you want to get to the love part – maybe the real love part – then it has to hurt to get there. It would be wonderful if I could wrap my life up like a story in the paper, and say that once upon a time David hurt me, and then I hurt him, but now everything's fine. Real life's never like that, though, is it.

He can say he's wished Jeannie on her way, but in my imagination I still see them together, with an intimacy that David and I never achieved. And we never even mention his secret crush on Hazel. But I can't forget about it, all the same.

'Stop thinking so much,' David says when he catches me staring at the wall.

'Put some electrodes on my head and wipe it all out then,' I tell him, 'because it's the only thing that's going to work.'

Then I take the last of his cigarettes and put the kettle on.

CHAPTER TWENTY-EIGHT

When I get home after work on Wednesday night, I fall asleep immediately because I'm so tired, then at about midnight I'm woken up by David cooking some horrible stew on the stove, with the windows closed.

'Sorry,' he says when I sit up in bed and peer at him with angry, half-shut eyes.

'What are you doing?'

'I'm hungry. Sorry.'

'Oh for God's sake.'

I try to go back to sleep, but I can't, so I get up and open all the windows.

'What are you doing?' he protests. 'It's freezing.'

'I need some fresh air,' I tell him.

Then he follows me round and shuts all the windows again. Suddenly I feel trapped.

I try to imagine what it must be like to be David at the moment, moving in here, being unemployed and surviving on a dream. And I try very hard to imagine what it must be like to be David, at nearly midnight, suddenly starving and feeling like a can of stew.

'I'm not much good at this,' I say eventually.

'What?' he asks, looking worried.

'This new phase in our relationship. I think I might be a bit too selfish.'

'It's just this place,' he says. 'It's too small for us. It'll be better when we move out and get our own place, won't it?'

'But you'll be paying for it all again. Because God knows I haven't got any money. And that means you'll be in control again.'

He gives me a look. 'You make me sound like your enemy, Linda. I'm not your enemy. I love you.'

'You've decided we're never going to get engaged again, so bingo, we're not.'

He shakes his head.

'Did you ever think about asking me?' I protest.

'Yeah, but you agree with me, don't you?'

'Don't assume, David. It's dangerous,' I warn him. I go to the window, open it and breathe out. I feel suffocated.

He puts his food down and comes over.

'No, get away,' I say. 'You smell of stew. You honestly do.'

'Sorry,' he says again.

'And stop saying frigging sorry. God. I've got to go to work tomorrow.'

And I do, the next day, after a rotten night of dreams about Evan, where I'm back in the cinnamon bath with him. Worse still, Evan comes in at lunchtime with a batch of photos of The Buzzcocks.

'I got these in Manchester the other night,' he tells Howard. 'Fancy a drink, Linda?'

I look at my desk, which is covered in press releases and half-finished crosswords that I have failed to construct. And I look at him, with his blond, spiky hair and his neat, creased pants and brown Hush Puppies. And then I think about David and the stew.

'I've got loads of work to do, sorry,' I say. And he leaves, with another cheque from Howard in his hand.

'Well done, Linda,' Howard says when he's gone. He is eating Gentleman's Relish from Fortnum & Mason, spreading it on crackers he keeps in a drawer. His dog loves the stuff, so it seems to be getting half of the crackers.

'I have done well, haven't I?' I confide in him. 'I've mastered the art of Evan management. I must be the only female music writer in London who's done it.'

'And how is it going with David returned from the wilderness?' Howard asks.

'Oh, I forgot I told you that. It's good, actually. Really good.'

'And he still doesn't have a job?'

'No, but he'll get one. I'm pretty sure. Yeah, I think he'll get one.'

Howard doesn't look convinced. Then he eats another cracker, and I wonder what he's thinking about – although with him, it could be anything from hammocks, to bidets to Terminal Sausage. Jon calls him the most inscrutable Englishman never to have visited the Orient. Maybe that's why the Sony Walkman people in Japan are always on the phone to him.

Later on, Jon gives me his copy of the new Joe Jackson album to tape.

'Seeing as you're the resident feminist, I thought you might like it,' he says.

I don't understand what he means until I get it home and play it to David. There's a single on it called 'Different For Girls.'

'I don't get it,' David says at last, when I've taken the needle off the turntable.

'What don't you get?'

'Does he mean men are only after one thing, and they're all the same, or women are only after one thing, and they're all the same?'

'Don't you like it?' I ask him. 'I love it.'

He makes a face. It's a face I'm beginning to recognize, because he's invented it for those situations when I play him records from work and he doesn't like

284

them but he thinks he should because it's an all-new relationship now.

'Don't make that face.'

'What face?'

And then we both go to bed, because there's nowhere else in this place to have sex. It's not like French films where people dart into the kitchen, or dangle from chandeliers, or try it in the stables, or experiment in the attic. There is only one place in this pink shoebox to do it, and it's the most obvious one. No other possibilities exist, because David's head would be wedged against the sharp corner of a plaster wall, or my feet would be hitting the plumbing under the sink.

'I've been thinking about you all day,' David says.

'Have you really?'

'It's like bolts from the blue – I go off for a job interview and you come into my head. I wait for a bus and you come into my head.'

'So did you go for an interview today then?'

'Miles away. In Croydon.'

'A bank in Croydon?'

'An insurance office in Croydon.'

'Bloody hell.'

He sits up. 'I've got a confession to make, Linda.'

'Oh no.'

'I was studying philosophy, after you left. I did it part time.'

'Did you?'

'There was an evening course at the college, and I thought sod it, I've always been curious. So I signed up.'

'Trying to pick up chicks.' I try to make a joke of it.

'Trying to make a difference to my days.'

'And did it have anything to do with sex?'

'Why?'

'It's so different with you now. It's like being in bed

with – I dunno. Some sort of professor. I mean, I'm not complaining.'

'Is it better?' he asks after a long silence.

'Much better. Oh God, I wish I hadn't started talking about this.'

'No, go on.'

'It's like you're more serious about everything somehow. Like you're working at it. You never used to be like that.'

'And you're thinking, Jeannie did that, and you hate it,' he says.

'No I'm not,' I lie.

'Well, she didn't,' he says, at last. 'Not strictly speaking. It's not like I met her, and she taught me new tricks.'

'I think I'm going to be sick,' I protest.

'No, we've got to talk about it, Linda. It's important. But what I'm trying to say is, I do want to take it more seriously with you now. I can see how intense you are about other things.'

'What, like music?'

'Yes, like music, and your job at *NWW*, and I think, why should sex be any different for you? To be honest, I feel like I've got to compete – you light up when you put a record on, and I need to be able to light you up as well.'

There's a pause then, and I snort with laughter.

'God, I sound like a tosser,' he sighs.

'You are a tosser.'

Then we do it again, but this time it's a case of once more with feeling.

'They had showers as well as baths when I was in Australia,' I say, much, much later.

'Meaning?'

'If we ever get any money, I'd like a shower. I think it would be nice to have a shower together.'

'You haven't watched *Psycho* lately, have you?'

I laugh. 'I'm just saying, you're working on the sex and music, I'm prepared to work on the house idea,' I say.

'You can get as far as the shower part then?'

'Yeah, I can get as far as the shower part. And I'd say that's progress, wouldn't you?'

'So if I get a job, and some money, you'll let me buy a house, on the condition it's got a shower in it?'

'Don't scare me. Just let me get as far as the bathroom first, OK?'

The days drift past after that, and so do the leaves, and then people start saying things like 'Hasn't the year gone quickly' and 'Only two months until Christmas', all of which makes me think of my dad, because David and I have always had Christmas with him, at home.

'I'll ring him,' I say when David nags me about it one day.

'You should go down and see him,' he says.

'All right, all right.'

So on Saturday, just to shut him up, I call Dad, warn him I'm coming home and make my way to Victoria Station.

As usual, the weather is better on the coast than it is in London, and the dismal grey skies that I left behind at Victoria have become magically sunny, for the moment at least, when I finally step off the train at the other end and climb on a bus. The bus driver knows me, because he works with Dad, and he greets me by name when I climb on.

'Hello Linda. Long time no see. Are you down to see your dad, then?'

When I finally arrive, the house is the same as ever – there's a copy of the *Sun* on the kitchen table, and the clock on the wall still has the minute hand snapped off. The smell of fried bacon hits me the moment I walk in the door.

'Nice to see you,' Dad says, and he puts the kettle on. Then he switches the TV on and we watch the news; we both agree that Mrs Thatcher is the most terrifying woman in England, so at least we agree on something – and then he finally says something about David.

'I hear he's moved back in with you.'

'Yeah. To save money really.'

'Oh well, give it time.'

I nod.

'He could get a job on the buses,' Dad says, 'if he gets desperate.'

'Thanks,' I say. 'I'll tell him.'

And that's it. No screaming matches. No plates of curry flying across the kitchen. No dramatic scenes, or accusations. The people who write soap operas about family life get it so wrong most of the time. It's not about blood, sweat and tears, it's about the TV always being on and nobody saying very much.

When I leave, I sense Dad breathing a sigh of relief. His duty is done, and so is mine, and nobody's conscience is guilty. Even if there is still an old Vesta Paella stain on the wall.

On the train back, I realize that there's always a rulebook. Everyone, especially your parents, and your grandparents, and even your great grandparents, *always* has a rulebook. It's like that Joe Jackson song. There are always maxims and old wives' tales about love – words of caution and words of wisdom.

When my mother was alive, she used to say lucky at cards, unlucky in love – and vice versa. Which was no help to me at all when I used to beat Hazel at Snap. My Dad thinks the solution for me and David is to give it time. Howard says, three strikes and you're out. And then there is Evan, who doesn't believe in anything at all, beyond a bath and a photograph, and the new

Stranglers album. So who are you supposed to believe?

On the way back home, I stop at Victoria and decide to go for a walk, all the way past Buckingham Palace. I suppose Prince Charles is inside there somewhere, playing his cello in the dark, and worrying about the fact that he's past thirty and not married. There are probably rules for him as well – and imagine what rules. I mean, I agree with the Pistols, it is a fascist regime in there, and it probably did make me a moron, but just imagine being *Charles*.

'It must be worse for Prince Charles,' I tell David later, when we're both watching TV in bed, and eating what he calls my very interesting baked beans on toast.

'What's Prince Charles got to do with it?' he asks.

'I had a walk past Buckingham Palace this evening, after I'd got off the train. And I was thinking about him.'

He snorts.

'You're such an anarchist, Linda. I'm frightened to be in bed with you.'

'I just feel sorry for him that's all.'

And that's a mistake, really, because although David's left the Labour Party – or at least the Jeannie branch of it – I get a nice big juicy socialist lecture for the rest of the evening.

'I'd really rather be watching that *Porridge* repeat on BBC 1,' I say, when he's finally wound down.

He looks at me.

'I've got to get a job, haven't I. I'm driving you mad.'

'Yes you do, and yes you are. Thank God you said it first,' I tell him.

'And how was your Dad?' he asks, leaving this question until last, in case it was an absolute disaster.

'Same as ever. It was fine. He said he can get you a job on the buses if you need one,' I say.

He nods, and we avoid looking at each other.

The postman comes the next day, bringing a letter from Jeannie with him. I spot it a mile off. Loopy handwriting I've never seen before, Sussex postmark, and the sort of writing paper I can imagine someone like her using. Sensible, grown-up, serious paper. Not the usual stuff with flowers all over it that Hazel uses.

'Here you are,' I say, throwing the letter at him as I get ready for work.

We've almost created a routine together now, from the ashes of our old lives. It consists of me doing mad things like cleaning my teeth while I'm putting the kettle on, to save space at the sink for him, and David lying in bed until the last possible minute, as rigid as an Egyptian mummy, to give me more room to get dressed.

'Jeannie,' he says, looking at it.

'You're getting The Post-Relationship Letter, aren't you?'

'Shut up.'

'Why can't she just ring you up?'

'And have you slam the phone down?' David counters.

'I don't care enough to slam the phone down, if you must know,' I retort, and I try not to look as he opens the envelope and sits down to read it.

'You're not going to believe this,' he says at last, folding the letter and putting it in his pocket.

'Yeah? What?'

'She's moving to London.'

'Oh well, that's her choice.' I'm being impressively cool about this, I think. Like Grace Kelly mixed with Siouxsie Sioux.

'She's been offered a job with Labour head office,' he says.

'What, with the comrades?' I try to make a joke of it. I think it's hilarious the way they write letters, addressing each other as comrades.

'She says she wants to have dinner with me,' he finishes.

'Not lunch then, dinner. That's a night-time activity.'

'Come here,' David says, and pulls me back into bed with him.

'I can't. I'm half dressed for work.'

'Yes you can. God, look at my boring day, Linda. You're the only exciting thing about it, and you're about to vanish.'

I grab the letter off the floor and scan it – I might as well get it over with, and the fact that David lets me immediately makes me realize there's nothing serious in it anyway.

'Bla bla bla, hope you're happy in your new life, bla bla bla. Oh well, that's nice,' I say.

'She's not moving to London because of me,' David says. 'So get that out of your head.'

'Of course she's not, David. She's just going to become the next prime minister, that's all. The next prime minister who also enjoys listening to reggae.'

He smiles and kisses me goodbye. And it's a proper kiss, which goes on through two songs on the radio and one set of ads.

'We're like a laboratory, aren't we?' he says when I finally pull away.

'Full of strange, bubbling things in test tubes?'

'Just one big chemistry experiment,' he explains.

'Yeah I know. If the ingredients didn't keep changing and blowing up, there'd be no chemistry at all.'

Then I kiss him again, and eventually manage to make it out the front door.

'Dalek I Love You have changed their name,' Jon says, when I land in the office after the rush hour on the tube. My days are starting later and later at Wardour Street, but nobody seems to mind. The newsagent distribution cheque came in for Howard the other week, and it was wine and Brians all

291

round at L'Escargot, so I gather he must be doing well enough not to care about small details like punctuality.

Dalek I Love You changing their name could ruin my crosswords forever. There were endless Doctor Who clues I could use for that band. And the *NWW* readers knew all of them, judging by the competition entries.

'The thing about daleks which nobody realizes,' Jon adds, 'least of all Doctor Who, is that they can't climb stairs. When exactly will one of his idiot female assistants point that out to him?'

'Yeah, well none of the idiot *male* assistants ever have either, Jon.'

Now that *NWW* has a regular following, Jon has become the target of fan mail, which is making him more arrogant than ever. He gets the same bloke in Huddersfield – an ageing ex-Punk called Nigel – sending him at least two letters a week, and occasionally girls write in, wanting to know if he's got a girlfriend.

'I live in the hope that one day something similar will happen to me,' Howard sighs, sorting through the morning post.

'You want my aura to rub off on you?' Whitten smirks from across his desk.

'Urgh, I wouldn't want anything of yours to rub off on me,' I say quickly, because baiting Jon is a habit. And then I remember how he wanted to sleep with me a few months ago and I go bright red. It's incredible. I'm a music journalist – I think I can call myself that now – and I live in London, and I share my flat with my boyfriend, and we have serious conversations about politics, and yes, I still go red.

'How's it going with Julie then?' I ask Howard a little later.

'Love has disappeared with the autumn leaves,' Howard sighs.

'That's a shame.'

'We both felt the same way.'

'Oh well. Not a shame. Quite lucky then, really.'

'It didn't disappear with the autumn leaves, it disappeared once she'd got the percentage worked out in her contract,' Jon says, once Howard has left the room.

'Cynical.'

'It's the truth,' Jon protests.

When I am at home in bed with David that night, Jeannie rings up to check whether he got her letter. I suppose she got my name from Directory Enquiries. I feel so sick, I can't even speak, not even to tell her to sod off when I realize it's her.

The only thing I can do is hand the phone over to David and crank up the volume on The Beatles. I've been listening to them a fair bit recently, because it's on the music Venn diagram David and I share. God knows, The Beatles must be on everyone's music Venn diagram.

While John Lennon bawls out 'I Am The Walrus', David makes those 'Mmmm,' and 'Mmmm I know' and 'Yeah' sounds that indicate the other person on the end of the line is doing a lot of talking, extremely fast. He's also smiling to himself, which I hate, and not looking remotely bored or put upon, which I hate even more.

'Well she's full of surprises,' he says when he finally puts the phone down.

'What's the surprise?' I ask him.

'She's moving in with a Labour MP,' he says.

'Who's he then?'

'Very high up in the party. He lives in this whacking great house in North London.'

'How socialist of him.'

'It's not just a case of moving in either,' David

293

explains. 'I mean, I don't think they're just flatmates, I think they're having it off as well.'

'Good,' I say, despite myself, and turn my back, taking The Beatles off and putting them back in their record sleeve.

Jeannie must be one of those revolving-door women. They come in quickly on the back of other people's break-ups, and then when they break up with someone, they're in a brand new bed before the dust's even settled on the old Valentine's Day cards. Annoyingly, they also hang around at the start of the next relationship as well.

'What are you thinking?' David asks.

'How many sacrifices I'm making for you. That's what I'm thinking.'

He says nothing then, and I wonder if I should put The Beatles back on. Ah, The Beatles, the soothing Beatles. They say they have that effect on us because Ringo's drumbeat is the same as a human heartbeat – or was that something Jon Whitten made up one day?

'No more sacrifices,' David says at last.

'No, I don't mind really. I mean, I want to give things up for you. I feel I owe it to you. I do love you, David.'

'I feel the same.'

'Well, then.'

'I want us to feel free this time round,' he says. 'I don't see the point of love if it doesn't translate into freedom.'

'I've got a job,' David tells me, a couple of days later.

'Oh my God. Fantastic. What is it?'

'More money than before. But this is London, so you know . . .'

'Come on. What is it?'

'Estate agent. Try not to vomit, Linda.'

'Don't be silly. I'm not vomiting. I'm not.'

'They said I was a natural. It's in Clapham.'

'Wow.'

'And the first bedsit I find under £25,000 with a shower is ours, as well.'

'Well how can either of us resist, then?' I hear myself telling him.

CHAPTER TWENTY-NINE

Most of David's new job happens on Saturday mornings. For a few weeks I'm left in bed on my own, then one weekend I give in and I follow him round on his house inspections, just to keep him company.

The Damned have a new single out called 'Smash It Up', and I'm obsessed with it. It's like Hazel's theory of falling in love. You can't get over the last compulsion until a new one comes along to replace it. The only way I can get 'I Am The Walrus' out of my head now is to detonate it with The Damned.

I still can't understand a word David Vanian sings, but I woo-woo along with the chorus anyway, as David shows a young married couple an old flat in Brixton one morning.

'The area will go up one day,' he tells them, and I think he even believes it.

The young marrieds can't really afford the place, you can tell, and I suspect they're only viewing properties this Saturday because there's nothing on the television.

'And you've got your own washing line,' David says, pointing to it stretching from one flat to another across a filthy concrete yard.

'Oooh lovely,' says the woman, and my heart goes out to her. Imagine a life where you get excited about a washing line. Even worse, her husband is beaming as well. Imagine a life where you *both* get excited about a washing line.

To kill the boredom, I find myself chatting to the wives – always the wives – while David shows their husbands around the properties.

'Do you work together?' they all ask me, and I try not to laugh. Sometimes they ask me what we did last night, and when I tell them that I went out to see Destroy All Monsters, or Penetration, they change the subject quick smart.

One Saturday I make friends with a woman called Sheila. She's looking on her own because her husband's away in Ireland on business.

'I just know I'm going to bugger this up,' she says, immediately endearing herself to me. 'I haven't got a bloody clue about property.'

David does her a favour and inspects the flat she's looking at – a crumbling heap in Stockwell – with extra care, making notes on the clipboard and measuring everything with a tape.

'Thank you,' she says gratefully. 'I really am clueless. But I saw this in the paper and I knew my husband would kill me if I didn't go and at least have a look.'

Sheila and I talk about her pregnancy for a while – she's got a lump the size of a watermelon under her jumper.

'No cigarettes is the worst part,' she tells me while David pulls open the kitchen doors and crawls in under the sink with a torch.

'What about the morning sickness?'

'Haven't got it. But I'll tell you what I have got – I've developed this horrible urge to lick the tar on the roads.'

'You're joking.'

'No, really. If someone doesn't stop me in the next

ten minutes, I'll go out and lick half of Stockwell.'

Sheila's a fan of The Police, so I promise to lend her all their albums to tape; because they're saving up for the baby, she and her husband have both got a ban on buying records and new clothes.

'I'm not sure what I can do for you in return,' she says. 'Maybe you can come over for dinner. We're in Gipsy Hill.'

'Thanks,' I say. 'I'd like that.'

On the way home, David makes more notes in his diary while we jolt around on the bus grinding its way up Camden Road.

'That was all a bit too normal for you, wasn't it?' he grins.

'Sod off.'

'All these married couples with babies on the way, looking for a good first investment property.'

'Well, when you put it like that.'

'And now we're going back to the pink pleasure palace,' he smiles. I've seldom seen David looking so happy.

'I expect you'll get first pick of all the flats, won't you?' I say.

'Unofficially, yes. Every job's got its perks. You take home Police albums. I can bring home houses.'

'Stop boasting, you tosser.'

I close my eyes as the bus stops to eject a few pensioners and pick up some noisy teenagers in an unfair exchange.

'What I'd really like', I say, with my eyes still closed, 'is a place where I can wash my hair without bumping into the oven.'

'You need a place where you can get away from me.'

'Where we can get away from each other.'

'A place with a shower.'

'Abso-bloody-lutely.'

'Somewhere I can play "Smash It Up" at full volume

and you won't want to throw your shoes at the record player.'

'Yes.'

'How much was your commission on that place you sold yesterday?' I ask him.

Later, much later, when we've had cauliflower cheese – a Venn diagram compromise dinner – and we're watching the news, David digs me in the ribs.

'You don't know any mothers, do you?' he asks. 'I bet Sheila's the first mother you've really talked to.'

'I've only just met the woman.'

'You hit it off straight away.'

I shrug. 'Well that's progress for me then, being friends with a *mother*.'

David takes our plates and washes them up in the sink.

'Bugger,' he says as he accidentally squeezes hair conditioner in instead of washing-up liquid.

'One day we'll have a shower,' I whisper. 'A shower like warm rain on your back. And a dishwasher.'

'Oooh, you've changed, Linda Tyler,' David says, putting on a stupid voice.

'I'm just turning into you, that's all,' I say. 'It's like when Doctor Who changes his face every few years. Your face is changing into my face. It's all the sex we're having.'

'Maybe.'

'There's no maybe about it, David. We're merging. We're melting. We're like baked beans and cheese, when you can't tell what's the cheese and what's the baked beans any more.'

'Bloody writers,' he says, making a face. 'I never should have encouraged you.'

CHAPTER THIRTY

Terminal Sausage have entered the Top 40, so Howard's decided to throw a party.

'Does this mean more sausage and salami from Fortnum & Mason?' Jon asks as we sit around the office on Monday morning. I'm beating up a story on Siouxsie Sioux, who has collapsed with hepatitis and been taken to hospital.

Howard's party also involves a live performance from Terminal Sausage, and he wants me to film it.

'Why me?' I complain.

'Come on, it's not hard, holding a Super 8 camera. Anyone can do it,' he says.

'Why not get Jon, or Cindy, or—' I manage to say it, 'Evan.'

'Oh well then, I'll get Evan to do it,' Howard says, throwing a cracker to the dog.

'Good,' I tell him. But at the same time all I can think about is a party with both Evan and David in attendance. There's no way around it. If I don't invite David he'll find out about it and stop speaking to me, and there's no way on earth Evan won't be going – the combination of loads of women and free food and drink will be far too much for him.

'I've never been to a party in London before,' David says when I tell him about it. We're both sitting in the flat with our coats on because the two-bar radiator has died.

'Well it's exactly the same as a party in Withingdean, except the drugs will cost more.'

'Where is it?' he asks.

'Howard's hired a place round the back of Covent Garden. There'll be food as well. His mother's got an account at Fortnum & Mason.'

'Very handy.'

'Evan will probably be there,' I tell him, and try not to breathe in too quickly when I say it.

'That's all right.'

'Good.'

We catch each other's eye, and look away again, because neither of us can think of anything to say.

On Friday, which is party day, Howard is nowhere to be seen. Jon is listening to the new Cabaret Voltaire album, which he proclaims raw, ripe, revolutionary and rectilinear, so I suppose he must have got himself right royally ripped again this morning.

Cindy and I go home early to get changed, leaving Jon with Howard's dog – he's been given the task of babysitting it.

'This dog's developing a fondness for synthesizer-based pop, have you noticed?' Jon asks as the spaniel curls up underneath the record player.

Cindy makes a face as she stomps out ahead of me in her fluffy mules. 'Gaaad he gets on my nerves,' she says. 'Him and his tosspot theories.'

It seems her fling with Jon is now officially over. I can't say I'm surprised. I only ever gave it six months. I thought it would all be over by Christmas. I could see it wasn't long for this world. I knew it wouldn't last beyond 1980. And it hasn't.

I suppose the attraction for him was based partly on her unavailability. Her art room door was always closed. And even when she was bending up and down

301

in a short skirt, looking for the coffee mugs in the kitchen, she was always out of reach. God knows what the attraction was for her. The fact that he knows really, really long words? The attractive layer of dandruff on top of his leather jacket?

I go home and get changed into a red vinyl pencil skirt, black tights with seams up the back, Princess Anne court shoes that I've painted silver, and my favourite old 1940s green tweed suit jacket. The party is in full swing when David and I get there, a little after eight o'clock. Howard seems to have invited most of London, and word must have got out about the piles of free sausages and salami, because almost everyone has turned up. Everyone who's anyone in our funny little London world seems to be here tonight – except Jon, who has staggered home to his sick bed to recover from last night's Black Beauty binge.

'I asked that Clare Grogan girl to our party as well,' Howard tells me, 'but she said she had to do her homework.'

'Oh well.'

'I'm completely over Julie now, you'll be pleased to hear,' Howard tells me as I squint at the makeshift stage, where Julie – looking portly, and dressed like Queen Victoria in mourning – is setting up her drumkit.

'Congratulations,' I reply.

'And I do like that chap of yours, David,' he confides.

'I'm glad.'

'You seem more settled with him somehow.'

'Oh well. That's a relief for everyone then, isn't it, Howard.'

Just before Terminal Sausage start their set, Evan arrives with a bottle of Scotch in his hand, a Super 8 camera slung over his shoulder, and a tiny, excited-looking red-haired girl hanging off his arm. I watch him saying something to her, and then she disappears to the food table, and he comes straight over.

The introductions are horrible.

'David, I'd like you to meet Evan. Evan, this is, er, David.'

They stare at each other.

'Nice camera,' David tries first.

'Any idiot can use one,' Evan informs him, and I realize he's rolling drunk. At the food table, the red-haired girl is hopping around, chatting to record company people and trying hard. I feel sorry for her. Especially when I think about the treat that doesn't await her when she finally gets into bed with Evan tonight.

'Linda tells me you're from Australia,' David tries again.

'Blind Freddy could see that.' Evan laughs, and takes a swig of his Scotch.

'Evan's under instructions to film the band,' I tell David, and then I rock backwards as Evan suddenly shoves the camera into my hands.

'Here ya go,' he says.

'Don't give it to me! I don't know what to do with it!'

'It's simple,' he slurs. 'Just push that button there, and make sure the light's switched on at the top, and don't wobble around too much.'

'Oh no, Evan. That's not fair.'

'I've got other fish to fry,' he says, aiming for the red-haired girl at the food table.

And so I am stuck with the camera in one hand and a drink in the other, while David stands about looking out of place – which he is, despite the new skinny leather tie he's bought. We watch as Evan pushes the red-haired girl into a wall and kisses her. She looks as though she'd like to ask for some oxygen.

'That's a classy guy you chose to have a fling with,' David says.

'Shut it.'

'Funny tight trousers he's got on.'

'He's a Mod.'

'Oh *right*, he's a *Mod*. Well that explains it then.'

'You just don't get it, do you?' I hear myself snapping.

'Have another drink, Linda. You might as well – they're free.'

'No, I think I'll go and film the band, as a matter of fact. Stay here and mind my handbag, would you?'

And so I leave him nursing a pink vinyl handbag, two beers and a plate of sausages. It will serve him right, I think, if nobody goes up to talk to him.

The best place to film Terminal Sausage seems to be from the side of the stage, so I start there, and then I get bored, so I move behind a pot plant and shoot them from behind the leaves.

It's fascinating, seeing things through a camera. I can understand how Evan became addicted to it. And it's even more fascinating watching him through the camera lens, swaying slightly as he tries to kiss the red-haired girl again, and making faces at me when he sees me filming them.

Seeing a band is rarely interesting just because you're watching the people up on stage. It's often about the other things that are going on while the band is playing – like people snogging each other, and fighting with each other, and doing drug deals, or getting smashed and pushing their way through the crowd to the front row. I try to find all of that now, with the camera, moving around the room like a spy and zooming in on the most interesting faces.

Some people get annoyed and look away, and others play up to the camera. The best people are the ones who don't even notice you're there. I see Cindy's feet, in a new pair of zip-up white boots, and I film them as well.

'Get behind the band,' she advises me. 'That's the best spot in the room, and you'll get the light as well.'

I take her advice, and climb up onto the stage, not caring whether people can see me, or what the band thinks. From behind the drum kit, you can see Julie's hands, in her funny black fingerless gloves, and every time she smashes her drumsticks down on the snare, the light breaks up for a second. I film that, and then I decide I want to get the crowd's-eye view of the whole thing, so I crouch down underneath the singer's face, and film upwards.

'Want a drink?' one of the roadies asks me when I move to the back of the stage again. I film that as well – him passing me a bottle of vodka, and me swigging it.

Drinking and filming, filming and drinking, I haven't had this much fun since I bought my first record player and started singing into my hairbrush.

I've already worked out how this little film is going to run. I need something at the beginning, showing people wolfing down sausages, so if I wander over to the food table and do that bit next – it can be stuck up the front when the film's edited.

There isn't much sausage and salami left by the time I wobble my way over there, but there's a plate upside down on the floor. I crawl under the table on my stomach to get it. As a bonus, there's also an untouched glass of shandy under there as well, so I put the camera down for a minute and knock it back.

Just then, a pair of feet, in unmistakable brown Hush Puppies park themselves in front of my face. Evan bends down, grinning at me and pointing.

'Your film's going to be underexposed.'

'No it's not.'

'Yes it is.'

I slide out, and notice that the red-haired girl is nowhere to be seen. 'You're enjoying yourself, aren't you?' Evan concludes.

I shrug. 'It's better than listening to the band.'

'I talked to your boyfriend,' he says.

'Did you?'

'About Australian property prices mostly. He got quite excited when I told him how cheap it is to buy a shack in Urunga.'

'Yes, I can imagine he would.'

'He's a breadhead, Linda.'

'So what? You're a—' I grasp for the word.

'I'm a root rat,' he laughs.

'No, I was thinking of something more poetic, but I'm too drunk. God I'm going to be sick tomorrow. I've had Scotch, vodka and shandy.'

'Well you *think* it's shandy. It looks like piss to me.'

'Oh, go away.'

Over in the corner, Howard is talking to David, so I get rid of Evan and wander over. I'm about to run out of film, so I suppose I'd better get Howard on it, before it's all over.

'She's making a documentary on us,' David warns Howard as they sit together, side by side, on rickety wooden chairs. Howard's tie is loose, which is always a sign that he's had a few.

Amazingly, David doesn't seem the slightest bit pissed off that I've spent most of the night ignoring him.

'We've just been discussing Evan,' Howard tells me.

'Better not get that on camera,' I say. 'He can probably lip-read.'

'We were trying to find the right word for him,' David smiles.

'I think he's just found it for himself,' I interrupt them. 'Root rat.'

'A fine Australian term, no doubt,' Howard cuts me off, 'but I was thinking more in terms of itinerant. I think Evan is an itinerant.'

'Whatever you want to call him is fine by me,' I tell

him. 'Now, can you take this bloody camera off me, it's killing my shoulder.'

A few days later, when I am compiling the cross-word – (7 Across, Bob Geldof's least favourite day of the week) – Julie comes in, with an enormous crocodile handbag. She smiles in an embarrassed way at Howard, and then crosses the room to talk to me.

'We absolutely love it,' she says, and gets three rolls of Super 8 film out of her handbag.

'Do you?'

'The boys think it's brilliant. Can you put it all together for us? If we pay you?'

Across the room Howard can stand it no longer, and leaps up from his desk as if someone's put a firework on his chair.

'Julie my sweet, are we entering into a business discussion?' he interrupts. 'Because if we are, I'm afraid the manager does rather have to be involved.'

Julie stares at him with her mouth slightly open. She's got so much lipgloss on, her upper lip is reflecting the office lights.

'It's all right,' I tell Howard. 'I don't want any money.'

Julie smiles then, and shuts her mouth.

'More crucially than the money, Linda, is the question of the film itself. You know, I'd like a friend of mine at the BBC to edit this. His name's Mick Powell. I went to school with him.'

From his desk across the other side of the room, Jon laughs.

'What?' I demand.

'Catch *you* letting someone else edit your stuff?' he grins. 'Howard, you've got more chance of getting Linda to hand her bloody crossword over for editing than you have of getting her to let someone else cut her film.'

Julie looks at me with big brown cow-like eyes. 'Me

and Howard can discuss this another time if you like,' she offers.

But Howard waves her away. 'No, no, it's fine. OK Linda, what about if I just get Mick to help you? I'm sure you can go into the BBC one Sunday when there's nobody there.'

'Oh all right then,' I say, trying to sound casual. 'And by the way, any chance of getting paid for this, Howard?'

'We'll talk about that later,' he says quickly.

Howard and Julie disappear to the pub after that, leaving me to construct more crossword clues with no help at all from Jon.

'Women are amazing,' he says.

'Yes I know,' I tell him, to shut him up. But he goes on regardless.

'You and Julie, just now. *Hilarious!* It was like watching two lionesses set up a goat before they go in for the kill.'

I make a face at him, and try to match a Gary Numan clue with a Debbie Harry clue.

'I mean,' Jon continues, 'you've both got what you wanted in ten minutes flat. You're in at the BBC, just like that, and she's got her film clip made. And Howard doesn't even know what happened.'

'If I can make a film clip out of that stuff, it will be a miracle,' I tell him.

Jon puts Cabaret Voltaire on the record player and lights a cigarette. 'It's the future of music, believe me,' he says.

'But you're always wrong about the future of music, Whitten.'

'Imagine it, Linda. No more live gigs. No more standing around listening to shite musicians while some bloody gorilla sends you deaf at the mixing desk. You'll just turn on the telly and there it'll be. A music film clip. You'll never even have to go and see the bloody band play. Trust me. It's the way it's all going.'

'What utter crap you talk,' I complain. 'Rock'n'roll will never die. Now, will you please let me get on and finish doing this crossword?'

At lunchtime, though, I can't help myself – and I call Annie, and Hazel, and my Dad – and I tell them I've made a film. My fingers are already itching to have the camera back.

CHAPTER THIRTY-ONE

Everyone's talking about a secret Jam gig tonight, down at the Marquee. They've been billed as John's Boys, but every Mod in England, and a few skinheads, has lined up on the streets outside, by the time I finally arrive with Evan to cover the gig.

'This could be our cover story, Linda,' Howard told me yesterday. Then he remembered the time he saw The Jam busking round the corner and nearly signed them – but didn't. 'You know, I could have had the Jam as well as the Sausage,' he said while the spaniel looked up at him mournfully.

Even though Evan and I get to the Marquee early, the crowd is still pushing its way up the street. You can almost feel the electricity in the queue – not that it's a proper queue, more of a hustling, noisy mass of people in parkas and pointy shoes, all stinking of chips and cigarettes, and laughing, and gossiping, and shouting at each other.

There's the familiar Jam logo, painted drippily in what looks like strawberry conserve, on a dozen bootleg T-shirts being flogged at the door. And there are fans with a little money and a takeaway curry – just like the song – wolfing down their Chicken Korma with one hand while they hold out the other for an ink stamp.

Everyone knows it will be hours before Paul Weller, Bruce Foxton and Rick Buckler appear on the stage, but still people can't cram inside fast enough. A girl in a white shiny PVC mac who's done too much of something she shouldn't is in tears.

'But you have to let me in!' she cries to the doorman who tells her to hop it, and jerks his thumb, while simultaneously edging her away from the door with his leg.

And then it's push, shove, drink, smoke, drink, drink, drink . . . until Evan disappears with his camera, which is always a sign that something is about to happen.

I'm in the loo when the band finally comes on stage, and the roar outside is so loud it nearly knocks me against the hand-drier.

Push, shove, apologize, don't apologize, but whatever you do, just get down the front. It's been like that at every gig I've ever been to, and it's the same tonight – even if I am supposed to be working.

They play ' "A" Bomb in Wardour Street' and 'Down In The Tube Station at Midnight' and another roar goes up. A Skinhead and a Mod are fighting behind me, and I can barely be bothered to switch my attention, even when the bouncers move in.

And, then it's David Watts and 'In The Crowd'. Four songs that tell us we all come from the same place, even if half the crowd did arrive here on a fast train from Upminster.

People have to be peeled off the front of the stage after the encore, and one of the toilets in the Ladies is now overflowing like the fountains in Trafalgar Square, but nobody minds. It's just that kind of night.

When I finally get home at 1 a.m. – leaving Evan on his way to a coffee bar in Soho with two girls from Amsterdam who want to follow him home – David is waiting up for me.

'A nice cup of cocoa,' he says. 'It'll only take me five minutes. Stay there. It's coming.'

'How can I ever thank you?' I yawn.

He kisses me. 'Was it good?'

'It was bloody *great*.'

'Did Evan get his photographs?'

'Yes thank you very much, Evan did get his photographs. And then he went off up Soho with two Dutch girls. I think they were about sixteen years old.'

David smiles.

I sit down on the bed and pull my boots off. My feet are killing me. I pushed down the front for the encore, and some idiot in brothel creepers brought his foot down hard on the side of my ankle when he was trying to hoist his girlfriend up on his shoulders.

'I was thinking what a good film tonight would have made,' I say.

'You've got a real bee in your bonnet about that film camera, haven't you?' David replies.

'I can just see it all in pictures, David, in my head. Much easier than words. You know, I can never do music with just words. Not properly. I've tried and I've tried, but it's like trying to pin down a butterfly. You'll never get the essence of it with a typewriter. Never. I mean, how can you get The Jam on a piece of paper?

'I read Mick Farren and Julie Burchill, and they come close. But whenever I try, it's like something that gets translated five times over, once removed. I make it sound like old cardboard when I write about it. When I had that camera the other night, though, I felt like I *had* it.'

'You should do a proper camera course then,' David says.

'Every time I contemplate learning anything, I have flashbacks to Graham Hayes and "Two Little Boys".'

He laughs.

'No really, David, I hate learning. I don't like teachers.

And I dunno, I think it would be more interesting to see films made by people like me, who don't know what they're doing. Does that make sense?'

'Maybe. It depends what it looks like on the telly. I think you should get a proper camera, though. Learn to do it professionally.'

'Well watching my film of Terminal Sausage on TV couldn't be any worse than watching Pan's People jig around on *Top of the Pops*. Could it?'

David pauses. 'I'm not sure I agree with you. I quite like Pan's People. Especially the little blonde.'

I scream then, and smother him with the pink blanket.

The next day I go into the office and find Jon on the phone, hustling for free entry to the Buzzcocks and Joy Division gig at the Rainbow on Friday night. I'm torn between that and Squeeze, who are on at the Hammersmith Odeon.

'God it's hard, having this much music in my life,' I moan to nobody in particular.

Jon sniffs. 'All the more reason for you to be more selective, Linda. You're like a bloody music Hoover, you are. You just suck everything in.'

I stare at him, but he's already got his back to me, putting some new band called Scritti Politti on the record player.

'I'm not a music Hoover,' I protest as Cindy clacks out of the art room and asks us if we want any cawfee.

She's changing her look, slowly but surely, so she looks less like she could be the sister of someone from the B52s and more like one of the blokes in Joy Division. Like every other vaguely arty person in London, she has become obsessed with Ian Curtis.

'Joy Division are so dee-pressing, but they're so fantaaastic,' she sighs.

She's dyed her hair back to brown, which was probably its natural colour in the first place, and has started wearing black men's shirts buttoned up to the collar and grey school uniform skirts.

'Ooh, I like the St Trinians look,' Howard said the day she marched into the office wearing black school shoes as well.

'Saint what?' Cindy asks.

'Oh, I'm sorry, I forget you're American.' Howard sighed. 'Poor old you, never to have the sheer bliss of knowing what St Trinians is.'

Jon flips over an album on his desk after he's put in his coffee order. 'You'll like this, Howard.'

'Will I? And more importantly, do they have a manager?' he asks, pulling the dog up on his lap.

'It's The Pop Group,' Jon explains. 'A song called "We Are All Prostitutes".'

Howard whistles through his teeth.

'They're right,' Jon mutters, with a far-off look in his eyes. 'Selfridges is the new Westminster Cathedral.'

'Is that something you just made up, or are you reading it off the sleeve?' I ask him.

'Well that's certainly right for my mother,' Howard muses, 'though of course I would never tell her that Fortnum & Mason is now the equivalent of a cathedral.'

'I think capitalism suits you,' I tell Howard. 'You're a natural capitalist. It's like being a natural Damned fan. You're either born that way or you're not.'

'Well thank you,' Howard says, spooning more marmalade into his mouth and giving some to the dog. 'Oh, I nearly forgot – the camera.' Howard digs around in a plastic bag on the floor and produces it for me.

'Wow, *high-tech*,' Jon observes.

'Is this for me?' I ask, like a six-year-old sucking up to Santa.

'Yes it is.' Howard waves me away. 'It was my father's. It's been in the attic with the train set since Princess Anne's wedding, so you may as well have it.'

314

I hold it up to my eye and frame Jon in the corner, and then Howard sitting down with the spaniel, and then all the posters on the walls.

'You're in at the BBC by the way,' Howard adds, though I can tell it's not by the way at all – he's been planning this for days, as a treat for me.

'Oh my God.'

'No problem at all, just sneak in after they've all gone home. This chap I went to school with – Mick – he'll show you what's what.'

He gives me a piece of paper with his phone number and name scribbled down, and beams.

'This is great, Howard. Thanks.'

'I could tell you were enjoying yourself the other night,' he says. 'You looked quite natural using the camera, didn't she, Jon?'

But Jon is ignoring both of us and reading the cover of The Pop Group album.

'I thought you looked as natural as a film director,' Howard goes on, 'as I look as a filthy capitalist.'

Just then Jon puts the new Damned album on the turntable, and we all sing along – despite ourselves – to 'Smash It Up'.

CHAPTER THIRTY-TWO

As an early Christmas present, David pays for me to go on a film course.

'It starts on 30 November,' he says, 'and it goes every Friday night. So I thought I'd better give it to you now.'

'Friday nights? David, I can't do it. I've got to go to gigs.'

'It finishes at eight o'clock, I checked. Then you can go out afterwards. Maybe you can take the camera out with you. I'll be at home.' He coughs. 'I'll be quite happy at home.'

The course sounds quite good, even if I am having nightmares about Graham Hayes. It has lots of vaguely famous people recommending it, anyway, and the brochure looks glossy and impressive.

'You could be the next Woody Allen after this,' David says.

'As long as I don't drop the camera on the floor,' I tell him. But later on, when we're both in bed, I look at him when he's asleep and silently bless him. I haven't even *thought* about his Christmas present yet. But he must have been thinking about this for ages.

I prod him, just before he falls asleep.

'Thanks, David.'

And he blinks at me, then smiles, and turns over.

* * *

Howard tells me I can go and see his friend Mick at the BBC in the first week of December to edit the Terminal Sausage film.

'Half the staff are away, so Mick said you should have an editing suite to yourselves. He's looking forward to meeting you,' he says cheerfully. 'He does all your crosswords in the paper, you know.'

'God, how embarrassing.'

I picture Mick – an upper-class twat who's probably got a fake mockney accent, to match his fake mockney name. His mother's probably the Countess of Durham, and he probably goes to work in a lilac shirt, tossing his golden locks.

And then, after that ungenerous thought, I have to run to the toilet to be sick. It's been like that every day lately. I've even had to leap off the tube halfway through the trip to work, just to rush outside and get some fresh air.

After lunch Howard gives me the number of his doctor. 'Dr Newnard will sort you out,' he says. 'Use my account.'

'God, thanks Howard. But you don't have to.'

'No, no. He's an excellent fellow. Very good for tummy trouble. I expect it's the hamburgers from that place over the road. I gave one to the dog and he was as sick as a – well, as sick as a dog, actually. Do you remember?'

I do remember. And just the thought of his dog vomiting in the office makes me feel queasy again. But Howard's got it wrong. It's not the hamburgers over the road that are making me ill. I'm pregnant.

'Fantastic,' David says when Dr Newnard confirms what we've known all along. 'Isn't it? I mean, don't you think it's fantastic?'

'Yes it is,' I say slowly. I suppose I'm in shock.

'I mean, I'm sorry I did it to you, Linda. When we

317

hadn't planned it. I accept all responsibility.'

'Yes. No. Don't be silly. It's my fault as well.' Somehow I'd never got around to going on the pill again when David and I got back together. And clearly his withdrawal technique wasn't quite as good as he'd thought.

'You're happy about it, aren't you?' David asks.

'I smile. 'Yes.'

Having a baby. I suppose it had to happen. Everyone else, except Hazel and Annie, did it years ago. In Withingdean they start churning them out at the age of eighteen, and most of the girls I went to school with have had three by now.

David has to go back to work, so we walk into the first coffee bar we see so that we can quickly talk it through.

He orders us both strong black coffees and lights up a cigarette, then puts it out again.

'Don't be stupid,' I say.

'No, I'm giving up smoking,' he replies. 'I've just decided. Because of the baby.' And despite himself, he grins.

We stare at each other, and I wonder who's more in shock, me or him. I can already see him doing calculations in his head. If he takes all his savings, and if he gets promoted at work, or if he gets a better paid job at another agency, then . . .

'I'll have to give up work,' I say. 'So that's one less income.'

He nods.

'I can't go to gigs with my stomach sticking out. I might get squashed.'

When the coffee arrives, I start to feel trembly.

'I love you and I will always do the right thing by you,' David says. 'By both of you. The baby and you.'

'Oh please don't start calling it a baby like that, David. I'm terrified.'

'Well me too, if you must know,' he says. 'But we can't be. It's not a good time to be terrified.'

'What will Dad say?'

'He'll be happy. He'll be pissed off we're not married, of course, but he'll be happy. You know he will.'

'What about Hazel?'

'Oh for God's sake, stop worrying about other people.'

'I'll never be Lester Bangs now.'

'And who's Lester Bangs when he's at home?' David tuts. Then he changes his mind and lights up a cigarette after all.

'What about all the films I want to make?' I ask him.

'You can make them,' he says. 'Come on, you're making it sound like having this baby is a tragedy.'

I feel my heart beating faster and faster as the coffee kicks in. It was a mistake. I shouldn't have ordered it.

'You bought me a film course and I can't even do it,' I say. I feel tears starting to prickle in my eyes.

'Linda. Don't be silly.' David reaches across the table and squeezes my hand.

'I've finally got a life I like, and I'm going to have to give it up.' I really am crying now.

'Let's go home,' he says gently.

'No, you've got to go to work. If you don't go to work, you'll lose your job, and then what'll happen? I'll be getting my nappies donated by the Salvation Army.'

In the end, David takes the afternoon off work, and so do I, admitting to Howard that I'm pregnant before he has a chance to rant on about hamburgers again. We need to be somewhere quiet, away from everyone, tucked away with each other, to take all this in.

By teatime we're still lying in our pink bed whilst the wind howls outside the front door.

'Put your coat on the bed,' I tell David. 'It's so cold

319

in here. God, why did I blow all my money on a trip to Australia when I could have had a proper fire?'

David laughs. Then we are both quiet for a while; I turn on my side and try to imagine what it will feel like to carry a baby into next summer.

'Whatever you want to do, you know I'll stand by you,' David says quickly. 'Just in case you're changing your mind.'

'I know. But I wouldn't do it to you, David. I wouldn't have an abortion. You'd hate it.'

'I'm just saying, if you don't want to go through with having it, I'll understand,' he says at last.

'Don't give me that crap,' I say. 'You'd never get over it. And it would be the end for us.'

I get out of bed and do the only thing that will return me to the real world – put 'Brass In Pocket' on the tape player.

'I'm keeping it,' I say at last. 'We're keeping it. It's a shock, that's all. I'm very happy. Happy for me, happy for us.'

'Fantastic,' David says.

We lie in bed listening to Chrissie Hynde, and I think of Kipper the cat at home, and about ringing Dad up later and what he'll say. The first thing he'll say, of course, is that we should still have a white wedding. And I dunno, maybe we should.

CHAPTER THIRTY-THREE

Mick Powell from the BBC is the love of my life, and I work that out in the first five minutes of sitting in his office. He's tall, and he wears Doc Martens – one of his socks is on inside out, and his hair is short, dark and spiky. So much for my vision of a golden-locked twat in a lilac shirt.

He keeps his coins in a jam jar on his desk, just like me. He talks fast, just like me, and in an accent that's not a million miles away from mine. He tells me he got a scholarship to Lancing and he hated it – except for Howard, who used to make him laugh. He says he's living in Shepherds Bush at the moment because he can't be arsed finding anywhere else, and his flat is horrible. He's got a Clash poster on his wall. He thinks my writing in *NWW* is fantastic and he wishes that Howard would let me do more, because Jon Whitten is crap. He goes to gigs every night after work, just like me. He hasn't got a girlfriend. And that bit is something he lets me know about in the first five minutes too, which is all the encouragement I need to start dreaming.

'I like your school tie,' he says.

'It's not my real school tie, I bought it at a jumble sale.'

'I love jumble sales,' he says.

I nod.

'What I like best about them is fighting the old ladies,' he goes on. 'People go on about boxing, but it's nothing compared to being mown down at Shepherds Bush church hall on a Sunday morning.'

'Those old ladies are tough,' I agree. Our eyes meet and we smile.

He gets a bottle of Scotch out of his desk drawer, says he's going to make an Irish coffee and asks me if I want one. Then he trundles up the corridor with two mugs, leaving me staring at the wall, with a racing heart and an exploding head.

There are people you tell everything, and people you tell nothing, and Mick is one of those people you tell everything. When he comes back, he pours the Scotch into the coffee cups, and before I know what I'm doing, it all comes out. My job in the Chinese restaurant; the songs that changed my life; the job application; my mother; my trip round the world; Evan, and Penny, and David.

'So do you still live by yourself then?' he asks.

We've just got to the part in my life story where I've come back from Australia.

'I live with David,' I own up. 'We got back together in the end.'

He nods, as if he was expecting me to say that, and I look at the floor.

'And why did you do that?' he asks. 'Sorry, just tell me if I'm being nosy.'

'No it's OK. I mean, I like talking to you,' I blush. 'What happened is, he lost his job, and then he realized he didn't want Jeannie any more—'

'The one with no bra?'

'Yes, her. And then he moved back in with me.'

I end the story there. I can't bear to tell him the rest at the moment.

Mick shows me some tapes he's made of various

bands this year. 'I've got some older footage too,' he says, adjusting the volume on a small TV set in the corner of the room, 'and that'll be the really important stuff. 1976 and all that.'

'Do you think so?'

'I know so. The Victoria and Albert Museum is already looking at Punk clothes for its archives. Can you believe it? I know that, because my ex-girlfriend works there.'

Ah. The ex-girlfriend.

'My love-life hasn't been anywhere near as inspiring as yours,' he says, half smiling and looking out of the window. 'I was with Alice for two years while she was finishing her MA at Cambridge. She decided she wanted to move to Paris, I didn't. And then she got a pair of glasses and for that, among other things, I went off her. She came back to London to work at the museum.'

'What kind of music did she like?' I ask.

'Ah, the all-important question.'

'Let me guess. She was into jazz?'

'God, how did you know that?' Mick laughs.

'I like your film of Howard's group,' he says when the silence between us has hung in the air long enough.

'Wow. Thanks. Do you really?'

'Your voice on the page is similar to your signature on the film.'

'I didn't even know I had one.'

'Put it this way, you've been using your camera the same way that you use your pen when you write reviews. I've read most of them so I can tell.'

I smile. He's read my stuff.

'It's a bugger that the band are so dire,' he says.

'Dire's the word.'

'But if you want to, we can do something with this footage that will make them look good. Really good.

And you're in luck. Everyone's away over Christmas, so there's plenty of empty edit suites around the place.'

I think about David and what he would say if I spent every day of his Christmas holidays at the BBC, and I think about the baby I'm carrying, and I try to bring myself back to the real world for a minute.

'It's really kind of you,' I say.

'I'll be here anyway.' Mick coughs, and I wonder about his life since he broke up with jazz-loving Alice with the glasses.

'I'll try to come in,' I tell him. 'My boyfriend probably won't like it, but I'll try.'

'Are you wanted at home then?' Mick fires back, and I can tell he was trying to turn it into a joke but it's come out all wrong.

'I just found out I'm pregnant,' I tell him the truth at last.

I can tell I've lost him then, and suddenly lost everything else as well. Just by the way he looks at me – or rather the way he doesn't look at me. It's like someone pulling the plug on a record player halfway through a great song.

'Congratulations,' Mick smiles, and offers to make another cup of Irish coffee.

I shrug, and feel the atmosphere going flat. 'It wasn't planned.'

'Often the best things in life never are,' he smiles, and I can tell that apart from being good-looking, and funny, and clever, and single, and into The Clash, and all those other things, he's just plain nice as well. But he doesn't want me any more. Or, at least, he doesn't want me with David's baby.

When I leave Mick's office, just before lunch, I make a sharp turn into the ladies' toilets in the BBC reception area and cry my eyes out, and then I throw up.

There are plenty of songs about the joy of recognizing

324

the person you're meant to be with for the rest of your life. But where are the songs about finding them and then losing them, all in the space of an hour and a half? Maybe you have to turn to country and western for those kinds of songs. Maybe you have to dispense with pop music altogether.

I look at myself in the mirror after I've washed my face. This is probably the prettiest I'll ever be. I've been living on the best music in history for half a year and I will never look better than this. I'll probably never be as interesting either. I will never be more tailor-made for Mick than I am at this moment. I'm meeting him at the best possible time of my life, in the best possible way. And the worst time as well.

'Sod it,' I tell the mirror, and make a face at my reflection.

There's no point in even *thinking* about David or the baby in this state, because Mick has managed to blow both of them right out of the water. I know he has, because I can still hear his voice in my head, and I can still see his face, and I can still remember the way he used his words and the things that he said.

Panicking, I try to think of reasons not to want him – and fail. Maybe he's disastrous in relationships – *yeah, but so am I.* Maybe he's got some terrible medical condition – *yeah, but I'm pregnant.* Maybe his ex-girlfriend is a pain in the arse and she haunts any-one new in his life until she's forced to give up. *Yeah, but I was like that, too, when Jeannie came along.*

The fact is, I have just met exactly the right person. I can't lie to myself about it, I just know. And I know this in a way I never did with David – that's the killer.

'Well done. Good girl. That's brilliant,' I tell the toilet bowl, feeling another wave of nausea hit me.

As I hang my head and retch again, I realize I can give up on the idea of editing the film clip with Mick if I want, but I may never have another chance to do what I really want in life, which is make films about music. I think I've recognized a pattern by now – you only get one chance to get lucky, and if you turn your back on it, you'll lose it for ever.

When I've finished vomiting, I dash out of the BBC foyer, turning my face to the wall, pretending to look at all the blown-up photographs of Michael Parkinson and Morecambe and Wise, so none of the girls at the reception desk can see my eyes.

Outside, it's freezing. It'll be Christmas in three weeks. And I still haven't got David his present. He's given me the film course so that I can follow my dreams; I haven't even had the imagination to think beyond a Boots' gift basket for men. Buying a present for Mick would be easy, I think, and I don't even know him. If he was mine, I'd give him a jumble sale present as a joke, and then I'd give him The Clash bootleg tape that Jon sold me a few months ago, and maybe the new album as well, *London Calling*. I haven't heard it yet because Jon's got the only advance copy, but he says it's the best thing they've done. In fact, he thinks it might just be the best record ever made.

To keep myself sane, I go back to the office, where Jon is moaning about some Irish band called U2 who Howard made him see last night.

'There were nine people there at the Hope and Anchor. Nine!' he complains.

'Do you think they have a manager?' Howard enquires hopefully.

'I don't care if they do. I give them until Christmas. Wailing Irish navvies.'

'Wow, Christmas is three weeks away, Jon,' I say. 'That's your direst prediction yet.'

The situation at home with David is mad, and the thing with Mick is mad, but the office feels safe. Wonderfully, comfortingly safe and secure, with familiar joking and smoking, and Howard's jar of marmalade on the desk, and Cindy sashaying around from the kitchen to the art room. I thought I'd never say this, but it feels like I belong here now. I wonder about the baby, and how long before it will start to show. And then I wonder about Howard, and how long he can keep me on for before it's time to say goodbye.

'Some nice fan mail for you this morning,' Howard says, throwing me a couple of letters. One of them is from the mentally ill person in Nottingham who thinks I'm working for Satan, but the other one is a genuine 'you are fab' letter, as Jon sneeringly calls them. The person who thinks I am fab is a girl in Liverpool who works in a fish and chip shop and wants to know how you become a writer. My heart goes out to her. And I say what I always say, which is crap, 'Start with your local newspaper and see if they need a helping hand on your school holidays.' It's something that a careers officer told me once when I was at school, but with untold millions unemployed, I wish anyone luck in finding work experience on a newspaper, even if it is a crap local one.

'How was Mick?' Howard asks.

I nod.

'He's such a nice fellow,' he adds. Then he gestures towards the door. 'Come and have some lunch with me, Linda, I need to talk to you.'

I nod again, while Jon pretends not to notice, and Cindy hovers in the art room.

Outside, we pull our coats in tight against the wind, and bowl down Wardour Street towards Oxford Street.

'Look at all these places closing down,' Howard tuts as we pass another boarded-up restaurant.

'Everything's getting turned into a sex shop,' I tell him. 'It's the only thing that people are enjoying any more.' And then I remember I'm pregnant, and I blush, while Howard smiles.

We find a deserted sandwich place and sit down.

'We haven't had a chance to talk, have we? I mostly just want to congratulate you,' Howard says, and leans across the table to peck me on the cheek.

'Thank you.'

This morning's tears in the BBC toilets threaten to well up again.

'I haven't told Jon or Cindy. Do you want me to? Or would you like to have the honour?'

'You do it. But not yet. You're supposed to give it three months, aren't you?'

Howard nods. 'Of course.'

I haven't really thought about the chance of miscarrying. But the idea is dismissed as quickly as it crosses my mind. It would be terrible. Awful. I'm not even going to think about it.

'I'm afraid we can't keep you on indefinitely, Linda,' he says at last.

'I know. I thought that. It's fine.'

'I'm so sorry.'

'No,' I shake my head. 'You can't send me to gigs with a bump. And when it's born, I can't leave David in to babysit every night.'

Howard sighs. 'Thank you for making this so much easier.'

After that, and a few more cups of tea, we push our way back to the office, fighting the wind, and the dust cloud of rubbish that has blown up from the gutters on Shaftesbury Avenue. When we get back inside and hang up our coats, Jon is playing *London Calling* on the record player.

'That's an Elvis album cover, isn't it?' I say when I see the sleeve.

'Yeah, brilliant rip-off,' Jon agrees. 'And wait until you hear it.'

'Well I'm sort of relying on you for that pleasure,' I tell him.

In response, Jon turns up the volume, so we can all

hear it. And I think about Mick again, and I think about the gigs we'll never go to and the films we'll never see, and then I think about the baby and how much David loves me.

After work, I find a phone box and call Mick at the BBC.

'I thought it might be you,' he says when he answers the phone.

'I can't do it,' I tell him. 'I can't make the film with you. In fact, I'm not sure I'll ever come back to the BBC again, even though you offered. I'm really sorry.'

He pauses. 'Is anything wrong, Linda?'

'Yes. Lots of things are wrong. But I can't tell you why. Does that make sense?'

In the background, I can hear someone trying to come into his office and talk to him, then going away again.

'I may as well be honest then, if I'm not going to see you again,' he says.

'Yes?'

'I feel as if I know you.'

'I know.'

'And if things were different, then life would be different.'

I breathe out. Thank God. It's mutual. He knows it as well.

'David sent in the letter that got me the job on the paper,' I tell him. 'I threw it out because I thought it was crap. He was the one who got it out of the bin and stuck it in an envelope and posted it to Howard.'

'Yup.'

'For Christmas, he's given me a film course. I didn't ask for it, in fact I told him I didn't want to do one, but he paid for it anyway.'

'Yup.'

'And I'm having his baby. And he wants to buy us a house. So—'

329

Mick interrupts me. 'It's OK. You don't have to explain yourself, Linda.' Then he adds, 'What were the ten songs that changed your life?'

'Eh?'

'On the job application you sent to Howard. What were they?'

And so I reel them off. 'Revolution Number 9', when I lost my virginity. 'Itchycoo Park', when my mother died. 'Ballroom Blitz', when I got caught shoplifting. The Damned. The Who. And all the rest.

'Fuck it,' Mick says.

'Why?'

'You've got at least two of my songs. Fuck it.'

'Really?'

'Not that I've ever had to make that kind of list, but if I did – well, "New Rose", that's one for a start. And "Waterloo Sunset", it's the most romantic song ever written.'

'I know,' I say. 'I know it is.'

And then we say our farewells – and they really do seem like farewells – and hang up.

When I get home, David has been to WH Smith and bought a couple of baby books. He's also made me some chicken soup, put all my records back in their sleeves, and he's bought me a bunch of flowers.

'I'm not going to do that thing at the BBC,' I say lightly.

'Oh. Why not?'

'It'll take up too much time over Christmas.'

David smiles at me. 'Whatever you say. I thought you were the workaholic in the family, though.'

The TV is full of ads for special holiday programmes, and the weatherman is making jokes about Santa having snowed-up chimneys in Scotland. I try to imagine what Christmas will be like in the future, when our kid is ten years old, and we'll be wrapping up toys to put under the tree.

'David, what do you think toys will be like in 1989?'

He shrugs. 'Same as they are now. Why?'

'I'm just wondering what our future child will be playing with, that's all.'

He hugs me. 'Don't worry about the future. All I'm worried about is whether the Tories will still be in power.'

I smile. 'All you ever think about is bloody politics, David.'

'And all you ever think about is bloody music.'

He wants to have sex after that, and I don't, so we end up sitting up in bed together, him with his pyjama top off, me with my pyjama top definitely on. It feels like we've been doing this for years – probably because we have.

'What's the real reason you're not going to do the BBC thing?' he asks after a while.

'What do you mean?'

'Come on. What is it?'

I shake my head. 'Stop being so nosy. Look, go outside, I bet you it's snowing. Go and have a look.'

Then I roll over and fall asleep, tucked into his side, where I always seem to have been.

CHAPTER THIRTY-FOUR

The first time David asked me to marry him, it happened on the beach at Brighton. The second time he asks me, it happens outside a Police gig at Hammersmith Odeon. These days, The Police fit into our musical Venn diagram of course, and afterwards, in the rain, in the street, he turns to me and asks the question.

'Did Dad ask you to?' I say.

'Come on, Linda.'

'No, did he?'

'Well I had to ask him first, of course. For permission.'

I make a face. 'Not again. That's the second time you've done that. Can't you just have used the permission from the first time? And why do I feel like this is the Middle Ages and my first name should be Maid?'

'Don't be like that.'

'Dad must get a bad case of *déjà vu* whenever you turn up at the front door.'

'Well sod it then,' David says, and turns his back on me, walking ahead to the bus stop.

'Thank you!' I call after him. 'Thank you very much!'

And I mean it, I really do. But that's about *all* I feel. Sincere and politely enthusiastic gratitude for an offer I probably don't deserve.

David comes back to get me. 'I'm giving you the option,' he says, 'that's all. I didn't want it to be a case of you having to ask me. I thought I'd do it for you. And I knew there'd be a fifty-fifty chance you'd say no.'

'Oh for God's sake.'

'What?'

'Stop being so bloody understanding, will you?'

It's a stand-off, and we both know it; we break away again, this time with me walking ahead.

'You know it will end up in bed,' he yells after me, 'because it always does!'

I shrug.

When he finally catches up with me, though, I can see that I have hurt him. At least four of the worry lines in David's forehead must have been caused by me.

'You were the one who said we should never have got engaged,' I say.

'That was before you got pregnant.'

'I don't see how it will help, that's all. It might make Dad feel better, but who knows? Maybe he'd rather we didn't. Did you ask him?'

'Not really.'

'Well, then. I mean, Hazel might enjoy it, because she could get herself a bridesmaid dress and chuck a lot of rice around. But really, David, I don't mean to hurt your feelings, but I can't see the point.'

We keep walking, heads down against the cold, hands deep in our coat pockets. David and I both have colds, so we're sniffing as well, groping for tissues every five minutes and sneezing. It's not what Aphrodite had in mind when she dreamed up love between man and woman. And it can't be what Cupid envisioned when he first started flinging arrows everywhere.

'What are the ten songs that changed your life, David?' I ask him.

'Don't be stupid. Why?'

'Just wondering.'

He thinks about it. And then he thinks about it some more.

'Why do I get the feeling that this is some kind of trick?' he asks at last. 'You're making me paranoid, Linda. What is this, a test?'

I shrug. 'Don't then, if you don't feel like it.'

But I can tell the gauntlet has been thrown down, and sure enough, after we've walked along to the next bus stop, he's come up with two of them.

' "Ballroom Blitz", because that's how I met you.'

'No come on. Be honest. That's cheating.'

'All right then. "Just The Way You Are".'

'Billy Joel. Oh God, David, you can't be serious.'

He gives me a look. 'So you're absolutely right about music, and I'm absolutely wrong. Even when it comes to my life, my choices, my personal preferences. Linda, you're a bloody music Nazi.'

I jut my bottom lip out then, and David begins to sing the words about some woman being told not to go changing. Whatever that means.

'But it's such a crap song, David.'

'There, you see. I'm absolutely wrong about music, and you're absolutely right.'

'Don't you think that music should be used to say something halfway decent?'

'But that song does. It's about loyalty.' He gives me a look. 'And love.'

'It's bland pap designed for AM radio stations. It's about some poor bitch being commanded to stay exactly the same for the rest of her life, so some hairy bloke with a medallion can feel secure.'

'Billy doesn't wear a medallion.'

'It's crap. There's so much good music around. It's just . . . anodyne.'

'Is that a word you learned off Jon Whitten?'

'It's so depressing, David. I can't believe that you think Billy Joel's music has changed your life.'

'The title of the song reminds me of us. "Just The Way You Are". We're not trying to change each other, are we? It's a good thing.'

'Oh God.' I make a face, both to him, and to myself.

'Are you feeling hormonal or something?' He pats my shoulder.

'No.'

'What is it then?'

'Nothing,' I hiss. And all the time I'm thinking about Mick and two of my all-time favourite songs in his head.

'Music's just music, Linda. You won't like The Jam for ever. When the baby's born, you'll probably start liking nursery rhymes.'

I think I'm going to cry then, but I don't.

And he just smiles kindly, as he always does.

'So it's a no to marriage, then?' he says.

'I don't want to talk about it.'

'Thought so. A no. Based on the fact that you think I'm a total prat for liking Billy Joel. Brilliant. Very mature.'

And then we kiss, and miss each other's mouths, and blink in the street lights until a bus pulls up, with headlights blazing, and a tired, white-faced driver waits for us to get on.

EPILOGUE

I can't quite believe it, but on Monday morning at exactly 10 a.m., I will have been working at the BBC for twenty years. I've been here for so long that I've seen cats and dogs get born on *Blue Peter*, and then be buried in the garden outside. I've been here so long that not only have we gone digital, we've also staged an OB of the Queen's Golden Jubilee. In 1979, needless to say, none of us crazy young anarchists thought there would actually *be* another jubilee. Embarrassingly enough, the first documentary I made at film school – the one that actually got me into TV in the first place – was just about that. It opened with 'Rule Britannia' being played backwards, and a picture of the Queen Mother's head on a dartboard. And now look at us. More people watched Ozzy Osbourne doing the Golden Jubilee gig at Buckingham Palace than turned up to see The Sex Pistols at Crystal Palace.

Because I've now been at the BBC for two decades, my department decides to throw drinks for me on Friday night to celebrate. And I go along with it – not because I think they're trying to suck up to me, of course – I know they're only doing it because someone's discovered a few boxes of champagne they'd forgotten from an old *Absolutely Fabulous* party.

'Well, someone's got to use it up,' says Phoebe, my

PA, who is far more cluey than me. She has pigtails, which she tweaks whenever she gets stressed. She's stressed now, I can tell. But then, she gets stressed about everything. 'Here you go, Linda, you have the first glass of bubbly. After twenty years of this place, you bloody deserve it.'

And then everyone makes that weak 'Raaay!' noise you get whenever the numbers are too low, and people are too sober to celebrate properly. A cake is even wheeled in, and it says *LINDA* with a big number *20* under it, in pink. Pink is still my favourite colour, of course. I did go off on a black tangent for part of the eighties, but like most good things, pink stayed around long enough to make a comeback.

Because my anniversary party coincides with the launch of a new music programme on another channel, a TV set is wheeled in, so we can all watch – and criticize.

'Oh no,' someone groans as the titles flash up. 'That wanker Jon Whitten's producing. I might have known.'

I smile and take another glass of champagne. It's one of those shows where women are reduced to rotating on a stage with their arses sticking out, and men sing songs about their heartfelt admiration for the women rotating on a stage with their arses sticking out. The audience are wearing FCUK T-shirts – how incredibly radical of them – and later on, in lieu of anything interesting to say, the presenter tells us there's a Kylie tour rumour.

'Tell me where she's rumoured to be touring,' someone says, 'and I'll make a note not to be there.'

The whole time I worked with Jon Whitten, he only ever made two accurate predictions about the music industry. First of all, he got video right. And secondly, he once told me that when music got too political and scary – too powerful really – the corporates would start pumping it full of sex to stop people thinking too

337

hard. Jon Whitten might have been wrong about everything else, but he certainly got that right. This new programme isn't so much a music show as timid porn for spotty teenage boys, set to nursery rhymes.

'Mmm, listen to those lyrics,' Phoebe nods, twisting her pigtails as the next band is wheeled onto Jon Whitten's programme. 'La la la la, oooh baby you're hot. That's original. And are those girls in the band pretending to be lesbians as well? I thought that was last month's thing!'

'And now,' says the presenter, 'a hot Eminem tour rumour.'

'Oh for God's sake,' Phoebe groans, 'is there nowhere safe on the planet any more?'

I see Jon Whitten from time to time, at music industry events. He's still single, which is terrifying when I think about all the ambitious young women who want to get jobs on his show. And I see Mick, too, sometimes, at industry functions. He never really dealt with the eighties – well, how would any Clash fan have coped with Duran Duran? – and he eventually left the BBC to go off and work on documentaries about bees. He's still single too. And that's equally terrifying. For different reasons, of course. Of all the men I've tried and failed with in the last twenty years, Mick is still the one I can't bring myself to think about. And yet there are days when I think about him all the time. He's in America now, working for CBS.

In the middle of a conversation with one of our floor managers, I am interrupted by Phoebe, rushing in from my office, twiddling her pigtails.

'I think it's your daughter,' she says breathlessly. 'The call's from Australia, and it's a bad line, but it sounded like her.'

I stagger over in my new high heels – they're far too tight, as everything from bloody Prada is – and take the call.

'Ivy?'

'Mum!'

'Are you ringing to congratulate me on twenty years at the BBC? It must be about 5 a.m. there.'

'No, Mum, I'm ringing to tell you that I'm getting married.'

I try not to sound too shocked. I suppose I've been expecting it. 'Congratulations, Ivy. That's great.'

'I asked *him*.'

'Good for you.'

'Shall I put him on for you?'

I say yes, put him on, and then I have the usual stilted conversation with my daughter's boyfriend, who is twenty-two years old, like her, but has the vocabulary of someone half his age. I don't know what she sees in him, apart from the fact that he's always dragging her off to exotic places like Australia. But then, maybe all mothers feel like that.

'You'll probably think we're too young,' says her boyfriend.

'Oh no,' I lie.

'But we're very much in love.'

'Oh good.' He's embarrassing me now.

'And Ivy and I are thinking of moving here. If the immigration department will let us in.'

'Oh well, see what happens,' I say cheerfully. The thought of Ivy moving so far away is too much to bear at the moment.

'We stayed with your friends in Sydney,' Ivy's boyfriend tells me.

'Penny and Evan?'

'I got my hair cut in their salon. Well, one of them, anyway. They're all over Australia aren't they?'

'Yes. When Australia gets split ends, it basically goes to one of Penny and Evan's salons to have them cut off.'

'They look alike, don't they,' says my daughter's boyfriend.

'They always did,' I tell him.

And then Ivy is put back on the phone, much to my relief. 'We want to get married in some old kind of stately home. In England. And we were wondering if you knew anywhere.'

'I'll have to ask the location manager. No, hang on. I'm sure Hazel and David will have something on their books.'

'In Brighton?'

'Anywhere you want. You know what they're like. They've got a database that covers half of Europe. How do you think they got so bloody rich?'

Then we talk some more, about the weather in Australia, and the constant rain in England, then Ivy says her money's running out on the phone card, and she hangs up. I'll have to check my e-mail in the morning. There's always e-mail these days, thank God.

I call Hazel, on her mobile. She's having dinner with David. They are the only married couple in England I know who still regularly go out to dinner with each other.

They ended up together, of course, just as the eighties began, and shortly after I gave birth to Ivy in hospital. Hazel held one hand while I went screaming into labour, and David held the other. The nurses couldn't believe it when I told them that she was my best friend, and he used to be my fiancé, but then nobody ever understood the way the three of us got on together. 'It's unnatural' my father said at the time – although he's OK about it now. Typically, it's only taken him the last twenty years to adjust.

What he didn't understand at the time – what nobody understood in fact – was that I never wanted anything but happiness for David. And the best way to provide that, all those years ago, was to open every

340

door I could for him and Hazel. He was right all along. They were made for each other. All that Jeannie bollocks, and even the time back with me, were just distractions.

'But how did you know your instincts were right about them?' Ivy asked me, years later, when she was old enough to hear the whole story.

'I didn't, but I thought it was worth the gamble. And anyway, look at them. Can you imagine your father ending up with anyone else?'

Now, on the mobile, Hazel is putting on her posh estate agent's voice, until she realizes it's me and relaxes.

'Ivy's getting married,' I tell her, getting straight to the point.

'What? It's very noisy in here, Linda.'

'Ivy's engaged!' I yell, above the din of the restaurant.

'Oh my God!' she squeals, and passes the phone to David.

'Linda. It's me,' David says. 'Did she call you from Australia?'

'Yes. She was going to call you next, but her phone card ran out.'

'But what do you think?' David asks me, sounding worried. 'She's so young!'

'I know, I know. But we've been through this before. You know what Ivy's like.'

'Yes, but—'

'But nothing. She's made her mind up. But listen, David, they want some nice, empty stately home to get married in. Is there anything on your books?'

There is a roaring, restaurant sound for a minute, while David is talking to Hazel, and then I get the annoying beep which means their mobile phone has just dropped out. I sigh, hang up, and go back to the party. I'm sure they'll call back, once they've gone home, and give me a list of a hundred abandoned country piles.

Ivy is the first of David's children to get married. After David and Hazel finally got together, it took them another five years to have children – both boys, as it turned out. I nearly laugh, imagining the scene between David and Hazel in the restaurant now. He'll be trying to tell her that Ivy's too young, and she'll be cleverly distracting him by talking about all the money the wedding is going to cost.

'Hey Linda,' my PA says, giving me a look. 'Is everything OK?'

'Absolutely fine, Phoebe. Don't worry. I'm coming back to the party. I just had to do the family thing.'

She pulls her pigtails, and smiles.

Back in the office, more champagne and cake are being passed around, and some of my colleagues, who've just heard about Ivy, start congratulating me, and another glass of booze is put in my hand.

'I bet it makes you feel old, though,' one of the staff says, and I pretend to kick her.

'Anyway Linda,' says one of the young production assistants, changing the subject, 'so how did you start with the BBC anyway?'

'Just luck,' I tell him. 'I started making film clips with someone's father's Super 8 camera. It had been in the attic. I got into film school, made some bloody awful documentaries, and then some even worse music videos ... and eventually I ended up here.'

'Someone said you're going to make a programme about 1979,' the production assistant persists. I quite like him. He came here on work experience, with a Mohawk – which I guess is a post-post-post Punk retro-irony statement in a league of its own. And he does the washing up in the tea room too, which is another reason to feel sympathetic towards him.

'Nineteen seventy-nine was a great year for music,' I

342

tell him. 'That was the year we got "Rock'n'Roll High School" by The Ramones, "London Calling" by The Clash, "Smash It Up" by The Damned, "Oliver's Army" by Elvis Costello, "Eton Rifles" by The Jam, "Heart of Glass" by Blondie, "The Great Rock'n'Roll Swindle" by The Sex Pistols and "Making Plans For Nigel" by XTC.'

'Right,' he says, twitching in vague recognition as I mention The Clash and the Pistols.

'It was a very good year for music,' I tell him. 'But a very bad year for my love-life.'

He laughs at that. 'So are we going to include your love-life in the programme, Linda?'

'No, of course we're not, you little tosser. That's the trouble with the BBC these days. It's not about music any more, it's always about everyone's sex life.'

He laughs again. 'Can I work on the documentary?' he asks.

'Yes. Learn about how corporate rock nearly went down the gurgler for ten minutes. That'll entertain you.'

He gives me a blank look.

'Believe it or not,' I tell him, swaying slightly in my heels, 'there was a time when a band could do a fifty-fifty deal with its record company. And there was even a time when people thought that the love of music was more important than the love of money. But anyway.'

The production assistant knocks back his champagne, trying to catch up with me.

'It wasn't just about the bloody badges,' I tell him. 'And you know something else about 1979?'

He shakes his head.

'Plain girls made it into the charts. Singers who couldn't really sing didn't become famous. And you could produce your own magazine on the photocopier at work, too.'

The production assistant gives me a nervous look – I suppose I am sounding a bit pissed and belligerent now – and makes his excuses, and wanders away.

'None of this *Pop Idols* crap!' I yell, in a decidedly 1979 way, as he disappears from view.

As I wander back to my own office, to try another call to Hazel and David, I find myself thinking again about the year that changed everything.

It sent Howard broke, of course, because *NWW* never did work out – despite those early, encouraging sales – and all the money he eventually made from that terrible band Terminal Sausage eventually got spent on bailing himself out of bankruptcy. He lives in Italy now, and he's still flogging bidets. He married an Italian, too, a porky creature in a black headscarf who looks not unlike Julie from Terminal Sausage, though I have no idea if she can play the drums.

For Cindy, I suppose 1979 was her chance to try out London for a while. Needless to say, after a year of strikes, freezing temperatures and general poverty, she liked it so much she moved straight back to Detroit. None of us ever heard from her again.

1979 was certainly kind to David in the end. When he bought us a deserted squat in Notting Hill just after Christmas Day, he was after a cheap place for Ivy and me. He wasn't looking for an investment property, just the beginnings of a home. When I left him, though, he hung onto it. And then two years ago, he and Hazel sold it for a fortune. Between them, they've bought and sold about twenty properties in twenty years, and David was right about Brighton. It did go up. As Ivy always says, when she wants to have a go at me, there's the *rich* branch of the family, and then there's the bloody Linda Tyler branch.

I had another dream about Mum the other night. They hardly ever happen these days. She was coming towards me holding an ivy leaf in one hand and a horseshoe in the other, so I suppose she was trying to tell me about Ivy's engagement. The horseshoe was the right way up, thank God, so I assume Ivy will be OK – unlike her mother, the queen of all pre-marital disasters.

Someone asked me the other day whether I minded being a single mum, before it became fashionable. It was one of those eager young female BBC researchers who occasionally lurk in the corridors, waiting to pounce on you, so they can grab a bit of your life for their files. You'd think that I'd crawled far enough up the hierarchy to avoid such indignities, but nobody's immune in this place. If you've got anything vaguely resembling *material* in your personal history, they'll be onto you in a flash.

'I didn't mind being a single mum, no,' I say, when she asks me.

'And what about the father of the child?' she goes on.

'Don't be so nosy. Look, he stood by me, all right? We had an arrangement.'

'And then what happened?'

'He married my best friend.'

'Ouch,' says the girl, making a sympathetic face.

'There was no ouch about it. It worked out well for everyone. I'd learned to stop being jealous, you know.'

She was satisfied, then, so she shut up and walked away, but I could tell from the way she was waving her clipboard around that she thought she was onto something good. I couldn't blame her, I suppose. I expect I was like that, too, over twenty years ago, when the gods smiled on me for the second time in my life, and I finally got my break here.

I decide to get some space and air, and leave my office, slipping out of the fire escape door into the BBC grounds. It's raining today, but the sun's trying hard to shine at the same time, so all the trees and flowers look soft, and unfocused. I love it when it's like this, when you can walk out into the garden and lose yourself among the taxpayers' daffodils. You can even forget you're in the middle of London.

I wonder about the music Ivy will have at her reception. If I know her, she won't even have thought about it. Her lack of interest in bands is probably the only disappointing thing about my daughter. Me, I'm more like Morrissey. He told the *Observer* the other day that he never fell in love with people or places, he fell in love with singles. He also said that pop music had been a lifetime's preoccupation for him, at the expense of everything else he could possibly name. I know exactly what he means.

David once said music didn't really matter. He said it was like supporting Man United, but it isn't, and that's why I couldn't marry him in the end. It had nothing to do with Mick, and everything to do with that bloody annoying Billy Joel song. That's what I should have told the young BBC researcher the other day. *That*'s why I ended up as a single mother.

The rain starts coming down harder until it's impossible to stand unprotected any longer, so I hunch down and run for shelter under the nearest oak. The water starts leaking into my eyes but I keep thinking of perfect songs for Ivy's wedding reception. Oh, the joy of a song list. Is it pathetic for me to feel more excited about planning the music than anything else about this wedding?

Then Phoebe runs out with a phone message, pigtails flapping.

'Are you coming back into the party, Linda?' she calls. 'Some bloke called Mick rang too,' she says, 'calling from LA.'

'Oh yes?' I refuse to give anything away. But I know exactly which Mick she means.

'He says congrats on doing twenty years at the BBC. Someone in the office told him about the party. And he says he's coming back to London next week and he wants to catch up. Here's his number.'

I take the piece of paper from her hand, which is covered in biro messages to herself, and put it in my pocket. Then Phoebe goes back inside, and I let the rain fall into my eyes, until the daffodils become a blur.

THE END

I'M A BELIEVER
Jessica Adams

'AN ORIGINAL AND ENTERTAINING NOVEL ABOUT
LOVE AFTER DEATH'
The Times

Is there love after death?

Read it and believe!

Mark Buckle thinks he's an ordinary bloke. He teaches
science at a junior school in south London. He'd rather
read Stephen Hawking than his horoscope column, he's
highly suspicious of Uri Geller, Mystic Meg and feng shui,
and he wouldn't be seen dead at a séance. Most
importantly, he absolutely, positively doesn't believe
in life after death. Then, one terrible night, Mark's
girlfriend Catherine dies in an accident and his
whole world is thrown into chaos.

Within days of the funeral Catherine appears by his
bedside and he finds himself communicating with her from
beyond the grave. Then, just when he's beginning to adjust
to life with his ghostly girlfriend, she decides to send him
someone new to love. . .

I'm a Believer is a funny, moving and compulsive novel
about love, life and what lies beyond.

'THIS IS A HEART-WARMING, FUNNY BOOK WITH A
SERIOUS CORE, CHALLENGING OUR MODERN-DAY
CYNICISM AND LACK OF BELIEF – NOT JUST IN GOD,
BUT IN ANYTHING AT ALL'
Glamour

'WITTY AND REFRESHING'
Vogue

0 552 77083 3

BLACK SWAN

TOM, DICK AND DEBBIE HARRY
Jessica Adams

'THOROUGHLY GRIPPING, YOU MUST READ THIS'
Heat

The lead singer of We've Got Blondie's Drumsticks and
We're Going To Use Them has a problem. He only wants
one woman in the world. And that woman is Debbie Harry.
Unfortunately, he works in a bank.

His brother has a problem too. His wife has gone missing –
on his wedding day.

Meanwhile, the best man is wondering whether it's okay to
live with a woman old enough to be his mother.

Welcome to the world of Tom, Dick and Debbie Harry.
Three men. Six women. One small town. And a sexually
dysfunctional Australian sheepdog.

'WARM, WITTY AND WISE'
Cosmopolitan

0 552 14721 4

BLACK SWAN

SINGLE WHITE E-MAIL
Jessica Adams

'SEXY, FUNNY, SMART. FOR ANY WOMAN WHO HAS
EVER BEEN SINGLE'
Cosmopolitan

Saturday night is a nightmare when you're single. Saturday
night is for couples and everyone knows it.

Victoria 'Total Bloody Relationships Disaster' Shepworth is
single and knows all about Saturday nights alone. A broken
relationship with the guy she thought was 'the one' has led
to a string of disastrous dates. Now she's fed-up with being
on her own and is once again in search of the man of her
dreams. But life begins to look decidedly more interesting
when she becomes involved in an internet romance with
glamorous Frenchman, Pierre Dubois. Little does she know
he could be closer than she thinks. . .

'A VERY FUNNY NOVEL FOR THE 90s WOMAN – READ
IT AND RECOGNISE YOURSELF'
New Weekly

'ADAMS' DEBUT INTO THE LITERARY WORLD IS
FRESH, FRENETIC AND FUN'
Elle

'SHE GIVES NICK HORNBY AND HELEN FIELDING A
DAMN GOOD RUN FOR THEIR MONEY . . .
THOROUGHLY ENJOYABLE'
Daily Telegraph

0 552 99830 3

BLACK SWAN

A SELECTED LIST OF FINE WRITING
AVAILABLE FROM BLACK SWAN

99830 3	SINGLE WHITE E-MAIL	*Jessica Adams*	£6.99
14721 4	TOM, DICK AND DEBBIE HARRY	*Jessica Adams*	£6.99
77083 3	I'M A BELIEVER	*Jessica Adams*	£6.99
99313 1	OF LOVE AND SHADOWS	*Isabel Allende*	£7.99
77105 8	NOT THE END OF THE WORLD	*Kate Atkinson*	£6.99
99863 X	MARLENE DIETRICH LIVED HERE	*Eleanor Bailey*	£6.99
77097 3	I LIKE IT LIKE THAT	*Claire Calman*	£6.99
99979 2	GATES OF EDEN	*Ethan Coen*	£7.99
99990 3	A CRYING SHAME	*Renate Dorrestein*	£6.99
99954 7	SWIFT AS DESIRE	*Laura Esquivel*	£6.99
99898 2	ALL BONES AND LIES	*Anne Fine*	£6.99
99656 4	THE TEN O'CLOCK HORSES	*Laurie Graham*	£5.99
99890 7	DISOBEDIENCE	*Jane Hamilton*	£6.99
99885 0	COASTLINERS	*Joanne Harris*	£6.99
77109 0	THE FOURTH HAND	*John Irving*	£6.99
99867 2	LIKE WATER IN WILD PLACES	*Pamela Jooste*	£6.99
99977 6	PERSONAL VELOCITY	*Rebecca Miller*	£6.99
99849 4	THIS IS YOUR LIFE	*John O'Farrell*	£6.99
77106 6	LITTLE INDISCRETIONS	*Carmen Posadas*	£6.99
77088 4	NECTAR	*Lily Prior*	£6.99
99952 0	LIFE ISN'T ALL HA HA HEE HEE	*Meera Syal*	£6.99
77087 6	GIRL FROM THE SOUTH	*Joanna Trollope*	£6.99
99903 2	ARE YOU MY MOTHER?	*Louise Voss*	£6.99
99780 3	KNOWLEDGE OF ANGELS	*Jill Paton Walsh*	£6.99
99723 4	PART OF THE FURNITURE	*Mary Wesley*	£6.99
77107 4	SPELLING MISSISSIPPI	*Marnie Woodrow*	£6.99